MORE DEADLY THAN THE MALE

Rod Hacking

To Lynne White and David Walker

(the female of the species is as lovely as the male)

WHEN the Himalayan peasant meets the he-bear in his pride,
He shouts to scare the monster, who will often turn aside.
But the she-bear thus accosted rends the peasant tooth and nail.
For the female of the species is more deadly than the male.

Rudyard Kipling

Beforehand

Eight o'clock was briefing time in Number 10, and he entered always by the back door where his car waited for him. Once inside he was customarily greeted by the Cabinet Secretary and led upstairs to the Cabinet Room where the Prime Minister was waiting for him, sat in the middle of the coffin-shaped table. The Cabinet Secretary sat next to the PM with the Chief of the Defence Staff on the other side and this morning they were honoured (in her eyes anyway) with the presence of the Home Secretary, whom Rob thought little of.

'Good morning, sir,' began Rob, making sure the other three knew that their presence was merely tolerated and not necessary.

'You have all heard me say before now that there is a growing conviction among the counterterrorism police and ourselves that somewhere in the country there is one person who manipulates the forces who constantly threaten our society, someone who oversees and directs operations and who for convenience we call Mr Big. The evidence suggests that this person is in regular contact with and may take instructions from ISIS.

'With your agreement, sir, I want to make finding this individual our priority. I realise that other matters may need attending to from time to time, but I want to put 5 on a war footing until we can apprehend or otherwise rid the land of this person.'

The Prime Minister nodded his head.

'You must do everything you need to, Rob. Getting him is a matter of urgency and you have my complete agreement that you give all resources to

1

this. Will 6 know about this?'

'Only if they need to and I don't think they do. It is vital that this remains only among us five here and within the Service though at some stage the Commissioner and Head of Counterterrorism at the Yard will need to know, but only when I say.'

'And how is Benjie?'

'He was fast asleep when I left home, sir. But sadly not at half past two.'

'And Caro?'

'Still a walking miracle with her hearing though complains whenever she has to attend a concert of her sister's music, as she did last week, that it means she can hear it. When she was completely deaf, she always thought it was bound to be good. Now she can hear it she's not quite so keen.'

'I was at that concert,' said the Chief of the Defence Staff, 'and I regret to say I know what she means!'

They all smiled.

Rob rose, and asked permission to leave.'

'Thank you Rob, and good luck.'

'Thank you, sir.'

He bowed his head and accompanied by the Cabinet Secretary left the room, descended the stairs and left by the back door.

Chapter One

No one doubted that he was clever. He had a Ph.D and had worked in a university and liked those around him to refer to him as "doctor". He began his "minimum of 35 years" in HMP Woodhill and later moved to HMP Whitemoor, both high security establishments. It was in the latter, out on the bleak Cambridgeshire Fens, that he received information which just might enable him to do what he knew he had to. He received information from one of the brothers that in Rampton, the high security prison hospital, there was a staff member who, for the right amount of money, paid upfront outside, was willing to be careless in such a way as to allow someone out. Money he knew how to find. The problem was getting into Rampton.

The prison computers prevented access to porn, violence and a large number of Islamic websites, but he had no difficulty finding a considerable amount about mental illness, and it took over two years of learning his lines and giving a daily performance of schizophrenia to achieve his end, feigning psychosis. Increasingly his behaviour was becoming more and more disruptive and the prison authorities feared they were getting out of their depth with him, so brought in a psychiatrist from Peterborough who on the basis of a number of meetings gave a diagnosis of schizophrenia and borderline personality disorder and recommended a transfer to a place where he could be treated properly. It still took ages, but one morning he was informed by one of the deputy governors that he was going to be moved on the following day to Rampton Special Hospital. He was greatly relieved for he had feared they might move him either to Broadmoor or Ashworth.

Rampton's patients are among the very worst in terms of the terrible crimes that they have committed, but was considerably more comfortable than Whitemoor and no shortage of brothers with whom he could associate and share Ramadan and discuss the teachings of the Koran. However, from the beginning he faced a major problem. The doctors here were much more used to dealing with the sort of major conditions that he had striven to imitate to get here, and he quickly became aware that they were not convinced that he was suffering from anything at all and agreed that he should be moved to another

High Security Prison, probably Wakefield. That meant time was short.

The officer was called Mike O'Donnell, a registered mental health nurse and senior member of staff, who had worked there for many years, and was regarded highly by superiors and colleagues alike. One morning he came into Shafiq's cell.

'Good morning Shafiq Zaman,' said the prison officer. 'I am here to tell you that you will be leaving us next Monday.'

'Oh. I wanted to ask you a question, Mr O'Donnell,' said Shafiq.

'Ask away.'

'Although it is no good to me in here, I possess a large amount of money.'

'Don't you think you should use it to pay compensation for the lives of the two young women you killed when you planted that bomb?'

'Regrettable collateral. It wasn't my fault, they happened to be in the wrong place at the wrong time.'

'That must be a great consolation to their parents.'

Shafiq continued, ignoring the sarcasm.

'The thing is, Mr O'Donnell, that I've come to Rampton especially to meet you. I have worked very hard to bring this about. What's your normal rate?'

'My normal rate? What do you mean?'

'£50k?'

O'Donnell paused.

'I have absolutely no idea what you are talking about, so don't waste my time.'

'Asif Mohammed paid £50k I am reliably informed and that knowledge could get you into very serious trouble, Mr O'Donnell. In fact it would get you into prison in a role completely different to your present one.'

'Are you threatening me?'

'Certainly. What else do you think I'm doing? But as I have nothing to lose by doing so, it would be quite easy for me to ask to see the governor and that would be the end of you.'

'I think you might find that the governor hears all sorts of stories from scum like you and treats them with the contempt they deserve. Even if what you were saying was true, you'd never be able to prove it. I've given years of service here and you murdered two young women and exploded a terrorist bomb, so who is she more likely to believe?'

'You're quite right and I shouldn't have asked but do tell me how Mrs O'Donnell and your daughter Gail at Cambridge are doing? We live in a world where all sorts of bad things happen and so I hope they both take good care to protect themselves. I gather Gail is at Sidney Sussex College.'

O'Donnell wanted to kick the shit out of him, the repulsive rat.

'You're leaving on Monday and the poor sods somewhere else will have to put up with you and your fuckin' evil religion.'

'You do know that you just committed a hate crime, don't you?'

'I would happily hang the lot of you.'

Shafiq Zaman thought for a little while.

'£75k is the most I can manage to get to you. £75,000. It would set you up nicely.

O'Donnell thought about the money.

'Don't go away,' he said, his voice laden with irony, as he left the cell, returning about 20 minutes later.

'You will need to get this sorted today and I will need to hear from my Bank in Moldavia by tomorrow that the money is in or it's off. If it arrives late you'll be at Wakefield on Monday and I keep the money. And you do exactly what I say.'

'Your wife and daughter will be hoping I can trust you.'

'You're a double murderer and a Moslem extremist, and far as I'm concerned you're the scum of the earth. You have no choice but to trust me, I know you are computer literate but remember that anything even remotely suspicious will be picked up by our boffins who watch over all our IT.'

'I can assure you it won't be.'

On Sunday evening there was always a staffing problem at Rampton and tonight was no different. Shortly after supper there was a fight on a landing which demanded the attention of some of the staff. It was nothing serious but at the same time the door from the kitchen to outside, for just a very short while, was left unlocked. It was the sort of silly mistake that might well happen when short-staffed, and Shafiq Zaman was already a long way from Rampton when roll-call noticed his absence. There had been a car bearing a taxi sign which picked him up and drove him across the Midlands to a house in Wolverhampton.

Mr O'Donnell met with the governor on the following morning.

'How many could it have been, Mike?'

'Five men were on kitchen detail and they all deny that they went out the door at any time let alone left it unlocked though one of them must have either forgotten or is not telling the truth. They all remember that there was a fight of sorts on a landing which may have distracted them and allowed one of them to overlook for a few seconds the locking of the door. But short of putting them on the rack I'm not sure what else we can do.'

'They'll have to be interviewed by the police, as I'm afraid you too will be, given that you were the senior officer at the time.'

'I'd anticipated that. Will they be the Leicester boys and girls?'

'No. Given who Shafiq is, it's being taken over by the counterterrorist squad from London. Their supposition is that this was not a chance escape but something planned so they will not be interested in the question of who might have forgotten what but a conspiracy.'

With money and new clothes, on the Monday Shafiq Zaman took the train to Crewe and then the bus to Nantwich, where he paid a visit to the Post Office to consult a copy of the electoral register, where he found the name and address he was looking for. Although his face had been on television news in the morning, no one looked twice at him. Before he made his way to the house he sought, he called into a hardware shop where he bought a knife. The time had come for the will of Allah to be fulfilled.

Chapter Two

Those who knew them always smiled when they were seen together, and members of their choir enjoyed their presence as their very own Sharon and Tracey. Sharon once tried to explain that her name was taken from an ancient Israeli love poem: "I am the rose of Sharon", but no one believed her and neither did she herself. She and Tracey rather enjoyed the joke but made an agreement that if ever a woman called Dorien tried to befriend them, they would murder her!

Tracey stopped the car in the drive at precisely 9.30 but had to sound the horn after three minutes. She was a natural-born timekeeper and whatever else her closest friend might be, Sharon was not and Tracey couldn't imagine how she managed to run a school. However, she came in response to the summons carrying her bags.

'I think you're early,' lied Sharon and in return received a look, which enabled them to start their journey to Leicester with a laugh. Sharon was wearing a tight t-shirt and skimpy shorts, which Tracey hoped she would change out of before the first meeting after lunch, but knowing Sharon as she did, thought it highly unlikely. Sharon, she knew better than anyone, was a law unto herself and many had been the times when they had gone together to some function or other, and Sharon had turned up wearing entirely inappropriate attire. That came of not having a husband. Geoff would never let her out of the house looking like Sharon.

They drove past St Mary's Church.

'God, isn't it a monstrosity?' said Sharon.

'Are there any nice buildings in Nantwich?'

'No. I suppose that when I came, I was expecting the place to reflect being part of wealthy Cheshire. I was taken aback when I had to face the reality.'

'There was a great battle of Nantwich here during the Civil War,' said Tracey.

'Yes, January 1644. The trouble is that the Town Council haven't yet got round to clearing it up.'

'Was coming here to live disappointing?'

'I've got used to the place now – sort of. And I would have never met you, my very best friend in all the world as children in your play school probably say to one another. I was reading something in the paper this morning endorsing the idea of the wonderful loving nuclear family and of course there are many examples in which parents and children flourish happily, but more than ever the story is very different, even in Cheshire, as I am probably well placed to know. We have more than a few girls from multi-father families and many single or separated mothers even in our posh school.'

'So what's happened, and I say that rather than asking what's gone wrong, because it may not be wrong?' asked Tracey.

'Oh, I have no doubts that it has gone wrong though there are lots of contributory causes and I'm afraid Pandora's box is now permanently open and quite empty. If he thought immigration was only going to be a big issue in this country, Enoch Powell got it wrong, as any visit to a European country will confirm, but although even now he is still derided and hated as the racist I don't think he was, he could foresee that the country would change and not necessarily for the better when there would no longer be any sort of unifying belief and shared values. What he didn't recognise was that television would undermine these things far more than immigration, and social media even more so.'

'Do you see it as your job as the head of a prestigious school to seek to inculcate those older values in your girls?'

'No chance. I would estimate that a high proportion, perhaps 90% of the students make extensive use of the internet and social media. It's most unusual and refreshing when one tells me she doesn't.'

'And what about a racial mix?'

'Oh yes. There are some from the Far East, unbelievably hard-working, some of African origin and they too work hard and usually want to study medicine or dentistry. We have quite a few of what I would never call in public, "in-betweenies", mixed race and almost always quite beautiful, and we also have a lot of girls from Moslem families who come equipped with a hijab. In fact my head girl for this next year is one of them. She's called Faridah and a real treat to be with you and exerts her influence on the school quietly but definitely.'

'How did she get appointed?'

'The senior management team meets to consider possibilities, and then I vote.'

Tracey laughed.

'Do you mean only you vote?'

'No not really. In the end it's settled between the two deputy heads and me but they're always so anxious to please, in effect it is.'

'I know what you mean about mixed race girls being so attractive and it's little wonder they appear on tv so much, but they do so very often seem to come from broken homes.'

'It's an urban problem and not unlike the issue of Moslem men using and abusing young white girls. Boys of mostly West Indian origin, the ones who speak the patois of Jamaica though they've never been there, like sex with white girls but as a point of principle won't do so wearing a condom as it's not masculine, so we have lots of inbetweenies.'

'They are quite often our best athletes.'

'Well you would know that. By the way, which route are you taking?'

'I've no idea. I just do what the sat nav says. Have you ever been on a singing week before?' asked Tracey.

'Once, and it was held in Eton College of all places. The beds were so uncomfortable that I slept on the floor of my room, but the quality of the teaching made it worthwhile. Clive does well with our choir, but a professional singing teacher can give you so much more and bring out of you things you never knew you could manage. Have you done one?'

'No, but I'm quite excited by it though I hope the beds will be better than you had at Eton. Like you I value Clive but I wondered how he feels about our going on the course, that he might think it was criticism of him. When I was a gymnast, if I had even said "Good morning" to another coach I might have been cast out of the team.'

'I spoke to him and he said he was delighted and that it could only strengthen the choir.'

'I hope he'll never want the choir to sing the awful Finzi piece we've had to learn for working on this afternoon and evening,' said Tracey.

'I totally agree and when I mentioned it to him he said it will have been chosen deliberately because it makes almost impossible demands upon our breathing and will therefore be an excellent place to start the course.'

The instructions for parking and the route to reception were clear and in a short while they were in their rooms – adjacent as they had requested. Each room was identical: a narrow single bed and bedside table and lamp, carpet, wardrobe, desk and chair, sink and en-suite. For any students wishing to sleep with a partner it would be a very tight fit! It was the long summer holiday so there were no signs of the students who might have occupied the rooms in the past year and they had been well cleaned.

It would soon be lunch but there was enough time for Sharon and Tracey to wander around and get their bearings. There was a host of rooms in which one-to-one work would be done and the Great Hall in which they could hear someone still tuning the grand piano. Much more important was the bar, and they had just enough time for an alcoholic boost to the system before seeking the dining room.

There were 45 of them on the course, more women than men as usual, more over 50 than under and many were regulars. Sharon even recognised a man she had been with on the Eton course a long time ago. There were however some younger women to whom both Sharon and Tracey thought they might be able to relate, although it was far from impossible that the younger women looking around might easily have included the Nantwich Two among the older!

Tracey's day was made when, over lunch, one of them recognised her from the 2006 Commonwealth Games in Melbourne, and in minutes the news had got round and she was regarded as a celebrity. She was even glad to be able to take refuge in the Finzi, which they worked on once the event had started properly, Hardly anyone over lunch had said they liked it, but in the hands of a professional conductor they modified their opinions.

After supper there was time for an outside wander in the grounds of the Hall of Residence, before they were due to give an "as if" concert performance of the Finzi. Sharon and Tracey decided to get some fresh air and walked on the grass towards some trees.

'Do men stare at you in the same way they do lots of other women when you're in your role as Headteacher?'

'You mean trying to decide if they fancy me or not?' replied Sharon.

'The only reason I ask,' continued Tracey, 'is that some of the men couldn't stop looking at you in your relaxed dress, and I just wondered whether they would stop doing so if they came to know the work you do.'

'My Shop Window, as I call the contents of my bra, for psychological reasons and to do with testosterone attracts male attention sometimes but all women surely have that, and indeed some dress because that is the attention they wish for, and perhaps that's what I'm doing today, but then again when do I otherwise get the chance to show off what nature has provided me with? Not at school, and wait until you see what I've brought for the formal dinner on Friday! I don't object to anyone staring, but if a man tried to grope they would soon learn my displeasure in the form of a very great pain in their balls. But, Tracey, it's your body I envy. You are so slim and lovely though I imagine you could never have been a top gymnast were it otherwise.'

'You're right, but at least we were actually women. In the World Championships I wasn't at all sure some girls weren't younger than they were meant to be. It concerned me, and especially when they were the ones who got the medals. Now we have Simone Biles from America, quite brilliant but . . . Well, let's just say it ought to make anyone involved in sport uneasy.'

'And what about Caster Semenya, the South Africa runner who wins every women's race she enters?'

'Some female athletes have always been quite masculine in appearance, especially weight lifters and shot putters from Russia and Eastern Europe, and some have failed sex tests. Caster looks like a man and runs like a man, and makes the rest who once were the best, look pretty average. They've introduced testosterone testing now, and she's fallen foul of that, but with trans people now demanding to run as women whilst retaining all the functions and muscles of a man and other things besides, it's got to be sorted out sometime soon.'

'It's certainly a problem for us at school. The governors have asked me what I will do if someone turns up looking for a place in the school who is a boy claiming identity as a girl.'

'What did you say?'

'I dodged the question a little by saying that we do not have the facilities necessary to accommodate such a circumstance and the answer would be No. The governing body seemed relieved.'

'Do you think of yourself as transphobic?' asked Tracey.

'I have no idea what the word can possibly mean, but if a man or woman has surgery, and takes the appropriate medication because they want to be different gender, then I have no objections. It's those who won't I just don't trust and I think putting a trans man with all his bits and pieces still in place into a women's prison, or letting them play in a women's cricket team is silly and dangerous.'

They had wended their way back to the Hall where they took their place for the performance of the Finzi. The conductor and pianist were chatting to the other three professional tutors on the course so within a few minutes the choir were getting restless.

The young woman sitting on Sharon's right turned to her and smiled'

'Hi, I'm Dee Bailey from Ilkley.'

'The gateway to the Dales.'

'That's supposedly Skipton but sometimes it's the traffic jam to the Dales. It's all the fault of James Herriot and the vets who've come after him, but if you know where to go you can still avoid the crowds, and the vets.'

Sharon smiled and made a mental note to meet up with Dee later and buy her a drink. In the meantime the pair were receiving a very dirty look from the conductor, who wanted to share with the whole choir some observations made by his fellow tutors, all of which were most helpful as they prepared for their run through, things which even Clive back in Nantwich might well have missed.

Afterwards they were to meet one to one with their appointed singing teacher to say hello and for the tutor to audition and make notes on what they heard.

They had allocated Sharon and Tracey the same teacher. Each student had been asked to prepare a song which would be sung unaccompanied so the teacher could hear whether or not a student could pitch a note. The friends had prepared together, and both chose Schubert which when the time came they regretted for neither had sung well, but the teacher was generous to both and said she looked forward to further solo work with them later in the week. Their primary target now was the bar, and for Sharon, meeting up with Dee. They decided to enjoy the warmth of the evening and sit outside with their drinks, Campari and soda for them both, whilst Tracey had been kidnapped once again by those men interested in her, their excuse being her experience of being a gymnast and a Commonwealth Games Gold medallist. Sharon looked over and could see that Tracey was adoring the attention.

'Do you have a family you're escaping from?' asked Sharon innocently.

'Ah, well,' she sighed, 'the answer is more complex than you might imagine.'

'You don't have to tell me.'

'I'm perfectly happy to do so. Some time back I visited a Travel Agent in Bingley. Do you remember Travel Agents? They arranged holidays for people in the days before they thought they had learned to do so themselves on-line and mostly screwed up the arrangements they thought they had cleverly made and mostly hadn't as they often discovered on arrival. I was served by a pleasant man and it turned out he was not an assistant but the owner, having inherited the business from his father. The holiday arranged, I was about to leave when he suddenly invited me to have dinner with him. He was quite a bit older than me so I was flattered. He was great company, and he tried nothing on at all. This was repeated several times and on every occasion he was well behaved, even refusing an offer to come back to my flat. Then, one evening in the middle of the meal (for which he always insisted on paying), he asked me to marry him. I was taken aback, to say the least. I had always assumed that these days marriage was something that followed an extensive period of cohabitation. He had held my hand, but no other part of me, but he convinced me of his sincerity and spoke of his wealth, which, he said, after our wedding we would share. The other odd thing was that although in his late 30s he still lived at home with his parents, and when I asked him his thoughts about where we should live, he replied that we would live with them, which I thought a bit weird. But I was completely won over when I met them, and by the fact that he was a true gentleman. Invitations went out and everything was ready and it took place in the Devonshire Arms Hotel in the Dales, truly a wonderful and romantic setting which must have cost his parents an absolute bomb. Graham told me we would have to delay our honeymoon because of work arrangements, which I didn't really mind, and he promised me Bali, so I spent my wedding night in the home of my parents-in-law.'

'Not exactly the best aphrodisiac.'

'In the circumstances I don't think any kind of aphrodisiac would have done.'

'Oh?'

'I'm afraid so. Not then, not never. He is impotent.'

'That explains the pre-marital chastity,' said Sharon.

'Yeah, at least it wasn't something wrong with me.'

'So what happened once this came to light?'

'I left three days and two sex-less nights after my wedding and went to see my solicitor.'

Dee drained her drink.

'My turn,' she said. 'Same again?'

Sharon nodded as Dee rose and went inside to the bar and soon returned.

'That's a ghastly story, Dee, and thank you so much for telling me. It's getting dark and we have an early start, but if you can bear being bored by it, sometime tomorrow I'll tell you all about my own utterly disastrous experience of marriage.'

'Oh shit, I am sorry about that, but I'd be fascinated to learn a little of how

the woman wearing by far and away the most provocatively sexy clothes here
became a head teacher of what I gathered from your friend Tracey earlier, is
something of a very posh private school for girls.'

'It is, but is it all over with now – your annulment, I mean?'

'The law proceeds very slowly so I'm still waiting although there has been a
generous financial settlement already made.'

The two women stood, each emptying their glass and returning it to the bar.

'So now to bed with Fauré,' said Dee.

Sharon was about to say something funny but tactless about Fauré being
more use in bed than Graham had ever been, but thought better of it, though it
amused her all the same. As she walked along the corridor towards her room
she was caught up with by Tracey.

'I lost sight of you after supper because some of the tenors claiming to love
gymnastics held me captive, though to be fair to them, they were nice and we
did eventually talk about other things. What about you?'

'Sitting outside with someone called Dee, both of us pouring Campari down
our throats to help prepare for singing tomorrow. Have you phoned home?'
asked Sharon.

'Oh no, I never do. We can always make contact if we need to but when I'm
away, I like to be right away. Home doesn't exist.'

They reached their rooms.

'Do you want a call in the morning?' asked Sharon.

'No, I'll use my phone.'

'A fellow student in teacher training with me went to spend a month in an
American school doing a placement. The teacher in Kentucky she was staying
with could hardly believe his ears when, before she went off to bed on her first
night there, she said to him, "Can you knock me up in the morning?"'

'What happened?' asked Tracey, laughing.

'She never said, though I'd love to know.'

Chapter Three

Sharon had risen early for as long as she could remember, probably because her dad always had and she grew up loving the time they had talking together in his study before breakfast, and always remembered the smell of his pipe tobacco – *Erinmore Flake*. The pattern of an early rise had continued, though after her dad died she didn't feel disposed to continue the pipe smoking on her own. It provided her with her own time before being overwhelmed as she would be once in school. Sometimes she just sat and read a novel or read poetry aloud. It would be different if she had been married and had children, but almost 600 girls were waiting for her when got to school, so perhaps that was enough.

On this morning she read a little and then showered. Looking out of the window she saw rain which decided her choice of clothes, a little more conservative than those she had worn on the previous day, but she smiled at the thought of the dress she had brought for the Friday night course dinner! Sharon had never in her life ever wanted to be a man, and took great delight in her femininity, something she recalled each morning when putting on her make-up and dangly ear-rings. She knew that at her school in Chester there were parents who looked askance at the head teacher dressed flamboyantly as she often was, but her aim was to show the girls of the school that it was possible to combine intelligence, hard work and great enjoyment. She wanted them to work hard but also to play hard. She knew that not all the governors approved, but she didn't care because she knew she was right and the consideration that mattered was that the girls instinctively understood this and her example meant that the point did not have to be laboured. She thought that what she sometimes experienced, sixth form girls asking where she had bought this or that item of clothing, would not be happening in a boys school!

Sharon and Tracey went into breakfast together.

'What time is your individual session this morning?' asked Tracey.

'Ten o'clock, and yours?'

'Eleven, but I'll go to one of the spare practice rooms and get prepared.' They collected a tray each and made their way to an empty table.

By coffee time it had stopped raining, and the sun was doing its best to emerge. Dee was sitting by the window looking out as Sharon approached causing her to turn and smile.

'Shall we risk the weather and go out?'

They smiled at one another and Dee stood up, leaving their coffee cups on the table, and went outside where, now, the sun had won its tussle with the clouds.

'How was your solo session?' asked Dee.

'Worth every penny. She notices everything and knows the best way of dealing even with tiny faults. I could feel my voice improving as I tried to put into practice what she was telling me. And you?'

'The same. He was great and, as you say, worth the course fee just for that. I'm already looking forward to my next session tomorrow. I hope the members of the Skipton Choral Society notice the improvement.'

'Well, that's why we've come. And now I should fulfil my promise to let you know something of my story after you were so generous last night in telling me yours.'

'It doesn't have to be quid pro quo you know. I'd love to know because I like you, but please don't feel you have to do so. The way you responded to me last night was a gift in itself.'

'I'm perfectly happy to tell you anything and everything, though as in the case of most of us, most of our lives are spent distracted from distraction by distraction, as T S Eliot maintained.

'My beginning was straightforward with good parents whom I loved and they loved me. It was a comfortable beginning and I enjoyed school, an all-girls school, and then went to university in Exeter to study English. After my first degree I did Research and even got awarded a doctorate for work I did on some obscure 17th century English poets whom I still love. Then my tutor decided I would make a better wife than an academic, and foolishly I accepted.'

'How old were you?' asked Dee.

'Twenty four on my wedding day but a very young twenty four. I knew a great deal about love in poetry and prose but nothing at all about it in my own life. I was advised by just about everyone not to marry Jimmy, but I was flattered and probably desperate so I took no notice. Then, just six weeks after the wedding, I discovered why some of those who had been advising done so. Jimmy apparently spent much of his time screwing young undergraduate girls, two of whom had abortions. If I'm totally honest I was a failure in bed, a big failure and I hated every moment of it, so perhaps Jimmy sought from others what I couldn't provide. I left Exeter and Jimmy for good.'

'O God, Sharon that makes my experience pale into insignificance. What did you do after you left Jimmy?'

'I went back to be with my parents on the Isle of Wight who welcomed me with open arms.'

'Were they retired?'

Sharon laughed.

'No. My dad was still functioning as a GP and we used to joke with one another as to which of us had the more right to call ourself doctor'

'Who won?'

'Me of course, every time.'

'Are they still alive?'

'No. They both died just six months apart. They lived for each other, and mum just didn't want to live without dad.

'Life's not been much of a bowl of cherries for you.'

'Should we expect it to be? I'm often amazed when bad things happen how shocked, even devastated, people are, as if they had never imagined life is exactly like this: a series of random happenings which we have the capacity to screw up even when they're good.'

'Have you tried men again?'

'No. I may flirt like anything and wear outrageous clothes, but I think I'd run a mile if any came near.'

'And what happened to Jimmy, if I may ask?'

'Somehow or other he got drawn into Islam and converted and though as white as you or me, was radicalised, and my ex-husband was the man you will have heard described as the Portsmouth Bomber, the one who planted a bomb at the Naval Base, killing two teenage girls, whom he described in court as unfortunate collateral.'

'O my God, Sharon.'

'He received a minimum sentence of 35 years in prison, and I neither know nor care where he is. I would be very happy for him to have been executed, as I would all Islamist terrorists. Our soldiers are allowed to kill them when overseas and I wonder why we should not do so at home too. I have often thought about those girls at the beginning of the lives. Why should a shit like him continue to live and breathe the air he chose to deny to them.'

Tracey, newly released from her solo session, saw them and went out to join them.

'Hi,' said Sharon, seeing her approach. 'How did it go?'

'Well, if today's composer-conductor is better than that, he will have to be very good,' replied Tracey. 'I came out feeling quite exhilarated. She was so encouraging and made me think I am a better singer than most of the time I fear I am.'

'Isn't that what a good teacher is meant to do?' asked Dee.

'I suppose it is, but when you find someone who really does it, you feel just great.'

'Let me go and change,' said Sharon. 'I'm far too warm, but I'll be back in a moment or two and I believe the bar is open.'

'Campari and soda?' asked Dee.

'I might manage that,' said Sharon, heading towards her room.

'What about you, Tracey?'

'Oh just a St Clement's, thanks. Alcohol now might make me very sleepy this afternoon, and I want to have all my wits about me. I'll get us a table by the window.'

Dee soon arrived with the drinks and had followed Tracey in going non-alcoholic.

'Do you work, Tracey, apart from being housekeeper, mother, nurse, cook and many other things?'

'Yes. I work full-time as the leader of a children's playgroup, something I began and really enjoy. There's something disarmingly direct about children and I often come home and tell Geoff something one or other has said in the day which can be so very funny. And the other thing is that you learn a great deal about how things are in their homes because they tell it as it is, which if I passed such things on to their parents would embarrass them greatly.'

'I bet it's exhausting work.'

'I have a great staff of part and full-time helpers, without whom I could never manage, but being here and able to stay awake in the evening is a luxury I haven't known for some time. And what about you? How do you earn what you need to come on a course like this?'

'Have you heard of *Betty's*? It's a company of high quality bakers in a number of places in Yorkshire, with lovely but expensive cake and tea shops. I'm the manager of the Ilkley branch and spend most of my days dressed up to the nines in a posh suit, and being nice to everyone.'

'Not dressed like this,' said Tracey, looking towards the door, from which Sharon had returned wearing a skirt so short it might have been a belt. She sat down and almost emptied her glass in one go.

'Right,' she said, I'm all set for lunch and a day's singing.'

'The question is whether the rest of us will be ready for you,' said Tracey.

Chapter Four

The singing over for the day, Tracey and Dee were sitting at a table whilst Sharon queued to get the drinks. They commented on the way she seemed so natural and interested in the people with whom she engaged in conversation, not least a couple whom they had both thought could bore for England. Now she had the drinks and came over to them.

'Sharon, your ability to relate to everyone is impressive,' said Dee.

'I've always followed the advice of George Burns: "Sincerity - if you can fake that, you've got it made."

'I suppose that's true of me too. No matter how difficult or horrible I find customers I have to smile and be as helpful as I can, often more than they deserve,' said Dee.

'What a joke,' said Tracey. 'My customers see through bullshit straight away and they're aged from one to five.'

They all laughed.

'I have to confess,' began Sharon, 'that I'm unfamiliar with your part of the Dales. I've been to Swaledale and Wensleydale where I once had an almost disastrous encounter with a large sheep with huge curly horns.'

'It'll have been a Swaledale tup and he probably fancied you!

'Oh. Do you think I should be flattered?'

They all laughed.

There was a tannoy call for Dr Sharon Mason, asking her to come to Reception.

'Perhaps there's a rule about the length of skirts,' said Sharon as she rose and went out towards the Reception area. When she got there, she was greeted by two police officers, a man and woman, carrying large guns.

'Hi. I'm Sharon Mason.'

'I'm Sergeant Sandra Lovell and this is PC Andy Gill, and we're from the Leicestershire Police Armed Protection Unit.'

'Protection?'

Yes, I will explain. First, can you tell me what you know of James Elliot, your former husband, also known as Shafiq Zaman?'

'He was my tutor at Exeter and supervised my PhD. He is very clever and he is a great loss to the academic world. He became a Moslem, and I converted to marry him but after just six weeks I left him and reverted to my maiden name of Mason. I assumed he had been radicalised, as it is known, because the Jimmy Elliot I married might have had great difficulties staying out of the beds of girl students, but would never have planted the bomb in Portsmouth which killed two young women. I know nothing further about him and don't want to.'

'Most recently, said Sandra, 'he has been in Rampton Special Hospital, having somehow convinced the medics at HMP Whitemoor that he needed psychiatric attention. The doctors at Rampton believed he was putting it on, though they couldn't work out why, and decided to move him yesterday to another high security prison, but somehow or other on Sunday evening he absconded, and extensive investigations are under way there to find out how. But what matters, Sharon, if I may call you that, is that you are kept safe. The problem you and we face is that your former husband has become obsessed by and made it clear to others in prison that because you have renounced Islam, under Sharia Law, you are an apostate and have to be killed. It is our belief that this is the reason for his coming to Rampton, that there is a security weakness which he knew about, and sought it simply intending to bring about your death.'

'How did you know where I was?'

'The same way as he did. Colleagues in Cheshire went to Nantwich and were told by a neighbour that you were here on a course, but that a man she recognised from a photograph shown to him had asked the same question of her an hour or two earlier,' said Sandra.

'So what happens now?' asked Sharon.

'You go to bed and try to get some sleep, and we shall remain at either end of the corridor. I need you to understand that Shafiq has shown himself ruthless and ready to kill. We will protect you.'

'I'm here with my closest friend, Tracey, who is in the room next to mine. I shall want to tell her all this, and I think I can with some certainty say she is not a Moslem sleeper agent.'

'We would prefer you to say nothing to anyone,' said Sandra. 'In the morning you will be taken somewhere safe. Until we can locate him it is best if no one knows what's going on and she may well be at risk.'

'Sorry, but I *shall* tell Tracey. She knows about the circumstances of my marriage and what happened afterwards. She will want to come with me – that's for certain.'

The bar had more or less emptied now. Andy led the way, followed by Sharon, with Sandra bringing up the rear. Once in the corridor Andy continued to the end and waited by the fire door. Sandra remained by the entrance door and Sharon went straight to Tracey's door and knocked and was quickly let in.

Sharon quickly told her.

'Oh my God. Wherever you are going tomorrow, I'm coming with you.'
'I have told them that already. We can work out logistics in the morning
when we know what's happening. It strikes me that the safest place for me and
you, is to be placed in Rampton so that the silly bugger would have to break
back in to accomplish his murderous intent.'
'Mention it to the police in the morning and see what they say – if you
dare.'
They laughed. Sharon now left Tracey and made her way next door to her
own room and received waves from Sandra and Andy.

The Leicester University campus was extensive and in the middle of the night
it took Shafiq considerable time to find out where the course was taking place,
not least because as he discovered there were quite a few residential events
taking place at the same time. Eventually he found a public noticeboard
containing all the details of these events and there was what he wanted to find:
The Choral Singing Course in the *Wyggeston & Queen Elizabeth College*,
which was very useful as it would provide an easy exit for him.
Because it was a warm night a window into the kitchen had not been
properly shut and he was in without fuss of any kind, though the door to the
dining room was locked. He noticed hanging from a row of pegs a number of
short white coats which he assumed were worn by the waiters and he took
one. It would be the perfect disguise as no one ever took any notice of waiters,
and a plan was forming in his mind. There was a notice on the wall which
indicated the time of breakfast and he remembered that Sharon was always a
very early riser so it could be done quickly before too many others were there
with her.
Unsurprisingly there was a mosque on site and following a sign he made
his way there and found it open. Removing his shoes he entered and
completed his morning prayers. In term time there would quite a lot of fellow
Moslems gathering here, especially on Fridays but this was mid-vacation and
the number of brothers using the place would be small. His prayers finished,
he made his way to the back and sat against the wall and fell asleep, having
first set the alarm on his watch.

The night passed without disturbance of any kind and Sharon had found that
sleep had come much more easily than she might have thought possible in the
circumstances, though next door it wasn't the same for Tracey. When dressed
she texted Sharon and asked if she could join her. Out in the corridor there
was just one officer, the man, present, and soon she was in Sharon's room.
'There's only one of them now,' she said urgently.
'I know,' replied Sharon. 'They've been taking turns doing a recce outside
all night and when Sandra gets back, she'll be able to tell me if it's safe to join
the others for breakfast. They're really nice but they'll be leaving soon and
replaced by others who will move us to wherever it is they have in mind.'
'They've not picked up anything about Shafiq?'

'If so they haven't told me.'
There was a knock on the door.
'Come in,' said Sharon cheerfully. It was Sandra.
'Our replacements are almost here so Andy will lead and I'll follow you into breakfast and we'll get some ourselves. We will stay near you at all times and if you receive an instruction from either of us, obey it immediately. May I just quickly change my clothes here? Appearing in full uniform holding big guns might unsettle your fellow singers.'
'Be my guest', said Sharon, who had not noticed the holdall Sandra had brought in with her.
She did something to her "big gun", presumably applying the safety catch, and placed it into a special holder which she locked. Beneath her tunic was a holster and gun which she removed and then removed her t-shirt replacing it with another. Her tunic trousers she replaced with jeans but fixed in place a sort of belt with an attachment which allowed her hand gun to sit invisibly in her pocket.
Sharon watched Sandra intensely as she went through the undressing and dressing process.
'Do you like your work?' asked Tracey.
'Yes. It's very much a hot and cold job in that most of the time nothing happens and the only time you use your weapon is in the firing range, but all of a sudden something happens and you have to be on full alert and ready to act.'
'Do they do psychological testing for those in your unit?' asked Sharon.
'You're not kidding. Getting in is not easy, and neither is staying in as you are tested continuously.'
'Is it dangerous?'
'It can be though you never operate single-handedly.'
'Have you got a family?'
'I have three boys and a husband, and trust me, when I am at work, I am much safer than I am at home.'
They laughed.
'What does your husband do?' asked Tracey.
'He's a copper too. That's quite common. Much higher rank than me. So at work he can tell me what to do and I do it. If he tried that at home he would regret it.'
There was a knock on the door.
'Who is it?' called out Sharon.
'Andy.'
'Come in, Andy,' said Sandra.
'Ready for breakfast?'
'Okay, Tracey, will you please lead the way into the dining room and when you've got your breakfast choose an empty table and start to eat?'
'Ok'
Tracey went out and did as she had been asked. A couple of minutes later

Andy followed her and chose a table where his view of everything and everyone was ideal. Now Sharon and Sandra went into the dining hall more or less together. Sharon joined Tracey whilst Sandra went to sit with Andy. A few moments later, Dee entered the hall, and seeing her two friends, joined them. Sharon looked across at Sandra who surreptitiously nodded her approval.

'Hi there. Is everyone ok?' said Dee.

Tracey and Sharon murmured a reply of sorts.

Shafiq looked in the window briefly. He could see Sharon, as usual dressed like a whore. He put on the white waiter's coat and made his towards the dining room though the kitchen, making sure his knife was ready to hand. Those working in the kitchen didn't recognise him, but he was not challenged as they regularly had casual labour coming and going. At least he was white, which made a nice change, in Leicester.

What followed happened so quickly that most of those present hadn't even realised that anything had happened until it was over. They may have been eating their breakfast but both Andy and Sandra never lost focus. The waiters coming in and out of the kitchen wore white jackets and were mostly non-white. Sandra was alerted to the presence of a newly-entered white waiter who seemed to have little idea of what he should be doing and mostly stood by the door into the kitchen doing nothing. Her alert had now become a definite unease, and she decided to get up and approach him. Then he suddenly made a move towards the table on which Sharon was sitting talking to her friends. Before he could complete the phrase "Allahu Akbar" he lay dead on the floor two feet from the person he intended to kill. Sandra later said that as she had stood she had seen the knife in his hand. Her gun was in her hand in a moment, and she fired twice. Both bullets entered his heart.

Andy cleared the room in seconds and made the call for immediate backup, but the danger was over and the mission completed. Sandra had returned to her table to complete her breakfast and asked Sharon to come and be with her, her back to the body of Shafiq.

'I hope it won't mess up your course too much, Sharon, but in a short while this place will be awash with men and women in white suits. I will have to surrender my weapons until an investigation can be carried out but you will be required to make a statement as well as the two women with you. To be frank, these things have to be done but I imagine it will be straightforward, not least because there are CCTV cameras in here and I was given authority in advance to shoot to kill. Are you staying or will you want to get home to recover from what was a very close shave with death?'

'Before I decide anything, I need to have some time with Tracey. She may want to go home and as we're here in her car, I may not get the choice.'

'She had her back to him so probably saw nothing before the gun fired. Though she probably saw his body afterwards.'

Sandra's radio burst into life.

'Are you ok?'

'Yes, my love, or yes sir, if you've got your uniform on.'

'I miss you in bed when you're on nights.'

'There's someone listening, my sweet.'

'I don't care.'

'You'll never get to be Chief Constable.'

'Sandra, you know as well as I the identity of one Chief Constable who rose to the top by frequenting the beds of those that mattered.'

'You are not doing likewise!'

'Well, get on with the de-briefing as soon you can. The gang should be with you soon, and then get home and get some sleep. And . . . Well done!'

'Thank you, my love.'

'Was that anyone you know?' asked Sharon with a broad smile.

'No idea who it was!' said Sandra with an answering grin. 'Now look whatever plans you and Tracey devise, you can't leave until you've been formally interviewed, nor your friends. I'm sorry about but I have no control over it. Ah, I can hear the cavalry arriving, late as usual. They will have been having breakfast.'

'Sharon did look behind her as walked towards the exit and the corridor. As she approached her room she could voices from next door and knocked.

'Come in, please,' said Tracey's disembodied voice, she and Dee sitting close together on the bed and holding hands.

'Oh Sharon, are you alright? It's a stupid question, but you know what I mean.'

Sharon joined them on the bed and Dee took her hand.'

'So now what?' asked Tracey.

'We will have to give a statement and after that it's up to us to decide but Tracey I'm totally dependant on you. If you decide to go home, I will have to come with you.'

'I think it has to be your decision, Sharon. Whatever you choose I will do as you wish.'

'What about you, Dee? They will want a statement from you as you saw it all happen from where you were sitting,' said Sharon.

'But I saw nothing at all because I was eating my breakfast and we were engrossed in conversation if I remember.'

'Yes, we were,' replied Sharon.

'What I don't understand is how he got here. Wasn't he meant to be in a high-security prison?' said Tracey.

'You mustn't underestimate how clever he was. He managed to get himself transferred to Rampton by acting as if he was schizophrenic and in need of psychiatric care. He absconded and made his way to Nantwich only to be told I was here. By then the police were on his trail, and that trail ended here. I had become a Moslem and then renounced it. I had sealed my fate: I was an Apostate and had to die. Well, what are you thinking, Tracey?'

'As I said, I'll do what you want. After all you were little more than a second away from death.'

'I really don't want to go back to Nantwich. It's possible that this will be on the news and in the papers.

'Sharon, if you want to be away from here, and I can understand why, I would be perfectly happy for you to go to Wharfedale for recovery and rest in my flat in Ilkley,' said Dee.

'Dee, that is so kind of you,' replied Sharon. 'I shall have to inform the police as they need to know where I shall be, but I'd really like that. What do you think, Tracey?'

'It makes a lot of sense and I'm perfectly happy to sample the delights of *Betty's.*'

'I can give you the key and directions,' said Dee, ' but be warned about the parking which is a nightmare.'

'Yes, it would be something of an irony to miss being murdered only to get a parking ticket,' said Sharon.

There was a knock on the door and when invited to do so a lady with bright red hair came in.

'Hello, I'm detective sergeant Andrea Lovesome.'

'Isn't your hair somewhat unusual for a detective,' said Sharon.

'I lost a bet with some colleagues and this was the forfeit.'

'I rather like it,' said Dee.

'Well now, which of you is Dr Mason?'

'That's me, though I prefer to be called Sharon.'

'We need to go and talk, and then I'll return for you two.'

Sharon left the room with Andrea and they went into the dining room, occupied by several men and women in white.

'Oh, I'm sorry Dr Mason, before we start can I ask you to do something not very pleasant and that is to identify the body still lying on the floor?'

'I was expecting something like that.'

Andrea led her to where the body lay covered in a sheet. When the sheet had been removed she saw that the body had been turned over and was now lying on its back. Andrea pulled back the sheet.'

'It's many years since I last saw him and his beard wasn't so extensive back then, but yes, this is my former husband Dr James Elliot or Dr Shafiq Zaman as he became. I'm sure he will be enjoying the 72 virgins he is entitled to as a martyr in Paradise; he enjoyed then on earth.'

Andrea smiled and then restored the sheet to cover the face and led Sharon to one of the practice rooms so she could make a statement but first ordered fresh coffee for them both. What she didn't report to Andrea, and it was uncomfortable to recognise it herself, was that the real shock of the morning was not the shooting or his attempted murder of her, but the reaction inside herself to the sight of Sandra undressing in her room. It was a feeling she had never known before and she found it completely unsettling.

Chapter Five

Leicestershire Police sorted everything at the University. Sandra was given leave but wholly exonerated in using her firearm and would return to the unit. CCTV had shown without a doubt that her every act was professional and skilled from the moment she clocked what was about to happen to when she fired to protect the target who might otherwise have been killed. As a matter of form they offered her counselling but turned it down because she would be with her best counsellor later in bed, and as he was a Chief Superintendant, no one argued and beside, it was not the first time she had used her weapon to kill. She had done her job, that for which she was trained and was undisturbed by it.

The investigation into how Shafiq Zaman got within two metres of Sharon Mason, when he was supposed to be a resident of a top security prison, because it covered several constabularies was put into the hands of a squad from Scotland Yard, led by Detective Chief Inspector Tom Buddle. He put together a small team who made first for HMP Whitemoor, staying overnight in the nearby town of March where the fleshpots, he told them, were non-existent or, even worse, were existent but the domain of Fen women which they should go out of their way to avoid.

Tom knew that the chances of discovering the link to Rampton were slight. There was no way any of the Moslem brothers would provide them with the information he sought, and he would not waste time pursuing the impossible, though several inmates proudly volunteered that they knew Shafiq was indeed aiming to kill his apostate former wife, something for which they honoured him. Shortly before leaving Whitemoor on the second afternoon, Tom received a call from his boss in London.

'Yes, guv.'

'From March you're to go to Peterborough railway station and collect someone. You won't miss her. She's very tall, very black and very good looking. She will come with you to Rampton and possibly return with you.

Whilst you are there she will ask you to take into custody a prisoner she will identify but don't ask me or her why. All I know is that she's a Colonel in the military and has served in the very worst bits of Afghanistan with distinction and if *I* have to call her ma'am, and I do, so will you all.'

'No problem guv.'

'If she thinks it necessary, she will take full command and even you Tom, will do as you are told.'

Tom laughed.

'As if I would do any other!'

'As if!'

Once on their way one of the team said, 'How on earth can people stand living round here? It is so unbelievably flat.'

There was no question of them missing Martha outside the station. She refused the passenger seat upfront and joined the others in the back, which impressed them all. Equally impressive was the fact that she withdrew from her bag a book and proceeded to read. Most officers would be sick if they tried to do that, but she quickly gave the impression of being fully engrossed in her reading.

'Is it good, ma'am?' asked one of the men with great daring.

'I tend to read novels that aren't too demanding of my emotions or contain violence or things such as we are doing today. I ought really go back to reading the books I read as a child, you know, like *Swallows and Amazons*.'

Do you mean, ma'am, that you share T S Eliot's view that humankind cannot bear too much reality?'

'Well, don't you feel that, the need to get right away from your work?'

'Oh yes. I love my job but I could only do it provided I get away from it regularly.'

'I've never seen you doing it!' said another of the officers, and they all laughed, including Martha.

It was clear that they liked her and equally clear that they all fancied her like mad.

In Scotland Yard, two geeks, Mike and Eamonn were super-competent at their job and were looking for links of any sort that might relate Zamal to his escape route. The door opened behind them, lighting up for a moment the many computers and devices they were working on.

'Hi guys,' said the woman as she took a chair a placed it between the two men. 'I'm Alpha 3 today.'

'And it's good to have you with us, Kim,' said Eamonn.

'Have you got anywhere yet?' she asked.

'There's a huge amount of traffic which is making it difficult,' said Mike, and I assume those we are looking for will be using more and more sophisticated security programmes. That won't stop us of course but it does slow everything down.'

'There will be something coming out of Rampton from a PC without protection. It's the one we need to find.'

'We've checked every message out of Rampton and there's nothing to be seen.'

'H'm,' said Kim. 'Suppose someone looked at something totally innocuous that had been deliberately created for the purpose allowing someone who knew how to replace code?'

'Thats odd,' said Eamonn. 'I noticed a little earlier that someone in Rampton had looked at an online comic, a title I'd never heard of, something intended for children aged about six and I imagine there would be no restrictions on that in prison.'

'Get it back,' said Kim.

It took Eamonn a little while to find it.

'It's been deleted but my machine has saved it.'

'Show me the code,' said Kim.

'There we are. The last two lines are in a different code: "Rails on Ruby Framework". Do you agree?'

Mike and Eamonn both nodded, a little stunned by the speed Kim had recognised the format but they knew her well enough to know she would be right.

'Ok,' continued Kim, 'which of you two clever men is going to translate it first?'

They set to work at once but after only a couple of minutes she stopped them having already done it.

'It reads: "75 to" a series of numbers I take to be a bank account with IBAN and BIC Codes."Urgent. Sunday evening. Car 7.30."

'It's a clever way of doing it,' said Mike.

'So we need to find, and by we, I mean you, where it was deleted and that's immensely important. I will chase up the bank details here and now but then we need to find who it was in receipt of the £75,000 which, I assume was what was paid for letting Shafiq out. I'll work on that by seeing if the far distant Bank, wherever it is, sent a reply indicating receipt of the money, which would be necessary for whoever it was leaving the door open for Shafiq. Then we shall have to search high and low in the Retford area to see where that communication was sent.'

For almost an hour they worked in total silence, then Kim spoke.

'Moldavia. That's where the money is and from what I can see it's not the first large amount paid in.'

'Where the hell is Moldavia?' asked Eamonn.

'Hell may be about right. It's between Romania and the Ukraine, and I hope it stays there. Now I need only find a return email and we shall be winning.'

Silence returned until Mike burst out.

'Jesus! I can't believe this, so Eamonn, please check it for me and I'll move it to one of your monitors, but if I am right we are dealing with someone or people in Ilkley in the Yorkshire Dales. ISIS in Ilkley somehow doesn't feel right.'

'You're not kidding,' said Kim. 'What's the world coming to?'

'It's very near to a huge Islamic population in Bradford,' added Mike.

'Ok. Find the computer and let the guys at Rampton know you have found out the approximate location of two machines, one in Yorkshire and the other close by, possibly in Retford. I shall head off there now. Call me when you have the precise location. When I'm with the device, I'll make contact. You've done really well. I really love working with you two. Thank you for your patience and tolerance. Oh, by the way, 14 down on today's Times crossword over there is "cyclamen"; good clue though.'

She stood up and left. Mike and Eamonn looked at each and smiled, and then set back to work.

None of the team had been in Rampton before and they knew it contained some of the most dangerous and unpleasant men and women who had been taken before the courts and sentenced to many years in prison, others having whole life tariffs, having done dreadful things to other human beings. The team were familiar enough with high security institutions but this place was different. Strangely, and unexpectedly, it was a more peaceful place than many though that belied the level of security and they noticed the greater use of CCTV cameras everywhere including in the toilets and showers, given that in the latter of these in other prisons acts of violence by prisoners on others prisoners were often committed.

'This is horrible,' said one of the team, 'I can't even have a piss without being watched.'

'Yeah,' replied one of the others, 'but from what I hear they're not queueing up to watch, after one of the women nurses said there was nothing worth looking at.'

'Oh shit, that's what my wife says too. Fortunately my underage teenage girlfriend is impressed!'

They weren't the first investigators to be there in response to Shafiq Zaman's disappearance. One of their tasks today, under the guidance of Martha, was to arrest and remove a prisoner. He looked disturbed and the men in the team wondered why the black woman wanted him and where she was intending to take him. She took him to the governor's office, presumably to complete the paperwork, and then took him outside to the vehicle which no one in their right mind would call secure. Whilst there she took a call and went back in to speak to Tom.

'I have something for you. Not a name as such but an address. However, you are to meet Alpha 3 to whom I've just spoken on the phone, at Retford Railway Station at 6.30. She has all the information and on the way you can drop us off at the Premier Inn.'

'What? With an extremely dangerous patient from Rampton, ma'am?'

'Yes, apparently there's a football match he wants to watch on the tele tonight.'

When they got outside the "prisoner" was swigging a can of Guiness and chatting nineteen to the dozen with Alpha One who clearly knew him well, but she was offering no explanations and all they knew was that his name was

Barrie which most certainly was not the name he had when he was arrested inside the prison.

After calling in at the Premier Inn, Kim was not quite as easily identifiable at Retford Station as Martha had been in Peterborough but she recognised their vehicle and waved them down.

'Hey, Kim,' said one of the men. 'I haven't seen you for ages.'

'Alpha 3,' said Tom.

'Don't be daft, guv. It's Kim, and we were at the College of Policing in Coventry together. In her final papers she got the highest marks for everything and she was brilliant with computers. Just about everyone asked for her help at sometime or other.'

Yeah,' answered Kim, 'like removing all traces of porn when wives and girlfriends were dropping by.'

'Can you really do that?' asked one of the men to general laughter.

'So what are you doing now? I heard that you'd left the force.'

'Something like that.'

They knew to ask no further.

'What do we need to know?' Tom asked Kim.

'We're convinced this is the home of the person who let Shafiq Zaman out of Rampton on Sunday evening for a large amount of money. I shall know certain when I look at the computer, so please as you search the house, do not under any circumstances touch a computer, printer or any other accessory. It's now possible to set them up so that they wipe the hard drive clean if moved.

'I don't imagine the lady of the house will give any trouble but if I'm right the man we need to speak to will arrive from work once we are already inside, provided of course that this vehicle is completely out of sight.'

As Kim had forecast entry was easy and straightforward and didn't require weapons. The door was answered almost as soon as Tom had rung the doorbell. The woman inside gave her name as Kath O'Donnell and said her husband Mike worked at Rampton Hospital, and should be back soon. She asked what it was all about and gave a good impression of not knowing anything.

'What's Moldavia like?' asked Kim.

'Not really the place to go for a holiday to be honest, but Mike likes it for some reason or other.'

'Whereabouts do you have your computer, Mrs O'Donnell?'

'There are two upstairs, one used by Mike, and the other belongs to our daughter at Cambridge, and is locked away in a cupboard in her room. We also have 2 iPads and two mobiles.'

'Thank you,' said Kim, 'I'll wait for your husband and let him show me.'

Tom pointed out that there were too many of them and so asked four of his men to stand down and secure their weapons in the vehicle and wait there.

They remained perfectly quiet for almost fifteen minutes when they heard the front door key and the door close behind him. Mrs O'Donnell had been told to shout her normal words of welcome and encourage her husband to come into the room. He had a surprise.

'Good evening, Mr O'Donnell. You might recognise us as some of those who've been with you at the hospital today and we thought it would be pleasant to come and visit you at home,' said Tom.

'I think it would be a good idea if I telephoned my solicitor and asked him to join us,' said O'Donnell.

'Please do so, but don't forget to ask what topping he would like.'

'What on earth are you talking about?'

'Pizzas. I can't expect your wife to cook for us all, and as it's likely we shall be here for some considerable time, we'll call Domino's and get them to deliver. Don't worry, I'll pay. So let's have your order. In the meantime, sir, please come and take this seat. If you need to pay a visit, that's fine, but I'm sorry to say that the door stays open, and my good friend Beta Two here has already brought the recording equipment we require from our vehicle and set it up.'

'Am I under arrest'?

'Why would you be, sir? Have you done something? No, you're not under arrest, but it will be easier for all of us if we can have a chat here. If that's not acceptable then we will have no choice but to take you to London this evening.'

'But you can't do this. It's harassment. The Police and Criminal Evidence Act does not allow it.'

'You're perfectly correct, sir. But we are questioning you under the terms of the Terrorism Act and we are counterterrorism officers. Please call your solicitor if you still wish to do so.'

O'Donnell did, but there was no reply. He left a message.

'Isn't that always the case? Now before we begin and our pizzas arrive I would like you please to accompany this lady to your computer, hand over your iPad to her and provide her with access to your daughter's PC. There will be some passwords required, though I don't think that would be an intractable problem for her if you refuse. I certainly wouldn't let her near mine.'

O'Donnell's own computer elicited little, nor did his iPad, but his daughter's PC was a different matter altogether and would require bagging and removal, but first Kim made contact with Mike and Eamonn who were having to work late. Together they unwound the knot of codes that had been deliberately but inexpertly designed to conceal and confuse. It was good, but still the work of an amateur., and took the three of them hardly any time at all given the work they had done earlier.

She called for Tom to come upstairs to see what she had unearthed. Shafiq Zaman had arranged for O'Donnell to receive £75,000 paid into a bank in Moldavia in return for a door from the kitchen to remain unlocked for no more than 5 minutes on a Sunday evening when staff were short-handed and a fight arranged to distract attention. There was no indication that Zamal had informed O'Donnell of his murderous intentions once he was out.

'Anything else?' asked Tom.

'Yes, there was a much earlier occasion which put £50,000 into the same bank account.'

'O'Donnell's put his prices up, there's inflation for you. It was almost certainly Asif Mohammed who absconded some months ago. I shall charge O'Donnell now, though not his wife at this stage, and we'll get off to London tonight.'

Gently but firmly Kim looked up at him.

'You can do these things when you are told, sergeant.'

Tom was taken aback.

'Of course.'

'Please can you ask one of your team to bag everything.'

'Yes, ma'am.'

No need for the ma'am bit. More important than anything we've done this evening is the question of whether my pizza has been kept warm.'

'Mrs O'Donnell put it into the oven for you.'

'At least she won't have to holiday to Moldavia any more.'

'Is there anything further on the Yorkshire connection?' asked Tom.

'Not yet, but I imagine that once these machines are in the hands of the two wizards I've been working with at the Yard, we'll know considerably more. Now, food.'

'Where will you stay?'

'Don't worry about that. I have friends who will have arranged something.'

'Are you military? I know you were once on the force.'

'I was and I enjoyed every minute of it, working in a team with lots of banter. Nowadays I have to work by myself much of the time but I do spend time in the Yard still and enjoy my visits.'

Tom smiled to himself in the recognition that Kim had told him precisely nothing. They went downstairs together where Kim nodded at Tom allowing O'Donnell to be charged, handcuffed and taken out to the team vehicle and secured. The computers and ancillary equipment were bagged and also placed safely in the vehicle. When her pizza was finished, Kim helped Mrs O'Donnell with the washing up, which amused her, as it was something her husband had never done even from day one and he had not bought them a dishwasher.

Kim called Martha reporting on their evening. Martha asked to be put on to Tom.

'Thank you very much for your work today and for putting up with me. You have been thoroughly professional throughout and I can tell how much your team respect you as I do. I very much hope we can get to work together again.'

'Thank you ma'am.'

'The prisoner we arrested for you in Rampton today. Do you need us to

transport him?'
'No thank you. I think he's probably fast asleep in the room next to mine. I'm pretty sure I could hear him snoring.'
If anything, Tom was more confused than ever.
'When Alpha 3 is ready she will let you go.'
'Yes ma'am.'
He handed her phone back to Kim.
'I have to say, Kim, that I greatly admire the way you don't make a fuss about anything. You just get on and do it.'
'Thank you, but weren't we all taught to be like that?'
'Yes, of course, but we have to work in situations where nerves are constantly on edge and we're given the sort of equipment that is designed to kill. See you here later and a car will collect you.'

'It's terrible I know and don't tell anyone, but I've become highly proficient at forgetting to carry my firearm to work with me in the morning.' Kim confessed to Tom.
'You're licensed?'
'Tom, I'm a senior officer.'
'Forgive me.'
'No need, but I will dismiss you and let you get going. I hope we meet again soon.'
'Me too, Kim!'
'Be gone.'

Within five minutes a marked police car had arrived outside from which Martha emerged and entered the house.
'Hi, Kim, you've had a long day though by all accounts pretty successful.'
'So far, but we're still needing to trace the link with Yorkshire.'
Martha turned to Mrs O'Donnell.
'It's my belief Mrs O'Donnell that you knew nothing of this but you may well be asked by Nottinghamshire Police to attend a police station, answer some of the same questions that we have asked you and make a formal statement. Try not to be anxious about that but it has to be done. They will also inform you how and when you can see your husband, but I have to tell you that based on evidence we have found, it is likely that he will receive a substantial prison sentence.'
'Is that grounds for a divorce?' asked Mrs O'Donnell, with a strange note of hope in her voice.
'I think only a solicitor could answer that but if you're looking for an opportunity, there no time like the present, though not literally at this time of night. Solicitors are like doctors in that you can't get them when you most need them.'
They laughed and went out to the waiting car which drove them to their Premier Inn.

Once there the two women sat together in the foyer, both dead tired, but needing a cup of tea and a de-brief.

'I think we take you for granted, Kim, but that's because you never seem to fail the service. Once again thank you.'

'Thank you Martha, I appreciate that.'

'There's one knot left untied, however, and it's this odd connection with Yorkshire.'

'Unlikely though it is, the contact was operating from a place in the Yorkshire Dales, called Ilkley.'

Martha at once reached for her bag and pulled out some papers which she looked through.

'Oh shit,' she said. 'There was a person on that course in Leicester where Zamal was shot dead, who came from Ilkley. She made a point of befriending the intended victim, and after the event, sent her and a friend to her home in Ilkley to rest and recover. And I sanctioned it.'

Chapter Six

Unusually but understandably, the two friends had said little on their way up the M1 and then via Leeds, along Wharfedale through Otley to their destination. That morning Sharon's former husband had been shot dead a couple of feet away as he was moving in to kill her with a knife. Only the diligence and skill of the police had saved her life. There was another matter on her mind from all that happened during the morning though it was something she could never speak of to anyone and it was the thing she kept returning to in her mind: it was the sight of Sandra, a married woman with three children, in her underwear. It had almost felled Sharon and left her quite shaken. She was sure she had never had a lesbian thought in her head, even in the all-female environment in which she worked, though equally, since her catastrophic wedding to Jimmy, neither had she ever had a heterosexual thought.

As they entered the town they saw a supermarket, the name of which they did not recognise – *Booth's* – but which when they had called in to stock up, they discovered was perhaps the best they had ever entered and, on enquiry, discovered it was a small company mostly in Lancashire who prided themselves on being the best. Waitrose had tried to take them over, but the owners, a Lancashire family, were not for selling.

Dee was quite right. Ilkley was as lovely as the parking was lamentable, if not worse, and they were too late to go into *Betty's* beneath Dee's flat but she had insisted they go down for breakfast each morning as the famous Karl, he of the dancing shoes, had been told not to charge them, however many breakfasts they had, though both Dee and Karl knew one breakfast a time in this establishment was enough for anyone.

Dee's flat was cared for and furnished to the highest standards with comfortable armchairs and sofa, and the largest television screen either of them had ever seen.

'She must be well paid to be able to afford stuff like this,' said Tracey.

'I think it might be the product of her divorce settlement,' replied Sharon, 'but did you notice in her bedroom the small Israeli flag? Don't you think that

a bit odd?'
'Now you come to mention it . . .'
'Are you wanting food? asked Sharon.
'I would rather do some serious drinking and allow myself to get picked up by some fit young Yorkshire lad who might be into gymnastics when I've taught him a thing or two.'
'Spoken like a happily married mother of two, if I may say so. I'm proud of you. But back from fantasy land, Tracey, would you manage *Piccolino Ilkley*, the Italian I spied as we drove up Brook St?'
'Trust a teacher to ruin my evening! Yeah, why not?'

The synchronised awakenings happened at 4-00 am. Dee heard a loud thumping on her door and having not locked it suddenly found the overhead light turned on and two people standing above her.
'We're armed counterterrorism officers and we have reason to believe that you have conspired with others to bring about the escape from prison of a convicted terrorist. We require you to accompany us for questioning.'
'Do tell me how you manage to do it so very well?'
'Do what?'
'Talk through your arse. Are you able to tell me if this is a dream,' asked Dee, 'as I would love to go back to sleep,'
'Please dress now.'
'Officer, I am wearing nothing under this sheet and I do not want to waste what I've got giving you a thrill in the middle of the night, so either find me a woman officer or drag me out stark naked and screaming "rape".'
The other officer spoke.
'You go, I'll stay.'
Her gender was in no doubt.
'Do you people do perpetual night duty?' asked Dee.
'Don't you start! My husband claims I only applied for the job to get away from being in bed with him.'
Dee laughed.
'True?'
'Well, lets say I like him to think so – especially on the nights when I am there and he's worked up an appetite!'
'By the way, I imagine you'll want my iPad and mobile, both of which are charging under the desk over there.'
The officer picked them up and immediately bagged them.
'Do you think I'll need my coat?'
'Bring everything."
'And will you be putting handcuffs on me because I'll put my gloves on if you are?'
'Having seen you dress completely, I do not think you have a concealed weapon and as you will be sitting in a car which can't be opened from the inside, I might spare you that at this time of the morning.'

Dee was in for a long drive. In the driving seat, was a woman who seemed to be in charge and who they called 'sarge'. Dee hoped that steady movement of the vehicle would get her off to sleep again and decided that wherever they were taking her was where she was going and that therefore making any kind of fuss was pointless. The only conversation that took place was when the woman officer who had been in her room incongruously asked Dee where she had bought the blouse she had put on.

'Strange to say, I bought it in M&S. Their women's clothes are not all that good these days, but I liked it straightaway, and it was quite cheap. I was pleased with it.'

'I bet you were. It's ever so pretty.'

The officer in charge spoke, 'I've stopped going to Marks,' she said. 'And it's a real pity. I still get my bras and pants there of course, like everybody else, but I'm afraid that the competition has really knocked them sideways. But no company has a right to eternal life.'

One of the male officers sighed audibly.

'Shut up you,' said the one in charge. 'These things are very important as you will find out when you get married, if ever!'

By the time they drew close to their destination Dee had told them all about *Betty's* and the three women were chatting about their own favourite cakes and pastriesu

'But really you must make every effort to get to Yorkshire,' said Dee. The shops and tea rooms are wonderful and I don't just say that because I work I work one of them. Harrogate is still the best and there's almost always a pianist who plays along while you indulge.'

The officer in the front passenger seat could not resist a comment.

'When I was at my interview for counterterrorism, the boss said it was often highly dangerous work with highly dangerous people. Dee, you've now got me terrified of cakes, cups of tea and blouses from M&S!'

It was Tracey who first heard the noise at the door. She looked down from the sitting room and could see police officers below. She opened the window and shouted down to them not to damage the door as she was coming to open it. By now Sharon had appeared, and greeted the police officers as they came into the sitting room.

'I'll make some tea,' she said, though one of the officers insisted he accompany her.

The officer in charge asked the others to do a full recce.

'I know you're only here to recover from what happened yesterday but we've received information that leads us to search this flat.'

'Does Dee, the owner of the flat, know about this and shouldn't we be asking if you have a warrant, but to be honest, though I've seen them on television I've no real idea what one is or how on earth you might get one. On tele they don't seem to have any difficulty getting them, so why bother?'

The senior officer laughed.

'No, we don't have a warrant as this operation comes under Terrorism legislation.'

'Well, please leave things as you find them and in the meantime ask any questions you may want. We're getting used to you lot coming into our lives at daft times. But have you come all the way from London just to give us an early-morning alarm call?

'No we're based in Leeds.'

'It's meant to be good for shopping. Is it?'

'My girlfriend says it's not bad. How much do you know about the flat owner?'

'Hardly anything other that she is the manager of Betty's downstairs, had to have her marriage annulled having discovered that her husband was lacking lead in the pencil department. Apart from that I know nothing, though there is one thing odd about her. In her bedroom there is a small Israeli flag, but why it is there and its significance I couldn't say and she never mentioned Israel or politics to me, but it wouldn't suggest Islamic sympathies.'

The tea came and the whole team came together in the sitting room.

The senior officer pointed to a mac computer.

'Have either of you had cause to use that whilst you've been here?

They both shook their heads and then the senior officer's phone rang.

'Delta One.'

Sharon and Tracey looked at one one another and giggled.

'Ok,' said the officer, and returned his phone to his tunic and looked at the two women.

'Alpha 3 will be here shortly, having been brought from Retford. Her instructions are to examine the computer and if necessary to take it away. She will also need to look at the iPads or whatever you have, and your phones.'

'What odd names you have. I've met no one called Delta or Beta before,' said Tracey with a perfectly straight face.

'There are several reasons why we use monikers, but chiefly to protect the identity of officers. I don't even notice it anymore and just take it for granted.'

'And does it achieve its ends?'

'Yes. There are times when anonymity in court, for example, is necessary, for protection from criminals and the press – unless, like me, you think they are one and the same. I sometimes think that those working our in Press Office have the most difficult job in the service, and that consideration should be given to arming them permanently.'

They heard a car arrive outside. Minutes later they were aware of someone coming up the stairs and then a woman entered the room.

'Wow,' said Tracey, 'where on earth did you get that coat?'

'Yes, it's really nice,' echoed Sharon.

'I got it in *Zara*, and it's particularly useful for a journey such as I've just made in the middle of the night. Just look at the lining.'

'Was it expensive?'

'If I can remember aright, it was £159, which I thought was not bad. Do you want to try it on?' she said, passing it to Tracey who at once disappeared into it.

'Oh this is lovely.'

'It'll be a little too small for me,' said Sharon, but when I get home, or more accurately, if I ever get home, I'll check their website.'

'Do you buy a lot of clothes online?' asked the woman.

'No, but when you live in Nantwich there's not a lot of choice locally and it's not easy shopping where I work being a teacher, as I would keep bumping into my girls.'

Across the room stood a fully armed police officer who like a colleague just arriving in London with a woman prisoner, couldn't believe what he was hearing. He was meant to be keeping watch over two women who might be involved in a terrorist plot, who had been joined by someone believed to be one of the greatest technological experts in the country and almost certainly worked for the Security Services, and here they were discussing clothes shopping at getting on for five o'clock in the morning!

Sharon however, was having huge difficulties of her own. What she had experienced the previous morning when Sandra was undressing and dressing in her room was nothing compared with what the arrival of this woman was doing to her. What was happening?

'I'm Kim,' she said.

'I'm Tracey and this is Sharon,' said Tracey, 'but I thought we had to call you Alpha 3.'

'It was my operational moniker whilst I was working in Nottinghamshire. Now I'm Kim. And this I take it is the computer I've been called to see. It's good, an iMac but not the Pro version. Very heavy and a good-sized 27" screen. The first thing I have to do is to enter without a password which is easy enough but first I'll run through the various start-up keys with a little gizmo I have with me plugged in the back, which will tell me most of what I want to know.'

Her keyboard speed was rapid and occasionally she made approving noises. Finally she pulled out her gizmo and started the computer in the usual way. The normal apple appeared, and the screen came to life.

'Amazing. The computer password has been overridden by the user so she wouldn't have to use it when she turned on and left it that way when she went away. That doesn't strike me as the activity of someone who might have something to hide though it could just could be a bluff, even if I doubt it, but I'll do a fuller check now.'

'Can you tell me the age of the device?' said Delta 1.

'Oh yes. The first day it was used was April 6 this year and I can tell that this has not been amended in any way. Could someone make me a strong cup of tea, white, no sugar, please?'

Sharon went out to the kitchen, stopping to pop into the loo where she could see that her face was flushed. Eventually she arrived back with tea for Kim. Her hands were shaking.

Kim went quiet for about half an hour, plugged various things into the back of the mac, put on earphones, then turned on the adjacent printer which she loaded with A4 paper, and sat back as page upon page spewed forth. When it had stopped, she spoke again.

'Nothing at all. This machine has not been used to communicate with anyone in Retford, and as I electronically dismantled that computer last evening, I knew exactly what I was looking for. Nor do I need to to look at your iPads and phones. All of which is good news for your friend Dee though it's not good news for you and your team Delta 1, nor for me, because it means we have a curious coincidence on our hands, because somewhere in this town there is a far from innocent device being used by those working with terrorists who attempted to murder you, Sharon. That computer has to be found.'

'How can you do that? Just about every house in Ilkley will have at least one machine?' asked Sharon, 'and my other question is to ask whether this means I'm still not safe?'

'I would say you are perfectly safe. No one here knows you, including the person using the offending computer, so I don't think you need worry.'

'I agree,' said Delta 1

'Does your wife or partner call you Delta 1? said Sharon with a smile, 'It might be sexy for her to do so!'

'Does your husband call you "Dr Mason"?' he replied.

'As he was shot dead by a counterterrorism police officer yesterday morning, I rather think he doesn't.'

'Oh shit. I'm so sorry. I wasn't thinking.'

'Don't feel even slightly bad. I'm only winding you up. We were divorced a long time ago, and he was after all just two feet away from killing me with a very nasty-looking knife. But the 19th century novelist Anthony Trollope records that Mrs Grantly always called her husband, the Reverend Theophilus Grantly, "Archdeacon", even in bed.'

They all laughed and it helped Delta 1 feel better about his faux pas.

'I've finished and urgently need sleep,' said Kim, though first I need to speak to London and arrange for Dee to be safely transported back to Leicester University or here, as she wishes. You and your men, kind sir, can stand down and make your own report. You will still need me here, so I shall find somewhere to stay.'

'Please stay here, Kim,' said Sharon. 'There's Dee's bed and I can't think she would begrudge her rescuer the use of it.'

'Thank you.'

'And you can have a special breakfast in *Betty's* below,' added Tracey.

'Ooh,' said Delta 1, 'is there any chance of my staying for breakfast too? I've heard about breakfasts at *Betty's*.'

In a chorus, the three women looked at him and said 'No!'

He looked crestfallen.

Kim spoke on her phone to someone who was clearly important and could make appropriately important decisions. Dee would be informed straight away that she was free and that arrangements would be made to transport her either back to Leicester or home to Ilkley, whichever suited her.

Having given that news to Tracey and Sharon, Kim declared herself dead to the world and made her way to Dee's bedroom.

'Wake me up in time for *Betty's*,' she said, and was gone.

'Do you know, Tracey, I think I have led a very sheltered life, all things considered,' said Sharon.

'Me too, I'm pleased to say. I must phone home in the morning and let Geoff know all about what's happened. I assume we'll be returning home tomorrow, or is today already?'

'Who knows and who cares? I'm doing a Alpha 3 and following her to bed,' but not saying what she was thinking, which was that she wished she could do so literally. The thought terrified her but she knew she couldn't deny it was there. She shook her head and wondered just what was happening to her.

The aspect of the whole business which made Dee most cross was not being dragged from her bed and transported to somewhere on the outskirts of London, or even being locked in a cell. All these things she could manage with equanimity. No, what really made her cross was being awakened sometime after five o'clock in the morning to be told it was all a mistake and that later she would be taken wherever she chose to go. She was not surprised because she knew there was nothing she had done or was involved in for which she might be arrested by the counterterrorism police of all people. She repeated now like a sort of mantra, 'I did try to tell you: I'm the manager of *Betty's*.' She was given back her phone and iPad and she greeted their return with, 'And who could I possibly call at this time in the morning?' Just before she put her head back on her pillow she was struck by the remembrance that they had said they would take her wherever she wished to go. She had always wanted to go to New York and perhaps she should try it on, but she was asleep again less than five minutes later and when she woke up in time for breakfast she thought she would stick to Ilkley!

Although still very tired from the adventures of their night, their jaws all dropped when presented with the breakfast menu, even though they didn't make it downstairs until half past ten. They had introduced themselves to Karl who welcomed them warmly.'

'I'm afraid we have an extra body with us, Karl, but I know Dee wouldn't mind her being included in your special offer.'

'Dee? When you say Dee, do you mean the Dee who has just entered the tea room via the front door?'

They all turned.

'Jesus,' said Sharon, 'yes, she's the one I had in mind.'

At once they stood as Dee came towards them with open arms and a big smile.

'Dee, this is Alpha 3, but we just call her Kim. She arrived in the middle of the night and bossed all the counterterrorism police before closely examining your mac and declaring you not guilty,' said Sharon.

'Ah, so you are the one responsible for them (whoever they were) waking me up in the middle of the night with that news. It could have waited.'

'Hello Dee,' said Kim. 'This has been a right mess, and it isn't over yet though any part you three might have had is over, and thank you for the use of your bed though if it's any comfort I imagine I got less sleep even than you.'

'You're very welcome Kim, and all of you: welcome to *Betty's*. Before we talk, let's order breakfast. Karl is so slow it could be lunchtime before it arrives!'

'I heard that,' said Karl.

'I suspect you were meant to,' said Tracey, and they all laughed.

They ordered and already the place was filling up and the smells were simply amazing.

'How have you managed to get here so quickly?' asked Tracey.

'I rather expect Kim will know the answer to that.'

'If a major error is made, standing orders are to restore persons and property with the minimum of further inconvenience. Over a distance such as this both road and rail would not be considered, and as we are quite a way from RAF Leeming I don't think it would be by aeroplane, so I would guess you came by helicopter and almost certainly it would have put you down at the nearest hospital with a helipad, which I assume would be the Airedale General in Keighley.'

'Had someone told you that, or was it just a guess?' asked Sharon.

'Neither, it was just obvious.' She smiled at Sharon who could barely cope with it. This is getting silly, she thought.

The others sat there in amazement, their silence now broken by the arrival of food and drink. Sharon and Tracey had the English Breakfast, Dee had the Swiss Breakfast Rösti, whilst Kim had gone for the crushed avocado on toast served with bacon and poached eggs. Coffee followed and little was said as they indulged themselves. Only afterwards did they try to catch up with what they had been doing in the past 24 hours.

'So what now for you, Kim?' said Tracey.

'The job's not finished even though you have been excluded from suspicion. We need to find a particular computer here in Ilkley, and I have two colleagues on their way at this moment to work on it with me.'

'Would it be helpful to use my flat upstairs as a base for what you want to do?'

'That would be very kind, Dee. It would just be the three of us. Any involvement of counterterrorism police would only take place at the location we indicate.'

'Will it take long?' asked Tracey.

'As long as a piece of string. We will only be able to locate it when it's in use which may severely limit our activities. So that will allow me a day off relaxing in Ilkley and I must say that this breakfast has been the best of all possible beginnings. It's quite possible that I shall go back to bed.'

'How did you get into all this technology expertise?' asked Tracey.

'I learned most from my dad who was one of the first to build his own computer, with help from his daughter of course. What he was doing was extremely in advance of what others were doing. At Uni I studied Computer Studies though it was frustrating because my teachers were streets behind dad, so in the main I did my own things and made various pieces of equipment which most certainly were not on the syllabus. I did get a degree but I didn't care about that. Instead I decided to do a Robin Hood. I could have sold what I was making to the highest bidder or turned it into a business, but instead I opted to make good use of it by joining the police.'

'I take it you're still with the police?' asked Tracey.

Kim smiled at her.

'No,' came her reply, which was the moment of realisation for Tracey that she would get nothing further out of Kim who had a clear way of ending a discussion simply by the tone of her voice.

Sharon and Dee had listened intently to all that Kim had said, especially Sharon who hung on her every word and watched intently now as she left the room.

'I feel I must apologise, Dee, for everything that's happened and ruined the singing course for you,' said Sharon.

'It's not exactly your fault, it's the lunacy of Islam.'

'Did they take you to London?'

'I don't think it was in London itself, just somewhere on the outskirts. I heard it referred to a couple of times as the "Conference Centre" but I saw various non-civil aircraft as they led me to the helicopter this morning, so I presume it's an RAF base.'

'It's a strange life,' interjected Tracey. 'How long someone like Kim can keep it up, I wouldn't know but you must function on massive bursts of adrenalin, and develop the capacity to manage without sleep for long periods of time. It also strikes me as highly dangerous and we probably don't know about a lot of the things they are doing all the time.

'Kim told me that she met up with her boss in Retford, who was in Rampton Hospital to remove a prisoner who wasn't a prisoner at all, but one of their own people who had spent a period there undercover. Only the governor knew who he really was, though even she didn't know why he was there. That is real commitment'

'Gosh, that must have been risky. Imagine what might have happened it it had become know that there was a stool-pigeon in there with them. They're not nice, the prisoners in there,' added Sharon.

'I know,' said Tracey, 'but who do you think Kim works for if she's not with the police any more? If they could lay on a helicopter for you, Dee, they must be high-powered.'

'The Security Service, I suppose,' relied Dee, but it doesn't feel right in

Ilkley to have James Bond lookalikes around the place. It's not the right sort of place to have terrorists resting up but we're pretty close to Bradford with its huge Asian population so I suppose they must always be on the watch.'

'Dee,' said Tracey, 'may I ask you a question about something that intrigues me?'

'Of course.'

'It's the Israeli flag in your room.'

Dee laughed and at the same time Kim returned.

'Tracey's asked me about my Israeli flag which I'm sure you've noticed in my room, Kim. At least it indicates I'm hardly pro-Palestinian. Ok. Some years ago, for my holiday, I joined a tour to the Holy Land, as they called it. It was horrendous and put me off religion for ever. It's difficult to know which was worse: the places we visited or the people I was travelling with. We began in Galilee, which was not too bad, and then travelled south down the Jordan Valley and visited Jericho, Qumran, the home of the Dead Sea Scrolls, the Dead Sea where we were invited to swim, and then Masada. In terms of the places visited, that day was the best by far, mainly because none of the visits were to Christian sites which are almost always ghastly and tacky . When we got to Jerusalem I developed a mysterious set of symptoms and stayed behind in the hotel on the next morning. They went off doing religion again in the coach, whilst I visited the Israeli Parliament, the Knesset, and whilst there got talking to a number of young soldiers with whom I went for a meal in the evening. They were smashing lads and all of them doing compulsory national service and not one complained about it - in fact, quite the opposite, they were all proud to be doing so. Our conversation moved me and I wondered why the political and military issues as seen by the the young people of Israel, all of whom spend time on the front line each year, were not reported adequately here.

'On the following day they collected me from my hotel and took me to a place called Yad Vashem, a Hebrew title meaning "a monument and a name" and is the official Israeli memorial to the Holocaust. It wasn't anything like I had visited before, and I mostly went round in a numb silence and tears, especially in the extraordinary monument to the children who died. After that, my soldier friends had received permission to drive me south to the area into which Palestinian rockets are fired every day, and once again this is rarely reported here.

'I came back radicalised, as it is called, though largely unable to do anything other than become a Friend of Israel and oppose anti-semitism wherever it is to be found, and not least in the Labour Party. I've heard it said, believe it or not, that some Labour people blame the Jews for losing them the last election. If that's not anti-semitism, I don't know what is.'

'Thank you for sharing all that with us. You're quite a woman, Dee. There's something else I want to ask, if I may?'

'I haven't any other flags in case you wondered,' said Dee smiling.

'Tracey has told Geoff that's she coming home but I don't want to go yet as there's so much on my mind and I wondered how you might feel about having a lodger for a while.'

'I would love it, but what about your work?'

'I will ring the Chair of Governors and tell her that I'm traumatised by the attempt that was made on my life and that I must stop for a while.'

'Will that work?'

'I couldn't give a fuck if it doesn't to be perfectly honest.'

Dee rose from her chair and walked across the room to Sharon and and gave her a big hug and kiss on the cheek.

'Welcome to Ilkley,' she said.

Kim had not taken her eyes off Sharon since she had returned to the room, and did not do so now. Sharon did likewise.

Chapter Seven

Tracey prepared herself for her journey back to Nantwich and loaded her bags into her car which was parked quite some distance away. Sharon accompanied her to the car park.

'It's been a terrible week, Sharon. We left Nantwich full of hope about the singing course never even imagining that what happened might do so, or anything like it.'

'Yes, I came extremely close to having my throat slit and were it not for the professionalism and skills of Sandra that would have happened. I keep reflecting on that and it makes me more determined that ever that however short or long the time left to me I have to make the most of it.'

'I think you should find yourself a man to love and be with. You know how much I adore Geoff and I think we give each other the means of thinking being alive is worthwhile.'

Sharon laughed.

'I know you do, you soppy date, and it's a shining example of what love means to all who know you. But I shall bear your words in mind. Now, my darling Tracey, drive safely as you make your way back to your lover who is also your husband, you lucky thing, and call me when you arrive to let me know you are there safely.'

'I will and what are you going to do this morning?'

'Dee says she has shopping to do but I won't offer to go with her, so I might persuade Kim to have coffee with me in *Betty's* and then perhaps have a walk down to the river.'

'You like her don't you?'

Sharon nodded. 'Yes, very much.'

Tracey smiled and put her hand on Sharon's arm in affection.

Disappointed that she was having to travel alone, Tracey set off for Nantwich, via the M62, M60 and the M6 (according to she who must be obeyed – or sat nav as she was known), though she was not altogether surprised that Sharon couldn't face going back during the school holiday. Although nothing had been said, Tracey sensed that something was troubling her friend and a few days in the Dales might be just the right medicine. Tracey herself, on the other hand, couldn't wait to get home. Considering what she had witnessed at breakfast on just the day before, what she needed was normality with Geoff and the boys, and then with the children in the play school. A simple world.

It was a nice day for driving and there was good music on the car radio. She had decided that before she set off properly for home, she would go and visit nearby Haworth, the home of the Brontë sisters, and visit the museum. She could quite easily take a couple of hours out.

Although she was well aware that nourishment back then was as nothing compared to now, she was nevertheless taken aback by just how small the sisters must have been to wear the clothes she saw, and also extraordinarily resourceful to survive the solitude and cold, but she loved every moment of her visit and bought a copy of *Brontë Letters* by Juliet Barker, always a good read. She decided on a cup of tea before setting off and began the new book which she was already finding fascinating reading just two pages in.

Kim was more than happy to go along with Sharon's suggestions and after a disgustingly enormous toasted teacake each they began their walk down to the river and the old bridge.

'Is your dad still alive, Kim?'

'No. He was just 60 when he died, I'm sorry to say. Believe it or not he died of lung cancer having never smoked in his life but if your number comes up you have to go.'

'What of your mother?'

'It may sound melodramatic, but I have no idea whether she is alive and although I suppose I would like to know and even see her, she and my dad split up when I was just two and she left me with him. I often asked him questions but he wouldn't answer them, and there are no photographs, so I don't even know what she looks like.'

'I could help you find her if you wanted, Kim.'

Kim stopped and turned towards Sharon.

'What a simply wonderful thing to say,' she said and took hold of Sharon's hand which made her almost want to explode with joy. Holding hands they continued down to the river. They received some funny looks from residents of Ilkley, but neither cared.

At the river, Sharon told Kim about her own parents and the calamitous marriage she had made and her inability to perform in the bedroom.

'I've never told anyone,' said Kim, 'before now. My own involvement with men was no more glorious than yours. Police College is notorious for sexual involvements and there's a kind of unwritten rule that the women attending are there first and foremost for the benefit of the men.'

'They must all be Moslems then, for that's exactly what Jimmy said to me when I told him I was leaving, but I was even lower than that.'

'My problem at college was not that I fancied other women recruits, but that I really couldn't stand the thought of doing something physical like having sex with a man, and though I know and like a lot of good and obviously attractive men, I feel exactly the same now about women.'

Sharon wanted to know whether Kim still felt the same about women but she wasn't saying. They continued to hold hands all the way back, but what was really going on in Kim's head? Sharon knew that she was in love, but how the hell do you say that to the object of your powerful feelings when she is a woman? She might not be surprised when a 16 year old came to see her at school and admitted to having a crush an another girl, and this had happened more often than she might have anticipated when she had come to the school, but now she was a head teacher in her forties in love with a female member of MI5! How the sixth form would laugh if they knew, though respecting them as she did, she knew they would also be extremely caring and understanding.

As usual on the M62 there were carriageway repairs (though whenever did a carriage ever come this way?) and on this occasion close to Rochdale, Tracey's car drew to a halt behind a lorry of some sort. Whether something distracted the lorry driver following and he wasn't aware of the stationary vehicles ahead, would have to wait for the inquest but he was probably still travelling at 50mph at least when he ploughed into the back of Tracey's car. The car was crushed, and it took almost three hours to remove the body. The lorry driver was taken to hospital and later charged with causing death by dangerous driving. The car registration number had provided the police with the identity and home address of the owner, and local officers called to inform Geoff who knew at once their visit was not social. He led them into the kitchen.

'Ok, tell me,' he said.

'I am so very sorry to have to report, Mr Adamson, that your wife was involved in a serious road traffic accident on the M62 motorway near Rochdale and our colleagues in Lancashire Police have told us that such was the nature of the collision, death will have been instantaneous. The road is still blocked.'

Geoff felt totally numb. Such things happened all the time but why to his wonderful Tracey?'

'Would you like us to make contact with anyone for you, Mr Adamson?'

'No, but thank you for coming so promptly. Our sons will be home soon. They've been on a summer holiday football course. Thank you.'

Geoff stood and prepared to show the two policemen out.

Tracey had spent longer in Haworth than she had intended and left her car in a large car park at the bottom of the steep hill but as she approached she couldn't quite remember where. She wandered around for a while, trying desperately to recall where it was, and then realised why she couldn't find it: it was gone. Compared with modern cars it didn't have any anti-theft devices and of those parked around her it must have been seen by the thief as a soft touch. She decided first to check with the man who had issued her ticket earlier, but he confirmed that no car had been towed away.

"Oh shit,' she said, as she took out her mobile and called the police which was easier said than done. It was not exactly an emergency, so she dialled 101. It took ages to get through, past the automatic voices, to a real live person, even though Tracey was not quite sure about the "live" in that description. He took the information but could offer no help as to what she should now do, so it left her with no choice but to call Sharon, explain what had happened and say she would get a taxi back. Dee was having none of it and within five minutes she and Sharon were in the car on their way to Haworth. On arrival they found Tracey sitting on a wall speaking on her phone and holding open her new book looking as if she didn't have a care in the world.

Geoff was utterly distraught and had no idea how he would possibly tell the boys or the other members of the family. He couldn't even ask Sharon, Tracey's closest friend, to call in because she was away in Yorkshire, staying behind and not returning with Tracey. As far as he was concerned, this was the end of the world. He went to get himself a stiff drink and in so doing saw their wedding day photograph and another of the gold medal winner in Melbourne.

The phone rang.

'Hello.'

'Hello darling, you sound miserable.'

'Tracey? Is that you? Is it really you?'

'Of course it is. Who else would it be?'

'I don't know, because the police have only just left after telling me that you were killed in a motorway crash this afternoon.'

He burst into tears.

'Oh, I can't tell you how wonderful it is to hear your voice. Where are you?'

'I'm in Haworth main car park, from where my car was stolen sometime in the past two or three hours, and I'm waiting to be picked up by Sharon and a friend we met on the course, to be taken back to Ilkley. Why did they say I was dead?'

'Because someone is, presumably, your thief. They still hadn't been able to get you out of the wreck, they said, but used the number plate, which brought them here.'

'Oh Geoff, you poor thing, you must have had a terrible shock.'

'I did and I imagine there'll be an inquiry as to how it can have been allowed to happen. If so, I shall want to be there.'

'Look, my love. I have no car now and can you let the insurance people know? I hope to be back tomorrow. I'll get the train to Manchester and then to Crewe. Might you be able to meet me?'

'If you wanted, I would drive up to Ilkley and collect you.'

'No. I'll come home by train. I couldn't face being on the M62 where the person died. I can get a taxi or train to Leeds and the Manchester train from there. Here they are, so I'd better go, but whatever else I am, be assured I'm not a ghost.'

'Thank goodness for that, though there will be one family facing tragedy and loss tonight.'

'Yes, I know, but not ours.'

Whilst Dee and Sharon were rescuing Tracey in Haworth, Kim's colleagues had arrived and begun setting up their equipment, the irony being that most of it had been designed by Kim. They took over Dee's internet connection. They worked hard but their efforts bore no fruit and it became increasingly likely that their chances of discovering the computer used to communicate between Shafiq Zaman and Mike O'Donnell would depend on when it was next in use and they were pinning their hopes on the evening, perhaps after whoever it was returned from work. They made the even more important decision to go downstairs and enjoy afternoon tea in *Betty's*. All three of them longed for the Pink Champagne Afternoon Tea but decided in the end to "make do" with sandwiches, a scone with clotted cream and strawberry jam, and then cakes. They were however at a loss to know what sort of thing an Engadine Slice was. They caught the attention of a waitress who was, like the others, immaculately attired.

'Our Engadine Cake is made by hand with layers of rich hazelnut meringue, almond paste and buttercream, topped with almond Florentine,' she said proudly. 'It comes originally from Switzerland.'

'Did you bake it?' asked Eamonn.

'Oh no, I just serve it.'

'That is such a pity as if you had said yes, I was going to ask you to marry me.'

The waitress laughed and pointed to his wedding ring.

'What would your wife say?'

'Who cares, if I was married to the woman who could make that!'

'If you like, I'll go into the kitchen and bring the pastry chef. He's twice your age and hasn't much hair and a tummy that makes him look pregnant, but I'm sure you'll be very happy together.'

They all laughed so loudly that everyone turned to look.

'Do you know, I might have second thoughts about that.'

Arriving back upstairs they found Sharon, Dee and poor Tracey, who for their benefit had to tell the story over again.

In Nantwich, Geoff was still struggling with his emotions. Although it had ended well, that didn't compensate for the shock that he had received when he had opened the door to the police. More followed. Shortly after the boys had returned from football and been told the saga of the afternoon, the front doorbell rang, and standing there was a reporter he recognised from the *Crewe Chronicle*.

'I'm so sorry to hear about your tragic loss, Mr Adamson.'
' Tracey is not dead, she's in Ilkley, and I have spoken to her since the time when her car was crushed on the M62. It had been stolen and tragically, whoever stole it must be the one who was killed, but she is fine, just annoyed that her car was taken leaving her stranded. All being well, she's coming home tomorrow by train.
'I'm more concerned to know how it is that you knew about Tracey's alleged death.'
'I make use of a scanning device as does every local journalist but you didn't hear me say that
'Well, please leave me be right now.'

The three women, too late back to benefit from the afternoon tea enjoyed by the others felt very envious until Dee, having taken herself off downstairs, returned laden with goodies left over at the end of the afternoon service.
As they indulged, Kim suddenly said to Mike, 'Mike, what are you getting on your screen – A4 69 D3?'
'It's still booting, so I assume it's a PC. How long is it to Christmas? It might come sooner.'
'It's new,' added Eamonn, 'but I've got a hold on it and recorded it.'
'Distance?' asked Kim.
'Less than 400 metres.'
Kim stood and went in search of one of her home-made pieces of equipment, with which she returned, and asked Mike to move. She was his superior officer, and without demur he did so. Kim's gadget was fitted into Dee's mac causing the screen to behave in ways Dee had never seen before. Kim turned to Dee.
'Don't worry Dee, it'll be ok, it's just a sort of sophisticated GPS.'
'No problem.'
Sharon and Tracey looked on at the screens and equipment. There suddenly appeared on the screen a browser that Dee knew wasn't hers. Dee typed something and at once there appeared what she was looking for.
'There we are, guys. It's what we're looking for – the children's comic with the changed code used from Rampton. Mike, can you give uniform a buzz and tell them we shall need them soon.'
'Yeah.'
'Eamonn, swap seats and narrow it down.' She turned to the three women. 'Have you ever noticed how on film or television, police officers don't ever need to go to the loo?'
"That's not right, Kim,' said Sharon. 'Scott and Bailey seemed to spend all their time there. I think it was to drink cranberry juice for their more or less permanent cystitis, but of course it was written by a woman, Sally Wainright.'
'I'm going now. It's all this excitement.'
Kim left the room to laughter. By the time she returned Mike was back, in Eamonn's seat, and Eamonn using Kim's equipment had the location exactly.

'Kim this is an amazing piece of kit, and you designed and made it yourself?' asked Eamonn.
'It's how I wile away evenings in my lonely bedsit.'
'I don't believe a word you're saying.'
'Neither do I,' said Kim. 'Start packing your stuff and I'll go out for a little walk and do a preliminary risk assessment.'
After Kim had left, Tracey said to Eamonn, 'Is she really that good?'
Both men nodded.
'The best I've ever come across and some of the stuff she has designed and uses could be marketed for a fortune. It is so clever.'
'But she's not with the police?'
'She knows a lot about police procedures so maybe once she was, but who she works for now is best not asked, and speculation is contrary to the Official Secrets Act. But whoever it is who employs her, they've got the best, and she must be the first person ever to do a risk assessment in t-shirt and shorts!'

Kim crossed the road outside *Betty's*, giving the appearance of a visitor out for a stroll in the warmth of a lovely summer evening. She continued to amble until she came to Ridding's Road, where there was signpost directing to the *Abbeyfield Home*, a company for which she had great respect, her aunt living in one near Banbury. She walked up the road looking constantly at the target dwelling. Once past she continued to make her way so that she could do a full recce of the rear. It was the thing she had been trained to do when she had first joined the police. She was now licensed to bear arms and on a matter such as this knew she should be doing so but preferred not to, for on such an evening a jacket would immediately have aroused more suspicion that not.
On her way back she noticed that the light had gone on upstairs and wondered if that showed that the computer had now been turned off. When they got to it she would have to insist it wasn't touched or removed until she gave the ok. Ironically, it was in the home of a corrupt police officer that she had first come across the simple device that could wipe a hard drive clean simply by moving the computer. Subsequently she had come across others like it and so had given a lot of time to putting together something that when plugged in could detect the mechanism and enable her to stop the process. On that first occasion she was quite fortunate to have made the discovery immediately before attempting to move it. The corrupt officer had still many years of prison to endure, not least of because of what the computer hard drive contained. She had been very lucky, but was quite happy for everyone to think her very clever!
At the bottom of the road she noticed three newly-arrived unmarked cars parked with their occupants still inside all carrying guns which she thought might be something of a giveaway to anyone passing and looking in. She knocked on the window of the first car.
'Good evening, gentlemen. Alpha 3. I've done a risk assessment and it will be straightforward. No one is to even touch the computer until I'm ready. That

is very important. Nine of you might well be an overkill. He's an elderly
Egyptian and I would imagine he hasn't the first idea why we are here or
remotely interested in him. So you will be gentle with him and that is an
order.'
'Ma'am. I suggest you and I wait until we have control. I was told you
would be armed.'
'Look closely, though not too closely please, at my t-shirt and shorts and
ask yourself if it's likely that I have a concealed Glock about my person.'
'I'd be willing to search her, sarge,' said one of the men in the back.
'You should be so lucky!' said Kim with a huge grin.
The others all laughed.

It was beginning to get dark when the five of them, watching something old
on the enormous tv screen, heard Kim coming up the stairs. She came in
smiling.
'I'm ravenous. It's not too late to get some food. I'm sure Dee can take us
somewhere.'
'Yes, of course,' replied Dee.
'It's still quite warm out there so we won't need coats.'
Bistro Saigon was a new experience for them, apart from Dee, who was
recognised and greeted warmly by the staff. Tracey had been a little wary of
the thought of Vietnamese food, but was completely won over by what she
had.
'Sad to say,' began Kim at the end of the meal, 'our business in Ilkley is
now concluded, and three of us have to leave in the morning. Mike and
Eamonn go back to Scotland Yard, and I have an appointment in Leeds which
I hope won't prevent me also getting back to town by tomorrow evening. Are
you still hoping to get home tomorrow, Tracey?'
'Yes. My husband offered to come and get me but it will be easier by train
with just one change, provided of course I don't get killed again.'
'I can't begin to imagine what Geoff must have gone through after the
police had called,' said Sharon.
'Nor me. I know you guys work for the police, but this was a terrible
mistake to make.'
'It was,' said Eamonn, 'and there will be an internal investigation I'm sure.'
'I'm sure you're right but internal investigations rarely come to more than
the most general of conclusions. I hope that at the very least your husband will
receive some sort of apology and even some compensation, you know, like
letting him off his next parking ticket.' added Kim. 'But back to tomorrow,
why don't the four of us go by taxi together?' said Kim.
'The men gave their approval, as did Tracey.
'And then, Dee, we will at last be out of your hair.'
'I've really enjoyed having you. At least I've got Sharon for a while longer,
but where are you two men staying?"
'In July it wasn't easy finding anywhere with accommodation, so we're

getting a taxi to the Travel Lodge in Keighley, and we can come back from there and collect Kim and Tracey in the morning.'

'No, you're not,' said Dee, 'I'll drive you there and at this time of night you'd be lucky to get a taxi, and I'm cheaper.'

Having collected their bags from the flat and aiming to collect their equipment in the morning, Mike and Eamonn left with Dee.

'Kim,' said Sharon, 'I couldn't help but notice that you said nothing to your men about what happened whilst you were out earlier.'

'Oh, they're not my men and in any case their job was done. Worrying about someone else's job is something they teach us to avoid. Plus, where I work, nobody says anything to anyone that they don't need to know. But in the present circumstance because it has all been about you, Sharon, I'll tell you.'

'Do you want me to leave?' asked Tracey.

'There's no need though once you've heard what I have to say, you'll all be covered by the Official Secrets Act.'

'What does that mean?' asked Tracey.

'In this instance very little. In the 1960s, believe it or not, it was an infringement of the Act to inform anyone of the position of the Post Office Tower in London.'

'You're kidding,' said Sharon.

'No, though no one was ever prosecuted for it, and as I have already said, the matter in hand here is pretty minor. The man lives alone, his wife having died, and I would guess that he's about 65. He is from Egypt and has a son living in Cairo still. He uses his computer, so he maintains, to pass on messages that are confidential so no one can trace them and he has built up a considerable clientele which, he thinks consists in the main of errant husbands and sometimes, wives. He says he never looks at the messages which are all written in Arabic anyway. When I told him what the messages contained it amazed him that one person was giving another £75,000 simply for leaving a door unlocked. Put like that, I agree. Anyway, we shall need to speak to him again in the morning, and I will have a longer examination of his computer, but I just have the feeling he is as innocent as he came over. He's been taken to Leeds and, sadly, will spend the night in a police cell, but I wouldn't be at all surprised if your staff downstairs are not serving him afternoon tea tomorrow.'

'Apart from the fact that my former husband was killed trying to kill me, would you think this is what you would call a result?'

'That will be for my superiors to judge. I came to do what I was ordered to do, and did it. As for you two, Sharon and Tracey, it must have been the oddest few days imaginable. A dose of normality will do you both the world of good.'

Or not, thought Sharon, who already was dreading the thought of Kim leaving in the morning. Perhaps the shock of what had happened in Leicester was doing strange things to her but once she was in her bed the thought of losing Kim led to tears. She felt again like one of her own adolescent students at the mercy of her hormones.

Life would often be so much less painful if only we had access to the thoughts of others enabling us to reach out to them when that might be what they wanted, thought Kim, sleeping as she lay less than a foot or two away from Sharon in the next door room.

Chapter Eight

Sharon and Dee were up early to share breakfast with Tracey and Kim before the taxi arrived with Mike and Eamonn. The equipment was loaded.

'Have a good journey, Tracey,' said Sharon as she hugged her tightly, 'and give my love to Geoff and the boys, who will all rejoice at having you back from the dead.'

'The boys will have forgotten it within five minutes of my arrival, I can assure you,' said Tracey with a smile. 'Anyway, enjoy any food you can get downstairs during your stay and I'll see you at the weekend.'

Dee gave Tracey a hug.

'Do you know,' she said, 'I'm sure we did this yesterday. I wish you better luck today.'

For the moment Kim had popped back to her room to do a final check to make sure she had forgotten nothing. As they came down to the taxi, Kim kissed each of them, but Sharon wondered if she was right in thinking her kiss was a tiny bit longer than Kim gave Dee. Kim got into the back seat with the two men, leaving the front passenger seat for Tracey. Kim opened the window and said to Dee, 'You'll get paid for everything – eventually.'

'There's no need.'

'There's every need, Dee.'

With waves, the car set off straight ahead, taking the back road through Ben Rhydding before joining the main A65 avoiding most of the traffic which the driver knew would be heavy at this time of the morning.

'I know they had it relatively easy last night, as befitting Ilkley, being admitted without any hostility but often their work must be scary, and as we saw in Leicester they have to be prepared to use their guns, and use them efficiently, by which I mean they have to hit their targets first time, and that must take a great deal of training and practice or else it could be one of them next,' said Dee.

'Or me,' said Sharon.

'As it nearly was.'

'You're not kidding.'

'I heard Tracey say that she is expecting to see you back home at the weekend. Is that your plan? I'm not trying to get rid of you, I only ask so I've got the information in my head?'
'I don't know where she got that from, but it wasn't from me. '
Dee smiled and put her arms round Sharon.
'You can stay here forever if you like.'

By late morning, Sharon was dog tired and whilst Dee was out doing the shopping she went and lay down properly on her bed. She did not wake for almost 2 hours and, as is often the case when we sleep in the daytime, whether in a chair or by total immersion in our bed, she woke up feeling even worse than she had before lying down.

She lay looking up at the ceiling, thinking of that dining room and her near-death experience at the hands of the man whom once she thought she had loved, even despite his involvement with girls in the six weeks of their marriage. Her divorce could only be classed as an absolute failure on her part. She should have been able to keep him to herself alone and even to this day was ashamed that she had not managed to do so. It was, however, a reality that she had failed him in bed. When Dee had told her of her experience of an impotent husband it tallied with her own experience of being not totally frigid but nearly so. For that reason she had not repeated the experience with any other man. Now her parents were no longer alive she was completely alone with no one to love her. She was respected, even admired, in Chester, for the way she ran the school and had greatly strengthened the teaching staff and returned fantastic exam results and university entrances to Oxbridge and the best Russell Group Institutions, "real universities" as she was given mischievously to call them. She had once heard parents unaware of her nearby presence describe her as "wonderfully dedicated" to teaching and her girls. That was the moment she knew it was over.

She had cried all the way home in the car. She didn't want to be wonderfully dedicated, respected or admired. What she wanted was really quite simple: she wanted to love and to be loved. And now she had lost even the hope she had felt in Kim, who was now lost to her and probably already back in London. Lying back on her pillow she thought she could what sounded like crinkling paper, sat up and removed her top pillow. There was a piece of paper. The words she recognised at once. They were from *Sonnets from the Portuguese* by Elizabeth Barrett Browning, in this instance Sonnet 43.

How do I love thee? Let me count the ways.
I love thee to the depth and breadth and height
My soul can reach, when feeling out of sight
For the ends of being and ideal grace.
I love thee to the level of every day's
Most quiet need, by sun and candle-light.

I love thee freely, as men strive for right;
I love thee purely, as they turn from praise.
I love thee with the passion put to use
In my old griefs, and with my childhood's faith.
I love thee with a love I seemed to lose
With my lost saints. I love thee with the breath,
Smiles, tears, of all my life; and, if God choose,
I shall but love thee better after death.

As Sharon read, she wondered how it had got there. Most obviously it would have to have been Dee who could have easy access to the bedroom at any time. But she hoped it had been placed there by Kim, but couldn't see how it could have got it there unnoticed. And then she recalled Kim's final check before she left. She could quite easily have put it there then. But how did she get the poem and have time to copy it out? She could hardly carry it around with her "just in case".

Sharon found it difficult to settle. Her mind kept going over and over the sonnet under her pillow. She looked at Dee's books but found no anthology from which she might have copied the words. Her mind went over and over the Browning poem, arguably the most wonderful love poem in the world. She was already convinced that she had seen the last of Kim. What was going on? In the end, and much to her self-disgust she spent most of the with daytime television on Dee's huge screen, which, sadly, did not serve to improve the quality of the programmes.

Dee arrived back laden with shopping and dry cleaning – her uniform for her return to work.

'Do you foresee a lifelong career with *Betty's*? asked Sharon.

'Well, I had hoped there might be a possible new life and identity, you know, getting married and having children, but that didn't quite work out, did it? I would like to be whisked off my feet by a handsome customer to a new life but it's looking increasingly unlikely. So I go on here in the absence of something better. My parents who still live in the village I grew up in would love me nearer but I want more, much more, from life than spending my days caring for them as they prepare to depart.'

'Have you thought of doing something totally different with the OU for example. I've known a good many people who have begun study for a degree and found that it changes a great deal for them. There's dozens of possibilities. You might have to go into Leeds or Bradford for tutorials but they're a great chance to meet other students. They don't do Summer Schools any more, not least because they tended to be a large-scale opportunity for extra-marital sex and led to a number of breakups.'

'What a pity,' said Dee. 'I rather think I might have enjoyed that.'

They laughed.

'I'm serious though. The quality of what they offer is very high and I think you would enjoy it. Have a look online sometime. But saying what you are is also very much how I feel about my own life. Until last week I was a divorcée and now I'm a widow. Perhaps I can try on-line dating and see who bites. Work-wise, as I sure by now you've gathered, I cannot face returning to being the head teacher of a posh girls' school in Chester, much though I adore the students and will greatly miss them.'

'Is it restlessness?'

'I think its more than that even though I can't immediately put my finger on it.'

After supper she received a telephone call from Tracey to say that she had got home without being killed, and that it was wonderful to be back with Geoff and the boys, and was very much looking forward to her return. Sharon said that she may not becoming back quite as soon as that as she had spoken today to the Chair of Governors who agreed a period of compassionate leave to recover from all of that had happened.

The school had recently suffered the loss of its Bursar, and Sharon had been especially keen on saying to her staff that looking after themselves was very important. On this occasion, however, she was not thinking of compassionate leave but of leaving completely, though this she had not communicated to the Chair of Governors nor Tracey. Here, she decided, was far enough away, not only from Chester but from the entire world of private education to give her space to consider what might follow.

For now, there was no indication whatsoever that Dee had left the poem, no hints of any kind or smiles of a certain kind which made it more likely that it must have come from Kim, but it was no easier understanding how that could have happened and what, if it was from her, it could possibly mean for the future.

After her phone call, Sharon suggested to Dee that they might go out for a walk as it was another lovely summer's evening, and possibly stop off at a pub on the way back. Dee was more than open to that suggestion and thought a walk down to the river would be good at this time of the evening. They set off down towards the centre of town.

'It's very quiet without the presence of the forces of law and order,' said Sharon.

'Isn't it just,' said Dee, as they made their way down Brook St and crossing the junction into the unimaginatively named New Brook St. 'I would be most interested to hear from you, an astute judge of persons, husbands not included, what you made of Kim?'

Sharon hesitated but made it look as if she was thinking hard.

'First and foremost I felt that awe I always feel in the presence of a real professional, someone who has mastered their chosen field, and in her case is also leading the way for others to follow. I watched her at work on your machine and it was remarkable because she didn't have to do what I do, which is to constantly ring Apple for help or anyone else for that matter. The way she worked in a team also impressed me. She was quite happy for them to do most of the work and greatly encouraged them but knew exactly when to take over. She was completely in charge.

'The best teachers are like that and function with what I call a lightness of touch. They don't have to impose themselves (well they do sometimes on 3rd year girls!), because on the whole the girls respect and like them. It's been my aim at the school to gather together teachers who are exactly like that, so if Kim offered to come and teach information technology I wouldn't hesitate to take her on board.'

'And further than that?'

'Well, we never really saw more than that. It was obvious, or at least it was to Mike and Eamonn, that she had once been a police officer but was no more, and their conclusion was that she had probably been recruited into the military. The guys knew what a command was, and when she gave one, it was never questioned.'

'I must confess,' said Dee, 'that thought had never occurred to me, but apart from that did you get any feelings about who she was, and not just the work she did?'

'Well, as I say there was no real opportunity to find out those sorts of things. She is of course extremely friendly and a nice-looking person who dresses very well, suggesting she gets well paid. More than that, I just can't say. I have no idea whether or not she's married, but if she is it can't be easy sustaining that sort of relationship when you're a soldier with the speciality she has, as it could well take her all over the world, and she never mentioned children. The only clue was her joke about inventing equipment in her lonely flat in the evening. Why do you ask?'

'No particular reason, other than sometimes I saw her looking at you and I wondered if you had seen her doing so.'

'Not especially. Most of the time she was looking at the screens and then we all chatted together in the Vietnamese restaurant and I certainly can't recall receiving more attention from her than any other of us.'

'When you work in a setting such as I work in, you are constantly on the lookout and have to be, for the eyes of customers. Not everyone waves their arm in the air when they want attention, so when new staff begin I have to teach them all about the importance of the eyes. It's just that I thought she was looking at you rather a lot.'

'Well if she was, I certainly never saw it.'

They reached the river and walked onto the Old Bridge, a lovely stone edifice with three arches, where on the previous day Sharon had come hand in hand with Kim, who she longed for now.

'Do you come down here often? It's so lovely.'

'Not as often as I should, but I guess that's typical, to live near something that tourists come to see and locals don't.'

'Now I fancy a drink, how about you?' said Sharon, wanting to get away from the memories of the bridge and also from the hordes of midges.

'That is the most sensible thing you have said all day. Come on, let's go to the *Flying Duck*.'

Dee met up with some of her friends in the pub and introduced Sharon to them, some young men among them looking at her more than once. They were a friendly lot, exactly what Sharon had always been told about the people of Yorkshire, and they engaged in an interesting discussion about a man from Ilkley called Tom Jackson, who at one time had been the head of the postal workers union and became very unpopular in the country at large when he led a long strike in 1971, but who, afterwards, set up a second-hand bookshop here in Ilkley.

As they walked back to the flat, Sharon asked, 'Dee, were you born here?'

'Shush, no one must know, but I was born in Lancashire in a village called Hoddlesden, near Darwen and Blackburn. If anyone was to find out I am sure I would lose my job at *Betty's* which is a 100% Yorkshire firm.'

They walked up the road together arm in arm. Sharon's phone made a noise and she took a quick look.

'It'll keep.'

When they returned to the flat, Sharon said she would go to bed straight away as the alcohol they had just drunk was emphasising just how tired she was. Dee agreed.

'There are some things I need to do tomorrow, Sharon, so I may be out some of the time. Is that okay?'

'Of course it is. I am more than certain that I can find things to do, and your life must go on as normal as possible despite having me here. I imagine you will want to do some shopping so I will give you £50 towards it.'

'You'll do nothing of the sort,' protested Dee. 'for me it is just a treat having you here and having you here alive. It nearly wasn't so.'

'Well, let's hope we have a night not broken into by the police with guns.'

'It will make a change!'

They gave each other a hug and a kiss on the cheek, and Sharon made her way to her bed. When she got there she sat on it, took out her mobile and opened the email she had just received. To say that she had expected this communication would be to overstate, but to say that she had hoped to receive it or one like it, was another matter altogether. Sharon looked at it and read it again and again, eventually undressing and getting into bed and looking at it once more.

"10.10 train arrives Leeds 10.38. Join me in Portugal!!!".

The final word told her everything – The Sonnets from the Portuguese.

Eventually she replied with just one word: Yes.

Chapter Nine

Dee woke up earlier than usual, and her first thoughts were about her guest. She was more than happy for her to be here and stay as long as she wished but she also knew that she was a complex person. On the one hand she was clearly intellectually more than able and from having looked up her school on the Internet she could see what a terrific job she had done there. On the other hand she had made the stupidest of marriages and chose to wear the most provocative of clothes as if she was on the prowl for any man who would respond. As she had noticed in the pub last night, most men did but then she put up an impenetrable barrier between herself and them. It was just paradoxical but contradictory. Dee wondered whether she had done right mentioning the looks Kim had given Sharon but it seemed to elicit no response whatsoever which had reassured her. There was no obvious sign that she was a lesbian, and could in any case hardly work in a girls' school as she did if this was known to be the case. It was probably only in her imagination, anyway. Kim clearly lived just for her work. Dee made Sharon a cup of tea and took it into her and found her wide awake, sitting up in bed and reading.

'Is it good?' she asked.

'Don't laugh, but it's *Swallows and Amazons*, one of my favourite books of all time. When I wake up, I like to read something light to get me ready for my day as a head teacher. Arthur Ransome does the job.'

'Do you fancy breakfast in my workplace?'

'Not today. One can have too much of a good thing. Looking on the internet there's an Arthur Ransome exhibition at the Henry Moore Gallery in Leeds, so I thought I might catch the train and see for myself.'

'That's a good idea. What train do you want to get?'

'It doesn't matter.'

'Ok, I'll leave you to get up. Do have a shower.'

As Dee was leaving her bedroom Sharon thought to herself that the time of the train mattered a great deal and she was not intending to miss it, though she already had butterflies in her tummy wondering what she was going to discover at the other end of the line and hoping for a great deal.

The train had come from Lancaster and the state of the two coaches was awful, but as it was less than 20 miles to Leeds, she would put up with it though there was nothing she could do about it anyway. The Aire valley was not attractive and much of it comprised relics of the city's industrial past. People said Leeds was a vibrant and exciting city – not here it wasn't. People were now preparing to get off, and she stood up ready to join them and she could feel herself shaking as the door opened and waited her turn to step down onto the platform.

Tracey was feeling fed up. She had missed most of her course, her car had been stolen and this morning she was faced with a mountain of washing left by Geoff and the boys. She thought what seemed to please them most about her not being dead was that she became their housemaid and cook once again. She was missing Sharon but would make sure she telephoned her today to moan about the men. She hadn't expected that it would be like this for as she had sat on the train all she could think of was how wonderful it would be to back with them, and the normality she craved which had been snatched away in the past few days. Because of where she had been sitting at that breakfast table, she had seen nothing and only heard Sandra's gun. She hadn't even heard the assailant shouting and immediately they had ushered her out of the room and she did not see the body lying on the floor. There was no time for fear of any kind as it all happened so quickly but in retrospect, and now she was home she was recalling it again and again, it was as if her fear and anxiety had finally caught up with her, not least in the realisation that had not Sandra been present and armed, her closest friend, Sharon, would now be dead. That the man was dead did not trouble her at all, and she was glad of it, and knew that Sharon felt exactly the same. He had cheated and tried to manipulate her when they were married, and later had planted a bomb and killed two young girls. As far as Tracey was concerned he should be dead, and though she would never say so in polite company, meaning those espousing liberal views, she sometimes wondered whether it would be better to execute all terrorists. She couldn't see the difference between allowing and even encouraging our soldiers to kill the enemy abroad and killing the enemy at home. But she also knew that governments and political parties were terrified of suggesting such a thing. Perhaps, she thought, there should be a referendum, a thought that made her smile, or was it scream?'

As she was loading the second lot of washing into the machine, the telephone rang, and she very much hoped it would be Sharon.

'Hi,' she said enthusiastically into the mouthpiece without having looked at the name of the caller.

'Hello Tracey,' said an unfamiliar male voice. 'It is Marcus Drysdale here.'

'Marcus!' said Tracey. 'Gosh, it must be at least a hundred years since last we spoke. How lovely to hear from you.'

'As we get older,' said Marcus, 'there are so many people with whom one wants to stay in touch that it becomes more and more difficult. It's like

Christmas cards. Each year you have to trim the list. I can assure you, Tracey, that I have never forgotten you, nor have others, which is why I am ringing today to put to you a proposition.'

'I'm intrigued.'

'I am now a member of the board of UK Athletics, which I am enjoying very much. You would hardly recognise it from your days as it has become professional in so many ways, and we've been doing so very well in all the disciplines. What we want is to continue to do so, and, if possible, even better, though London and Rio were excellent. We have an outstanding group of young athletes though I would have to say that among the gymnasts we have done rather better with the boys than the girls whereas on the track, at the present time, it seems to be the girls who are leading the way. One thing that is so vital, and I am sure you will recall this from your own time, is to have experienced and reliable mentors alongside top coaches who are more than ready to push our young people sometimes too far and too fast.

'So we have been meeting in the last couple of days to discuss the best way of taking this on and putting forward suggestions as to who and what we are looking for. They have to be experienced athletes themselves to win the respect of those with whom they are working, tough enough to impose themselves when necessary, and gentle enough to handle the vulnerable. Are you with me so far?'

'Yes I am, in the sense that all you have said is sensible, but at the moment Marcus, I can't for the life of me see what it has to do with me. If you are looking for someone to offer my support, then you can have it though I can't imagine a single gymnast today has ever heard of me, but by all means use my name if it helps.'

'No, that's not what we have in mind Tracey and that's not why I am calling. The board feel strongly that you are the ideal person to use your experience as an athlete and Olympian and someone who won a gold medal at the Commonwealth Games. We want to appoint you as the UK athletics women's coordinator, the person responsible for mentoring our young women competitors as they face up to the challenges and opportunities of the next five years which will include one Commonwealth and two Olympics. I think I should tell you that although we considered quite a few names, some even better known than you, when the time came for a decision, you were the unanimous choice and they delegated me to make this call to you.

'You will be very well paid in this job and all your expenses will also be met in full and a house will be provided. During the Games you will be housed in the village so you can be on hand. There will be no coaching role for you as such but that doesn't mean your experience counts for nothing and I am sure that in the gym you will be of enormous help.'

'Marcus, Marcus, hang on. Are you being serious?'

'Yes. We want you. Wouldn't you welcome the opportunity to be back in the world of competitive sport?'

'Yes, but I'm totally out of touch and I know next to nothing about so many of the sports women participating in now. When they appear on *A Question Of Sport*, it's only Sue Barker that I recognise.'

'You would have no responsibility for women participating in anything other than athletics and gymnastics. I know you will need time to think about this, to talk it over with Geoff, and how you wish to arrange things in Nantwich and your office in Loughborough will be up to you. We are more than happy to help financially in any way we can.

'I want to stress again, Tracey, that the Board of UK Athletics wants you and no one else to do this job, and I am a member of that Board and wholly endorse their selection. I will call again on Monday and very much look forward to hearing you say that you accept. In the meantime, if there are practicalities you want to discuss, call me on my mobile. Hearing your voice again only confirms my belief that we've got this 100% correct. Ok. Bye.'

Tracey put the phone down more stunned than she had been at the time of the shooting earlier in the week. She had seen neither event coming and how on earth was she going to respond? She desperately needed to speak to Sharon but for whatever reason she couldn't get through. She would continue to try.

Dee drove into Skipton to meet some of her choir friends to tell them about events at Leicester which shocked them and to say that the intended victim was staying with her for the time being, a highly regarded head teacher of a private girl's school in Chester.

'You should bring her to choir tonight,' said one of the friends.

'If she stays a little longer, I may well do so, but I think tonight might just be a little soon. Also, she dresses somewhat outrageously and it might prove too much of a distraction for some of the men.'

'And maybe one or two of us women,' said another, resulting in general laughter.

Dee said nothing about counterterrorism police being in Ilkley. If she had, she knew she could rely on the word being spread rapidly and she wished to avoid that. The others returned to their work and Dee went to the Building Society down the main road to check on her balance and withdraw some money for day-to-day living. In a short while she was on her way back to Ilkley where she would call in at Booth's and do a big shop for Sharon and herself.

As Sharon queued at the ticket barrier she could see on the other side the reason for being there. She was using all her energy to show she wasn't shaking but it was a fruitless effort. She struggled to get her ticket into the machine until an elderly lady from behind in the queue did it for her. O God, she thought, I'm turning into a blithering idiot! She looked up and saw that Kim was laughing at her efforts. This being Leeds, no one took the slightest notice of two women holding and kissing one another for all they were worth. It probably happened all the time.

They said little though tightly held hands in the taxi that took them up past the university, Woodhouse Moor on to Headingley, before turning right and right again into Grove Lane.

'This looks nice,' said Sharon.

'Yes, it's held in reserve for when it's needed. It's not wildly convenient, but it's more than comfortable. Come and see.'

Kim took Sharon's hand again as they walked up the steps towards the front door, which Kim opened and led Sharon in. Once again they held one another and kissed.

'As always,' said Kim, 'you look amazing. I don't know how you do it.'

'Today I do it for you and no one else in all the world, besides which I shall soon be old and not worth even glancing at, so I want to take advantage of being forty four. And, I imagine, that means being quite a bit older than you.'

'Why? How old do you think I am?'

'I don't know. Possibly mid-30s and beautiful.'

'Wrong on both accounts. I'm 40 with a lifestyle that's starting to make me feel it. Beautiful I'm not, whereas you are, Sharon.'

'I'm sorry to correct you (as I sometimes say to my girls) but you're wrong. You are beautiful and there's an end to it.'

'Thank you,' said Kim, once again enfolding Sharon in her arms. 'Would you like a coffee over which we can catch up, and I must warn you I also have two apricot Danish Pastries with which I would like to tempt you.'

'You have tempted me ever since you walked in the door of Dee's flat in the middle of the night. Something happened inside me, something big, but on this occasion an apricot pastry will have to do.'

'For now . . . ' Kim's voice trailed away as she entered the kitchen.

With the coffee on the table before them, and clutching one another's hand, it was Kim who spoke.'

'I imagine you were a little surprised to find a poem under your pillow after we had left for Leeds.'

'I found it in the afternoon. It was one of those special moments in life when the most unlikely thing for which you might most long for happens. After you left, I knew that I was missing you a great deal though I could say nothing to Dee, who, if she had noticed my mood would probably have put it down to PTSD, and I guess in part that she'd be right. And then I found it and read the words. I remember thinking how brave you must be to write out and give me Sonnet 43 knowing nothing as to how it might be received. And here I am, 44 years old, and I receive my very first love letter and what a letter! I can't imagine that in these days of technological communication there are that many love letters written, but oh Kim, this one was wonderful beyond words. But didn't you fear rejection?'

'What I'm about to say is ridiculous I know, but intuitively I knew that what I was feeling for you was reciprocated. What is even odder is that I have never had feelings like these for anyone, let alone a woman before and I had become so wrapped up in my work I had given up the thought of having any sort of relationship with a man even if I had wanted to, and trust me, I didn't.

And amazingly, I wasn't shocked by my feelings because they felt as natural as they were unexpected. There came a moment and I think it may have been in the pub when I thought "O God, I love this woman and all I want is to be with her". No pressure, you understand!'
They laughed together.
'I found the sonnet on the internet and knew it had been written not for Robert Browning but for you and me. So thank you, Mrs Browning.'
Though she could not have known what she was disturbing, at that moment Tracey phoned.
'Hi Tracey, how goes it?' said Sharon not wanting to interrupt the moment.
Tracey told her friend what had been offered her (Kim used this as an opportunity to cuddle closely up to Sharon who was more than receptive).
'What are your initial feelings?'
'A combination of knowing it's totally out of the question and knowing that I have to do it.'
'How long have you got to make your decision?'
'Monday. When are you coming home?'
'I don't know.'
'Not at the weekend.'
'No.'
'Oh, are you still in Ilkley?'
'No, I'm in Leeds with Kim.'
'I thought she was back in London.'
'No, she's been held up.'
'Oh well, say hello from me. So what do you think? I want some sort of clarity in my mind before Geoff comes home.'
'Tracey, this is your last chance. I mean it. You and I both know much you love the world of gymnastics and athletics, and it's unlikely at your age, and I'm not being rude because you're younger than me, that you'll get another chance to give back to what has been so enriching for you. You do a great job at present in the playschool, but you can do so very much more. I nearly died this week, and you actually did in a strange way. I'm going to make a change, a big change, and so should you. Seize it with both hands.'
'And Geoff and the boys?'
'Are you really saying that a woman always has to subordinate her own opportunities for those of the man?'
'Well no, though that is still the norm, and what sort of change are you making?'
'Don't think about me and my life. Concentrate on your own, and make the right decision. Keep me in the loop, though.'
'Though if it happens, it'll mean being a long way from my best friend.'
'Do what is right, Tracey, and do it for you.'
She put her phone down after turning it off.
Kim looked up at her and smiled.
'You are so strong and supportive, Sharon. Wonderful in fact.'

Once again they kissed.

'I'm not sure I can believe this, my darling Kim. I had never thought I could fall in love with anyone and that for the rest of my days I would live alone with my books, and working in an all-girls school, never once did it occur that I might have a relationship with a woman, lovely though some of the older girls are. And then, in the twinkling of an eye, in the middle of the night, in the middle of Yorkshire, I knew that at long last it had happened. I was in love, there and then, and from that moment I longed for you, body and soul, though if I'm honest and in the hope it won't embarrass you, your physical presence so excited me. Suddenly I discovered what people mean by sexual attraction and I wanted to take you straight to my bed and make love, even thought I have no idea what that might involve.'

'Oh darling Sharon, you have been able to describe precisely what I also felt. I had got used to being non-sexual and although I have regularly been praised for my creations which have proved so very useful in my work, they are not much of a compensation for the absence of loving and being loved. When I entered Dee's room and removed my coat to let Tracey try it on, I wanted your eyes to see my body, to take it in. And how right that you should say it just happened at that moment, because that is how it was, and I want us to be together for ever. And as for knowing how women make love, I don't think for one moment that our love, longing and imaginations will let us down.'

Dee's phone was ringing.

'Sharon! I was getting a little worried in case you'd got lost in the centre of Leeds.'

'It's a great city with some smashing shops and I've decided to stay over until tomorrow. I can give you a ring when I'm on my way, but please don't wait in for me. I've got a key. You can have a nice quiet evening to yourself and you may not want me back tomorrow.'

'Where are you staying?'

'Somewhere in Headingley, near the cricket ground,. However, I'm sure I'll find my way back tomorrow though there's a big one-day match being played there and I just might try to get a ticket.'

'You'll be lucky, and how was the Arthur Ransome exhibition?'

Oh Dee, everything about Leeds has been marvellous. I'll tell you when I see you.'

'Ok.'

Dee had been disappointed earlier when she had arrived back to find Sharon not yet returned from Leeds, and now thought it odd that she wasn't returning tonight but staying over, but not properly revealing where. She knew that Sharon was unlikely to do anything foolish, but it was odd all the same. It was tempting to call her again and offer to drive in this evening and collect her to save her having to come back on the train, but she rejected the thought almost as soon as it had occurred to her. Instead, she would attend to one or two things on her computer and after tea perhaps wander to the house of one of her friends who lived nearby.

Tracey had become something of a nervous wreck in the time after she had spoken to Sharon and as the time for Geoff's homecoming drew nearer. The boys had spent the day at a summer club and arrived back ravenously hungry and wonderfully tired. She knew that they were adaptable lads and would probably cope with a move easily after inevitable initial protests. Geoff, however, was a different matter altogether. Her strategy was to wait until after tea when the boys would be occupied on their X-boxes or whatever they played with in the evenings before bed. She would then try to explain her thinking and feelings to Geoff, but that might just be like pulling out the pin from a grenade, throwing it and then discovering that the wind was blowing it back. At least he wouldn't be able to blame it on Sharon who was more than a hundred miles away with Kim, though as she reflected on that thought it most odd. Kim had said she would return to London on the early evening train once she had inspected the computer belonging to Mr Ali from Ilkley.

Geoff was the owner of a business selling, installing and repairing fitness equipment in gyms of various kinds, including several football and rugby clubs in the area. He was a stickler where timekeeping was concerned, for himself and those he employed, so she knew that he would be back from Crewe no later than 5.30. That didn't leave long and first she had to complete the food for them all, though at the moment she had no appetite.

Chapter Ten

Chapter Ten

'Kim?'

'M'm?'

They were cuddled up together on the sofa stroking one another's arms and kissing from time to time.

'There's something I need to tell you, if you're willing.'

'Tell me.'

'When I was training to be a teacher, I used to do a night shift every Saturday with the Samaritans in Liverpool. It was often demanding, but I felt I was doing something worthwhile. The nights were long: 10pm to 9am and two of us. Calls came in regularly until about 3 or 4, and then we might get a little sleep.

'I'd been doing this for about a year and was working alongside someone I had got to know well, when my phone rang at about 11-00 o'clock. It was a quietly spoken young woman and after some hesitation told me the reason for her call. She had already taken tablets, a lot of them, because she was determined to end her life and wanted me to stay with her whilst she died, talking her through it to the end, so she wouldn't be alone.'

'Didn't you try to stop her?'

'I tried again and again to persuade her to let me get help, but she wouldn't give me her address or permission to trace her phone number. As we spoke I noticed her speech beginning to slur, so once again I asked if she wanted help and she refused. Now there is a standing order at the Samaritans whereby if a caller wishes to end their life and is wholly resistant to offers of help, we must allow them to die. By one o'clock there was no further sound and eventually, after consulting my colleague, I ended the call, and moments later someone else rang and demanded my full attention.'

'I suppose it's possible that she didn't die and just slept it off, whatever it was.'

'I was certainly left hoping for that. However, on the local evening news programme on the Monday evening there was a report of the body of a young woman and her baby found dead in a flat in Wallasey, and that foul play was not suspected, which usually means suicide. The few details they gave indicated to me who it was and then two days later I received a call from the head of our Branch to say that the police had traced her final call to the Samaritans though as they will have known in advance, the Samaritans would not comment.'

'Sharon my sweet, that was just awful for you.'

'She hadn't mentioned a baby. If she had, I would have had no hesitation in getting the call traced and an ambulance sent at once to her as an emergency. I would also have suspected PND and have been able to use that to get help. She died and her baby died, just 5 weeks old and and had been fed crushed tablets by her mother in her milk.'

'Technically therefore she murdered her child.'

'And I was party to it.'

'No, you weren't, you really weren't. What you did for her as it is astonishes me.'

'Do you recall reading about the suicide of Sylvia Plath?'

'I've read something about it, but not a lot.'

'She was married to the Yorkshire poet Ted Hughes, later Poet Laureate. He left her after falling for a woman called Assia Wevill, a very beautiful German, and who soon became pregnant by him, although she had an abortion. Hughes had informed Sylvia of the pregnancy and it is certain that this played a large part in Sylvia's suicide. Hughes and Assia now lived together and had a daughter, Shura. He was a great philanderer and continued to have affairs, and in 1969, Assia committed suicide and took four-year-old Shura with her.

'For the rest of his life Hughes wriggled out of any sense of responsibility for either death, but I and many others choose not to read his work.'

'I should think not. But oh, I cannot imagine what it must have been like for you hearing from and talking to someone dying.'

'It is now some time ago, and isn't in fact the thing I need to tell you about. That is something that has happened much more recently, in June, so it's just a matter of a few weeks.

'The school bursar is, or was, Henry Ward, a retired accountant wanting to do something useful in retirement. I learned to trust and depend on him and he did his job very well. He was married, and they had two children living away, whom they often went to see. Henry was also treasurer of his local church which was quite a big affair in Chester, and also served as treasurer for the local counselling service. He often rang me at home in the evening to discuss financial matters, something I appreciated because I always felt school was too public to have those sorts of communication.

'One evening he rang to say that he had something important for me to know, but that it was nothing to do with the school. He said that his wife was away visiting their son in the Black Country and that she knew nothing about what he was going to tell me. To be honest, I wondered just what might be coming.

'Henry said that he had removed £60,000 from the Church funds and a further £25,000 from the counselling service, which had yet been noticed but would be tomorrow as the bank (and both used the same bank) had notified him they had an obligation to inform the officials of both when their current accounts fell below a certain amount. I asked him what he had done with it, and he replied that it had all gone on gambling debts. I asked about our own accounts but he said he had not touched them, not least because the removal of those sorts of amounts would require my approval. Despite his reassurance I knew I would have to check as soon as possible after the call was over.

He said that he would do the right thing which I assumed he meant coming clean and facing the consequences, but he had a different "right thing" in mind altogether. He told me he had already rigged up a noose in the scullery in which he was intending to kill himself, as there was no way he could face either the shame or prison. I did my level best so persuade him to let me come round, but he was adamant. No matter what persuasion I sought to use, he was resistant to it, and I knew he was probably drinking quite a lot as we spoke. I was on the horns of a dilemma in a enormous way. My Samaritan training told me to let him be if dying was what he wanted, but if I went round or summoned help, wouldn't I be condemning him to the shame or prison he dreaded?

'It was the man delivering the oil for their central heating tank who saw him hanging lifeless through the scullery window and he called the police at once. He had been dead some hours. Knowing what I didn't do when I could have done is the reason why I don't want to back to school. The police, his widow and the governors are all aware that I was the last person he spoke to. Did I know about the money? Yes. Did I know he was intending to take his own life? I prevaricated long enough for them to conclude that I had known and did nothing to prevent it. My Samaritan defence did not impress them, nor the members of Henry's family who are pressing for me to be charged with assisting a suicide. I have to appear at an Inquest with a jury in August.'

'When people are in the position that your bursars's family are in, the most natural thing is for them to want to hit out and divert attention from what he has done. You are an easy scapegoat but I can tell you for certain that the police and Crown Prosecution Service would not consider, even for a moment, that you assisted a suicide. Not everyone will share that view I'm sorry to say and local news outlets may, in the absence of any other story, make a great deal of it. You could certainly tough it out if you chose but whether the school governors would welcome adverse publicity by keeping you rather than accepting your resignation because you wish to free the school from that sort of attention, you will know better than me. But I think you did right all those years ago with the mother and baby, and now with Henry. Your role in each is a tribute to your extraordinary wisdom and understanding.'

Kim put her arm around her and held her closely.

'I knew at once that I loved you, and now I love you even more,' she said.

'It's odd. People speak of falling in love and literature uses it again and again as a motif, poets and novelists alike. I've tended to be more sceptical about it, probably because of my terrible experience of Jimmy. "But I was young and foolish then", wrote Housman in his brilliant poems, and truly I was.'

'I've not heard of him,' said Kim.

'He was a brilliant academic, a classicist, who wrote poetry that is sublime, mostly a response to the loss of young life in the Boer War and the ways of young men in Shropshire (his greatest work is called *A Shropshire Lad*). He was gay and fell hopelessly in love with a young man at Oxford with the unlikely name of Moses Jackson who did not or could not reciprocate, and it was something from which he never recovered.

"I think I am in love with A.E. Housman
Which puts me in a worse than usual fix.
No woman ever stood a chance with Housman
And he's been dead since 1936."

Kim laughed.

'Goodness,' said Kim. 'Can you recite lots of poetry by heart?'

'It was something we did a lot of when I was at school and my dad used to read lots of poetry of poetry aloud to me, which I adored.'

'And who wrote that one?'

'A nice lady called Wendy Cope'.

'And that reminds me,' said Kim reaching out her hand and drawing Sharon to her feet. 'I don't think I've showed you our room yet.'

Geoff allowed Tracey all the time she needed to report her phone call and its job offer.

'Can I do the washing up before we talk about this?' asked Geoff.

'We have a dishwasher you know.'

'Yes I know, but I always find washing the dishes a quite helpful distraction when I need to think. I always have, and indeed I'm pretty sure I washed the dishes before I came out to meet you that evening and asked you to marry me.'

'So that's why you smelled of Fairy Liquid.'

'Don't knock it until you've tried it.'

'The problem is that when you wash the dishes you only do half of the necessary work, and leave them for me to dry and put them away.'

'If you left them on the rack they would dry themselves.'

'Maybe if they were rinsed first.'

'You are aware,' said Geoff, 'that being difficult and argumentative may not help your case.'

'In which case, my love, get on with it.'

Dee was becoming agitated in her flat in Ilkley. She didn't know what it was, but something was wrong. She wanted Sharon back, though was wary of calling her again, though she might send a text later. Sharon was not on social media of any kind.

Dee put a ready meal into the microwave and turned on her computer. She looked at the cover of the curry that was rapidly heating and noticed that it was Halal, and she smiled. That's what came of living in Yorkshire. She turned on the television and turned out her curry onto a plate with the rice she had previously cooked. There was little on the news to interest her nor in the following *Look North* based in Leeds. She didn't go to the computer straight away but went first into the room that Tracey had used and pulled out a red rubber keyboard. With this she went back, sat on her sofa and began typing. It worked by Bluetooth and enabled her to sit in comfort as she did her writing. Tomorrow she was hoping for the return of Sharon. She also decided to send an e-mail to Tracey to congratulate her on her safe journey home:

Hello Tracey. Congratulations on making it home this time. The flat feels very empty without everyone in it. Sharon has disappeared to Leeds and is staying over somewhere but says she's returning tomorrow. Are you missing breakfast at Betty's? Sometime you must come and try it again. What an odd few days! Do keep in touch. Xxx Dee.

At home Tracey was still awaiting the arrival in the sitting room of the man doing the washing up. She therefore welcomed the distraction of the email from Dee.

Hi Dee, it's great to hear from you. Breakfasts are not the same in Nantwich. Sharon has disappeared from my orbit today. All I know is that she was meeting up with Kim whose return to London was delayed. No doubt she'll explain everything tomorrow. Lots of love, Tracey. Xx

Geoff came into the room with their coffees and sat down.

Dee, as she sat on the sofa, became agitated as she read Tracey's text. What the hell was Sharon doing with Kim and why hadn't she said anything? And why was Kim not back in London? She had finished her work here and surely there was nothing more to detain her. She had felt all along that Kim was a total bitch, the way she ordered the men around and constantly giving the impression of effortless superiority. What on earth could Sharon want with her?

Tracey turned off the television.
'So great washer of dishes, what is your verdict?' asked Tracey.
'Yes,' replied Geoff almost casually.
'Yes what?'
'Yes to it all. I think it will be wonderful for you because that is the world where you knew such joy and if I remember rightly, it was in that world where

you met your future husband, though I think repeating that is not to be part of your agenda. And I share the view of Marcus Drysdale that this is a job designed for you. You will love it and though I know it will involve quite a bit of travel, that's something you enjoy. I think it's great and I want to say congratulations.'

'Oh Geoff, thank you for your support. I would love to have a go at it but your work is here, so what are you going to do?' Driving from Loughborough to Chester every day would be quite a haul.'

'Not if I find myself a fancy woman in Stoke and stay with her during the week and come back at the weekend.'

'Oh Geoff, be realistic, there are no fancy women in Stoke.'

'You're right. Whenever I visit the Stoke City training ground where all their equipment is ours, I sometimes go into the town for some lunch. The women there are all quite scary. So Loughborough it will have to be but it so happens I've been giving a lot of thought to expanding the business. We enjoy a good reputation here and I've learned a lot. The Midlands and East Anglia are crying out for us.'

'Blimey, I hadn't realised there was quite as much washing up to be done as there obviously was!'

Geoff smiled.

'Now the hard bit,' he said. 'Let's get the boys down here.'

Sharon and Kim walked hand in hand towards Headingley. Kim had wanted to cook for Sharon but was persuaded that instead they should take advantage of the proximity of the restaurants up the road. Grove Lane gave way to Shaw Lane and ahead there was an extremely busy four-way crossing. It took a little while to manoeuvre themselves in accordance with the pedestrian lights but finally made it across the Otley Road and walked towards something called *Sukhothai Headingley*, a Thai restaurant Kim had seen and fancied. Even though it was quite early the place was almost full but they were squeezed in.

They ordered food and drink.

'Kim, can I ask you something embarrassing, well it is to me and I've always thought myself to be a woman of the world.'

Kim grinned.

'Of course you can.'

'This afternoon I experienced with you for the first time in my life such ecstasy as I have ever known.'

A man on the next table looked round briefly and the women were amused and delighted to see that he was wearing a vicar's dog collar. Sharon lowered her voice a little.

'What struck me was that I had no idea whatsoever and you did. You'd said this was new to you too, but it didn't feel like it, wondrous though it was.'

'I do wish we could have this conversation louder,' said Kim with a giggle. 'My darling Sharon, I have never made love to any woman other than you. Please believe that, and while we're on the subject there haven't been any men either. However, and I will admit this to you, from to time in my work with the service I am obliged to discover anything and everything that is stored or hidden on a computer. That's how I know.'

'But I assumed it was mostly men and women.'

'For a headteacher you are remarkably innocent.'

The food was so very good, incredibly tasty and spicy but without being especially hot as they might have experienced in an Indian restaurant.

'I think we should have afters when we get back, don't you?' said Kim looking Sharon straight in the eye, who actually blushed.

As they were leaving the restaurant Kim's work mobile rang.

'We don't want this,' she said picking it up. 'Alpha 3.'

'Alpha 2. I want you as a matter of some considerable urgency, by which I mean immediately, to make contact with Mike and Eamonn. I want them up with you in the morning. They will tell you more but your good work in Ilkley seems not to have finished. There's an echo somewhere. Is that the right word?'

'Well to be honest I thought it had all gone too easily. I'll call them now and liaise in the morning. Thank you Alpha 2.'

'In the meantime I hope you and your friend can have a good night together. Please take care of her. This has been an extraordinary week for her. One other thing, as she may have told you, she is involved in a matter at her school in Chester. I will do what I can to protect her.'

'Thank you.'

'Am I allowed to know what that was about?' asked Sharon as they began their walk back.'

'Of course not, but I'm going to tell you anyway but just let me make two quick calls first.'

'I always leave lines open after we think we've finished a job, just in case. I'm sure you've done the same, Kim.'

'Yes, of course, but in this instance I left it to you because back in London you would have the equipment and I was still with Mr Ali from Ilkley.'

'Well,' said Eamonn, 'it took him no time at all to be up and running again, which did make me wonder whether he might have received help. This evening there was an echo, someone close I think and in a hurry to get him to send something off, but in such a hurry as not to have full blocking in place which is how we picked up the echo. According to Alpha 2 we're Leeds bound in the morning.'

'Text me your arrival time and I'll meet you..'

Having taken their lives into their own hands they eventually made it across the junction and began the walk home.

'I will understand if you can say nothing, said Sharon.'

'I can't tell you everything because I don't know all that much but myself and the boys from London who will be with us in the morning are returning to Ilkley.'

'Will you use Dee's flat as the base again?'

'No. And neither my darling must you. In fact I want you to stay here at the flat because here you will be safe and looked after. The service knows that you're with me (and I don't know how but they do) and I've received instructions from the deputy head of the service herself that I have to take care of you, which was totally unnecessary because that is what I intend doing for the rest of my life. And then I was totally gobsmacked when she said that I was to let you know you're not to worry about the inquest as the service knows full well you are not even slightly involved.'

'How the fuck do they know all this?'

'Sharon my darling, you do know who I work for, don't you?'

'Is it the RAC?'

'O my God you've guessed. How clever you are. Now come on and let's get home.'

'One other thing, Kim. Are you a soldier?'

'Yes, I'm a captain in the army though I used to be a police officer.'

'And do you carry a gun?'

'When I remember but I'm hopeless at that, but I am wearing one now as one of my aims this evening is to protect you.'

'Ye gods! And you other aims?'

'I thought you might like to undress me and find it.'

'As you're an officer, how could I disobey?'

Chapter Eleven

Kim met Mike and Eamonn, and they all clambered aboard the rickety train bound for Carlisle which would pass over the Ribblehead Viaduct, unfortunately (for Eamonn) not with them on board as they had to alight in Ilkley. Kim had earlier booked them into the Tivoli Place Guest House, hoping that they would only require one night. Being away from Sharon was already hurting.

'Won't they think it odd that we have so much equipment with us?' said Mike.

'It's sorted.'

The men knew there was need for no more. Information strictly on a need to know basis, something they took for granted.

'Is there any chance of breakfast at *Betty's*?' said Eamonn.

'I'm not sure the hotel would welcome that. I will go and call on Dee this afternoon and let her know what's going on, and if you're good boys I might reward you with a cake.'

Sharon was missing Kim terribly and never more so than when shortly after she had left the doorbell rang and after he had revealed his identity, she admitted what she assumed must be a plain clothes policeman.

'Can I ask why I need a babysitter?'

'I have no idea but I obey my orders. I have to stay with you, toilets and showers excepted, at all times until I am relieved or asked to stand down. Please may I be permitted to call you Sharon?'

'Yes please, and are you known as Alpha Delta Beta 5?'

He laughed.

'I do have a moniker but I would prefer you to call me Liam.'

'Thank you, I will. Are we housebound or can we go out?'

'You are in charge, Sharon. If you want to go out then that is what we can do but if so I have to insist you do not leave my sight at any time, which means that before we leave, you go to the loo.'

'This is not a complaint about you, Liam, but aren't there any women

officers.'
'The counterterrorism force is engaged elsewhere, women included. I do personal protection, basically you and the manager of Leeds United.'
Sharon smiled.
'Are you armed?'
'I think you're intelligent enough to know that I can't answer that question though when I protect the football manager I usually do so in a tank!'
Sharon looked him up and down.
'Do you know what happened to me in Leicester?'
'Yes, I was told all about it in my briefing. It must have been frightening.'
'Not at the time because I had no idea it was happening until the shots rang out. Afterwards I quickly became a nervous wreck.'
'I gather he was your former husband.'
'We were only together for six weeks and he spent most of that time in bed with girl students at the university. I was exceptionally stupid.'
'I reckon a lot of couples could say that about their early days.'
Sharon's phone rang. It was Tracey.
'How was it?'
'The boys weren't all that keen but they'll come round. Geoff on the other hand was wonderful and is already looking forward to expanding the business in the Midlands, and I'm just excited about it. I rang my friend Marcus and have already accepted the job.'
'I'm so pleased, Tracey. It is such an exciting opportunity.'
'UK Athletics are going to announce it on Monday and they want me there for a Press Conference. And what about you?'
'I'm still in Leeds.'
'With Kim?'
'No, this time it's with a rather dishy man called Liam. Just him and me.'
'Fucking hell, Sharon, what are you like?'
'What's going to happen at the nursery?'
'In the short term, nothing. It'll go on as usual. After that I'll do some talking with the staff and mothers. They will want it to continue but we shall need to find a new leader. Oh, by the way, I heard on the local news that a local Church Treasurer has purloined £60,000 from his Church.'
'My question would be to ask whether a church should have such money in the bank in the first place, and not be using it for the benefit of the poor.'
'That's a good point. There was no more detail but I'll keep you in touch.'
'Make sure you do. Oh, Tracey, I'm so pleased for you. This is a wonderful opportunity, though tell me honestly what you'd have done if Geoff had been opposed.'
'Mercifully that hasn't arisen but I did give it thought.'
'I bet. Okay, speak soon.'
Tracey noticed Sharon had not mentioned when she might be returning, and Sharon noticed that as well. With Tracey gone did she need to go back at all?'

'Are you really called Sharon and Tracey?' asked Liam with a broad grin, as she put down her phone, 'and thanks for the unlikely description of me as dishy. That was quite some time ago, if ever.'

'Are you married or partnered?'

'Is that the word they use?'

'I think I might just have invented it.'

'It's good and I hope it catches on. But to answer the question, yes, I am married, and believe it or not I'm still married to the same person who was my girlfriend when we were both 18.'

'Blimey. In the police service that must be some kind of record. Children?'

'Three boys. One's in CID here in Leeds, another's at Armley Prison as an assistant governor, and the third is still at Uni in York doing biochemistry.'

'You must be very proud of them.'

'They're good lads.'

'And your wife?'

'A psychiatric social worker in Wakefield.'

'That must be a tough job.'

'It is and much more dangerous than mine.'

'You all make me feel quite inadequate.'

'But you're a headmistress. That is such a responsible job.'

'Alas, Liam, your age is showing. We're all head *teachers* now.'

'What a shame all the same. We went as a family to York once. Lovely city but horrendous traffic, so we went by train. Anyway as we were leaving the Minster, which is well worth a visit, I noticed a list of the vicars who work there. One had the title of "Vice Dean" and I thought this hilarious especially since I had had two years working in Vice in Wakefield.'

'Would you like a coffee?'

'I'd prefer tea, milk and one sugar, thanks.'

Sharon returned.

'If we go out, will you be looking for someone in particular?'

'My job is to suspect everyone and defend you at all costs and I will.'

'I sort of feel honoured but it's tempered with the knowledge that I was about 2 feet away from death the last time I was protected. Had it not been for Sandra you could be having the day off.'

'Sandra, I assume was the officer who took the assailant out.'

'That's one way of speaking of it. Her brain was in full gear despite having been on duty all night. She recognised in a flash what was happening and her aim was superb, I'm relieved to say, or she might have killed me and done his work for him..'

'We are trained not to miss.'

'I'll bear it in mind, Liam and that presumably is how you have three sons.'

'I'm shocked to hear a head teacher say such a thing, though reminds of a joke about the Pope in Ireland who was introduced to a woman with 12 sons. The Pope was impressed and "12 times and always a boy", and the woman replied, "Oh no your Holiness, lots and lots of times nothing at all"!' said Liam with a grin.

Dee heard the bell ring and wondered who it might be, hoping it might be Sharon. She walked downstairs and opened the door full of hope which died the moment she saw Kim.

'Dee, it's great to see you again,' and they air kissed.

'And you, Kim, though I thought you had gone back to London,' she said leading her up the stairs to the sitting room.

'In my work there's sometimes unfinished business, things that have to be tidied up. It's a strangely small world because when I was coming out of the Police Station I bumped into none other than Sharon who was on her way to book a ticket at Leeds Playhouse. I was surprised to find her still suffering from the aftershock of the attack made upon her in Leicester, but shock can be like that for some people, I suppose. She became quite tearful so I persuaded her to stay in the work flat I use. Then I learned that the counterterrorism guys had received word that she was still under threat, so she's now being guarded again. Must be awful for her.'

'Is she still in your flat?'

'I have no idea and no one will tell me, which is the point. I don't need to know.'

'It's just that I would have gone to see her and tried to cheer her up.'

'That's so kind. I'll mention it and recommend that they let you though I have no sway with counterterrorism. But I'll try my best as I know how over the moon she would be seeing you.'

Thanks, Kim. Where are you staying? You're very welcome to stay with me.'

'I knew you'd offer, Dee, and your generosity will not go unrewarded when I get back to HQ and complete my report.'

'I don't want anything. I was just so pleased to be of help. Now, how about a cup of coffee and a teacake downstairs?'

'Only if I can pay,' said Kim.

'Oh yeah. That's really likely, I don't think,' replied Dee with a grin.

True to her word, Kim arrived back with a cake she thought would soon disappear judging from the looks in the eyes of Mike and Eamonn.

'Anything?'.

'Not until five minutes ago.'

'Oh?'

'I've recorded it.'

Kim approached the machine on which the data was recorded, a machine she was more than familiar with having designed it. There was no doubt when she looked at the screen.

'It's gone to our friend Mr Ali, though he will again deny knowing the content. He hasn't sent it on yet, but as before he probably will later. We have to stop it at once and at the same time pick up Dee because there's no doubt that is where it came from.'

She took out her mobile.

'This is Alpha 3. It's go for both targets. Don't let either near their computers nor anyone else.

'Confirm go for both targets. Out.'

'A cup of tea and a piece of cake before we go for a walk. She has another keyboard we need to find and if that requires we take the place apart, then that is what we shall do.'

Liam suggested a walk in what he called Golden Acre Park, found to the north of Leeds on the road towards Bramhope and Otley. Liam drove them and turned off left into the car park, but made her wait in the car for three minutes while he logged every vehicle that came in after them.

'You can get out now. I will follow you, and if I give a command, don't stop to ask why.'

The Park was very lovely and unsurprisingly much frequented by the citizens of Leeds especially at the weekend. They had almost reached the turning point when Sharon's phone rang. She turned to Liam.

'I don't recognise the number.'

'What is it?' he asked, and she showed him.

'You can answer it but you mustn't speak.'

At that moment his phone also rang.

Sharon pressed the green button. She knew at once it was Kim.

'It's Alpha 3. Please say nothing at all. You must do everything your protection officer says.'

The line went dead. She had been impressed with Kim from the very first, and she was even more so now.

Liam had completed his call and he too, she noticed, had not spoken.

'We should move,' he said, 'though it's a pity because it's so lovely here. I'll be in front this time and let me know if I'm going too fast for you.'

'Am I allowed to speak now?' she asked with a broad smile.

'Oh alright.'

'I'll keep up with you. Do you know what's going on?'

'No. I just obey orders and need not worry myself about the rest. If I need to know I will be told.'

'Isn't that frustrating?'

'No. It's the best way of not passing intelligence on to undesirable ears. The fewer that know the better.'

They reached the underpass, and Liam asked her to wait while he gave the car park the once over. He then waved to her to come. As they left the car park Liam turned left instead of towards Leeds as Sharon had expected.

'Where are we going?' she asked.

'Just two miles up the road. My phone call told me to take you to what we call G4, the Forte Post House. Everything's been sorted in advance and trust me, you'll be very comfortable there. Your things will be brought later by my relief.'

They arrived and walked through the foyer, Liam stopping briefly to collect the key card. He opened the door of her room and saw at once what he meant by comfortable – luxury would have been a better word. She looked at the kingsize bed and imagined being in it with Kim.

'What now?'

'Nothing. I don't recommend you leave the room and knocks on the door I will answer. You might find that once on that bed sleep will catch up with you. If so, I will sit outside the door and leave you be.'

'Liam, I think I would trust you completely to stay in the room.'

'That's kind of you to say so, Sharon, but we have a protocol.'

'Of course. What time am I to expect your relief?'

'I think you'll get on well together if you can understand a word she says; her Leeds accent is very strong. Like you she's very feminine so you may want to spend the whole evening talking clothes.'

'What a terribly sexist thing to say,' she replied with a grin.

'Surely it's not sexist if it's true. When my wife and my sister get together I abandon any attempts at conversation.'

'What's the male equivalent?'

'Beer, sex and football, but not necessarily in that order, though to be honest there's only one of them that I care about.' It was his turn to grin. 'But may I please ask you a question and if you would prefer not to answer it, then I shall fully understand?'

'Ask away.'

'I'm here with you now because you're an apostate from Islam which according to Sharia law means you have to die, and some iman or other has issued a fatwa which strictly speaking has to be brought about by your husband, or some other. He died in the attempt, thankfully, but rooting out the mysterious "others" is what the counterterrorism team are doing even as we speak. Am I right so far?'

'It is what you would have been told this morning, but I'm still waiting for the question you promised.'

'You sound like a teacher I had at Meanwood School.'

'I wonder why!'

'I'll have you know John Craven went to that school.'

'In which case it did a good job with at least two of you. The question?'

'You're highly intelligent as shown by your Ph.D and now you are the headteacher of a highly regarded school so here it comes, why did you marry a Moslem which involved conversion?'

'I'm tempted to say that I'll phone a friend, but I'll have a go. The straightforward answer is that I was stupid. It's possible to be both intelligent and stupid at the same time, and I was. And I was stupid in many ways, because what I didn't know and many others did and never told me directly was that the man in question screwed his way round the undergraduate girls, both before and after we were married. I didn't give a shit about religion of any kind, and still don't, so it meant nothing to me becoming Moslem. He wanted me in a burka but I refused and was hit across the face for that, and I agreed to a hijab which was totally pointless because I had very short hair. I greatly enjoyed cutting it into pieces when I left. Six weeks I am glad to forget.'

'His ethnicity?'

'Oh, white British and a convert.'

Liam sat, thinking.

'Odd thing religion.' he said after a while.

'That's very profound, Liam. He should have gone to Meanwood School,' said Sharon, laughing.

By the time they had eaten all the cake, drank their tea and gathered their equipment, the counterterrorism squad had done their job.

Kim's phone rang.

'Delta 1. Premises secured and targets gone on holiday.'

'Thanks, Delta 1. Good job, Out. Ok buys, let's go for a walk in Ilkley. When we get to the junction, Mike, cross the road and go up Ridding's Rd. There should be a bobby outside. Go in and bag up the PC and bring it down to the flat. It will be easier to work with both to hand. The irony of the house in Ridding's Road is that it backs on to Ilkley Police Station.'

'No problem. Can the officer then stand down?'

'I'll call through and let them know. He'll get his orders.'

Kim and Eamonn turned into The Grove and the could see another police officer, this time a woman securing Dee's flat. She showed her the Security Service pass she always carried with her (just in case she got a parking ticket!) and Eamonn his Scotland Yard pass.

'A third member of the team will be joining us soon and should be carrying a bagged up computer and he also will have a Scotland Yard pass.'

'Thank you ma'am,' who was not sure how to address Kim.

Once in the flat went over to the mac she knew so well from earlier in the week. Nothing seemed outwardly different.

'Eamonn, can you set up, please?'

Eamonn smiled to himself because Kim was his only superior ever to say "please".'

The place was something of a tip and the house-proud Dee would have hated the sight. In the bedrooms things were even worse with every drawer emptied onto the floor and gone through, every item of clothing in the wardrobe cast out onto the overturned beds, mattresses cut open. Kim did not envy the team that would be coming to put everything together again in a few days's time, though in London she had seen evidence of their work and wondered if they could do the same with her flat!

Eamonn called her. She returned to the sitting room, where Mike was also now present.

'The message hasn't gone yet.'

'Ok, get them talking to one another.'

In a matter of a few minutes what they wanted was on both screens.

'She did it here then,' said Kim.

'But not using this keyboard and if there were others we missed earlier in the week I imagine that is why,' added Eamonn.

'So where the fuck is it?' said Kim. 'It looks like a bomb has gone off in the bedrooms and they found nothing but she may be cleverer than them. Can you get the officer from downstairs to come up.'

She came into the room.

'I may get shot for abandoning the front door, ma'am.'

'I'm Kim, and you?'

'PC 1062 Helen Boardman'.

'Well Helen, I'm way superior to anyone here in Ilkley and now you work with me, Mike and Eamonn.'

'That's the first good thing I've heard since I began in this job.'

Kim explained what they were looking for.

'You know Dee better than we do, so where is this thing concealed and I can't begin to emphasise how finding it is essential to national security and the lives of individuals because it is used to communicate terrorist information in Arabic on ordinary computers without leaving a trace.'

'There is no way she would have stored it here in the flat. Dee is really clever. If there was any any chance that you or others would come and take the place apart as you have done, then it will be elsewhere, and the most likely place is downstairs in *Betty's*. You can look in her office there but you'll not find it there either.'

'Because this is a counterterrorism operation you will not need a warrant,' said Kim to Helen. 'Take Mike who asked you to come here and enter *Betty's*. You will not accept No as an answer to any objection to your search and if they complain to the station I will deal with them and, trust me, they will not enjoy that.'

Helen and Mike left.

Kim and Eamonn heard the sound of a siren and looked at one another.

'Predictable,' said Kim, standing and going down the stairs. A marked car was just pulling up outside *Betty's* and by the time they were rushing towards the door of the shop Kim was blocking their way in.

'Excuse me, madam,' said the one with three stripes on his arm, 'please move now.'

'I don't think so, sergeant.'

'I beg your pardon. Move now or we shall arrest you.'

'My advice with the benefit of being your superior officer many timesover, would be that you return to your vehicle and drive somewhere else. I am in charge of an operation being carried out by the counterterrorism squad inside here searching for a device that has been concealed and which has already brought about the death of one Islamist in the last 3 days and will do so again if I do not get it before then.' She withdrew a card from her wallet and showed it to them. 'Now gentlemen, off you go.'

They looked at one another.

'Yes, ma'am,' said the sergeant, and both returned to their car and left, tails between their legs.

The "counterterrorism squad" consisting of a woman PC and a civilian working with technology at Scotland Yard were away for fifteen minutes before Kim heard them on the stairs. Coming into the room, Helen was carrying an evidence bag and Kim could see at once what it contained.

'This had nothing to do with me,' said Mike. 'Helen was brilliant and especially insistent that the assistant manager open all the staff lockers including those not in use. In one of the empty lockers Helen noticed that the base seemed a tiny bit loose and this is what she found there.'

It was red rubber keyboard which had been considerably modified by someone who knew what they were doing.

'Ooh, I like it,' said Kim. I must make one like it. Ok, Mike and Eamonn, put it to the test, please. Helen, please come with me.'

She led her to one of the bedrooms.

'O my God, what a mess.'

'Well they're nothing if they're not thorough,' replied Kim. 'I don't think the owner will be back for a long while. Now Helen, tell me about your future plans.'

'Er, hopefully a transfer to CID and eventual promotion.'

'And does that involve staying in Ilkley. A boyfriend or even a husband?'

Helen laughed.

'I'm not averse to the idea but the local talent is not up to much.'

'Do you think you'd be up to working across the whole country, doing work which might sometimes be dangerous but is very important?'

'I'll have you know that standing outside a door in Ilkley is very dangerous, I might die of sheer boredom.'

'Ok, I'd like you to come to London next week to meet someone in a coffee shop not too far from Parliament.'

'A coffee shop?'

'You can have tea of course, but yes it's important for people never to be photographed entering our building if they are new. I was interviewed in the coffee shop and others too. You will be interviewed by the Deputy Head of the service, a senior military officer who likes straight answers. You'll like her because everyone on our side does, but she's also as tough as they come. Please write down your full name and address and phone numbers and email address. I'll be in touch by Monday and all this will be squared with your superior officers by then. If you're asked anything, just smile and say you are bound by the Official Secrets Act and can say nothing. Oh, and by the way, you now are! Let's now be real feminists and make the boys get us both a cup of tea each.'

Chapter Twelve

It was just before seven o'clock when there was a knock on the door and Liam admitted Pamela who turned out to be everything Liam had said. Her clothes were the best, her hair was an amazing bright red and she was fully made up. Anyone seeing her would never have imagined her job nor that beneath her jacket and under her left arm she was equipped with a very powerful firearm. Sharon took to her immediately, though Liam was also quite right, understanding Pamela was not at all easy if you didn't hail from Yorkshire yourself, but it was fun trying.

Having ascertained from Pamela that she had not yet eaten, Liam suggested that they went to the restaurant which enjoyed a good reputation. They went out in a procession, Liam at the front and Pamela at the back. Sharon was reminded that it was in a eating place that she had been attacked and although both Liam and Pamela cleverly chose seats which would afford them the best possible view around the room, she was under no illusions about the risk she was living with again.

Once they had ordered their meal, Pamela said she would bring them up to speed.

'I thought Liam said you were not actually in touch with such things.'

'That comes with Pamela being a sergeant whereas I am only a constable.'

'Is that right?'

Pamela nodded.

'This afternoon two people, a man and a woman were arrested in Ilkley under the terms of the terrorism act. Both have been taken somewhere to answer questions. The flat belonging to one of them was thoroughly searched and it was only elsewhere that the technos found what they were looking for. They also intercepted a message giving what they thought would be your location in the Service flat, the assumption being that this was where you could be found. The message was never sent. I understand that a further arrest has now been made in relation to this conspiracy to kill you in Milton Keynes.'

'Milton Keynes?'

'But I've never even been to Milton Keyes!'

'Lucky you,' said Liam.

'That is the full extent of my knowledge,' said Pamela.

'Is there an order to stand down?' asked Liam.

'Not yet, and until then I shall stay with Sharon.'

'Sharon's phone burst into life, and she quickly picked it up in the hope that it would be Kim.

'Sharon, it's Tracey. You need to know that there has been a strange story about you on the television news this evening suggesting that you are implicated in the suicide of your school bursar, and I think it's fair to say his family are after your blood.'

'I would imagine they are saying I assisted a suicide, but did it also mention the amount he stole from the church and the counselling service, and that is was being found out that brought about his suicide. I was on the phone to him, it is true, but being 13 miles away from him would seem to preclude any possibility of my assistance. So don't worry on my account.'

'And do you know when you'll be back?'

'No idea, though I'm hoping to be in Loughborough on Monday.'

'O thank you. That's just wonderful. I won't ask where you are, but are you safe?'

'The most unlikely detective sergeant in the world, called Pamela, is taking good care of me. Just don't worry about the other matter.'

Pamela was smiling as Sharon finished her call.

'Looking as I do is often very useful in our work. I can go to places where other coppers can't.'

'I imagine you can but isn't it dangerous?'

'I get by,' and giggled.

Pamela's phone now rang.

'Papa Echo 1,' she said, but then clearly listened intently to the rest of the call.

'There we are, all done and dusted. I can stand down and you can return to Headingley with me, or stay here and wait for Alpha 3 who will be here a little later if you decide to stay.'

'I'll stay I think. It would be good to see Alpha 3 again.'

It's your decision but if that's what you want, then that's fine. I have a party I was going to have to miss, but now I can go.'

'But aren't you still on duty.'

'As I say I have a party to attend.'

'I'm being stupid.'

'You've had quite a week. Take your time recovering.'

'Thank you, Pamela and always take care in what you do.'

They hugged and then Pamela left, telling Sharon to lock the door and not to admit anyone who didn't call first.

Dee was somewhere in Wakefield though she didn't know that and was refusing to speak to anyone. Having spent some hours in a room without windows and a reinforced door, which also contained a CCTV, she was now led to another room equipped in much the same way but with a table and two chairs in it and some sort of recording mechanism. She sat on the bed by the wall and waited. A pleasant looking man in his fifties came in to the room and immediately went over to her to shake her hand, which she, having resolutely made her mind up not to cooperate in away, took hold of.

'I'm pleased to meet you,' he said. 'My name is André and I imagine you and I might get used to seeing one another over the next couple of days, though first I must apologise for what happened in the middle of the night when you were in Leicester and unceremoniously kidnapped and taken to the Conference Centre, but I do hope there was some consolation in being returned back home by helicopter, for which you have me to blame or thank, depending on the sort of experience it was.'

'I enjoyed it.'

'I hoped you might.'

'What's going to happen to me?'

'Shortly we will be collected and taken to RAF Digby and flown to the Conference Centre again. I shall be your travelling companion and I assure you that I am not armed, but others with us will be. Then after breakfast you and I will be able to chat further. One other thing before we get going. Is Dee short for Deema or Deeba? The latter means Obedience and the former Cloudy Rain.

It's Deeba.'

'What do you wish me to call you: Dee, Deeba or Dorothea, which is such a beautiful name?'

She blushed.

'Dee please. But how do you know about things like names?'

'Possibly because I'm a sad old bachelor who has nothing better to do in the evenings than read Arabic?'

'You're kidding.'

'No, I really am a bachelor,' he said with a smile.

'You know what I mean.'

'I read Arabic at University and I adore the countries and culture of the Middle East, and there is an enormous amount I love about Islam, believe it or not. Most of the time I hold it in great esteem. Regrettably some misguided and remarkably un-Islamic people don't see things that way and I try to use my experience and a little learning to find out why and what the implications are for others.'

Sharon had fallen fast asleep when at about 10-00 her phone rang.

'Hello?'

'This is Alpha 3. Is that the woman I adore?'

'I very much hope so.'

'I am about 20 metres from your door.'

'What are you waiting for?'

'For you to open the door.'

They were in each others' arms in seconds, their mouths joined.

'Oh I have so missed you today, despite Liam and Pamela, the last of whom I suspect may be the best plainclothes officer anyway, though trust me there was nothing plain about her clothes.'

'Sharon - stop talking. Do you want to stay here or go back the Service Flat in Headingley, always remembering that the breakfast here in the morning will be superior?'

'A Latin scholar would tell you that you have asked me a question in the form that expects the answer Yes, so Yes it had better be.'

'I was hoping you would say that but I was under orders to ask you.'

'Seriously?'

'Well, the person giving me the order doesn't know how much I am in love with you.'

'Pamela said, though her Yorkshire accent was so strong that I might have totally misheard her, that you wouldn't be able to tell me anything.'

'Did you know that the name Pamela means "Don't believe a word I say"?'

'No, bur perhaps the name "Kim" means exactly the same!"

Kim threw herself at Sharon and they had a wonderful tussle on the bed. It was Sharon who finally spoke.

'So . . . tell me something at least.'

'It has been quite a complex conspiracy but all those involved are now in custody. I'm sorry to say that Dee is one of them.'

'No!'

'Mike and Eamonn had picked up in London what is known as an echo on the Ilkley connection which they had left open which they do even after a find. I feared all along that it came from Dee and when I was present in the house of the old man we arrested the other day and then released it was on his machine but not yet forwarded because he was under instruction only to do so in the evening. That instruction was Dee's downfall because it pointed directly to her mac. But we found no trace of it and I suspected that she almost certainly made use of a extra keyboard modified to leave no trace behind. The boys and girls of counterterrorism tore her flat apart but nothing was found. It was Mike and a very able woman police officer who suggested it might be concealed downstairs in Betty's. It was near closing time so pretty quiet. Their attention was focussed on the staff lockers. Dee's contained very little, unsurprisingly, nor did any of those belonging to others. Then they asked to have the empty lockers opened, and the police officer, Helen, noticed something in the base of one of them and when she pulled it up - bingo!'

'Good for her.'

'No. Good for us. She will be coming to meet the Deputy Director next week. I think she has just what we require, and the idiots in Ilkley were using her to do nothing other than stand on guard duty.'

'Good heavens! Are you a recruiting sergeant?'

'All of us are called on to be on the lookout for potential recruits. Now, where was I? Oh yes, the modified keyboard. I'm pretty sure it's not Dee's work but that will I'm sure emerge later. We were able to get back from it a great deal relating to you. It appears that a fatwa, like the one on Salman Rushdie was issued by an iman in Milton Keynes, the site of Woodhill Top Security Prison, at the instigation of Shafiq Zaman. The man combined his work in the mosque with being Moslem Chaplain to the prison. Counterterrorism have already picked him up. Another one who was due to complete the demands of the fatwa is a Pakistani man in Bradford, now also with Counterterrorism. He was waiting for instructions via the Ilkley double act and I suspect it was to happen tonight. We can't know yet whether all the players are in custody but I suspect they are.

'There is one bright light however. The last message sent by Dee which we intercepted before it got sent to Bradford we assumed was the starting pistol and contained where you could be found. But she didn't say that at all, insisting instead that the fatwa had been withdrawn. I also found a diary in which she she knew she couldn't let anyone hurt you. The experience in Leicester made her realise that she loves you and cannot let harm come to you.'

'Where is she?'

'I have no idea, though it maybe that she's on her way to what we call the Conference Centre for what we call de-briefing. I gather she's already been seen by the very best of the inquisitors and he will be with her again in the morning. That is the story as I know, though others might know more.'

'Am I safe now?'

'Only if you promise to stay with me for ever.'

'You know I will.'

It was pouring with rain when they awoke, wrapped up in each other.

'We could stay in bed all day,' said Kim.

'I will second the motion but I could eat a horse and I need some breakfast.'

'You're very unromantic, Sharon.'

'I didn't say I wouldn't come back to bed after breakfast. In the meantime how would you like to join me in the shower?'

'Now you're talking.'

Chapter Thirteen

'Good morning, Dee. Come and sit down. I hope you were comfortable. Your breakfast was probably not up to the standard of *Betty's* but I've got used to it and I hope you may too.'

'How long am I going to be here?'

'Oh, that depends on how you and I work together today.'

'Ok. Where do we start?'

'How did it begin?'

Dee sat for a while in thoughtful silence.

'I got married. He owned a travel agency and asked me out a few times. Then he me asked me to marry him, but insisted I would have to convert to Islam and I did so, albeit unenthusiastically, exactly like Sharon had to do so, though I never told her. I was lonely and here at least there seemed to be a future of sorts. It was a very posh and expensive wedding in the Dales. The marriage lasted two nights as I discovered he was impotent.'

'That must have been a terrible shock.'

'It was grim. I cried for a week. About two weeks or so later someone rang from a mosque in Bradford saying that he wanted us to meet so he could apologise and talk through what had happened. He seemed very nice, so stupidly I jumped at it, desperate to talk it over with someone. We met in an Asian restaurant in Bingley and he was at once extremely understanding and very supportive and that was to prove my undoing. I was so very needy and here was someone so very caring.'

'Do you know his name?'

'He was just Mr Khan. We met a number of times and he came with a lady sometimes, though I don't think she was his wife – you can always tell the signs in the way they speak to one another. He was always much too polite. I can see now what he was doing, by which I mean he was beginning the process of drawing me further and further into the religion.

'They learned that I knew a bit about computers and asked me to send messages, because their own computers were being monitored by Special Branch. I was provided with a special keyboard which they recommended I

find a very special place to conceal and I did so in an empty locker at work downstairs.'
'Did you know the content of what you were sending?'
'None at all. Most were in Arabic which I cannot read.'
'So you didn't actually type them?
'My keyboard was modified to serve as a scanner receiving messages which came to my computer, so I didn't need to type but I could have done because the keyboard would translate if I wanted it to do so.'
'And did you?'
'Yes, just once. I sent the message calling off a further attack on Sharon. I said the fatwa had been withdrawn.'
'Had it?'
'Not to my knowledge and frankly (and please excuse my French) I couldn't give a shit!'
'Has it occurred to you that if you abandon Islam, you too will be an apostate?'
'I don't care. Sharon is now safe, and I have nothing to live for anyway.'
André smiled at Dee.
'How would you fancy a tea or coffee and then to stretch our legs outside and get some fresh air?'
'I assume I would have to be handcuffed.'
'Why? Are you intending to attack me?'
Dee laughed.
André turned off the recording equipment and led her out of the room to a sort of café, where they were followed a moment or two later by a woman, who had been listening to every word spoken and watching the interview on a screen in a nearby room.'

'That was a lovely hotel and I enjoyed every moment being there, and some moments even more than others.'
'Do you know, Dr Mason, that you have a singularly naughty mind for the head teacher of a posh school for girls.'
'Really? I'm sure I never had it until I met a lady who works for the RAC.'
Kim laughed.
They had reached the difficult junction in Headingley and Kim turned left and made her way to the Flat. She stopped the car on the drive, turned to Sharon, and took her hand.
'I think we have big things to talk about and leaving the RAC is just one of them.'
She leaned forward and kissed Sharon.

'That was really odd and utterly unexpected. We just walked together across the airfield. I wouldn't have expected that.'
They were back in the interview room.
'Why not? I had no grounds for thinking you might be dangerous or ready

to run away. I also think you recognise that your future prospects lie here and now, in our time together, and I was clear that you would not want to do anything to risk that. Also I wanted to clear your head in the fresh air, though not as fresh as in Wharfedale, because we have reached a key moment in our chat together, and that concerns your visit to the University of Leicester on a singing course.'

'I knew we would get round to that eventually.'

'Are you in fact a singer?'

'Yes, I'm a soprano with the Skipton Choral Society.'

'Are they any good?'

'Too many oratorios for my liking – Handel and Mendelssohn in the main, but singing is such a good activity to engage in that I always come away feeling better and they're a nice crowd.'

'I agree with you about Horrortorios, as I call them. If I hear *Messiah* again, I shall die.'

Dee laughed.

'So did you arrange to go to Leicester at the suggestion of your choir director?'

'How else would I have known about it? I'm sure Mr Khan wouldn't have know about it. Most choral music is Christian anyway. When I met Sharon on the first afternoon and going for walk and having a drink in the evening with her, I thought she was such a lovely person. I have never had feelings for a woman before but when I was with Sharon I could understand that I could have done quite easily and there is no way I could ever have let anyone hurt her. She's had a really tough time in so many ways.'

'And on the morning of the attack?'

'I was sitting with Sharon and her friend Tracey. What I saw was a white man standing among the waiters suddenly dart forwards towards Sharon followed by the gunshots. Whatever else I might have thought there was no way I expected it in such a public setting and even the two police officers were out of uniform which I understood to have meant that there was no risk whatsoever.'

'What were your thoughts about the dead man, Shafiq Zaman?'

'I thought then and believe still that he got what was coming to him.'

'When you were arrested and brought here in the middle of the night, what were you thinking?'

'The middle of the night's not an easy time to think straight and I was too stunned to think anything, other than in a conversation with two of the officers about buying bras, pants and blouses in Marks and Spencer's.'

'But what had you actually done? You had got to know Mr Khan slightly and passed on messages for him you could not and chose not to read, doing them a kindness because they were being kind to you, deliberately so because they believed you had come to need them? I'm not sure that amounts to a great deal.

'If you had to appear in court I imagine all you would please guilty to was

passing on messages the content of which you didn't know to Mr Ali across the road who actually sent and received them.'
'I would above all have to please guilty to stupidity.'
André laughed.
'I think the judge would say that if stupidity were to be made an offence, the courts would never be empty.'
'So what now?'
'Now I will disclose to you things you do not know and which may distress you considerably.'
'Oh!'
'They're about your marriage and legal annulment.'
'Go on.'
'You were not in fact married by the ceremony at the Devonshire Arms. There is no legal record to show that you were. The registrar was as bogus as was the certificate. The settlement after the legal annulment, which never took place by the way, was regarded as a necessary payment to keep you thinking it had all been done by properly appointed solicitors, and the solicitor you used was appointed for you. Is that right?'
'The gist! And what about Wazeer, my impotent husband? Was he in on this?'
'I'm afraid so. He is married with three children and lives in Halifax.'
'That explains why he didn't want to buy a house. Then she started laughing. 'What a twerp I've been. It's like falling for the three-card trick on a bigger scale but I have to admit they've been clever, not least in finding and choosing an idiot like me.'
'No, Dee. I won't allow that and your resilience and strength amazes me. You might yet be able to turn the tables on them if you are willing.'
'Oh?'
'My boss who has heard and seen us the whole time wants to come and chat with you. She is listening now. Even so I must tell you that not only is she likeable in every way, but is also a high-ranking military offer who has seen active service in some of the toughest parts of world, so can I recommend that when she comes in you don't challenge her to an arm-wrestle.'
Dee thought this quite hilarious.
'I'll try and will I see you again? I hope so.'
'Yes, you will, as I'm looking forward to being served breakfast by you in *Betty's.*'
He rose and left the room and moments later was replaced by the beautiful and tall black woman she had seen earlier. Instinctively Dee stood.
'There's no need to stand.'
She sat down herself and gave a big smile.
'I bet you regularly get told you could give Naomi Campbell a run for her money.'
'I wouldn't mind her money and I bet she never has to come here on a

Saturday morning but I'm not sure I can stand all the different clothes she has to put on each day.'
They smiled at one another.
'This is your second visit,' said Martha. I hope you've been comfortable and able to sleep.'
'Yes thank you. What do I call you?'
'You have a choice. I am a Colonel in the army, so you can call me that if you wish, but my name is Martha and I am perfectly happy for you to use that.'
'Thank you. One other thing. Should I have a lawyer with me? It never occurred to me before.'
'You've had one with you all the time so far.'
'Do you mean André?'
'Once upon a time he was a barrister and strictly speaking still is. If you want a lawyer you can certainly have one, though it would have to be a Service Lawyer for reasons of security and getting one at the weekend might not be easy and I'm sure both you and I don't want to prolong your stay, and in any case please trust me when I say that you don't need one, though we might need one to defend our wrongful arrest twice over.'
'Are you able to give me some sort of idea what is going to happen to me? How long in prison am I looking at?'
'Please,' said Martha, 'let's just chat and we'll consider those things a bit later. I must say, first of all, that the account of your involvement in all this makes sense and for what it's worth I don't believe that the evidence we have suggests you have lied to us. Nor do I think for one moment that you would be willing to hold a gun and shoot someone, or plant a bomb. You spoke about your loneliness and the catastrophe of your short-lived and now non-annulled non-marriage. I'm not a psychiatrist but I recognise that you were distraught, lonely and therefore vulnerable, an obvious recruit. And that is what they did and you were flattered by their attention and you found yourself involved, almost without knowing it. How am I doing?'
Dee nodded her head, her eyes having filled with tears.
'Leicester was the turning point in that you were brought facte o face with something of the reality of the worst of Islam. When you were brought here the first time we could see how you had been set up but at that stage we had nothing on which to hold you. It's clear you know a lot about Information Technology but you encountered back in Ilkley someone who knows considerably more than anyone I have ever come across.'
'Kim.'
'You must have felt you got away with it when the gentleman across the road was taken into custody.'
'Yes, I did, but I was already setting up my withdrawal from the whole thing.'
'Yes, we know that from what Kim has found on your computer. By the way when you get home, we would recommend a change to your email

95

address. The word is that you could quite easily cast your screen on to the largest tv screen in the world, which would allow you to send the biggest emails ever composed.'

'I didn't know you could do that. Perhaps Kim could give me a ring and tell me how.'

'If you are released without charge, are you assuming you will continue working at *Betty's*?

'I think I would have to do so, as I promised André a cooked breakfast.'

'Now, it's time for us to stop. I have to liaise with others and only then might there be the possibility of release. In the meantime I shall lead you back to your room and you will be served lunch there.'

'Thank you so much for believing me, Martha.'

They decided to walk to Headingley centre which could have been a disaster as England were playing a one-day match against the West Indies nearby at what was now called the Emerald Stadium but still known locally as plain Headingley. Before the game and afterwards the streets would be crowded. At the junction Kim pointed up the road in the direction of Otley.

'About 200 metres from here I'm told there used to be the best fish and shop in the world, called *Brian's*. Sad to say it's long gone. So let's walk the other way and pay a visit to the ubiquitous *Pizza Express*.'

'That's fine by me,' replied Sharon, 'and please hold my hand.'

Kim did so but first gave her a little kiss. And then Sharon's phone rang again.

'It's Tracey,' she said to Kim. 'Hi Tracey and how's the UK Athletics Poster Girl today?'

'Getting nervous about Monday but I wanted to give you some good news.'

'I like the sound of that.'

'It was on BBC Radio Stoke this morning. A policeman said the accusation against you that you had assisted a suicide was ridiculous and being discounted. Furthermore, if the family persisted in accusing you of something you could not possibly have done, they would be formally informed about the law on slander. How about that?'

'Tracey, that's good news, though I will still have go through the inquest, but thank you for calling and I'm still very much expecting to be with you in Loughborough on Monday.'

'Where are you now?'

'Safe and well in Headingley and walking hand in hand with Kim to *Pizza Express*.'

'Oh. I'm not sure how to respond to that. Will you be returning to work?'

'I'm on compassionate leave, following a murder attempt on me, if you remember.'

'Good. I'm certain the school will do anything to keep you. Any word on Dee?'

'Nothing as yet.'

Sharon reported the news to Kim.

'No other conclusion could have been reached.'

'Is this the work of the RAC?'

'The Crown Prosecution Service do not like anyone seeking to manipulate them but in this case it only required a lawyer to present the outlines for them to know there was no mileage in it whatsoever.'

They had reached the restaurant and went in, There were still plenty free tables and Sharon noticed that Kim deliberately but apparently nonchalantly chose one from which she could keep an eye on all comings and goings. There was music playing louder than Sharon wished but when she said so, Kim said that it served to stop anything they might say being overheard.

'We have some important decisions to make,' said Kim. 'Whilst you were not looking I tossed a coin, and I won, so I will bat first and say that since our first moment of shared being I have been utterly overwhelmed by the love I have received from you. As you know my life has not on the whole been satisfactory in terms of love and relationships and I now feel that these are the most important things not only in my life but in the lives of everyone. I truly would like to make a life with you, Sharon, and if that were to mean giving up what I am doing at present, then for me it would be a price worth paying.'

'I do hope you know,' responded Sharon, 'that if I were to repeat every single word you have just spoken they would be identical.'

At that very moment their food arrived and looked very good. Both women knew that the franchise worked on the basis of a limited but attractive menu across all their branches and it did well. As they ate their lunch and drank their wine, Kim looked up at Sharon.

'I'm just a simple computer nerd who used to work for the police as a constable. You have a PhD and are head teacher of a major private school for girls. I suspect you get paid very much more than I do. With all your intelligence, I think you should be the one to work. I am not abdicating my responsibilities but recognising that the most important thing in my life is not my work. To be with you I will do anything. So if you can get this sorted by the time we get back to the flat and have a clear plan of action, we can go to Loughborough on Monday in a happy frame of mind.'

Sharon was insistent on having Tiramisu as a pudding though Kim said she would abstain until the waiter came to take their order when she suddenly opted for sticky toffee pudding with ice cream!

'Oh Kim, I am stunned by your willpower,' said Sharon, laughing at her.

'Don't worry, I'm only doing it to stop you feeling guilty.'

'Oh my darling, such self-sacrifice. I have paper qualifications and they impressed my present employers when I applied for the job, but I have been foolish in ways that you never would know in my life. Only now, in meeting you have I finally come to my senses, and compared with that what is a PhD but a piece of nonsense and being a head teacher, nothing at all? If I were to be stricken with a fatal disease those things could do nothing for me, but the discovery of our love would have made being alive worthwhile.

They returned to the flat for a cup of coffee.

'Briggate is the name of a street in Leeds where there is a *Zara*. When we've finished here we could get a cab and pay a visit. I'd love to be able to buy you a gift.'

'That is a wonderful idea. I do love you.'

'And I you.

Chapter Fourteen

Martha reached into her bag and removed a phone which most definitely was not one anyone could buy in a shop, and dialled a number.

'Alpha 1.' said a man's voice.

'Do tell me, Rob, when I am Director will I be able to take weekends off, or am I permanently condemned to spend my Saturdays at the Conference Centre with nothing but garbage to eat?'

'I know, I know. Why do you think I gave this job to you and I'm here at home?'

'We're not there yet. Anyway I am releasing her into the safe custody of André and tomorrow they will travel by train to Ilkley. There are risks, as there always are when you tether a kid goat to catch a tiger, but a team will be there.'

'How many are you using?'

'Seven. Dee is not stupid and more than capable but all the same I want André there with her.'

'Has she told you everything?'

'I think she is quite without guile, Rob, but if she isn't then I think it will emerge.'

'Well, I will sanction the operation, though the chances of my not doing so in an operation set up by you are nil, as well you know. It really is the big one and if we can get this man it will save lives. A kid goat tethered to catch a tiger; take good care of the goat.

'Of course and in phoning you I am just protecting my back if it all goes tits up, and that reminds me, how is Caro getting on with breastfeeding?'

'She absolutely adores it and so do I, watching. There is one major problem I'm facing however, for it has become abundantly clear to me that I should never have married her. When we got married she was deaf and could hear nothing and that meant I could have music playing at any volume I wished and that anything I muttered under my breath she couldn't hear. But following her most recent operation I have come to realise what a mistake I have made. She doesn't pretend that her hearing is perfect, though the surgeon says it will get even better, but she now tells me to turn the music down except when it's by her sister Nadine, and then she tells me to turn it off! Just about everything I say she can now hear. Surely that's intolerable in a marriage!'

'And is she listening to you now?'

'Yes, and sticking her tongue out... All I can say, and she and you both should remember that I am the Director of MI5 and therefore very important, and so should be obeyed without question at all times. You and she are the bane of my life. All I can say is that I adore her more than ever. She has produced the most wonderful baby and the doctors have finally been able to work wonders with her hearing. May I use a colloquialism: "what's not to like?"'

'From Alpha 2 to a very happy and contented Alpha 1, my best wishes to the three of you, sir. Out.

Martha pocketed her phone.

'Kim told me that Dee's flat was taken apart by the counterterrorism officers and have left it resembling a tip. You haven't had any leave this year, André. How would you fancy a trip to Ilkley to give support to Dee as she tries to get everything sorted? The clean up team will come in early tomorrow instead of Monday – I will make sure of that, and you have an open budget to replace and repair.'

'I will happily take a week off, and she has promised me breakfast in *Betty's*. Shall I go and fetch her.'

'No. Let me do it.'

Martha rose and made her way through the labyrinth which is the Conference Centre to the holding rooms, in which the only resident was Dee.

'Do you fancy a cup of tea to wash down what you've just eaten – next time you come, make sure it's not a Saturday and, to be honest Sunday is not much better.'

'No offence, because you and André are such nice people, but as they almost say in parliament, "I have no plans for such a visit!".'

'Any chance of coming to work here and using your work skills to provide for us and the men and women of the Royal Air Force?'

'Are you being serious?'

'Well it has just come to me, but we've rather taken to you and so I believe would everyone else. Think about it and I'll do the same. Now you can leave your room for the last time and let's go for that cup of tea.'

Dee was beginning to wonder if she had suddenly moved from a nightmare to a dream, and dutifully followed Martha to the dining room in which there was only André, who at once stood up.

'Tea with milk but no sugar I believe.'

Having sat down her thoughts were racing about what Martha had just suggested. André returned with the tea and both he and Martha sat down.

'What would you do about food here at the weekends when it's occupied only intermittently and unpredictably?'

'It's surely not beyond the bounds of possibility to have available a range of quality ready meals chosen with care from the best suppliers, together with fresh fruit and various sorts of desserts. What you need is a much bigger and better microwave than the one that I can see from here, and perhaps two, one dealing with defrosting and the other with cooking, and who knows, perhaps even three. That I think would be infinitely preferable to the re-heated food we've been eating which always carries the risk of food poisoning.'

'Oh great! Now you tell me,' said Martha. 'You are presently manager of *Betty's* in Ilkley and on £27,000 plus the flat above.'

'I won't ask how you know that,' said Dee with a broad smile, 'but it's accurate.'

'Your pseudo-divorce settlement was generous.'

'Pseudo-annulment.'

'Of course. I realise that you live in the Yorkshire Dales and that must help compensate for what is a poor salary by London standards.'

'It might if I ever had the time to get out into them and in any case they are a little tarnished by the experience of my sham wedding in one of those dales.'

'Yes, I can imagine that,' said André.

'I can offer a starting salary of £50,000 if you would be willing to come and be Senior Catering Manager for the Centre and RAF Northolt.'

'Is this some sort of further interrogation technique?'

André smiled.

'There is another reason why you should consider this. There are going to be trials ahead at which you will be asked to give evidence, and if so there may be attempts at reprisals,' he said. 'You will be safer here than in Ilkley.'

'But where would I live? The money sounds good but would be less so if I have to pay London prices for a flat.'

'Definitely,' said Martha, 'and therefore I shall take you outside and show you the house you can live in, rent free. You will at all times be bound by the terms of the Official Secrets Act and receive positive vetting but we can that for granted as we know all about your terrible past. But, Dee, I urge you think carefully about this and then make contact and say Yes, because we think you might well be very happy and I think I know my people well enough to say that they will be too. On that subject, let's go and take a quick look at the property, and then I must go home to a husband and children who will be thinking I have abandoned them.'

'Gosh. I didn't see how you could do this job and be married with kids,' said Dee.

'The Director, my boss, is married to a truly beautiful young woman who was stone deaf from birth but who now, for the first time in her life can hear thanks to the surgeons in London for whom she used to work. It's not perfect but she laughs and says she misses the silence, especially when her husband is around! They have a new baby. So imagine fitting all that in to being Director of the Security Service as well.'

They looked at the house. It was small but it was a house and not a flat. As they came out the front door, she turned to look at Martha.

'I've thought long and hard about this, Martha (well for at least five minutes!), and the answer is Yes, but I would need to speak to *Betty's* before I could give you a starting date. I think my contract specifies a month's notice.'

'That will be fine but until you are in charge of catering, I will stay away at the weekends!'

Kim and Sharon were very much enjoying their shopping trip.

'I love shopping,' said Sharon, 'though it's never too painful if you're single and on my salary.'

'Could two shoppers live on it, even for a little while, until the other is also able to earn some money?'

'Is that a proposal?'

Kim smiled.

'Would you mind if it was?'

They tightened their hold of each other's hand. After many attempts with various coats, Sharon settled on a lovely brown knee-length one, and Kim took it away to pay for it. On the walls there were large photographs of models showing off the stock. When Kim joined her again, Sharon pointed to the photos.

'I do hope that when business improves they'll be able to afford models who don't look utterly fed up.'

'You're not kidding. There's not a single smile on any face, except yours I hope,' and handed her the bag containing the coat.

'O thank you my darling. I love you,' and there in the shop kissed one another, and when they parted could see that no one had been taking the slightest bit of notice. They left the shop and continued to walk up Briggate on to The Headrow and down to the Henry Moore Gallery. There were still many shoppers around. As they walked towards the Gallery, two young men, one black, the other white, approached them and blocked their way.

'A pair of dykes I would reckon,' said one to the other.

'Yeah, what they need is a real man.'

'Yes, we've been looking for one,' said Kim, 'but can't find any? Obviously not you two,' said Kim.

'You've got too big a mouth, bitch,' said the white one, who now moved right in front of her face. Sharon immediately tensed.

'Sometimes I think you try too hard, Craig,' said Kim.

'Just checking you're both ok, ma'am. And don't tell anyone, but we both felt too embarrassed to follow you inside *Zara*. We would have looked like suspicious voyeurs.'

'All voyeurs are suspicious,' said Sharon.

'Any chance of a cup of tea, Kim,' said Craig, 'and by the way this is Ed, based here.'

'Hi Ed. And this is Sharon.'

'I assumed so. Hi Sharon. It's good to see you alive and well.'

'Thank you, Craig. Where would you, Ed, recommend for a cup of

Yorkshire tea?

'There's a good place just about 100 metres behind you on the Headrow.'

At that moment a policeman appeared and said to Sharon. 'Are these men troubling you?'

'Yes, they are – could you please arrest them and charge them with overacting?' said Kim.

The policeman looked baffled. Kim removed from her handbag something Sharon couldn't see but it had the desired effect.

'My mistake,' said the policeman. 'Sorry ma'am.'

'Not at all. That you came straight to us shows you got it right. But thank you, and this is not meant to be even remotely patronising,' said Craig, 'but well spotted and well done.'

'I suppose we could make it even more realistic by screaming and having a struggle,' said Kim with a broad grin, 'but what we really want is a cup of tea.'

The policeman raised his arm and said: 'I recommend a place about 100 metres behind you but be warned, their cakes are very moreish.'

'Can you join us?'

'If only, but not on duty. Pity though.'

They ordered their tea and cakes and sat at the back.

'Now Craig, there must be a reason why you needed to speak.'

'Yes. Apparently you left your encrypted mobile in Headingly and Alpha 2 wanted to make contact.'

'Oh shit. That's a capital offence. So what did she say?'

'The message as I received it indirectly from Leeds Control is: "Betty is free and coming home. The Clean Team will begin in the morning and you are a naughty girl for forgetting your phone, and Dr Mason should give you detention!"'

They all laughed.

André was driving with Dee towards his home in Pinner, and they chatted all the way, about all sorts of things,

'It's a lovely house,' said Dee, as André pulled into the drive and stopped. 'Have you lived here long?

'Ten years, just about.'

'Is that when you started your present job?'

'Yes and no. I had worked in Northern Ireland doing much the same work, only not in Arabic.'

'Was it frightening?'

'Obviously when working with someone like you it's utterly terrifying but for the rest, honestly it's just like most jobs and you get used it, even if Belfast was a dangerous place to be if you were military personnel.'

'You were a soldier like Martha?'

'Trust me, no one is a soldier like Martha, but no, I was never in uniform though I was made to bear arms when I was outside the base. Kim, whom you know is a soldier – in army captain. She often has to bear arms though she's

confessed to to me that often forgets.'
'Did you ever have to use a gun?'
'No. I reckoned that if the boyos wanted me dead, they would arrange for it to happen and there would be no shoot out at the OK Corral, not least because no one ever taught me how to use it.'
They entered the house and after showing Dee around, fixed them both a g&t and they sat together in the sitting room.
'André, may I ask a very personal question?'
'I will answer before you ask it. No, I am not gay though many think I am, apart from the two at the top. People thinking the wrong thing about you can be very useful.'
'Are you or have you ever been married?'
'No, but across the years of my bachelor existence I have had women friends, some very close. My private life and that of my work I have striven to keep well apart. As I say, the boss and his deputy, Martha, know just about everything about me, and all my girlfriends had to be vetted even though I'm not sure any of them knew. You cannot be a security risk.'
'I must say how impressed I have been with the service (is that the right thing to call it?) except when they took me from my bed in the middle of the night and brought me to the Conference Centre, but I shall always be grateful to you for the helicopter ride home.'
The doorbell rang. André had a sort of television monitor by the door which allowed him to see what might be outside, but on this occasion he had no hesitation in opening the door.
'Stephanie, you wonderful lady, do come in and bring in your goodies.'
'Hi André, I haven't seen you for ages, I hope you haven't been on a diet', the woman replied.
It was obvious to Dee that Stephanie was bringing hot food.
'Does it look as if I have been starving myself?'
'I suppose not but it's the big danger of working in the City – all those working lunches.'
'You could well be right. Now this is Dee who is manager of a very well-known teashop and bakery in Yorkshire.'
'Is it *Betty's*.'
Dee looked at André who gave an almost imperceptible nod.
'It is.'
'Oh how I love going into *Betty's* in Harrogate. The teas, cakes, music and the loveliest toilets anywhere.'
Dee laughed.
'We must mention the loos on any new advert we put out.'
'I must go, said Stephanie. 'I think you will enjoy your dinner and it's been great to meet you, Dee, and even you, André.'
Dee looked at André.
'Is she one of your former ladies?'
'Let's say we've had our moments.'

'And how will she feel seeing me here?'

'Probably poisoned your food though the taste will be incredible.'

He wasn't wrong about the food. It was simply delicious and more than compensated for lunch!

Chapter Fifteen

André, understandably, recognised the faces of each of the seven men and women who, one at a time, regularly walked through their corridor ostensibly on the way to the Buffet Car. A woman with a trolley came round and André bought two coffees and two bars of chocolate for them.

'How would you rate the catering compared with where you work?'

'On here? It isn't catering or even an excuse for it. I am a bit puzzled why it is people seem to want to go to the Buffet Car and some of them at least twice.'

The journey was hold-up free and took just a minute or two over three hours. As the train approached the station in Ilkley, André noticed that a man and a woman, a couple of buffet-walkers as André thought of them were also leaving the train with them.

'Let's get a taxi,' said Dee. 'I know it's not far but it might mean we shall be in time to get lunch in my place of work before they move into afternoon tea mode.'

As they made for one of the only two cabs outside the station, a voice came from the one at the front.

'Hey Dee, we've missed you. Have you been abroad somewhere?'

The speaker was obviously of Asian heritage but he spoke so well it was most likely that he was the son of immigrants, and born here.

'Something like that, Paddy.'

'Paddy?' said André.

'Yeah well, my actual name is almost unpronounceable even by me, so at school I told everyone including teachers that I was called Paddy and it stuck. The only problem was when mum and dad came to the first parents evening and when teachers spoke of me to them, at first they assumed that the teachers meant someone else. Now, would you believe even mum and dad call me Paddy. Now, to *Betty's*, I assume.'

'Yes please,' and in they clambered.

'Two things to report. The first is that was a large cleaning company van outside your door early this morning. I assume you had arranged it.'

'To be honest Paddy, I'd left the place in a bit of a mess, so I arranged for them to come though I was amazed that they would do so on a Sunday.'

'It can't have been too bad as they were only there for an hour and a half. The other thing is that I saw Mr Khan knocking on your door on Thursday evening.'

'That's a great pity as I need to be in contact with him. Oh well, he'll no doubt be in contact again. And here we are – home sweet home, and still in time for some lunch.'

As they alighted, André reached for his wallet, but Paddy stopped him.

'No charge for that lovely lady, and especially not for such a short journey. Can I ask, are you her dad?'

'As far as I know both of Dee's parents have died and I don't think I'm a ghost, but I'm a sort of distant honorary uncle and I've come to do some Dales walking for a few days and eat lots of hearty breakfasts in the café behind me.'

'It's good to meet you. If you need a cab, Dee has my mobile number. Any friend of hers is a friend of mine.'

André waved as Paddy drove off.

Dee entered her sitting room to find things were mostly in the wrong place but at least the floor and windows were clean. In the bedrooms things had been put into drawers, but usually the wrong ones. The major problem was that all four mattresses had been cut open and though now back in place, stuffing was coming out. They would have to be replaced though André had insisted that this was not a problem and that he would make sure they were replaced.

Although Dee had warned André that the lunch offered would not match up to Stephanie's dinner of the previous evening, when he had finished he was fulsome in its praise.

'That was superb, and what a view from the picture window, but I sensed that all the staff seem nervous having their boss in to eat.'

'I should think so too, not least because they now know I shall be back in place tomorrow. One of my staff told me when we came in that they had no idea if I'd be back at all, let alone tomorrow.'

'Mr Khan must be well known if Paddy knows him.'

'He's the man with whom I used to meet for Asian meals in Bingley as I was being drawn in. More than that I don't know.'

'Don't you think it might be a nice idea to call him and say that had heard from a local cab driver that he had called on you? You might even suggest a curry in Bingley.'

'You don't think they might try to kill me.'

'You won't be alone in there, believe me.'

In a way Sharon and Kim were rather sad to be leaving Leeds but they had to travel down to the Midlands for the launch of Tracey's new career and life for her family. Sharon had booked them into a Premier Inn but had great difficulty getting the receptionist to grasp that they wanted a double bed and only one room. As yet they had not discussed Tuesday and beyond.

'The last time I was in the Midlands,' said Sharon, 'my former husband tried to kill me.'

'Oh, I'm so sorry my love. So much has happened and at such a speed that I haven't given you the time and space to talk it through.'

'Well, to be honest I've rather buried it inside me because as you say so much has happened, and maybe I need to process it a little longer before it might emerge into the daylight but I already know that when it does you will be the one with whom I shall want to share it.'

'I want to hear your own thoughts about our future,' said Kim. 'I've tended to think along boring channels of either I stay with the service and we live in the country somewhere outside London, or you continue as head teacher in Chester and I come to live in Cheshire with you. Or . . . Is there another possibility, that we both abandon our work and find somewhere we both love, get married and live there.'

'That would be asking a great deal of you, my darling. You love your job much more than I do mine and, although this may sound somewhat unexpected coming from me, you are serving your country in such important ways. Mike and Eamonn are really smashing lads, and they told me that you are the very best and way ahead of anyone else in the counterterrorism field.'

'You have a PhD.'

'They're two a penny these days, and besides which when did I last use it? Since becoming a head I have not taught anything related to my subject. I am only the senior manager.'

'And tomorrow Tracey begins her new life.'

'She deserves something good and she will be good at it too. She is patient and caring and one of the greatest encouragers I have ever come across. They will miss her at the Nursery in Nantwich as from the beginning she was the guiding light but like all good leaders she will always have been preparing others to take on that leadership role. Gymnasts and athletes will requires different attention I imagine, but they will all know that she has been through it herself and emerged a winner.'

'You won't be seeing quite so much of each other,' said Kim.

'But you know, we didn't see all much of one another anyway, usually only at choir and afterwards in the pub. Her's and Geoff's real concern will be getting the boys settled into a new school. The housing goes with the job so that's sorted. Then, of course, there are the Olympics to come soon, so she'll be travelling quite a lot meeting her charges and their coaches.'

'If, and it is only if, I were to stay in post and we find somewhere to live outside London, what would you want to find for yourself?' asked Kim.

'I wouldn't need to *find* anything, as you put it, because I already know.'

'Are you going to tell me what it is?'

'I might do . . . Oh, alright I will, but keep it a secret.'

'As I'm bound by the Official Secrets Act you're safe there!'

'I am going to write a novel, a historical novel about the poet George Herbert, his wife and her family into which he married. Sources are not exactly in great supply so it's an ideal setting for imagination.'
'You must do it, Sharon. It sounds so wonderful that when we get to Loughborough I shall be tempted to go on-line and order an advance copy.'
'You're only saying that because you love me.'
Kim glanced towards her partner.
'How did you guess?'

'Mr Khan? It's Deeba, back home serving coffee, teas and cakes again. . . A taxi driver said he saw someone knocking on my door whilst I was away and I thought and hoped it might be you. I have lots to tell you about my holiday and some of the people I met, in which I feel certain you will be interested and I wondered if we might meet for a curry in Bingley. . . Yes, Tuesday night will be great . . . eight o'clock.'
André smiled at her.
'That was pretty impressive. Keep it up and we'll have to promote you from Senior Catering Manager to Head of the Service!'
'What happens now, André?'
'What happens now is that you try to relax and prepare for your first morning back at work. I have to go out for a short while and for company you will have Shirley, whose face you might recognise.'
Just then there was a knock at the door down the stairs.
'It's ok, 'said André, ' I'll let her in and see you a little later.'
Moments later he was replaced by a woman younger than herself with a warm smile whom she recognised from yesterday's train journey.'
Hi, I'm Shirley.' Her accent was very Welsh.
'Hello, I'm Dee, obviously. Please come and sit down.'
'I just need to orientate myself first.'
She opened the door to the short corridor leading to the bedrooms and opened each door.
'Just the sort of preparations we get taught.'
'I'm impressed.'
Shirley now sat down.
'Do you work with André a great deal?'
'Hardly ever, more's the pity. We all love him.'
'I can understand that.'

André walked up the drive of number 15 which was divided into flats, and pressed the upstairs bell. A light come on in the hall and the door was opened by a young woman in jeans and tee shirt.
'PC 1062 Helen Boardman?'
'Yes?'
'I'm a friend of Kim's and I come bearing a letter of invitation to a coffee morning in Westminster for you, as she promised. May I come in?'

'Yes, yes, of course. I wasn't expecting to hear just yet.'
'We like to get on with things.'
'Clearly.'
'Though other things have also brought us.'
'A cup of coffee, tea or a glass of wine.'
'Actually a glass of wine, any colour, would be lovely.'
She went out to what he presumed was her kitchen and soon returned with two glasses of red.
'Kim says that your station here is still in the dark ages where women officers are concerned but that you stood out in ways that might be of use to us.'
'I take it you are talking about counterterrorism.'
'Certainly not. I am led to believe you saw the the state those boys and girls left the flat above *Betty's*.'
'M'm.'
'They do a good job sometimes, I suppose, but I wouldn't want you being one of their thugs.'
She laughed.
'Our service demands intelligence more than anything, the sort of intelligence that can make intuitive leaps of the mind. We also require courage and the capacity to deceive others when necessary. As yet you are not fire-armed licensed but you will have to be so as soon as you begin, if that is you want to begin.'
'Kim refused to say who she works for for, but intelligence, courage and deceit are the sort of thing only required by the Security Services.'
'I do like this wine, Helen. Might you top me up?'
She brought the bottle.
'My boss spoke to your boss yesterday morning. He said you were stroppy and capable of being a real pain.'
'I would put it another way and say that I certainly am especially when I have good ideas which he usually sits on and when I complain he says I'm stroppy.'
'Could you work in a team made up of men and women as cocky and able as you?'
'How would I know? I am the only female police officer in Ilkley and my colleagues only ever praise my tea-making skills though I will admit that they are particularly good.'
'It sounds to me that division should be informed, but that's not going to be your problem any more if you come to us. Our operational boss is a woman and outstanding – an army colonel who has done time in some of the worst hotspots. You'll meet her in the coffee shop later in the week.'
'Is that some sort of code, because Kim used the same words?'
'Not at all. It is literally a coffee shop and the Boss likes to meet new people there.
'Good Lord.'

'Oh I'm not sure she meets him there, but if he does I bet even he calls her ma'am!'

Again Helen laughed.

'Your station knows that you have left them today and that there are to be no questions asked, to engage in something very important and secret, but that you might be back next week – which I added just in case you don't wish to join us, though I hope you will. You start tomorrow. We are here doing something in which we are happy to include you.'

'As a test?'

'No, Helen. It's very real, and because you cannot be armed, it will be essential for us to make sure you're protected if the going gets rough. One of things you will come to realise is that in the course of your work you will often receive bizarre instructions, and you will obey them without question. Any former members of the military with whom you will find yourself working will do that without hesitation. There is no other way in which we can work.'

'Of course.'

'Now, tomorrow should be a gentle introduction. Two hours of babysitting while you indulge yourself on the delights of *Betty's* cafe. From 11 to 1 you will sit in a seat facing inwards so you can see whoever is coming in. You won't be alone but don't spend your time looking around to see if you can work out who is the other spook. In the unlikely event that there is trouble, your single task is to protect the manager, Dee, at all costs. Leave dealing with anyone who comes in to attack her to your colleague, your job will be to get her out of the way, into the kitchen or her office. Other customers will have to fend for themselves. Are you clear?'

'Yes.'

'Assuming nothing is going to happen we shall repeat on Tuesday, but for Tuesday evening we shall brief tomorrow night and you'll get details.'

'Ok.'

'Do you already wish none of this had happened and that perhaps being a PC in Ilkley isn't too bad after all?'

'I'm already looking forward to visiting the coffee shop in Westminster.'

André stood, placed his hand on her shoulder and nodded. 'There's lots of things you haven't asked me about. Helen, it's our job to find out things, and we know a great deal about you already, including your reputation at Coventry Police College, where it is said you defeated every other recruit, male and female, at Judo and scared the living daylights out of your self-defence tutor!'

'I learned sheep-shearing when I was a lass. Compared with a big old Dalesbred yow, handling and controlling police cadets, and even the tutor, was a walkover.'

'I must go,' said André. 'Eleven o'clock tomorrow. Dee won't know you're now working for us, so keep it like that, and make the most of the food on offer.'

Kim and Sharon had arranged to meet the Adamsons for a curry just round the corner from their hotel, on the Leicester Rd. Conversation was limited to the events of the following day, and Sharon could sense how excited her best friend was.

'This is such a great move, Tracey. I'm so pleased for you,' she said when they found a chance to be alone together in the loo (like Scott and Bailey?).

'Yes, and happily Geoff feels the same and is looking forward to his own new departure. The boys I'm sure will be ok. Oh, but I shall miss you, Sharon.'

'Maybe not as much as you might think. Kim and I are giving most consideration to the thought that she stays in her present job and I leave Chester to find a house together in the commuter land north of London. If so we can certainly make sure we find time to meet regularly.'

'Is this anything to do with the suicide business?'

'Not directly, but I don't want those events following me every day of the new school year which I rather think they will.'

'Will you still have to be at the Inquest and give evidence?'

'I have no idea, but I hope not. Kim thinks a letter might suffice.'

'Will you look for another headship?'

'No. I want to write a book on George Herbert.'

'And what about you and Kim?'

'What about us? We were both wanting love more than anything else, and we have found one another.'

Tracey put her arms around her friend and held her tight.

'That puts what I am doing tomorrow completely in the shade. I am thrilled for you both.'

Chapter Sixteen

The sight of Dee in her uniform was enough to set André's heart racing.

'God, you are so beautiful, Dee.'

'I bet you say that to all the girls in uniform.'

'I bet you I don't. What time do you start?'

'The shop opens at 9 o'clock but I begin at 7.30, though the bakers will have been in since about 5.00. My arrival is usually the signal for them to turn off Radio 1. I'm on today with my deputy so we can catch up with last week's business and turnover, material I need to let Head Office in Harrogate know before they find a reason to sack me. *Betty's* is a wonderful old-fashioned company which is why people love us, but is also just a company that has to continue to perform well and compete like all the others. Botham's of Whitby would love to take over our share of the market so we have to stay at the top of our game.'

'Dee, forgive me saying this again, you are beautiful.'

'Thank you André, and shall I see you downstairs today?'

'I hope so. I have one or two things to do but I would like to be back for afternoon tea.'

'Do you think this attire and frilly aprons on the others would go down well at the Conference Centre?'

'Dee, believe me, you in your attire would go down well anywhere. Not so sure about the frilly aprons given that most of your staff are men.'

'I must go. See you later.'

She came over and gave him a slightly lingering kiss on the cheek and momentarily held his head close.

Once the café was open, surprise gave way to amusement as time after time there came faces she recognised from her train journey on the previous day, almost all of whom chose to sit at the same table, the one which allowed the best view of what was going on and who was coming in through the short hallway where customers queued for a table. One face was very familiar

however, that of Helen Boardman, one of the local police officers.
'Hello Helen,' said Dee. 'Are you on a day off or a late?'
'Today, happily, is a day off and I thought I would come to my favourite watering hole, relax and have one of your delicious lunches.'
'Madam is very wise.'
'And where is the great dancer today?'
'Oh, Karl has sashayed out to the bank but he'll be back soon, or at least I hope so, or else I shall have to call upon you.'
'To hunt him down, to be his dance partner or to be a waitress in his place?'
'I'm sure I could find you an apron.'
'Alas I have to wear hi-viz at all times now.'
'Well, don't say I didn't ask! More coffee?'
'Yes please.'
They grinned at one another, and the day went by for Dee in her usual busyness, with a succession of oddly familiar faces coming and going.

The event was to take place in what is known as East Park, a part of the University Campus a little aside from the main body of buildings and student accommodation across the Epinal Way, in the National Gymnastics Performance and Research Centre, which delighted Tracey. In addition to her own introduction was to a be statement about funding for UK Athletes which would, in the way things are in the world, get a far bigger mention in the newspapers tomorrow than her own appointment.

She, Geoff and the boys were there is good time and met up with Sharon and Kim who both wanted to give her every encouragement they could muster. Someone from the Press Office came and took her away, however, and took her through all that was to come and how she should handle it, especially any questions about how a new job was being financed at a difficult time for UK Athletics, which she should pass over to the Chair. They were now in the hall and members of the Press were setting up. And there was one face she knew ever so well, and had known it a long time before everyone in the country who now knew it well though she still knew it by a different name. They ran towards one another and hugged.

'Oh, wow, Gabby Yorath, the only person I know to retire at the age of 17. Oh Gabby, it's great to see you and thanks for being here. You are looking fantastic.'

For Tracey it was a great occasion with so many familiar faces from the world of sport, and the filled the heart of Sharon with such joy for the woman who had been her special friend so long.

They met at *The Star*, not many yards from where the action was due to take place at the Asian Restaurant, and where they would eat at lunchtime.

'You are putting her in great harm's way, you know that don't you? You are my superior officer and I will do as you order, but I couldn't myself sanction this operation and I would like to have that formally on record,' said the counterterrorism commander from Leeds.

'As you wish, but your people won't be in any danger. I need you there to backup and cleanup. I take it you do want Mr Big?'

'But will he be there?'

'Not at first, but I suspect he will come all the same. Now, let's go to the curry house. It's Moslem and that means it's dry.'

'That's alright. For once I'm driving myself.'

'Is that either wise or safe?'

'I'll take the risk. What it means is that I'm the only one who knows about tomorrow, and nothing will go on to a computer in advance unless we choose it to.'

'I take it you have someone in mind.'

'A computer operator. If it is so, and it may not be, she puts nothing on the computer herself, but it's just possible she passes on what she reads and hears to interested ears.'

'Why don't you just get rid of her or hand her over to Special Branch?'

'She's Asian, Moslem and a woman. There's three reasons which outweigh a suspicion, or at least that's how the Chief Constable would see it, and in any case she can come in useful being fed misinformation.'

They had left the pub and were almost at the restaurant which they now entered.

At the present time they were the only customers, though it would get busier later. Before their curry, they ordered popadoms and fruit drinks.

André dropped his first popadom onto the floor. A waiter appeared at once to help André recover it.

'I will bring another, sir.'

'Thank you.'

'Now, do tell me how United are getting on in their search for a return to Premier League Status. I remember the great (not just good) old days of Don Revie, Bremner, Giles, Lorimer, Hunter, Charlton and the Gray brothers.'

His words were accompanied with a look straight into the eyes which told him that the banal was to be the sole topic of conversation, because André had presumably found something under the table necessitating silence on tomorrow's operation, presumably a microphone. So banality and fantasy reigned supreme as they ate their meals, including accounts of André's wife, a primary school teacher in Worcester and their three adult children and what they were doing in life!

Their food had been very good, but best of all were the sparkling fruit cocktails and they were honestly able to thank the staff for a highly enjoyable meal. Once outside they turned right into Leonard St and walked for about 200 yards before they spoke.

'It was such a pity that you dropped your popadom.'

'I know. What I saw was a "sub-min Lavalier" and I imagine they have one under every table. Not sophisticated but still effective and we can certainly make use of it. But tell me, for an op what is your customary circulation?'

Rod Hacking

'CC or ACC, Yard and Home Office liaison and Armoury (though they receive no details of what will be happening, where or when).'
'Any leaks won't be from them, hopefully. You have misinformed that you're raiding at dawn on Thursday and this will be confirmed by Dee at her meeting with Mr Khan on Tuesday.
'You're still leaving her on the front line? I'm unhappy about that. If the man you're hoping to get turns up, he will surely come with armed support.'
'She will be well supported inside the restaurant. Six armed officers will also be eating curry and talking all about rugby league and heaven knows what else. Outside there will be you and your team and two of us. She is not expendable under any circumstances. When Mr Big arrives and enters the restaurant, immobilise his car and take away the driver. If the big man runs out bringing her with him, he is to be taken out. No arguments.'
'You're the boss.'

They were heading down the MI towards London and after an initial conversation about how well everything had gone, Kim had lapsed into an obvious silence. Quite unexpectedly she turned off the motorway into the dark and doomed world of Toddington Services which has less life in it than a cemetery
'Do you need the loo?' asked a puzzled Sharon, but when Kim turned towards she could see tears cascading down her cheeks. 'What is it my darling?'
'It was seeing Tracey and all the other successful women so apparently happy and fulfilled by their commitment to what they do. Tracey has found the job of her dreams. Then I thought of how I was taking you away from such a good and important job of work, in which you obviously shine to live in a shit-hole like London, and you might never know where I was or what I was doing, and always the terrible fear that one day I just might not come home. And I love you so much and I just can't risk that. Everyone says how clever and wonderful I am in what I do, but it's been cover for the absence of the only thing that matters in this world and that is love. I had assumed that I was never going to get it, and then you turned up and my world has been transformed.'
Her words had emerged intermittently through the tears and some sobbing, but Sharon had taken hold of her and let her cry.
'My darling, Toddington Services is such an unlikely place for two people who love each other to make huge decisions, but let's do so together. You're right about London and the nature of your work taking you away to places unknown to me, and also the risks involved which I know are real. But you're not right about my work in Chester. Once the A-level results are in, I shall be ready to go though almost certainly they will demand that I stay until Christmas to give them time to replace me. I shall get oodles of sympathy from the attempt to murder me and the things that have been put about by the family of our former bursar. But I want what you want and that is each other. I

116

have a book to write and I cannot doubt you will soon find a way to market some of your amazing creations. We will be happy because we love one another, even if I have no idea where that might be located. Have you given thought to Iceland?'

She looked almost on the verge of tears again.

'Didn't they buy out Bejam?'

'Yes, but I bet you didn't know that the name Bejam, was formed from the names of those who started the business, all from one family: Brian, Eric, John And Millie.'

'Oh Dr Mason, everyday is going to be a a day of discovery with you.'

'As every night is for both of us at present.'

'Do you think we should return to the motorway and get on to my house?'

'What size bed have you got?'

'Kingsize.'

'Better than the double last night.'

'Oh I don't know. I didn't notice you objecting.'

'Well, consider this. I emailed the editor of The Times, who's daughter came to my school, and with whom I've always got on very well, to say I'm leaving Chester to move to London, and has he anything on the Education side he could use me for, and he replied during lunch today, offering me a job.'

'Gracious.'

'Don't be too surprised. I do have one or two skills, you know.'

'I know, and this could be a wonderful opportunity for you.'

'And for you to stay in the army.'

André had arranged a briefing for the team, and introduced Helen, who would be observing on this occasion. Typically he talked first about the menu assuring them that those inside would get something good to eat. Warning them about the little presence under each table of a microphone, they all knew what that would mean. He stressed as he had to counterterrorism that above all else Dee was to be protected, even if that meant the loss of the target. Also tomorrow, today's pattern of protecting in *Betty's* would be repeated.

André returned to Dee's flat and she had prepared supper for them.

'My team feel they're getting fat.'

'They don't have to stuff themselves,' Dee said, laughing.

'Oh no. They are doing it in the service of the Crown and feel they are therefore under orders to do so.'

'It's clearly a hard life in the Service.'

'It is, Dee. Just think of the sacrifice I am making having to be here with you and sharing your life and your food.'

'You are truly a martyr, André.'

'I know, but I can bear it. I have a question for you, and it concerns your taxi driver friend Paddy.'

'Oh?'

'I want you to call him and book him to take you tomorrow evening arriving at 8-00, but tell him there's no need for him to wait because you're hoping Mr Khan will bring you back. Tomorrow evening is the big event and in anything that might happen my team and that of others who will be surrounding you and are under clear orders that you are to be protected. Remember that as far as they are concerned it will be a debriefing, an attempt to discover what happened in the course of your trips to the Conference Centre. Tell them everything they ask. They will try to trick you on the basis of their existing knowledge which is why you must be straight when you talk about the place and both Alpha 2 and me, whose names they will know.'

'Ok. But will you be safe, André? If they know that somewhere close by is a top person in the Service, they might well decide it's your scalp they want and not mine.'

'There's one other point you might make, though best made only after you are joined by someone coming in late. Tell them you were refused Moslem dress when you asked for it, and you feel quite strongly that they were the ones who insisted you should stay in plain clothes, might it now be possible to adopt the proper Islamic dress for a woman?'

'In the light of what you have already told me, Mr Khan will probably be wanting to remove what you have on rather than adding to it, but if they ask you to stay as you are for now, it will mean that they have others things in mind for you as their spy.'

'By Wednesday will I be in a position to give in my notice?'

'You will, but tonight I want to you send a message via Mr Ali across the road.'

'But I haven't got my special red keyboard and the special form of Arabic would not be the same if you simply wrote it.'

'I will get in touch with Kim and ask her to write it and send it to here making sure it will have all the appearance that it is from you. I need to ask her something else as well.'

'I don't believe it,' said Kim as her work phone summoned her from the arms of Sharon, as they lay fast asleep together on the sofa. 'Hello André, you are just about the only person I would consider forgiving for phoning me at this particular moment.'

'I won't be long, Kim, but it's extremely important. Two matters. An op tomorrow in a restaurant each table of which is equipped with a sub-min Lavalier and a central box behind the counter.'

'God, they must be short of money.'

'What do we need to do if we want to record a particular table?'

'You have two options. The first is to get in there and put your own wire either under the table or, better, on someone. These days they are tiny and very effective.'

'And the other?'

'Much simpler. A helicopter very early in the morning at the Conference

Centre. Sharon and I will go there for lunch and as we talk rubbish and eat I will disable them all remotely. And then a flight home.'

'As you say, much simpler. Ok, I accept your offer. I don't want them finding even a tiny wire on Dee.'

'Dee? You can't put her into such a dangerous position, André. The risks are considerable. Has this been authorised?'

'By the Director and Deputy Director.'

'Ok, André. You said there were two things.'

'Yes, have you got the red keyboard from Dee's machine?'

'Yes.'

'And can you operate it?'

'I don't think I heard what sounded like an insult, André!'

'I didn't think you would. Please will you forward to Dee a message to go to Mr Ali and onwards which will show it originates in Dee's machine and not yours, in Arabic of course?

'I may make an official complaint about you for insulting me.'

'You are surely aware that complaints come to me in the first place?'

'Actually I do, but it would be fun all the same. Ok what's the message?'

'You know the format used and I suggest the wording is something like "Guest from 5 excited about op on Thursday." That should do it. I'll text your flight time.'

'That sounded important, my love.'

'It was just my personal travel agent arranging our transport for lunch out tomorrow.'

Chapter Seventeen

'Do tell me, my love, is this likely to happen on a regular basis? It isn't six o'clock in the morning yet.

'But at least the traffic's light and parking won't be a problem and the flight won't leave without us.'

'I remember feeling slightly envious of Dee when she had her helicopter ride, so I mustn't complain. Have you done it a lot?'

'Hardly at all apart from when I did a couple of weeks with the SAS in Hereford.'

'Jesus! Did you really? I imagine that was tough.'

'I was there to learn how to use firearms and they were great.'

Sharon loved every moment of the flight even if she was slightly taken aback by the fact that it was to be flown by two 10 year old boys (as they appeared to her but mercifully were not) who flew them to a private airfield where there were met by a car containing André.

'I am delighted to meet you, Sharon,' said André. 'You must be desperate for a period of the most boring normality.'

'You're not kidding, but I'm pleased to meet you, André. Kim says you're on the side of the angels but someone who makes me get up at four o'clock in the morning, is to my mind more of a fallen angel.'

André laughed.

'I rather think you and I will get on. Anyway it's literally a flying visit. We'll go to Skipton for a coffee and then on to lunch in Bingley before coming back here for the return flight. You'll be back in London by mid-afternoon.'

Just outside the mosque, two men were talking when one received a text.

He looked at it and said to the other that they had someone to visit and he handed him his phone.

'Yes and we had better go now.'

It was the first man who did the driving and the other somehow or other felt compelled to talk.'

'Tomorrow morning in Hull we begin preparations for the next big shock to the British establishment. Two suicide bombers in huge shopping areas where the infidel pigs gather to feast themselves. They will be more or less simultaneous and serve to remind the people of Manchester and Newcastle that they too are making war on Islam.'

'Have you got the bombers sorted?'

'Yes, Deeba in Ilkley who has totally outlived her usefulness and I thought the woman we are on our way to see now in Manningham, who's neither use nor ornament. For both the supreme sacrifice will be the most wonderful thing they can do for Allah and en route rid us of two women who are likely to be a nuisance.'

'Something has been afoot for a few days now,' he continued, and it may be we are near the climax.

Faridah's information is usually correct but I just want to check it out with her. Information has to be backed up with accounts of movement and behaviour. Fortunately she understands that so we will probably not need to be here long.'

She had seen them coming from her window and opened the front door before they got there. They greeted one another in Arabic but continued in English. She let them in and, having expected them, served them fruit drink.

'You are completely clear about this?'

'Yes, but I also know that they have in place a plan to take her from her flat in Ilkley early tomorrow morning. On this occasion she will not be passed on to MI5 but held locally.'

'I imagine that's because MI5 can't decide what to do with her which is why they keep letting her go, though I also have a feeling it may be to do with the fact of what we knew long before them, that she is much cleverer than she appears working in a café. And what about the armoury?'

'The J12 order has gone out. I typed it and sent it and received the coded acknowledgement but only for Thursday. I think they are expecting no resistance tonight in Ilkley.'

'I hope you are not putting yourself at risk of discovery.'

'We would like you, Faridah, to join us for a curry in Bingley this evening?.It would be better to have another woman with us and that would have the added advantage of your being able to recognise any of the counterterrorism squad if by chance they were attempting an ambush.'

'I would be honoured to do so.'

'Can you collect Faridah on your way to the restaurant, Mr Khan?'

'Of course. Shall we say just after half past seven?'

'I'll be ready.'

'According to Paddy, the MI5 old man is still with Deeba,' said Mr Khan.

'I'm perfectly happy for him to be killed. Would Paddy do it?'

'Paddy will always do as he's told.'

The men took their leave. In the car Mr Khan asked what should happen to

Deeba after this evening.

'It depends on what she has to say and whether we believe her. My only fear about her is that she might have been turned by MI5. But as I said earlier I have a rendezvous in Newcastle in mind for her.'

'Do you want me to take you home?'

'No. There's a reception at the National Science and Media Museum which I should attend and I'll call David to come and collect me in time to get to you by, say, 8.30. I'll get him to wait and he can deliver me home afterwards. I must be the only Moslem with a Jewish driver!'

Arriving at the museum, they shook hands.

The curry was good but the sparkling fruit juice with it almost exceeded the ability of either woman to describe it. Why would anyone want beer or lager when they could drink this? As they ate, Kim was operating a piece of equipment on her knee leaving Sharon to do all the talking which she was more than able to do, mostly about her future book on George Herbert. At one point, looking up at Sharon Kim said, 'No, you need to make what you're saying more boring. I'm becoming interested in George Herbert and keep losing my concentration.'

Sharon laughed.

'Do you think I can pass that on to a literary agent as a recommendation?'

After the meal they engaged the head waiter in conversation, congratulating him on the food and the restaurant. He seemed genuinely pleased and accepted a generous tip. By now the place was pretty full.

They arrived at the car and walked past it for at least 150 metres.

'I assume this is what they call subterfuge,' laughed Sharon.

'You're a quick learner, Dr Mason.'

'I've heard you say that somewhere else before now.'

'Shush. You mustn't make be blush when I'm on duty!' and they stole a quick kiss.

Once back at the car, Sharon was asked to sit in the front, whilst Kim gave André some lessons on how to work her machine.

'Is it one of yours, Kim?'

'Yes. I admit it's pretty basic but it's still remarkably effective against what they're using. Here you plug in your recording device and each of the 12 switches corresponds to one of the tables. Someone inside, and I'm assuming you won't leave Dee alone in there just needs to text you the number of the table you're interested in. Turn the others off and you will hear loud and clear. I can't see them using any other than Table 6. Above all, André, protect Dee, whatever happens.'

'I intend doing so, Kim. I promise you that. There's more to her story than you and Sharon know and when this is over I want her to be able to tell you it all herself.'

'Now, our fee. Two of us having to endure that curry, special clothing for the bitterly cold North, the machine and the ingenuity that went into it. I reckon it will come to the same as your fee for the helicopter ride, so shall we call it quits?'

They all, including the driver who was not supposed to be listening, laughed.

'Ok,' said André, 'let's get you two back to London, and there's a message for you. Martha would like to see you in her office at four o'clock.

'Are you wanting to give me your resignation?' – Martha's first words.

Kim was shocked by her words.

'I . . . Er . . . don't know quite what to say. Have you been listening to us in some way?'

'There's no way I could manage that without your help, Kim. No, I had a feeling that this was a possibility given that you are in love, a time when people perhaps over hastily make decisions. You and Sharon are greatly in love and I rejoice in that for you. After all these years I still love my husband very much, even though he complains that he never sees enough of me, even though at the end of a holiday he always seems glad to get me back to work and, I am pleased to report our Director is besotted with Caro and their baby, even though he complains about her being able to hear every word he utters now!

'I'm not at all sure however that Sharon will really want to return to being a head teacher, and so my guess would be that you would like a house in the country where you can snuggle up together and be happy. Is that any sort of reflection of your thinking?'

'It has crossed our minds.'

'Kim, if you choose to go, I would not even try to stop you, but I would first of all like to meet Sharon here, with you there of course, and see what alternatives there might be for you. Oh, and that reminds me, I'm meeting Helen Boardman in the coffee shop on Thursday morning, someone talent spotted by you.'

'I think she's good, Martha.'

'Yes, and so does André. So, do you think that Sharon might come in with you tomorrow and listen to what I have to say even if, afterwards you think I may be talking drivel?'

'I don't think there is anyone who would accuse you of that, Martha. But before I go, can I ask you an extremely personal question?'

'If the question is what I think it is, the answer is yes, for a short while, when I was at Sandhurst and feeling pretty lonely, especially being a black woman, but in those days if you were to remain, let alone get on, in the army, a short while in a relationship with another woman was all that was possible.'

'Thank you, boss. I hope you know how much I admire and respect you.'

'We shall see how much when I've finished with you and Sharon in the morning!'

The Director and Deputy Director had a glass of wine together in the late afternoon, to catch up with one another. On assuming office Rob had been knighted but was someone who wore such things very lightly, for her part, Caro thought being called "Lady Browning" was a real hoot and found it opened all sorts of previously tightly-closed doors, which with her long-standing gift for lip-reading gave her great power wherever she went, and friends and acquaintances alike took great care with their speech even on the other side of the room.

'Rob, there's something brewing this evening in Bradford being jointly run by André and counterterrorism. They are hoping to pick up the elusive controller linked to ISIS using Dee, of whom I have spoken to you, as the tethered kid goat. I have instructed that in every circumstance she must emerge safe and sound.'

'Won't they think we have turned her, which of course we have?'

'That is what she is going to tell them.'

'Ok, keep me informed, Martha. However the idea of André sharing control with anyone strikes me as completely hilarious but I know he will have thought it through and he did mention it to me. And what are you plans for Mr Big?'

'If we pick him up, he'll be taken to RAF Leeming, and brought to the Conference Centre overnight.'

'Well, good luck to them tonight. It would nice to have something positive to report to the PM in the morning.'

Most of them had done this sort of thing a number of times, but there was not a member of André's team not on edge as the time drew near to making their way to Bingley. They each knew the batting order of their entry into the restaurant and who their partner was. Dee had had little chance to think about the evening ahead as her day, like most of them, was just too busy to focus on anything other than immediate tasks.

She locked up and then made her way via the stairs to her flat which was empty, a source of disappointment to her as she had become fond of André and had enjoyed his presence enormously. He had reassured her that they would see one another later. It was only as she shed her uniform, showered and then dressed for the evening, that she began to go over in her mind her script.

André had wandered down to the river for a stroll and was observed doing so by Paddy, who let Mr Khan know that there seemed no chance whatsoever that anything involving André this evening, and that he and off-duty female police officer had gone in to the Flying Duck for a drink.

Paddy collected Dee shortly after 7.30 and they chatted all the way to Bingley, mostly gossip about the life and times of Ilkley. Paddy knew much more than Dee which he enjoyed recounting. Just before they arrived, Dee asked Paddy if he worked for Mr Khan.

'Now and again he sends me work, such as bringing you here tonight. He pays well but to be honest there's nowhere near enough work from him to live on. I do it because I want to support my brother Moslems.'

Paddy stopped some yards short of the restaurant. By the time Dee was standing on the pavement and waving to Paddy as he set off back to Ilkley, Mr Khan was already walking towards her and had in tow a young woman wearing a sky blue hijab.

'Deeba, how good to see you. Please meet my friend Faridah. Before we go in, and I'm sure you will understand, it will be necessary for you to go the toilet with Faridah, and she will give you a quick radio scan. I don't doubt you but we have to be doubly certain.'

'I don't mind that at all,' she replied with a smile.

They went into the restaurant and were shown to the table between the front door and one into the kitchen which two other customers eating their onion pakoras had already noted as number 6. Dee and Faridah returned from the toilet chatting amicably to one another and sat down.

'The only thing it registered was my smartwatch,' said Faridah, handing over the scanner.'

Once they had ordered, and Dee noticed that there were still four place settings, Mr Khan said to Dee, "If we had not got to you this evening, Deeba, we have it on good authority that counterterrorist police would have been disturbing your sleep and taking you away for a third time.'

'Oh no. Why would they do that that? They've had me twice already.'

'Well, you can perhaps help us understand that by giving us an account of what happened during your most recent stay at RAF Northam.'

'Northolt,' corrected Dee. 'It's the same airbase where Diana, Princess of Wales was brought after her death.'

'They don't seem to have minded letting you know where you were and what the place was used for – what I believe they call the Conference Centre.'

'I was the only occupant and everything seemed to be in the control of a black woman who moaned constantly about having to work on a Saturday. My main questioner, if that's the right word, was an older man who called himself André and who has accompanied me back to Ilkley, though there was no sign of him this evening when I got in from work and I know this sounds highly unlikely but I think he's developed something of a "thing" for our local woman PC, Helen. It's quite sweet really. But it was he who set about the task of recruiting me, "turning me" they called it, getting me to arrange a meeting with you to feed you exactly what they want you to know. "Fake news" he called it.'

Two rather boisterous young men came into the restaurant and were ushered by the waiter as far away as possible from Mr Khan's table. Moments later another man came in and was warmly welcomed by the staff and taken to be the fourth customer at Mr Khan's table. They all stood and shook hands.'

'I am pleased to meet you Deeba and you have already done much for us but before we decide what you might still be able to do for us, please tell me about your time as a guest of MI5.'

'No, it was the Security Service, not MI5.'

'Oh, sorry, my mistake.'

He gave a quick glance at Mr Khan.

In the far corner, the two most recent arrivals were having an argument about something that seemed to be getting a little out of hand. One of the waiters was about to go to them, but a raised hand from Mr Khan stayed him, and he himself went to the table.

'Gentlemen, please, no doubt each of you feels strongly about whatever sports team you were discussing, but please bear in mind that others have come for a quiet evening, and I should not wish to see you asked to leave.'

They nodded meekly. Another couple, a man and a woman now came in through the door, just as the couple that had been in earlier asked for their bill and prepared to leave.

'Thank you, Mr Khan,' said the man. 'Now Deeba, please tell me what you think they know about whatever might be happening here in Allah's own county.' Dee laughed.

'I think there is a lot of guesswork. They have a technology expert and I mean expert, who got into my system easily, who lives in London, I imagine, and is now living with Dr Sharon Mason, who was the target of Shafiq Zaman, in a lesbian relationship. The tech expert uses the codename Kim but I have not yet found out her real name or her address, but I am hoping to go and stay with them soon.'

'That is important. If she is as good as you say, then it might be better for us if she has a change of circumstance, sad though that might be for her lesbian partner.'

'They told me that the government is setting up a form of Jihadist reform programmes in prisons to replace the present scheme which has failed but that I was to tell you that an announcement about this will be followed by a long period in which the only thing that will happen is that imans presently licensed as chaplains will be completely withdrawn together with all arrangements for Moslems to pray and associate.'

'On their heads be it.'

'Oh and they have offered me a job.'

'Really? What sort of job?'

'Catering manager and housekeeper of the new Jihadist Control Centre in Tottenham. They will be moving out of Milbank in two week's time.'

'Are you interested in the job.'

'I would miss the Dales of course, but it could be enormously useful to have someone innocently walking around when things are being considered and plans drawn up.'

'Yes, especially as your computer work here is now what the English call "a busted flush". When they pick you up in the night, what will you tell them?'

'That I met with Mr Khan and passed on everything they asked me to in our favourite Asian restaurant in Bingley where I have eaten with him a number of times before.'

'What are your feelings about the Mason woman? Our brother Shafiq

Zaman lost his life simply seeking to impose Sharia law. Do you think we should seek to complete that fatwa?'

'You know the answer to that question because you know that I sent a message calling off any further attempts to kill her. Please do not lie or pretend to me. Sharon was appallingly treated by Shafiq Zaman who decided he could be married and at the same time screw any young student he wished. It was he who deserved to die not her. That is my personal opinion but it should, I think, go back to the iman who issued the fatwa and ask him. Remember I am nothing other than the manager of a posh tea rooms.'

They all gently laughed.

'And I,' said the man, 'am nothing other than a servant of the crown and the useful idiots who voted for me and my party, though tomorrow I turn importer and receive an important shipment of things we need. But Deeba, you have been a great help to our cause of seeking to establish Sharia law in this land. I think that as with Faridah here who also works under cover, your use in this new MI5 Jihadist Control Centre could be considerable. Once it is established you will be contacted as to the best ways of maintaining contact, and you and I might also be able to meet when I am in London.'

Dee thought she could sense from the way he looked at her body what those meetings might be for.

'I would like that very much indeed,' she said coyly.

At that precise moment the door into the kitchen and the front door to the restaurant opened simultaneously and two men stood in the doorways, now joined by the two formerly "noisy" men, and the couple who had just come in. They gathered close to the four persons at the table.

'All of you,' said the man in the main doorway, 'please put your hands up in the air where I can see them. You need to know that this building is surrounded by armed counterterrorism police officers. You will all now be taken in handcuffs to four separate locations so we can have a chat with you before you can be released.'

'I don't think you quite realise who I am,' said the man, now with his hands up.

'Identity will be established when you arrive at your destinations.'

The man looked across the table, spat at her and and said with real menace, 'Deeba, enjoy the little that is left of your life.'

Police officers entered and secured the four with handcuffs, and then one by one they were led outside and each put inside a different vehicle.

Dee found André and Helen inside her vehicle and her handcuffs were immediately removed.

'Who is he, André?'

'His name is Imad Hafeez, and he is the Member of Parliament for Bradford Central, member of his party's executive council and newly elected as Chairman of the Commons Home Affairs Select Committee.'

'You will have to rely on me to tell you what he said.'

'No we don't, thanks to the woman with the codename Kim, as you cleverly described her. And so we listened in, and may I congratulate you on how well you played your part, though I was surprised you knew about the Jihadist control centre in Tottenham given that it doesn't and as far as I know won't exist.'

'I'm quite good at ad libbing,'

'I take it he was surprised.'

'His face was a picture.'

'I was very impressed,' said Helen from the front seat.

'And to which location are you taking this prisoner?'

"Home, any good?'

'It'll have to do but I think I can be of much more use at the Conference Centre. Oh, and I think you may need to pay a call on my friend Paddy.'

'It's already in hand,' said Helen.

'I know you prefer to enter unwillingly in the middle of the night,' said André with his hand resting on Dee's arm, 'but this time, all three of us will go tomorrow by virtue of the RAF. Helen is about to meet Martha: Alpha 2.

Chapter Eighteen

'What is she like?' asked Sharon as they snuggled up to one another in bed.

'Everything you wouldn't expect to find in an army colonel. Yes, she's quite tall and doesn't suffer fools gladly, but she's unbelievably gentle and generous towards those who work for her. As a soldier she is more than handy with weapons of all kinds but I think she has this job because of the sharpness of her brain. It is assumed that she will become the next Director, not the first woman of course as there was Dame Stella Rimmington, but I'm told she's popular in Downing Street, and the boss has a wonderful habit of sending her if there's bad news to impart.

'Typical bloke!' said Sharon.

'Oh I can assure you that's not the case. Quite the opposite. He's extremely dishy, also military, but married to Caro who is stunning, who has been deaf from childhood until very recently. They married last year and have a beautiful baby boy, Benjie. Caro's sister is a well-known composer who teaches at the Royal College of Music near the Albert Hall.'

'And what is the colonel going to say to me?'

'Well, I have a well-earned reputation for wizardry with new technology, but as for prediction I'm just a beginner. When I took my first look at you, I had longings, but I couldn't have predicted this.'

'H'm.'

Intelligence Briefings in Downing St usually take place at 8-00am for 5, and 8-30am for 6, This morning Rob had already spoken to the Cabinet Secretary and said that we would not be able to brief the Prime Minister if anyone other than the Home Secretary and the Cabinet Secretary were present. There was no argument.

As was customary, Rob's car brought him round the back of No.10 where he was met by the Cabinet Secretary himself.

'Good Morning, Sir Robert, and how is the most important member of your household?'

'I was up changing his nappy at 2-30 and then his mother fed him. He went straight back to sleep and I did not.'
'As you requested, in addition to us there will only be the Home Secretary and Prime Minister, so I have arranged for us to meet in his private study.'
'Microphones?'
'No.'
Sir Edward knocked on the door and at once entered.
'The Director of MI5, Prime Minister.'
'Good morning, Rob,'
'Good morning, sir, and good morning, Home Secretary.
Rob sat down opposite the PM who was also in a comfy chair. The other two had to make do with chairs less so.
'I regret to say that I bring tidings of woe.'
'That's most odd because usually in such a situation you send Martha.'
'Indeed I do. She'e much prettier than me and I always hope it will be a sugarcoating to whatever she has to say. As the result of an operation run by ourselves with the help and co-operation of counterterrorism last night near Bradford, we have been able to take into custody the person who has been running a Jihadist cell responsible for a number of Islamic attacks in the country. He has links with Isis in the sense that he takes orders from them. Even as we speak his house is being dismantled. This morning he was due to receive a crate from a boat in Hull. Counterterrorism and bomb squad officers will endeavour to intercept and find out what it contains.'
'So far you have only provided good news. Where is the woe?'
'That lies in his name.'
'Ah. I feared it might.'
'He is Imad Hafeez, Member of Parliament for Bradford Central and newly-elected Chair of the Home Affairs Select Committee, so no doubt meeting with you regularly, Home Secretary.'
'Oh fuck!' said the PM. 'This could hardly be worse. Where is he now?'
'Locked up securely and guarded in Wakefield prison.'
'Has the new leader of the opposition been sworn in as a member of the Privy Council yet?' asked the PM.
'Yes,' replied Sir Edward.'
'Arrange a meeting behind the Speaker's Chair at 11.00. Privy Council terms and just the two us.'
'Of course.'
'Well, Home Secretary, it's for mornings like this that you earn your corn. You and Rob had better decide what happens next. Has he been interrogated yet?'
'No sir. He will be transported to RAF Northolt and I daresay we shall be able to catch a word with him there.'
'"To catch a word" – what a splendid euphemism. Now, where will you two go to do your thinking?'
'I think it would be best for the Home Secretary to come to Milbank. It

would not be out of the ordinary.'
'Ok. Keep me in touch regularly.'
The three of them rose and departed, leaving the Prime Minister to ponder events.

'Helen's phone rang at about 5-00am.
'Helen, it's André. You're got 20 minutes to pack and get over to Sharon's flat.'
That was all. No explanation of any kind. Oh well, she thought, that was almost certainly how it was going to be.
Dee drove. They were going to RAF Leeming and onto a flight to RAF Northolt. As they approached the guards on duty by the barrier, André leapt out and spoke to them, showing them something or other which had a magical effect, and the barriers were lifted. One of the guards told Dee where she should leave her car and then all three headed for the main building and in a matter of a very short while were in the air.
'I thought we were going by train,' said Dee.
'So did I, but it's quite likely that the package we picked up last night will cause us to be running around like headless chickens, and I had a call from on high telling us to get a move on.'
'I was a bit shocked last night,' said Helen. 'Being a woman officer in Ilkley mostly means road crossings and body searches of ladies suspected of shop-lifting.'
'Do you find anything?'
'Yes, I do. Shopkeepers have eyes in the back of their heads and know straight away if something has been moved or taken.'
'And what do these terrible villains say in their defence?' asked André.
'Mostly something like "I can't think how that got there", when I unearth something from inside their underwear.'
'And men?'
'I'm sure they shoplift too, but I'm not allowed near them, presumably because I might give them a thrill, or, of course, get one myself. I should be so lucky!'
They laughed.
It was daylight and sunny as the plane began its descent.

It was daylight and sunny in Wakefield too, though you wouldn't know that if you were in a secure cell within a High Security prison with an armed guard outside the door. The man inside the cell was far from happy, but would be even less happy were he to know that his house in Pudsey had been turned upside down in his absence, and that his wife was answering questions in Bradford. He had been a solicitor and knew that asking for a solicitor was pointless under the terms of the terrorism act. The only way he was going to come through this was to be as meek as a lamb and co-operative throughout.
His flight landed at Northolt at about 10.00 and he was taken straight to a

room in the Conference Centre. Less than 50 metres away Helen was ushered into the canteen and introduced to Martha.

'Good morning, ma'am,' said Helen.

'Martha will do. Events you have been part of have necessitated a change of location for your interview and we've brought it forward a day as you and I are both here. So tell me the truth about last night and what you made of it.'

'I was tense but I should think in that context that is de rigeur. I've not been in the presence of such firepower before which took some getting used to, but I was impressed that it was not used and for the most part well-concealed. The planning was good and it went like clockwork.'

'And could you see yourself as part of a team of men and women doing something similar, or might you prefer to remain in Ilkley with all its attendant excitements, not that the idiot in charge there let you in on them.'

'That's true. Inspector Markham was sexist and racist, but more worryingly he is one of the laziest people I have ever come across.'

'You're not firearm trained or licensed so if you want to come and see if being part of our setup is what you think you might be good at, and André's recommendation is not lightly earned, I would want you to start the course next Monday. It is intensive and demanding, but necessary.'

'My answer is Yes, Martha.'

'We have some accommodations available on a short-term basis, but the course takes place in Hereford with the boys and girls of Special Forces. All the paperwork will be ready in time. So, Helen, welcome to the Security Service. Tomorrow you'll receive a full security briefing. Now I have to attend to the gentleman whose aeroplane has not long since landed.'

Two cups of fresh coffee were brought in. The Home Secretary received hers sitting behind her desk and Rob sat immediately opposite.

'Who will be seeing him?'

'My two best inquisitors'

'And what happens if he doesn't speak?'

'With all due respect, Home Secretary, I've yet to meet a politician who could resist the chance to speak.'

'The good news from our point of view is that he belongs on the opposition benches.'

'That is of no concern to us, though members of your own party proposed him for the Home Affairs Select Committee and you therefore liaise with him regularly. I think we should keep party politics out of this. What he has been doing is tantamount to treason and I should think there is going to be a lot of fallout, wouldn't you?'

'How long will you be keeping him?'

'Until the inquisitors are satisfied we have enough to hand him over to the CPS and the Courts.'

'You think it will go that far?'

'Home Secretary, this man is the principal organiser of Jihadist terrorism in this country and he was due to be collecting from the docks in Hull this morning, which has now been intercepted, two suicide vests and the explosive device they require. On tape he admits to wanting to make Sharia Law the established law of the land and it is abundantly clear that becoming a Member of Parliament has been part of a well thought out plan, and because he's a Moslem, to whom everyone has to be nice, he has managed to get the most important job members of the House can elect him to. This is, I'm afraid to say, going to be difficult for the PM and you, though for all members of the House.'

She sat there thinking.

'Ok, I accept that this has to be faced full on, but perhaps we can drip feed the press with it, at first at least. I shall inform the PM of our conversation. In the meantime it's for you, Rob, to do your work to see whether we hang him out to dry or muzzle him.'

He stood.

'Thank you Home Secretary, I shall keep you informed.'

He turned and left the office, his car waiting for him.

'Christine,' he said to his driver once he had done up his seat belt, 'if ever you hear me say that I'm thinking of going into politics, you have my permission to shoot me.'

'It could never happen, sir. You're such a rotten liar.'

Kim put her phone down.

'There's no rush Sharon. We've been moved to the afternoon. Something big has arisen and we're not invited.'

'Have you seen this in the paper, Kim?'

'What is it?'

'It's a short piece reporting that the family of Henry Ward, my former bursar, have met with members of an organisation called Life, to see whether they could bring a private prosecution against me as, apparently, I assisted a suicide.'

'All you did was an extremely good turn to someone in need who trusted you, but I've had a thought as to how we can stop this completely.'

'Really?'

'Kate Howard is the Features Editor of *The Times* and lives a short distance away. I know she will be interested in this and will want to come and do a feature on you and the Samaritans. I'll give her a ring at work and see if she wants to call in this evening. You'll like her though we'll have to hope she doesn't bring her three small children with her – triplets. They were wonderful when born, but at four years old she can't wait to get them off to school next year.'

'I'll be guided by you. By the way, when I was in the bathroom I was listening to the radio news and there were reports of trouble of some kind at a mosque in Bradford with lots of police in attendance.'

'Thank goodness we are many miles away then.'

'I so admire you, my love, and all those with whom you work. It must be so complex trying to remain one step ahead all the time.'
'I think that most of our work is taken up with the struggle of not being one step behind.'
'Why don't you pour us both some cereal and come back to bed.'
'But you've just had a shower.'
'I can always have another, and this time with you!'
'Two bowls of cereal coming up!'

When André entered the interview room, Imad Hafeez was already hoping for release of the handcuff that was connected to the table. Seeing this, André asked the man on duty to release him and then indicated that he should wait outside the door.
'Good morning Mr Hafeez, my name is André and I am happy for you to use that name, as I know you are familiar with it. First and foremost, I hope you have had enough to eat.'
Hafeez nodded.
'If you need refreshment, please just ask and someone will bring it. Everything we say is being recorded, audio and video. Whoever might take my place will have heard and seen everything. I am here so that we can have a chat about what you have become mixed up in the hope that it might be possible to keep this out of the public eye. The government wants that, your party leader wants that and I imagine your constituents want that too. Incidentally, there has been a riot in Bradford this morning following the taking into custody of an iman. I have it on good authority that he will be released without charge shortly.'
'That will be a handy distraction from the disappearance of an MP.'
André replied in Arabic.
'Erm, I regret to say my Arabic is very limited.'
'Shame on you. But how on earth do you communicate with so many of your fellow Moslems here and in the Middle-East?'
'Many of them speak English. It comes from watching western television.'
'I want you to know Mr Hafeez that I wish to say nothing disrespectful about Islam. I studied Arabic at university and in the days before it became less safe to do so, I travelled widely in Pakistan and Egypt. Islam has so much that is good about it. What is perhaps less good are those radically misinterpret the Koran and in its name cause mayhem and kill those whom we regard as innocent.'
'I understand what you are saying André, of course I do. It's just that so many of those I represent and live among feel that this a society which hates them and hates their faith There are 26 bishops in the House of Lord without having been elected, simply as a matter of right. One or two of us who wouldn't say an Islamic boo to a goose, can be appointed, but only the Christian religion is given things by right.'
'I agree with you wholeheartedly not least because the House of Lords is a

joke. You however are an elected member of the Commons and sufficiently well respected to have been appointed Chair of a Select Committee.'

'I want to see the establishment of Sharia Law, not replacing but parallel to the laws of parliament. That is why I am in Parliament and I have worked very hard to get to the position I'm in.'

'You are here now however,' said André, 'because you sanctioned the execution of Dr Sharon Mason at the hands of Shafiq Zaman who managed to escape from Rampton High Security Hospital with money provided by you.'

'Zaman was a madman, an obsessive convert, more Moslem than the Moslems and to be perfectly honest I was just as glad that he was dead as the counterterrorist officers would also have been. The money he used dates back to his Portsmouth bombing and I was asked by Isis if I could put money in his bank account so he could get away, but of course he was caught. I did not know he was going to use it in the way he did. But, and here is the point, I authorised only the fulfilment of the instructions of the fatwa and nothing else. It said nothing about killing anyone and I would not have sanctioned that under any circumstances. I want Sharia Law but it won't be possible if I act against it.'

'When Dr Mason was in Leeds there was intel that her murder had been sanctioned once again, and this time from Bradford. I take it this was you.'

'There was something of a serious short-circuit of our system brought about by someone who knew what he was doing and destroyed our computer network, in Ilkley of all places! Messages got misunderstood, but I did not authorise any such killing and there was no fatwa issued for doing so.'

'If there had been, would you?'

'André, that is a totally hypothetical question.'

'I think we should take a break. You have a choice. Either you can return to your room and drink alone, or you agree to my staying with you, and we can talk about something completely different.'

'Please stay. I have heard your name many times and the odd thing is that your reputation is not normal for an interrogator.'

'I don't interrogate. I believe always that the best way for myself and another is to be as civilised as we can and engage in conversation. In my experience most people like talking about themselves and that includes those the newspaper like to describe as terrorists, and I always welcome coming to a deeper understanding of how it is that people have arrived at where they are, and usually it is most illuminating.'

'Amazing, but I would welcome hearing about your time in Pakistan and Egypt, and I would like tea with milk but no sugar. And you?'

'Oh they know.'

Someone came in with their drinks and they compared notes on visits they had made to various locations. Once they had drunk their tea André stood up, smiled at Hazeez and wished him well before leaving the room. Moments later his place was taken by a tall black woman whom Hafeez assumed to be military. She sat down.

'Good morning Mr Haffeez.'
'Good morning . . . Er what do I call you?'
'My husband calls me many things but most often it is Martha.'
Hafeez smiled.
'You seem to have landed yourself in something of a pickle, from which both you and I want to get you out of for a lot of reasons, but mostly because you are a Member of Parliament. At the very least you will lose your position on the Select Committee you have obviously striven for and possibly lose the whip, though that has not yet been decided on.'
'That is the least; what can I expect as the worst?'
'The Crown Prosecution Service will liaise with Scotland Yard and together they will decide what to do. We have done our job and now they will do theirs. However, I imagine they will wish to speak about the large container arriving in Hull this morning which you were due to collect and why it contains suicide bomber jackets together with the appropriate explosives included. In fact they will have many questions for you, some of which will require a lot of answering.'
'What is happening to the other three arrested with me last night?'
'The two women are not even remotely important, and having had the fright of their lives, or at least I hope so for their sake, will go back to their boring lives and leave the excitement to others though both have lost their jobs. Tafiq Khan is another matter altogether. He is, as it is said, "helping the police with their enquiries" and perhaps you should be hoping that in order to save time in prison he is not making it more difficult for you.'
'As far as I am concerned I am simply a casualty of war.'
'If I may say so, and I say it on the basis of front-line service in Afghanistan and Iraq, please don't fool yourself about that. I have seen and caused casualties of war and trust me, they don't look like you.'
Martha stood.
'You will now be taken back to your room and remain there until the politicians decide what is to be done with you.'
The guard came back in, attached a handcuff to the wrist of Hafeez and led him out and back to his room. Martha went into the Relay Room where André was closing down the recording system.
'Coffee? she asked.
He smiled his thanks, put down what he was doing and followed her through to the canteen, where their first sight was of Dee talking to those who would soon be some of her staff. André knew that she ran a tight ship in Ilkley and it was clear from what she was saying that her intent was to do so here too. She asked one of the men to go and attend to Martha, and carried on talking to the others. She was clearly intent on making a difference.
Martha brought her coffees over to André and sat down.
'Someone sounds as if she knows what she's doing.'
'About time too. What about the new police officer from Ilkley, Helen Boardman?'

'She's good. I've sent her back home to gather her things and return by Friday. She'll go to Hereford on Monday and for the time being can stay in a safe house. Much more worrying is Kim. I fear she may be coming to resign now she's found love, but we can't possibly let her go not least because in addition to her technological skills she is a singularly able talent spotter. She has to stay. I've invited her partner Dr Mason along to give her a feel of what we do and hope I can convince her to stay. In the meantime she is still caught up in an unpleasant accusation that she assisted a suicide which would have been quite an achievement at the distance of thirteen miles. I'll see what our lawyers can do. Now, let us turn our minds to our Member of Parliament.'

'You were much more direct than me and almost menacing, Martha.'

'Thats why you're so good, André. Getting them to speak is an art form you have in abundance and without which we can get nowhere at all. But what do you make of him?'

'There is enough there to get him to court and put away for a long time. It was clear to me in his arrogance that he is very much the national overseer. I didn't refer to the Portsmouth bombing but it wouldn't surprise me if he was the originator and instructed Shafiq Zaman to plant the bomb and rewarded him by letting him attempt to murder the apostate wife. Those going through his financial records should be looking for that. When Zaman was killed he was probably relieved.'

'I agree in every respect and feel we should throw him to the wolves and have him taken to Belmarsh. I'll let Rob know and he can pass it on to the PM. What happens after that is up to others though I suspect the Home Secretary will want his balls mounted on a plaque on her wall, and take all the credit! God, this coffee's awful.'

'I'll have a word. Go and make your phone call.'

When Martha left, André remained watching Dee at work and concluding her chat with them so positively and with great encouragement that they returned to work with smiles rather than frowns.

Dee came over to André.

'The coffee was awful.'

'I know, I tried to drink it earlier and nearly died. It will improve and I've already ordered some new equipment, but I have got one problem, André, I have nowhere to live as the house next door needs work done on it.'

'Cardboard boxes are what you need as they provide good insulation but take good care which shop doorway you choose to sleep in, as regulars can get easily cross. Or, there's the other option and that is that you move in with me and that we should set off for there now.'

Chapter Nineteen

'I shall be in soon but in case you wanted to make contact and report to our betters, André and I are convinced he's the UK overseer for ISIS recruitment and acts of terrorism, including the Portsmouth bombing. In addition, counterterrorism picked up at Hull docks a consignment due to be collected by him this morning. When opened it was found to contain two suicide vests with explosives ready to be primed. Bomb disposal dealt with them.'

'What's he like?' asked Rob.

'He's an MP so he's a slimy git even before we recognise the dreadful things he was doing.'

'Where is he now?'

'Still here but I want him moved to Belmarsh. The tapes and our reports will be ready to go with him.'

'It's a good job well done, Martha.'

'Thank you.'

'Ok. Make the arrangements to move him and I'll speak to the PM.'

'Good luck.'

'He won't like it but they will have to deal with it now.'

A call to Downing St revealed that the PM was not yet back from PMQs.

'Well get him back and at once. This is Code One and the Home Secretary will need to be there too. Act on this now and I shall expect the two of them to be present when I arrive in 15 minutes time.'

'Yes, Sir Robert.

André and Dee were making their way in from the Conference Centre.

'Is your work very demanding, André?'

'Getting people to chat by being everything they don't expect me to be is not, as in some ways it's just an extension of myself and I suspect they respond. The harder part is when I get them to talk about what they have done or are planning to do, usually involving the loss of innocent life and I have to restrain myself from wanting to attack them and do them a serious injury.'

'Have you ever done that?'
'No, but this morning I would have wished to do so. That is why I have made two decisions. I am going to retire. I have given it my best years and I want to make the most of what is yet to come.'
'And the second decision?'
'I'll tell you when we get back home.'
'I know what it is. You've repented of your earlier offer and you intend throwing me out on the street after all.'
'How did you guess, but the the good news is that I'll help you hunt for cardboard boxes!'
'Oh André, how will I ever be able to thank you for your generosity?'
They glanced at one another and grinned.

The Prime Minister and Home Secretary, together with the Cabinet Secretary were waiting for Rob to begin to speak in the PM's private office.
'This has to come to you, sir, before the Home Secretary. We have uncovered a Member of Parliament recently elected to a senior position on a select committee who is the overseer in the UK relating to and recruiting for ISIS. This morning two suicide vests were intercepted on their way to him, and we believe he financed the Portsmouth bombing and the escape of a Jihadist killer from Rampton High Security Prison so he could kill his former wife, whom he believed should die under Sharia Law. Intel enabled us to be prepared and less than two metres away from her with a large knife he was shot dead by a police officer in plain clothes. I think that there will be more to come and I have ordered him to be taken under armed escort to Belmarsh for further questioning by the counterterrorism inquisitors. Our part will then be over other than to recommend you meet very soon with the Attorney General.'
'The Leader of the Opposition went white when I told him and I suspect a great many members will do likewise. I know of course that you will give me no operational details but how did you get him?'
'A tethered kid goat to catch a tiger!'
'Was the kid goat at risk?'
'You don't want to know, sir. But there is one thing I would like you to do for us.'
'Please, go ahead.'
'This operation was led by a man who has served us, and therefore, the crown, for many years including in Northern Ireland and Afghanistan. He is the finest inquisitor I have known. I think the time has come for him to receive a K.'
'No question. Please give the details to the Cabinet Secretary.'
'Rob handed over a piece of paper.'
'As always, Rob, we owe you a great deal. Do you think we need a meeting of Cobra?'
'That has to be your decision, sir, but it is just possible that when news emerges there may be an Islamic backlash.'

Rob stood and departed. He was leaving them with one hell of a problem but that was why they entered parliament and sought high office. On the other hand he knew only too well that they would inevitably make some sort of balls-up as they dealt with it, especially when the Press Office got hold of it. He smiled at the thought and left the building by the back door. His car pulled out and turned left approaching Birdcage Walk. Rob asked his driver to stop at the junction.

'Are you alright, sir,' said his bodyguard turning round from the front seat.

Rob pointed.

'Over there, those two ladies. One of them works for me and is called Kim. I don't know the other, but please ask them to come here a moment.'

The bodyguard did as he was asked and brought Kim and Sharon to the car.

'Kim, hello.'

'Hello Director.'

'Introduce me, please.'

'Oh . . .yes, of course. This is Dr Sharon Mason, a head teacher from Cheshire, and the recent survivor of a terrorist attack in Leicestershire.'

'Sharon, I'm very pleased to meet you.'

'And me too, sir.'

'I hear you are on your way to Milbank, so get in and arrive in style.'

The driver turned left towards Parliament Square.

'Sharon, were you aware that Kim is the lynchpin of just about everything we do?'

'She's the lynchpin of everything I do too.'

'Have you any plans for Saturday?'

Sharon shrugged and looked at Kim.

'None, sir.'

'In which case I would like to invite you both to come and join my wife Caro and my son for lunch which if the weather is fine can stretch out all afternoon. Might that be possible?'

'It would be a pleasure, sir,' said Kim.

'Indeed it would, thank you,' echoed Sharon.

As they entered the house, they could hear the telephone ringing and André put his bags down in order to answer it.

'Yes, that's me.'

'To verify, we have had a visitor here at No 10. Can you tell me who that will have been?

'Sir Robert, I imagine.'

'Yes, thank you.'

'I am from the office dealing with honours, and the Prime Minister wishes you to receive a KBE for extraordinary service. Will you accept this?'

André looked towards Dee who was already on with making a cup of the tea for them both.

'I would be profoundly grateful to receive such an honour, but hasn't this happened very quickly?'

'That's because we are making arrangements for the forthcoming military investiture which, as I am sure you know is not, for obvious reasons, a public event. We think it would be desirable to include you in that given that you are quasi-military.'

'Yes, I can see that. I shall fit in with your arrangements.'

'Anything important?' asked Dee who had arrived with the tea. 'I'll make some lunch after we've had the tea and you still have to tell me your second decision which is probably that you've decided to move abroad and once again leave me to cardboard boxes.'

André chuckled.

'The phone call and the second decision are closely related, or at least I hope they might be. You see, Dee, a terrible thing has happened, utterly unexpected and wonderful. Perhaps the best way I can put is to ask if you would like to be known as Lady Beeson?'

'What are you saying, André?'

That phone call came from Downing St to say that the Prime Minister has seen fit to recommend me to the Crown for the receipt of a KBE, a knighthood, and that would mean that my wife would be entitled to be known as Lady Beeson, and so I am asking you, Dee, to become Lady Beeson, because I love you. I have never known anything like this, and it's true I'm quite a bit older than you but we could still have many happy years together. I made my mind up when you went into that Asian Restaurant alone the other night. I already had fallen for you but when I saw you behave so courageously, I knew I couldn't let you go and that I wanted to marry you.'

'If that is a proposal, then I accept with great joy in my heart. I am so lucky and I am now the happiest person in the world.'

For the first, but by no means the last, time they hugged and kissed.

'It's not what I expected,' said Sharon. 'There's less high tech here than in our IT room at school.'

'This is just the library. The real stuff, where I work, is upstairs but you don't have clearance to go there.'

'Is this where we are meeting Martha?'

'That's her decision.'

'And are you still intending to resign despite what the Director said?'

'I know only that I make no decisions without them being ours made together.'

Sharon took hold of Kim's hand and then kissed her.

'I gather you made a grand entrance,' said a voice behind them.

They turned to see Martha smiling at them.

'It's nice and quiet here so why don't we sit down? Dr Mason, I'm relieved you survived the attack made upon you.

'Yeah, I'm pretty chuffed myself,' she said with a broad smile, 'and there's a police officer called Sandra who saved my life I'd love to meet again.'

'That can be arranged, but I'm sorry about your singing course.'
'There'll be others.'
'Now Kim, have you thought further about your resignation which would of course be so lovely for you two in your house in the country, even if a total disaster for those seeking to defend the country and without that Kim person who was simply outstanding in every way as we have just seen in the arrest of the single most important organiser of Islamic terrorism in this land? No pressure you understand.'
Kim and Sharon were laughing.
'Even the Director considered the possibility of leaving when he met Caro.'
'Really?' said Kim.
'And although I don't know, because he doesn't tell me everything, as well as wanting you to meet the amazing Caro because that's a treat in itself, and of course his son and heir, I think he wants Dr Mason to see that being married to someone in the Service is by no means impossible. He, and all of us, want to keep Kim. I realise you have to return to Chester for a while in order to announce your departure.'
'Actually Martha, that may not happen and we are seeing someone later about that and the possibility of court,' said Kim.
'Good, well you have no charge to answer and if you need to, one of our lawyers will assist you and even come to be with you in the Coroner's Court. Now Kim, I regret to say that although you have not in fact actually resigned, I could not accept even it you did, and we are very much looking forward to seeing you back here on Monday. '
Martha did a military right wheel and was gone.
The women looked at one another and burst out laughing before falling into each other's arms.

Imad Hafeez had no idea what was going happen to him. Lunch was brought to him but the guard did not answer any of his questions. He would have liked to be in parliament for PMQs and hoped that when something was worked out which would bring next to no embarrassment to the government he might once again take his seat, though accepted that the Chair of the Home Affairs Select Committee would go. He imagined that even as he sat where he was some sort of deal was being worked out in Downing St. After all they knew that this all becoming public would shake the foundations of parliament, government and the opposition, all of whom he had duped, had out thought them all. It was all the fault of that woman from Ilkley.
Two men entered his room without warning, turned him and handcuffed him behind his back. They led him along a corridor and then outside to what was obviously an armoured van. He was taken inside and placed in a cage towards the front which was securely locked. Only then were his handcuffs removed. One of the men stayed with him in the back whilst the other closed and locked the door. Hafeez could see that the man within in the van was armed with an assault rifle of some sort, and noticed his finger on the trigger.

Outside he recognised the sound of outriders in front and behind. This was special status.

'Where are you taking me?' he said to the man.

'It's not my job to know,' he replied. 'It's best that way.'

Neither spoke again and the journey took well over an hour, but at last the vehicle stopped with its engine running, and then pulled forward.

The guard reattached the handcuffs and after receiving a security message then opened the cage as the van doors were opened revealing that they were in a prison yard. Hafeez was handed over to the prison authorities and disappeared in the main building to be the tedious process of reception which would have to be repeated each time he went out and came back in. Welcome to Belmarsh!

'Well?' said Sharon as they sat on the seat in the Tube at St James's Park station, 'Martha clearly has a will of iron and I suspect that on the whole what she wants is what she gets. And has she now?'

'I meant what I said earlier about this being a joint decision.'

Sharon answered the door and before her stood someone not much older in appearance than one of her sixth form girls, and with her a young man carrying a camera and some lighting equipment.

'Hello,' said the woman, 'I'm Kate Howard and this is Gerry Elven, and as you are not Kim, I take it you are Sharon Mason, whom we have come to see.'

'Hi there. You're quite right about who I am. Please come in.'

Once everyone was ready, which meant that each had a glass of wine, Kate (who now Sharon could see better and realised she was older than she had first thought) asked Sharon to tell her story. She began with her account of the phone call from the Bursar and the information that he had taken an overdose of tablets and wanted to talk to Sharon as he died, and how having once had a similar experience as a Samaritan, felt obliged to follow the same protocol, asking him repeatedly if she could get help for him or come herself, but felt she must allow him to do what he chose. She understood that he had stolen a massive amount from his Church and a local charity where he served as their Treasurer, but once they heard from the Police who had traced her number, that she had failed to intervene, the family diverted attention from the theft to her having assisted his suicide. The CPS said there was no case to answer and the coroner said he would accept a written statement from her at the inquest. The family were not satisfied and have said that with the support of an organisation they would press for a private protection. Sharon continued with the story of her marriage to the Portsmouth Bomber and her experience at Leicester University.

'I've often wondered what teachers did during the long summer holiday; now I know,' said Kate, 'and it's not as enjoyable as I imagined.'

'In fact Kate, it has been also most wonderful, because Kim and I have met one another, know how much we love one another and are now choosing to live together.'

Kate smiled.

'Well it's a happy ending and no mistake. But what are you hoping for from me?'

"To tell the plain unvarnished truth.'

'Everything?'

'Yes, everything. I know the school governors well enough to know that what they most dread is any sort of scandal to do with the teaching staff. They're not alone in that but they are particularly dependent upon attracting parents with money and know that any bad association will turn some away. I have been almost killed by a fanatic ex-husband for whose sake I became a Moslem for a short while, and who was a Jihadist bomber, then I have become embroiled in a very public accusation of assisting suicide. Perhaps all these things I might possibly survive, but to be a lesbian will be wholly unacceptable in an all-girls school.'

'You will be pretty exposed by what I write though I can promise that you will be completely exonerated and although Kim absolutely refuses to say who she works for, my guess is that I wouldn't want to get on the wrong side of whoever it is.'

'Oh come on Kate, it's only the RAC,' replied Kim with a large smile.

'That's what she's told me too,' said Sharon.'

'One other thing, said Kate. 'Is it the case that one of your closest friends in Cheshire is Tracey Adamson who wasn't killed in a fatal car crash (an odd thing to say) and has now become a key member of the UK Athletics set up?'

'How did you know that, if I may ask a journalist for her sources?' asked Sharon.

'Ah, I'm afraid that was me,' said Kim.

'It's a good job you work for the RAC and not something where you would have to keep secrets.'

'True, but at least I can change tyres.'

'That's alright then.'

Gerry had sat quietly throughout but now came into his own taking many photographs of Sharon, but none of Kim, and none together except from behind in which Kim's identity would be protected. Gerry then departed while the three women had more wine and conversation about many other things.

André and his his fiancée took a cab to a very special restaurant, which being a weekday still had a table for them. Dee would not release his hand and in fairness he didn't wish her to do so, and which of the two thought him or herself the luckier was almost impossible to say. Tomorrow André was intending to resign from the Service at exactly the time Dee was to join.

'André, I have to tell you something important,' said Dee after they had ordered and their wine had come.

'Oh my God,' said André, 'is it that your legs are both artificial and have to be unscrewed before bedtime?'

She grinned.

'I'm being serious.'

'In which case it can only be you are a trans woman, and that inside your knickers is a penis and testicles.'

'André, if I didn't want yours in prime condition I would kick you under the table! No, it's my name. I'm not really called Dee.'

'Oh I know that.'

'You do?'

'I know that your first name is Dorothea, one of the most beautiful names given by George Eliot to one of the most beautiful characters in all literature.'

'Well it strikes me that Lady Dee Beeson would sound odd, so perhaps now that I have met a man who has just said what you did, I should revert to my real name.'

Their first course arrived.

'Blimey, this is better than anything we ever served in *Betty's*.'

'Oh what you served was pretty good, you know. The success of the firm is a tribute to how much it is appreciated, but I want to hear what thoughts you have for our life together. You accepted a new job before this new development. If you wish to stay with that then I will go along with your decision.'

'Have you something other in mind?' asked Dee.

'How would you feel about leaving London completely and buying a home in Somerset or Devon?'

'André, I don't have much in the way of savings.'

'But I do, and a house to sell in London, with which we could buy ourselves something special. And once we are married I shall arrange to have my will changed wholly in your favour.'

'I don't know what to say. I mean I would love the idea of heading west and living together in the country, just being with you, and enjoying one another, but I made a promise to Martha and I spoke to all the staff.'

'It will take a while to sell and even more to find the right place to buy. It strikes me you could quite easily operate as a consultant at the Conference Centre because I'm convinced that even in a short while you could make important changes that would benefit everyone. Then we can move.'

'There is a question I must ask before we go home tonight. Are you too old to become a dad?'

'I'm looking forward to finding out.'

Chapter Twenty

'I liked Kate, but she's a journalist at the end of the day, and you know her much better than me, so will she exploit us for her own ends?' asked Sharon.
'It's possible, I suppose, for as you say, she's a journalist, but I trust her because we are good friends and even more because she needs me to fix her PC which she regularly screws up. She won't risk losing that! But have you decided yet when you're going to be in touch with your school governors?'
'Yes. I shall call the Chair in the morning'

'Cheryl, it's Sharon here.'
'Oh how are you? What happened must have such a terrible shock for everyone present but especially for you as apparently he was so close to you before he was killed. And to think he was your former husband. I don't think we knew that you had become a Moslem in order to get married. Still, the important thing is that you're safe and sound. And now this other business in which the Ward family are seeking to hold you responsible for Henry's death.'
'You are aware that the Crown Prosecution Service had ruled out any involvement on my part in his suicide?'
'Yes, but I can also see that they have a point. You were the only person who could have saved Henry's life and you chose not to, thereby not preventing if not actually assisting, albeit directly, his suicide.'
'Cheryl, are you aware how much Henry stole from his church and local charity, or the reason why he did so, which was to pay off his gambling debts, and the only reason we were spared at the school was because unknown to everyone, including you, I put a double lock on all our accounts? His family do not want this bringing out into the open air and therefore are diverting attention to me. To privately prosecute me that are receiving money from *Life* an organisation resisting any change in the law to do with assisted dying.'
'Are you talking about a lot of money?'
'£85,000.'
'Wow. Some gambling debts.'

'The Times is going to do a major feature on me very soon, given all that's happened. I haven't read it yet but I have great confidence in the journalist that she will support me in the face of the Wards and, judging from what I've read in the local press and television, give me considerably more support than I have received from the school governors, chief among them being yourself.'

'I don't think that's altogether fair, Sharon.'

'Really? Would you like me to read some of your comments? How about the one that says, "what matters above everything is the good name of the school which has a well-deserved reputation for excellence, not issues that staff get mixed up in. In this case we did not know that Dr Mason, the headteacher had been a Moslem married to the Portsmouth bomber and that she had not tried to stop Henry Ward's suicide". So tell me what's not fair about my commenting on your total lack of support?'

'You know the press twists our words?'

'I think then that a written statement denying that you said these things should go to the paper soon, preferably today. We need to close this completely before term begins. Oh, and I should tell you, that the article in the Times might be accompanied by a photograph of me and my fiancée, as I'm getting married.'

'Congratulations. And who is the lucky man?'

'She's called Kim.'

'She?'

'It's quite legal you know and criticism of it can be regarded as a hate crime. My contract says I have to give a term's notice, so you will have your lesbian headteacher, and everyone will be able to read about in *The Times,* until Christmas, if that is, I decide to go then. But don't be anxious Cheryl, people get used to all sorts of things these days, even a lesbian head of an all girls school.'

'Do you really want to come back, Sharon?'

'Of course I do. If you remember I am the most successful head teacher the school has had in a long time. Why would I not want to come back? And indeed I am planning on doing so next week. There's a lot to get through including examination results and I really like to be there for that. Furthermore it would be very difficult at this stage to replace me with someone comparable. The staffing situation in most schools is already settled for the new year. But you seem to have a hesitation?'

'I'm not the only one who knows what you have done for this school and replacing you, when the time comes will be extremely difficult. It's just that once you are here in Chester there will be a lot of talk, and you know as well as I, this is inevitable and because I think you could go to any school you chose, you might want to redirect your career by means of another big school away from the tittle tattle that will be here.'

'Oscar Wilde said there is only one thing in life worse than being talked about, and that is not being talked about, but I would be foolish Cheryl not to consider what you are possibly suggesting, which is that I either take extended sick leave or we draw up some sort of deal whereby I don't return and the governing body appoints someone in my place as temporary head – the obvious person would be Eleanor Shaw. That would give you time to advertise. But it will be expensive as I shall want full compensation for having to leave an extremely important and well paid position, and have to consult my lawyer about your words about me, which may be libellous.'

'I can't of course commit to the school to any such thing without the consultation with members of the governing body. I rather think, however, they will insist that in return for the compensation there must be no further publicity on your part.'

'The feature in *The Times* is not in my hands and will be published when it is ready. I have no say at all in its content but it is first and foremost concerned with the sullying of my reputation with regard to the suicide of Henry Ward by his family, and not concerned with the school at all. I do think you've all been slimy bastards in your total lack of support, but I wish to say nothing about the school other than to sing its praise. Why would I? I am really proud of what I've done and of what we as a school have created. Our parents can rightly feel it is a good place, if not a *very* good place, and if I am asked that it is what I shall continue to say.'

'I fully appreciate what you have said and I will endeavour to get as many of the governing body together today to discuss the matter in hand. But you know, it is all very sad because nobody thinks more highly of you than I do, and I know full well that the girls of the school feel exactly the same. You drive a hard bargain but your work here could not be faulted. Thank you, and presumably I can call you on your mobile wherever you are?'

'I'm in London and living with my fiancée. She is so lovely and I am so lucky. I look forward to hearing from you.'

André and Dee took ages to get into the building as Dee was coming with the intent of receiving the pass she would need to get in. Only when he insisted on phoning the Deputy Director were they finally admitted, and Dee was allowed a Visitor's Pass. The door to Martha's room was slightly ajar and André could see someone he recognised talking with Martha. He knocked gently, and they entered.

'So, André and Dee, said Martha, with a heavy heart, 'Tell me as if I didn't already know.'

'The time has come,' said André, 'to call it a day, and also to stop speaking in clichés. I want to retire with some life left, and this wonderful lady, who is as courageous as she is gorgeous, has done me the honour of accepting my proposal of marriage.'

'I'm profoundly shocked. Losing you André, well that's just bad luck, and we can easily replace you, but so many of us urgently need Dee running the Conference Centre. You are irreplaceable and this could bring the whole Service down.'

'I'm not going to let you down. It's going to take some time to sell André's

house not to mention to find and buy another for us, and during that time I will come and get everything, including the staff, sorted. Thereafter I will come regularly to check on everything. They're not a bad lot, they just need some leading and management, and I will then assist in the appointment of a new catering manager.'
'Of course, now I see your plan, André. You're marrying someone to do the Christmas cards.'
'Shush, Martha, don't let her hear.'
'What I do I hear is that soon you will be Sir André and Lady Beeson which is nothing less than you both deserve. We shall miss you André for there is no one quite like you but at the end of the day none of us is indispensable except perhaps Kim, whom you both know, and is also getting married.'
'Kim is?'
'Yes, to Dr Mason.'
'Sharon? That's wonderful. Thank you for telling me that. So she's giving up school.'
'Yes, it would seem so.'

Kim met up with Sharon for some lunch.
'And how was conversation with school?'
'As I thought. They see me now as a liability no matter how much I've done for the place but when I said I would be back in harness next week, the chair of governors almost died of fright, so I offered her a deal: a leaving package which would be my salary up to Christmas or I come back and stay at least until then and maybe longer. She said the governors would demand no press or tv interviews as part of the deal and I said that it was too late to stop *The Times* feature but that in effect the last people I wanted to deal with were journalists.'
'And what do you think they'll decide?'
'Oh, don't worry, my love. There's no way they'll want me back. I told her that I was getting married to you. That decided it.'

The Prime Minister and Home Secretary had no idea what to do. The Cabinet Secretary entered the room bringing with him the Attorney General, the Chief of the Defence Staff, and the Commissioner of the Metropolitan Police.
The Attorney General spoke first.
'This meeting is top secret. No recordings or notes may be taken.'
She looked at the PM.
'MI5, with help from the counterterrorism squad in Leeds,' began the PM, 'have not only located but have captured the man known as Mr Big, the coordinator of Jihadist activity in this country and supplier of finance '
'Yes, sir.'
'And has he been co-operative?'
'I gather not though his right-hand man, known as Mr Khan, currently helping the counterterrorist inquisitors in Wakefield prison has been much

more forthcoming. Plans were already in place for two suicide bombers, the two women they were with when they were arrested though those two knew nothing of this. One would be in the Metro Centre in Gateshead, the other in the Trafford Centre in Manchester. Each would kill many.'

'That would have been catastrophic', said the PM. For the benefit of those who do not know the man's identity our problem is that our Mr Big is a member of parliament and recently elected as Chair of the Home Affairs Committee which I suspect his being a Moslem had something to do with that. The Attorney General advises me that I cannot have him killed, in which Presidents Putin and Xi have a very great advantage. So are you ready to charge him?'

'Yes, sir.'

'Commissioner?'

'It's going to be extremely uncomfortable for Parliament, but short of arranging a road traffic accident which we both know would make him a martyr, you have no choice. Details of his capture and especially the role of the Security Services must remain concealed.'

The Attorney General nodded her head.

'I'm sorry Rob, no public praise for you and your men.'

'In fact, Prime Minister, it was almost exclusively the work of women.'

'I'm pleased to hear it,' said the Home Secretary with a broad smile.

'Who will actually charge him? said the PM.

'I think it would highly appropriate, sir, if I send two relatively junior female detectives to do it. If you remember that's how they broke Shipman because he thought he should only talk to the highest and most senior man befitting his status. It was a detective sergeant, a woman, who broke him,' said the Commissioner.

'You don't mind, Rob?'

'We don't have the authority anyway. Shoot him, yes, arrest him, no.'

'Commissioner, let me know when it has been done. I shall have to make a statement to the Commons and I suspect it will be to a subdued House, so I will get on with that now. The Press Office will have to brief the wolves but you can leave that to the Cabinet Secretary to sort out. Thank you, ladies and gentlemen.'

It was a sunny and warm Saturday as Kim and Sharon arrived at the house in Surrey. Outwardly for that area, the house was more or less typical, but once the gates were open and Kim drove in, Sharon saw some sort of sentry box concealed from outside and close by, an armed police officer. That was probably not normal, even for Surrey!

Earlier, Sharon had received a call from Tracey who wanted to report the news that the school in Chester had announced that they were looking to appoint a new head teacher to build on the superb work of Dr Sharon Mason who had now taken up new work in London.'

'I don't suppose they made mention of the amount I have made them pay

me for going now.'
'No. I hope it's substantial though.'
'Well, I can only hope it comes through soon as they will be taken aback by a feature article in *Times 2* next Thursday which will contain the news about Kim and myself getting married.'
'I don't know what Kim will wear, but you really must choose something outrageous as you did in Leicester. Do you know when it will be?'
'Soon, I hope, but don't worry, you'll be first on the guest list.'

Until he fell asleep, Benjie was the star of the show. Rob and Sharon talked a great deal about her new job as education correspondent for The Times and her forthcoming research on George Herbert, about whom he was surprisingly well informed and could even talk about individual poems. Caro gave Kim a detailed description of her ear operation and showed her on the iPad the surgeons in action.
'What was it like hearing?'
'Don't forget that I could hear when I was young, but it was most odd, like suddenly remembering something very important that you had completely forgotten. Rob's voice was as beautiful as I assumed it would be and Benjie will never know me deaf. I loved my sister's music when I was deaf but I think it will take a bit of time to grow on me now I can hear it,' she laughed, 'but the birds are wonderful even though they're silent for the autumn, but once spring comes I have a lot of making up to do.'
Sharon had been listening intently.
'There can be no doubting, Caro, that as some form of compensation for what you have had to endure in being without hearing, you have been given quite extraordinary beauty,' said Sharon.
'That's kind of you to say so but just as long as the Director of MI5 thinks so, I shall be satisfied.'
'He's pretty good looking himself, if you don't mind my saying so,' added Kim.
'He has to go away sometimes but they always leave me a nice man or woman with a machine gun to keep me company. And of course there is this little chap.'
'Might he get a sister or brother?'
'I hope so, but I keep telling Rob that if he can't perform now that he's now very old I'm sure one or other of the police officers at the door would help him out!'
'And what does he say to that?' asked Kim.
'Nothing at all but bedtime is usually more fun than usual!'
'I've heard a great deal about you, Caro, but all that I've heard is as nothing compared to meeting you.' said Sharon.
'I'm glad you've said that Sharon, because I feel the same about you. I think we're on the same wavelength and I feel certain we could keep a conversation going for ages. Our other halves can save the country from peril but we can

perhaps have some fun whilst they are doing so.'

'That would be great, though my life has gone through a transition in a very short time. I was almost murdered, accused of assisting a suicide and more or less forced out of my school because I told them I was marrying Kim. But as with you and Rob, so now I have Kim, and therefore I have only joy to come.'

Part Two

PART TWO: 9 months later

Beforehand

Nancy Carmichael had lived just off Commercial Road in the East end of London for a long time and was well-known in the local, especially the Irish community. They also knew of her favourite form of entertainment: picking up fit young men and taking them home with her. She was still remarkably good-looking for a woman in her fifties and if asked, might have suggested that she knew the elixir of youthful living and made use of it as often as possible. Only a very few knew that she had a formidable reputation as an executioner in the later years of the "troubles", shooting touts, the name given to informers in the back of their heads across the border in the south, outside British territory. It was believed she had shot 12 such people, including 2 women. The Irish government knew all about her and where she was, but wanted nothing to do with her as her arrest would stir up matters best forgotten. The British security services expressed interest in her from time to time, and on the last occasion of contact she had reported that she wanted a complete break with the past with the provos and the latest form of Continuity IRA. No one believed her.

She used the *Wig and Pen*, a popular local pub as her favourite picking-up spot and although she preferred no one twice there were some she brought home more than once. No doubt word circulated about her but she didn't mind provided there was a regular supply, though of late, and no one knew of this locally, she had taken to inviting a girl or two around.

Nancy could make a drink last a long time as she liked to be more or less sober when choosing her partner for the evening (they never stayed the night) and when she saw him enter the pub and order a pint of Guiness she was already decided. His hair was the same shade of red hers had once been (and for which she paid each month to keep it like that) and he was tall and carrying no spare flesh. As soon as he had taken his first mouthful she began to draw up her well-practiced plan. At first she turned away from him and began to chat to the person next to her at the bar or the barman or barmaid (*maid* being a somewhat inappropriate title for the girl on duty tonight). She then made a move for the door and suddenly stopped, turning towards the man.

'Hi there, you must be new or at least I haven't seen you before.'

There was still a little Irish twang in there.

'No, I'm visiting from Sligo.'

'Business?'

'In a manner of speaking.'

'I live a very short distance away if you'd like to be somewhere quieter and I have some of the black stuff on tap. I'd love to hear about the home country.'

The man finished his pint.

'Sounds like a good idea.'

They went out of the door together but no one noticed. It was just Nancy doing what Nancy did. They crossed the busy road and down a side street where Nancy lived. She opened the door and turned on the lights in the hall allowing her companion to follow her into the lounge.

'You have a nice home, Nancy.'

'Yes. I thought you would know my name. No one from Ireland ever comes into the *Wig and Pen* unless it's me they've come to see. And who are you – real name please?

He reached into his inside jacket pocket and pulled out his EU passport and passed it over.

'Brendan O'Callaghan,' she read aloud, 'and real name?'

'The same, though most folk call me Bren.'

'Ok. So what do you want?'

'I've nowhere to stay tonight and I wondered if I might qualify even though I'm 30.'

Nancy laughed.

'I'm always willing to make exceptions to the rule, but that's not why you are here. What you've been talking about is just a splendid opportunity someone suggested you might take advantage of. That's fine by me, but why are you here?'

'The Council has a little job they would like you to perform. It's more or less straightforward and something you've done before. It won't be all that difficult because the target lives in an isolated cottage on Dartmoor. He was with 5 in Belfast and has been with them since as their chief interrogator at RAF Northolt, and they have now honoured him with a knighthood to mark his retirement. We believe his security is more or less nil. He has a young wife.'

'What happens to her?'

'That's up to you.'

'And the reason why?'

'That's not for you nor me to know.'

'Ah! Well in that case the answer is simple. I've retired too, and the answer is No.'

'I don't think so.'

'Brendan, my dear boy, no one says that to me and that includes you.'

She stood, crossed the room and picked up her phone.

'What are you doing?' he asked aggressively.

'Hello Mavis, it's Nancy here. Have you got a free room for the night still? Yes, someone from home called Brendan O'Callaghan from County Sligo so you might get him to do an Irish dance for you. Smashing. He'll be with you soon. Yes, just one night. Bye.'

She put her phone back.

'It's a guest house about 100 meters away called The Happy Rest. Mavis is my friend and you'll get a good breakfast so be on your way.'

'If you don't someone else will.'

'You've never met André Beeson, have you? He is the nicest and best of people though I'm tempted to go and murder his wife and claim him for my own. Now Brendan, off you go. Out of the front door, turn left and first left again. And a piece of advice: give this shit up, the war's over.'

She heard the front door slam, and then again she picked up the phone.

'Hello Julie, it's Nancy. You'd be more than welcome to come and stay the night. Good. See you soon.'

Chapter Twenty One

Her husband had popped down the shops in the village and as he returned he passed a van coming down the lane from their house.

'Who was your visitor?' he asked.

'I didn't ask his name. He came in a large van, and wanted me to carry in 24 large boxes with your name on them. I apologised and said that as I was I couldn't help, so he carried them all in and put them in your study so you will hardly be able to get in. The piece of paper he gave me said it is the 60 volumes of the Oxford Dictionary of National Biography which must have cost a fortune.'

'You forget that I was a contributor so I get it at greatly reduced price.'

André stood still for a moment and then looked up at Dee who was smiling.

'What did you say to the man? Tell me again.'

'I told him that as I was I couldn't help.'

'And how are you?'

'Probably about six weeks, but . . .'

Dee could say no more as she found herself engulfed in André's arms and with a wet face from the tears running down his face.

'Oh my beloved darling, I thought nothing could be better than being married to you but this surpasses it completely. It is wonderful and to be honest I never assumed it would be possible.'

'Oh I don't know; you've tried often enough!'

'Anyone looking at you would know why! But when did you find out?'

'I've suspected something was happening for a few days and I knew my period was late and getting later, but it was only last night that I used a pregnancy test from Boots in Exeter. The two lines went pink and I wanted to tell you, but I decided I would wait until I had done a second test to confirm and when you left earlier that is what I did, and this confirmed it. André, you and I are going to be a mum and dad.'

'I think I might explode with wonder and joy. Do you have to see a doctor or midwife?'

'I need to call the surgery and book an appointment with the midwife, and she'll give us all the details of what we need to know and where the young

Blackburn Rovers supporter will be born.'
'Whereabouts?'
'The Devon and Exeter.'
'Have you spoken to them yet.'
'No, I wanted to wait for you.'
'Thank you. And does it necessitate cancelling this weekend's invasion from London?'
'No way, André. We haven't seen them since our wedding, and Sharon's got a great new job as Features Editor at The Times, and Kim has been promoted to major. We have to see them.'
'I do know that. I was just teasing, but this pregnancy lark, I suppose, means the end of sex.'
'I'm going to get you a book from Amazon called something like "Why you can continue have to sex as often as you wish during pregnancy, but not for six weeks after when you'll be totally knackered anyway". It's by Enid Blyton and the short title is "Five have a sex romp".'
André laughed and laughed.
'My love, I think you should write the book.'
'Whether I do or don't it's true, and sexual pleasure isn't just for men, you know. I fancy you no less, but just in case you think I mean now, the answer is that you have a lot of boxes to unpack and I have soup to make for lunch.'
André grinned.
'I admit the thought had crossed my mind but I'll save up the energy you always generate in me until later.'
They kissed one one another.
'Who would have thought that this could happen at my age?'
'André, lots of ladies would have liked to be in my position over the years including some I dare say, who sat across from you on the other side of an interrogation table. But I'm the one who won the race, like the sperm so generously donated by yourself into my vagina, swimming to be first at the winning post.'
'Ah, so that's how it happens. I did wonder,' replied André with a mischievous smile and the raising of his eyebrows.

Before engaging in soup-making Dee decided to telephone the surgery and arrange an appointment with the midwife. Amazingly she was in and able to speak directly with Dee.
'So how far do you think you're gone?' asked the midwife, having told Dee she was called Kate.'
'Six weeks and I've had two positives on my Boots testers.'
'Sickness?'
'None to speak of.'
'Then let's hope it stays that way. How many other babies have you had?'
'Hang on, I'm just counting...four, five, six, er none.'
Kate laughed.

'What I prefer to do is to come to you for our first meeting. It will enable you to be more relaxed and you'll be able to make me a cup of tea – milk, no sugar. I've just had a change of appointment, so would tomorrow morning at about 10:30 be ok?'
'That would be great.'
'What's your address?'
Dee told her.
'Oh! Does that mean you're Lady Beeson?'
'Yes, though to you, Kate, and everybody else, I'm Dee.'

After soup and a clearup they went up to bed for a rest but had none as they talked almost incessantly about what now lay before them.
'I know you were only joking, my darling, about my need of a book, but I'm not joking when I said that. I think a book or even a series, is what I need.'
'That makes two of us, André. I've never done this before either and my mum probably can't remember even if they lived nearer. I'll have a look on Amazon and see what there is.'
They heard a car approaching so rose from the bed and went downstairs. Through the window they could see that it was a police car and when the knocker sounded Dee went to open the door. Standing outside was a woman police officer who smiled broadly.
'Ah,' she said, 'Lady Beeson, you lucky devil, being married to my wonderful old friend, Sir André. You won the lottery and many are the ladies who hate you for it.'
'Let the rascal come in, Dee,' shouted André from inside, 'It's only Rowena Lehmann.'
'André, said the visitor, 'welcome to Devon and your wife, who if I may say so, is as lovely as the stories tell. It's a treat having you come to live here.'
Dee was feeling disorientated, as André could see.
'Darling, Rowena and I worked closely together at the Conference Centre for almost five years.'
'Where I gather you've transformed the food situation beyond all recognition,' said Rowena to Dee.
'It was pretty dire, but did you work with André asking questions?'
'Nothing so grand as that. No, I managed the place, apart from the dining facilities. I made sure it worked when necessary with adequate space for guests, and making sure the place was clean and the laundry done, and blood regularly washed off the floor and broken teeth picked up. That sort of thing.'
'That's by no means the whole truth. Ro developed an astonishing knack for chatting informally with those being held, usually about their families, and in that way we learned a huge amount we weren't getting any other way. And might still have been doing that now had she not broken a tooth on a chocolate bar she had brought with her for lunch because she couldn't face the food.'
'It's all true,' continued Rowena. 'So I rang my dentist only to find he was

on holiday but that there was a Swiss locum who could see me at the end of the afternoon. His name was Moritz and when I saw him I thought I would die so totally gorgeous was he, and as I sat there in the chair I was trying to work out what problem with my teeth I could need him for on the following day and the day after that. I needn't have bothered as it turned out as he felt the same way. So I handed in my notice, and we went off to live in Berne where we got married and I did a degree in criminology. Moritz could tell I was missing England and found the offer of a partnership in Exeter which has worked out well. I decided to opt for the police and entered the fast-track system which means I will be an Inspector before long. For now I'm but a humble sergeant with a rural operation.'

'"Humble sergeant" will never describe you, Ro. How is your daughter, by the way?'

'Beautiful and already bi-lingual, as we tend to speak German at home, which is not bad for a four-year-old.'

'What is she called?' asked Dee.

'Lotte, short for Charlotte.'

'Is there any chance of the three of you coming for tea on a Sunday? asked André.

'To talk babies, I imagine,' replied Rowena.

'How the . . . ? said Dee, stunned.

André began laughing.

'You haven't met Ro before, my darling, have you? She has one of the fastest minds I've ever come across, but tell us how you knew, Ro.'

'Simple really. As I came in I noticed a print-out lying on the printer shelf.'

'Told you.'

'Ro, you've been through all this before and I know hardly anyone here who has, so whenever you're passing and fancy a coffee, I'd be over the moon if you could come and help me talk through it,' said Dee.

'I'd be delighted to, and of course we'd love to come and share Sunday tea with the knight and his fair lady.'

'It's more red than fair, I think,' said André, 'but I'm dying to meet your dentist and daughter.'

'Ok, I'm off the weekend after this, so Sunday would be great. However I am here for another purpose as well, surprise, surprise.'

'I assumed there probably would be,' said André.

'It's just a security check. You can't just stop what you've been doing for MI5 for a long time, including time in Northern Ireland, and not expect the local force to exercise a measure of care for you. The Chief Constable, the two ACCs and me are the only ones who know about your past, but the boss is determined we look after you properly. I imagine you receive security info from the Service on a daily basis anyway, so we'll know no more than you, and we have no intention of installing a resident babysitter, but she's keen that nothing happens to you, and for what's it worth, I feel the same. But if at anytime you need to call us, I have some numbers, including my own. The other thing I have to check is the matter of a firearm. Do you have one?'

'Yes, indeed, the metal cupboard, duly locked in here in the corner. It's a handgun, a Glock 17, together with some ammunition and I'm told Hereford will provide more if I need it. They've also offered to take Dee on a course and we've thought about it but now she's pregnant it's on hold.'

'If you want, Dee, I'll take to our range in town and let you have a go.'

'Thank you. I might just take you up on that. Our friend Kim's coming tomorrow, and she's done Hereford, so I'll hear what she has to say.'

'The offer's there.'

After Ro had left them, Dee asked André if it was true he still received daily MI5 briefings.'

'Yes and no. They come to my computer every day but mostly I don't look at them.'

Chapter Twenty Two

Dee was up early. It was going to be a demanding day. Once Kate had been she would need to prepare for the arrival of Kim and Sharon whose train was due into Exeter St Davids's shortly after lunch. André had said he would collect them so as not to tire her and allow her to catch perhaps an hour's sleep

It was a clear day, not especially warm in the wind, but Dartmoor looked good and after breakfast she popped her nose outside to breathe in the clear Devonshire air. Almost as soon as breakfast was over, the dishes washed and dried, André was in his study opening more boxes though he had confessed to her that doing so was taking a lot longer than he had imagined, because he kept stopping at every new box, opened the volumes and was amazed by what he read and learned.

Almost exactly on time, a land rover pulled up outside the house, and out of it came a woman Dee assumed was Kate. She wore a dark blue uniform with a belt and was carrying a larger bag that Dee had expected. Kate was tall and a little chunky but not obese and wore a lovely smile as she advanced towards Dee.

'Hi Dee,' she said, 'as you've probably worked out I'm Katy Perry and we're going to be seeing a lot of each other in the months to come and we'll make a start this morning. Oh, and is my cup of tea ready?'

They shook hands and Dee summoned André.

'Good morning, Sir André.'

'They shook hands.

'Good morning, Midwife Perry.'

All three laughed.

'Can you make Kate a cup of tea, darling?'

'Of course. Black and three sugars?'

'That's it.'

'Kate, should I have made an appointment with my GP before being in touch with you?' asked Dee.

'I checked up and found that you have registered with them, so I spoke to Dr Dereham. She and I work closely together and she confirmed your referral to me, so that's sorted.'

'Thank you.'
André arrived with the tea.
'May I stay?' he asked.
'Of course, though you will quickly become bored because there are going to be a huge number of questions to do with Dee's medical history and they will last about an hour. We shall eventually need to go to your bedroom for an examination and you might want to be there for that, but, honestly, André, I feel you might spend your time more usefully, and if we need you we can call you. Dee?' said Kate.
'I'm happy with that if André is.'
'Definitely,' and he motioned to rise from his chair.
'Hang on,' said Kate. 'There's a first question I have to ask Dee. Dee, are you experiencing any form of coercive, physical or sexual abuse in your home?'
'No. Of course not.'
'What about you, Sir André?' she said with a straight face.
'Nothing coercive or physical but nowhere near enough of the third category!'
'You are dismissed,' said the midwife with a sly smile.
André returned to his boxes.
True to her word, the questions lasted the best part of an hour before Kate said she needed to do an examination and Dee led her upstairs where André joined them. Kate listened and looked and said nothing as she did so. First however, she was sent to the loo to provide a sample of her wee. Then she did her blood pressure and took some blood.
'I'll get it to the lab this morning so results will be there when you get to the maternity department. It just saves time. Ok, Dee, you can put your things back on but a visit to M&S for a bra that fits might be a good idea.'
Kate sat on the bed, and Dee joined her, André sitting opposite on a chair.
'You're further on than you thought as I could see straight away and although this can only be confirmed when you have a scan, I'm pretty sure that I could hear two babies in there.'
'Oh my God, said Dee, 'twins!'
André said nothing for a moment, before saying, 'You are sure it's only two?'
'No, you'll have to wait for the scan for that.'
'Aargh,' said Dee. 'Don't say that.'
'I'm going to call Exeter when we get downstairs and get you an appointment for Monday. I've done more than half their work for them.'
'Are you saying there's a problem?' asked Dee.
'Not at all, but when we're talking about multiple births we need to be absolutely clear as soon as possible so we can care for you appropriately, but there's nothing to worry about. Multiple births are pretty common.'
'I do wish, Kate, you would use a better phrase than *multiple* births. It makes it sound as if Dee's going to give birth to a litter.'

'I'm sure that all being well you'll be wonderful parents, and as well as you, they'll have each other to hate and love in almost equal proportions. I'll call Exeter and then must be on my way.'

She went downstairs and they could hear her laugh. When she had finished they came down and joined her.

'You'll have a hundred questions that occur once I've gone, but save them for the appointment on Monday at 11:00. Go to the Centre for Women's Health and head for Clinic One. They'll be expecting you, and in addition to attending directly to you, you'll no doubt find an auxiliary will give you the grand tour of all the facilities, at least those not in use at the time, but the website is superb and if you look at it you'll be familiar with the place even before you've seen it. There are loads of videos too trying to put me out of business. On which note I'll see you again soon after I hear from them how it's gone and they hand you back to my tender care.'

She checked she had everything in her bag.

'Enjoy your visitors and I'll call you. Bye.'

André and Dee echoed her farewell and in a matter of moments they heard the landrover turn and she was gone.

'Because I've got to and collect Kim and Sharon a little later,' said André, 'I won't have the stiff drink I deserve and desire. What amazing news. Oh, my darling Dee, you are so clever and it is wonderful. I am so pleased that I could almost do a jig if it was not for the fact that I have no idea how to do one.'

'Oh Sir André, I thought you could do everything.'

'Well clearly I have managed something.'

'And I need you to keep in practice.'

'There was a moment when I saw you in your work uniform when we were both in Ilkley and I knew I had never seen anything so beautiful, and when Kate was examining you earlier I thought back to that moment and knew that I was absolutely right, and I think that over the next few months you are going to get even lovelier.'

Dee was crying and came to her husband and put her arms around him and they kissed passionately.

According to the internet, the train was still running on time as it reached Taunton, so André set off for Exeter knowing he wouldn't have to hang about too much at the station. Dee assumed that after her morning's news there was no way she would sleep but almost as soon as her head hit her pillow she was gone, so much so that she wasn't even aware of the arrival back and her two women friends with whom not all that long ago, she had gone through so much. She had once had a massive crush on Sharon and had felt peeved that Kim had stolen her, but once she knew how much she loved André that was all forgotten. She very much doubted that Sharon would have managed to get her pregnant though at the time would have longed to give it a try. At the time Sharon had been head teacher of an independent girls' school in Chester, but since getting together with Kim was Features Editor for *The Times* and also writing a novel. The rumour was that she was also now a close friend of the wife of the Director of the Security Service. For her part Kim was regarded as the principal technology officer in the service and had quickly been raised to the level of major in the army. Where Sharon exuded femininity, Kim was more discrete about hers, though when she had come to Dee's and André's wedding you wouldn't have known it was the same Kim, who had smiled to herself when she saw Sharon proudly showing her partner off and to be fair, she looked amazing. Dee hoped that Sharon and Kim would themselves marry soon and make it the fashion show of the year, with Kim as the sexiest major in the army.

As Dee emerged from her sleep she could hear voices and it took her a minute or two before she realised that it was André, Sharon and Kim that she could hear. The news Kate had left behind was going to take a great deal of getting used to and she determined as soon as possible to let her two sisters know – but would swear them to secrecy with regard to their mum. She touched her tummy and could hardly believe that inside there were two minuscule forms of life growing each day. Her eyes filled with tears at the thought, and more tears when she thought how wonderful this was for André too and for them together. Tears dried up, she prepared herself to go downstairs to see two of the other people she loved so much in this world. She felt, however, that perhaps she should hold back on the baby talk given that Kim and Sharon had no children though it was not an impossibility if that was their wish. At the moment what she was hoping for was news of a marriage.

Hearing her footsteps on the stairs they both shot out of their chairs. Kim reached her first and was almost as tearful as Dee had been upstairs.

'Good afternoon, Major,' said Dee.

'Good afternoon, Lady Beeson.'

They laughed and hugged again, and then it was turn of Sharon, which Dee, if she could dare admit it to herself, was most looking forward to. They held and kissed.

'I gather we're here on a very special day,' said Kim, taking no notice of the special hug and kiss enjoyed by Dee and Sharon, having known for ages how Dee had once fallen for Sharon, but knowing too that she was the winner of that particular race!

'Twins, at least,' Kim had continued, laughing and taking hold of Sharon's hand to draw her away from Dee.

'No', said André, 'only twins will be allowed and I'm hoping for boys.'

'Nonsense, André, and you know it,' said Sharon, still being held by Kim. 'You love girls and ladies and look at the one you have fallen in love with. She is so beautiful and you are perfect for each other. I feel the same for Kim.'

'Well, now the mutual admiration club has finished its meeting, let's have some lunch,' said André.

After lunch the three women headed out on to Dartmoor. There was a climb and then a valley beyond in which to their initial shock and then delight, they put up a fox which took off before them.

'Is it like the Yorkshire Dales?' asked Kim.

'If you remember, I was mostly never out in the Dales because of the demands of my job, so even in the short time we've been here, I've done more walking than I ever did in Ilkley. It's nowhere near as crowded and I've discovered that André knows far more about country life than I would ever have thought likely.'

'Does André know that he has about seven months of normal life left to the pursuit of any serious study he might wish to engage in?' said Sharon. 'Once twins arrive, life is going to change for both you in a considerable way. Wonderful yes, but from what I've seen in others, utterly exhausting.'

'I don't think he minds. For him almost every day is a new experience. Yes, he has his books and plans for writing, but he seems to have taken more to doing nothing, to sitting outside and identifying birds or gently walking down the lane and engaging anyone he meets in conversation.'

'You could easily get lost up here, not least when the weather suddenly changes as I imagine it might very well do, such as now,' said Kim.

Sharon suddenly kissed her.

'You're the soldier, Major. We'll follow you back down.'

'H'm. I haven't got round to doing map-reading yet.'

'That's ok,' said Dee, laughing, 'we haven't got a map, but I know exactly where we are: we're here! All we have to do is get there.'

Wherever *there* was, it was quite invisible because of the rain, but Dee had no doubts of the way back, and they were all soon able to see the house, where they arrived soaking wet.

'You were quite right, Sharon, about the weather suddenly changing. Even a map would be little use. Only those who have often trodden the land are going to be safe, which is why I go up every day and familiarise myself with it, and until my body and its contents won't let me, I'll carry on doing that. I want the twins to grow up knowing and loving the moor.'

'They went towards Honiton for Dinner, as Sharon and Kim had asked them to book somewhat special for Dee and André to be their guests, and they found Deer Park Country House was everything they might wish for. It described itself as a "boutique" restaurant which led André to admit that he expected it to sell 1960s clothes and Mary Quant among the waitresses. He hailed a passing maitre d'.

'What does it mean by calling this a Boutique Restaurant?'

'Strictly speak, Sir André, the whole house is a Boutique Hotel, and it refers to the size and intimacy of the place.'

'Is this a new terminology?'

'No sir. It goes back to 1984 when two entrepreneurs opened a hotel in New York and compared it to a boutique.'

'I congratulate you on being so well-informed.'

'Thank you Sir André, but it's something I get asked so often that I made sure I could answer it. I try to attend regularly to the sorts of things someone

might ask.'
'And how did Exeter fare today?'
'Exeter City lost 3-1 away to Port Vale, but Exeter Chiefs beat Harlequins 24-12 at Sandy Park.'
'Bravo,' said André with a huge smile, and the other three joined him in delighted applause.

On Sunday morning, after a long and slow breakfast, Sharon and Dee went out for a walk together, leaving the major and the former Chief Interrogator of MI5, to have a conversation.
'You said in your email, Kim, that Rob had insisted you and I have a conversation, and it can only be about technological and security matters. Am I right?'
'Whispers in the wind.'
'Grade?'
'Two/One, from your old friend, Nancy Carmichael, albeit indirectly from one of ours called Julie Dickinson, who keeps a close eye on the Irish community, and on Nancy in particular. She reports a visitor from Sligo wanting Nancy to come to Devon and show MI5 that they are far from finished in Ireland and can take out anyone they choose, and who better that someone who was in Belfast and is now a knight of the realm.'
'How the hell did she manage to get that much out of Nancy? I never could.'
Kim laughed.
'You never engaged in pillow talk with her.'
'Good heavens. Nancy must be changing; in the past it was young and fit boys only. Well good for Julie. Any more?'
'Nancy refused point blank and threw the guy out and called Julie because there was now a gap in the bed.'
'Ah, what we have to be prepared to do for the Service.'
'Nancy apparently thinks the world of you.'
'That's because I kept her out of prison.'
'I didn't know that. Anyway, Julie seems to have squeezed out of her the information that CIRA might have a go at getting at you anyway.'
'There are a number of questions which even Nancy would not be able to answer, such as where their info came from about my knighthood and where we live. That would suggest some sort of inside information as I cannot believe we have been followed from London to here. It means that once again there is a loose tongue that will have to be tracked own. In this you are going to be as important as you were the last time you enabled us to track down a traitor.'
'I accept that and Martha has already called together a small group of us to meet together this week. The information about you could quite easily have come from the finance department. After all it is hardly hardly a state secret. Someone could have revealed this with the minimum of pressure from a

boyfriend or lover.'

'I am grateful for this information but was there something else intended by *your* visit, a visit from the principal technological officer in the Service?'

'Caro knew Sharon and I were coming and mentioned it to the Director, who for that reason summoned me to the top floor where what I have passed on to you was told to me. Sharon knows nothing of it, by the way. It is likely that this has already been passed on to the Devon and Cornwall Police. The boss wanted me to do a security check which took hardly any time at all as there is no security. He also wanted me to make sure Dee receives some basic weapon training, but I gather that may be underway with the police.'

'Yes, and now I understand why this was pressed upon her. Do you think we need more than that?'

'The Director said that he thought you would be reluctant to accept cameras and the like.'

'I am retired and I am living with a beautiful young wife, now pregnant. We want to live and love simply with our children, not in a prison or Fort Knox.'

'I fully understand and I agree. Besides which, setting anything up here would be a ghastly eyesore and draw attention to you and encourage local burglars. You are also too far away from the local police to make it worthwhile for me to install even a sophisticated alarm to summon immediate attendance because immediate would probably be quite a long time.'

'In other words we're on our own and reliant upon native wit.'

'Of which neither of you are lacking.'

'Let this be a lesson to you too, Kim. When you've worked in the Service you take your past with you. My reputation was as an easy-going gentle interrogator, and that was so in Northern Ireland in my time there, and yet I'm under threat. But if anyone would ever dare to put my beloved wife and children-to-be under a similar threat, I would not hesitate to kill.'

Kim reached out and placed her hand of his arm.

'I never doubted it.'

'But tell me about you. Together you are clearly so very happy, but you must realise that your work puts you both at risk. Martha sees you moving upwards, even as a future Director, and I'm not trying to flatter you, because I've heard Martha say it. But you have to ask whether your love could withstand that. Downing St every morning briefing the idiots, as I call our politicians who are totally under-equipped to make the decisions demanded of their office; constant meetings with allies and with the US of whom we are unsure; travel here and there; and a wife as lonely as Sharon admits Caro is. All that may only come at a heavy price, which is why, having met Dee I decided to quit.'

'It has already meant closing down the possibility of a baby which I would have wanted. Sharon is a little older than me and feels IVF is something she cannot face. I could possibly, but even I'm getting older and I'm unsure I could go through all that would be demanded of even one cycle and I've met women who when they've reached the third cycle just cannot face any more, but that almost certainly indicates I'm not as desperate as others clearly are. Sharon and I discuss it regularly.'

'You know, I'm sure, that Dee once had a crush on Sharon. When we were out last night I think I did as well. She is incredibly attractive in just about every way, if you don't mind my saying so, but so are you, and between you I find your joint formidable brain power quite scary.'

Kim laughed.

'You are a flatterer Sir André, and I might add that as a definite lesbian, I find Lady Beeson fanciable even on a rainy day.'

'H'm, this is turning into a very worrying conversation and as I can hear approaching voices, perhaps we should begin speaking about the forthcoming cricket tour to Australia and the selectors' choice of spin bowlers.'

'Ah well, one of my subordinates, Eamonn, with whom I've worked a lot talks about little other than cricket when we're not active, so I might just surprise you what I know about the relative merits of Leach, Rashid and Ali, though to be fair, I have no idea who he's talking about!'

The pair of them dissolved in fits of laughter as the front door opened.

'Ah ha,' said Dee, 'caught you enjoying yourselves when you said you had some matters to clarify about the Service.'

'It was indeed Service business we were discussing. Agents Leach, Rashid and Ali are being considered for a special mission in a far-off land, and we were considering their merits.'

'Oh, fair enough,' added Sharon. 'For a moment I thought they were the names of spin bowlers.'

'Oh, Sharon, you always spoil everything by being so clever.'

'Just a lucky guess, that and the fact that I have more time than you to read the whole paper in the morning, including the sports pages.'

All four now laughed, enabling André to get up and put the kettle on for tea and cake. He was also cooking their evening meal and the conversation did not dry up once throughout. There were a number of electrical faults which Kim was happy to correct for them and Sharon waxed lyrical about the countryside around them asking if she might come again soon to explore it, an idea Dee and André were both delighted about, and even Kim seemed to encourage.

Chapter Twenty Three

After Mass, three men gathered for a Guinness.

'I don't exactly know how many executions the woman performed for the provos but I'd be surprised if it wasn't at least a dozen,' said Tomas. 'And there were the two Americans which were hushed up. How she got away with it, I'll never know. I've always thought the CIA would come for her.'

'We sent that idiot doctor over to get her to go to Devon but he failed, so we're getting him to go to England again, this time to Devon. The former MI5 interrogator, Beeson, is the target we are talking about. He lives on Dartmoor and the Council thinks it will be good for the cause to take him out and show that we are still a force to be reckoned with, but the doctor won't be alone. There is someone else going.'

'Have the Council agreed?' asked Terry.

'Yes.'

Tomas and Terry knew better than to ask who, or for that matter, when this was going to happen. If Eamonn spoke it was enough for them, though it never occurred to them that he knew far less than they imagined. The Council of which they spoke was nothing even remotely like that during the troubles but the fewer that knew that the better.

Over supper Dee had talked about how her Lancashire mother might respond to the news of her pregnancy.

'I shall leave telling her for the time being because I just know she will be here before we know where we are. Probably she would fly from Manchester to Exeter and then take a taxi, and, once here, getting rid of her would be difficult to say the least. André's very good with her because he's a knight of the realm and she takes notice of him, but if she were to stay a long time I would end up poisoning her.'

'How many brothers and sisters have you?'

'Two of each, and Hermione had to beg her to go away when she was pregnant.'

'Hermione?'

'Oh yes. Hermione, Hippolyta, Dorothea, Oberon and Fyodor.'

'Fyodor – in Lancashire?' asked Sharon, somewhat stunned.
'What about Oberon or Hippolyta?' asked Kim.
Dee began laughing.
'The thing is that everyone knows what my mother is like. Mrs Bucket off the tele had nothing on her and so we all quickly adopted practical alternative names, and now it's only mum who uses the names when she phones us. Thank goodness for that and yet despite that, the people of Hoddlesden continue to love her and she knows they laugh behind her back for it and doesn't mind and has said that, on the contrary, some have said they wished they knew as much about books as she clearly does.'
'She sounds like quite a lady,' said Sharon.
'Oh she is that,' burst in André, 'but having her here from now to the birth and beyond would be an unkind thing to do to the people of Hoddlesden who clearly need her more than we do – a lot more than we do – trust me!.'
The three women all laughed.
'I miss my mum a great deal,' said Sharon. To the very end of their lives she and my dad were devoted to one another and she gave every possible ounce of support to him in his work. He disliked the new NHS contract because he functioned best as a family doctor who never minded have to respond to night calls or at the weekend. I let them down twice. In the first place I didn't apply to Cambridge, and then I married the wrong man altogether. It only lasted a very short time but they never said anything even remotely like "told you so". They simply welcomed me home again and cared for me. It was considerably more than I deserved and they were wonderful.'
'How did they respond when they knew that the man you had married was the Portsmouth Bomber?'
'Needless to say, we had lots of visits from the police, but their care and support never wavered, even though they were profoundly shocked by what Jimmy had done, and the deaths of the young girls he had caused.'
'As Dee knows only too well,' said André, 'my wonderful mother and I were extremely close. My dad had disappeared from the scene before I ever knew him. I don't think she ever liked or trusted any man thereafter, apart from me, so there was no likelihood of her installing a man in the house on some kind of permanent or semi-permanent basis as my step-dad. She decided that her future lay in screwing men in return for letting them screw her. So, she became a prostitute. We lived on a council estate in a grotty part of Leeds and very cleverly she worked out a deal with the fleet of taxis in the city. Using her own house meant she could charge a lot more than girls only offering the backseat of a car or a "knee trembler" up a back alley, and of course it was very much safer than being on the streets. I never knew anything about the finances, but I do know it seemed to provide us with a healthy income for the eight years she did it.'
'Eight?' said Kim. 'How old were you?'
'Seventeen when she decided to declare her innings closed. I adored that woman and until I met Dee she was the most courageous and beautiful woman

I had ever known.'

'But did you know what she was doing with the men arriving by taxi.'

'Of course. She never hid that from me or pretended she was telling their fortunes so noisily upstairs. I simply admired her and thought the world of her. A couple of times she asked me to bring water to the room, when a "guest" felt faint, which I always thought was a hoot. Usually the man skedaddled pretty quickly when I appeared. She told me once that it wasn't just the money, she also enjoyed the sex and she truly believed that doing what she enjoyed also provided an important service. She told me that some of the men who came regarded her as primarily there for them to talk to. My mum was quite a lady, believe you me, and like you, Sharon, I really miss her. It would have been wonderful for her to come to the Palace for my K.'

'When did she die, André?' said Kim.

'While I was at Oxford, of which she was so very proud. She developed a brain tumour and never recovered. Nowadays she might have stood a better chance, but what a life and I'm so very proud of her. You would have been astounded at the number of sheepish looking men who turned up for her funeral. She didn't smoke and she didn't do drugs. She was simply amazing.'

That's wonderful, André,' said Kim, 'and I would love Sharon to turn that into a story; it would be fabulous. My own parental story is so much more dull in comparison. It was just normal except for the huge amount of time I spent with my dad in what started as *his* workshop, then became *our* workshop and then became *mine*. I learned so much from him and my mum was so supportive. When I got to uni I was simply wasting my time doing the sort of things I had been doing with my dad when I was ten. I'm not boasting but I was streets ahead of everyone else, including the teachers, and I know it sounds daft, but most of the time now my mind is looking around thinking of new ways of doing things.'

'Sounds like bedtime must be fun for you and Sharon,' added Dee to the laughter of them all.

'I'm not complaining,' said Sharon, 'but all those electrical wires and pieces of equipment can be a little off-putting.'

Their laughter continued.

Following an unexpectedly good night's sleep, Dee and André dropped Kim and Sharon at Exeter Central Station to await their train back to London, before going, somewhat nervously, to the hospital. They found the Centre for Women's Health without difficulty and then followed the signs to Clinic One. Before they even reached the Reception area a lady approached them.

'Hello. Welcome. You must be the Beesons.'

They greatly appreciated that she had not used their titles with so many people around.

'Come and have a seat and we'll just complete the inevitable paperwork, though Mrs Perry has done most of it for us.'

It didn't take long. Both of them looked round and felt very much that the atmosphere was conducive to feeling relaxed.

'Have you had a chance to look at our website?'

They both nodded.

'Well, you've probably had the virtual tour but Nurse Jenkins here will give you the quick once-over and show you everything apart from rooms in use. After that we shall get you in for your scan and then a meeting with your obstetrician Dr Timothy, who despite the name is a woman. Between you and me she greatly enjoys confusing everyone. She insists she has a brother called Timothy Timothy but none of us believe her. She's quite brilliant at her job though and is the senior consultant and you'll see her most times you come in.

The tour was fascinating to both Dee and André and Nurse Jenkins was able to answer all their questions helpfully. The place had a wonderful feel and Dee enjoyed being with other young women, each of whom, judging from outward appearances, were in different stages of pregnancy. Only the sight of enormous bumps alarmed her!

The tour completed, they sat and had a drink, but were then led into a room with slightly subdued lighting, a bed and complex machinery along side. To greet them was a cheerful young woman with a broad Devonshire accent.

'Hello, I'm Sam, the sonologist, which means that I do your scans and help you to see what I can see, which aren't always the same thing. So I just need to know your name and date of birth, and can you identify this gentleman who came in with you?'

'Yes, he's the man who got me into this state.'

'I'm glad to hear it. I have to ask, just in case he's come in off the streets. Ok, Dorothea, please climb aboard.'

'Dee, please.'

'Can you lift your blouse up and let me see your tummy. The gel may feel a little cold but really it's not too bad. Ok, let's get scanning.'

It took longer that Dee had expected and Sam said very little as she worked and looked at her screen.

'Your midwife was very clever to pick up two heartbeats so early and you may be relieved to know it's not triplets. It's definitely twins although we shan't know their gender for another ten weeks. If you both remain here I'll go and collect Dr Timothy for you to meet her and let her explain what we can see.'

She left the room, and Dee gave André a worried glance. There was hardly time for them to speak before the door re-opened and following Sam into the room was a woman of about 40, dressed in blue scrubs.

'Hello, I'm Ruth Timothy, a consultant obstetrician. Congratulations on your pregnancy and I shall be looking after you. Because she's very much more able at reading a scan than I am, I shall ask Sam to describe what she can see.'

'I'll highlight what we need you to see,' began Sam. 'Yes, there are twins, what we call monochorionic twins, which means that they share a placenta and will be identical. If you look here you will see that this twin is a little

Rod Hacking

larger than the other. Over to you, Ruth.'
'Actually the disparity between them is not too great but it's there. It's caused by an imbalance in the blood vessels from the placenta to the twins, meaning that the bigger is getting more blood than the smaller, whom we call the donor twin, which results in the bigger getting too big and the donor growing too slowly.

'This is called Twin-to-Twin Tranfusion Syndrome or TTTS for short. It's not common but neither is it rare. Your twins are not that different but my sharp-eyed friend here saw it straight away.'

'Is it dangerous?' asked André.

'Well it's not what either you or I would want for your pregnancy, but I really don't think we should be in panic mode right now. My judgement is that you are about 10 weeks pregnant and the TTTS is present and what we shall have to do, I'm afraid, is to bring you in here every fortnight for a scan. On your next visit I'll bring along the head of our fetal centre and compare notes with him. He's much cleverer than me.'

'If it is TTTS is it likely to speed up as it were, and if it does what would happen then?'

'We might consider sending you to Bristol to the Regional Fetal Medicine Centre. It they think it appropriate they will drain off the excess urine being produced by the bigger baby and which will be making it harder both for the donor baby and you. There is another treatment possible, but it would mean having to go to London. They make use of a treatment which involves inserting a laser into your womb and cutting those tubes which are taking the excess blood from the donor. We don't do it here yet, but what they do is amazing and they have good results, though at the moment the babies and placenta are too small for the procedure.'

'Might my babies die?' asked Dee.

'Might my wife die?' added André hurriedly.

'To the first question I can only say that I pride myself on doing the very best we can for all mums and babies. Some babies are in a far worse state in the womb than yours. As for the second question, all I can say is that maternal mortality rates are higher in this country than in some other countries but I don't have any reason to think that you have any underlying cause which give you or me any cause for anxiety. Now, I have another patient as does Sam, so I will ask you to meet with my Registrar, Dr Samuels, and he'll be able to answer further questions and provide you with lots of information to take away. The internet also has a lot on TTTS, but you are not yet typical, so don't apply everything to yourselves, and I ask you especially to stay well from American websites. I mean that. So see you in a fortnight.'

Sam helped Dee clean up.

'Take no notice of her. She's forgotten more than I know about reading a scan and the Fetal Centre director knows just how brilliant she is. You are in the best of all possible hands, and I've seen babies like yours just continue almost as normal.'

They met with the Registrar who looked as if he was about 12 years old but clearly knew his stuff and as they left, the Receptionist handed them a reminder of the next appointment and pointed out that they would also hear on-line. Holding hands tightly they walked in silence to their car. Thoughts they might have had about some lunch in the city were by silent consent abandoned. Once in the car Dee burst into tears and fell onto André.

'Oh André, I'm so sorry to have failed you.'

'Dee, you've done nothing of the sort. These things happen and we are in excellent hands for ensuring the best outcome. Ruth Timothy exuded confidence and she thought there was no need for panic of any sort and what dies it matter if we have to pop up to Bristol once in a while, that's nothing. We can face this together, all four of us, and we shall.'

She looked up at him and kissed him.

'Thank you my darling. Let's get home.'

Chapter Twenty Four

Once back up on the moor, Dee recovered a little, aided by a lovely albeit cold day. Almost as she walked through the front door, her phone rang. It was Kate.

Hello Dee, I've just heard from the Unit about your visit today. I can call in to see you at about half past four provided there's a mug of tea awaiting my arrival. Can you both manage that?'

'Oh Kate, that would be great. Thank you.'

'Ok. See you then.'

'Kate's going to call in for a mug of tea at half-past four,' Dee said André.

'It's all very impressive care, I must say.'

After a piece of toast each, André persuaded Dee to spend an hour or two resting in bed and she was happy to do so. He had other business to attend to.

Once he felt Dee was asleep he telephoned Ro, who immediately asked him if everything was ok.

'No one is at present seeking to kill me, if that's what you mean, though I need urgently to talk to you about that, not least because although I've now had a briefing from the Service, I suspect you already knew and didn't want to say anything in front of Dee.'

'It wasn't graded "immediate".'

'Well, I think we both need to hear it from you and your thoughts about how we should prepare ourselves, including getting Dee ready and able to use a firearm. On top of that we've had something of a setback this morning at the hospital. It seems the identical twins are drawing from just one placenta between them, and one of is drawing more blood for growth and development that the other. It's potentially very serious.'

'Oh what a bore.'

André smiled.

'You could say.'

'It will mean more trips than most mums-to-be have to make into Exeter for scans, but it does mean you will get first-class attention. Which consultant did you see?'

'Dr Timothy.'
'In which case you've got the very best. Look, I'm tied up until about seven but I can call in then and in the meantime I'll fix up a visit for Dee to learn which end of a gun to point with.'
'Ro, you always were brilliant, and clearly still are.'

Dee slept on, and it took André with a cup of tea to summon her back to the land of the living.
'The world looks different.'
'It's bound to, but Kate will be here soon and later Ro is going to pop in to see you.'
'I'm so sorry. André. I feel as if I've let you down.'
'In the first place you haven't let me down at all. Our twins are still there and the doctor didn't seem like she wanted to panic, so as far as possible I don't think we should either.'
'Have you been reading what the Registar gave us?'
'I've glanced through it but to say I've read it would be to say too much. What I saw was interesting though. I had never heard of it before and when I went online I selected the wrong entry: the Tonic Tensor Tympani Syndrome and couldn't quite understand why it was all to do with ears!'
'Darling, however did you do your old job? Did you ever question the wrong prisoner?'
'Oh, quite possibly, but if so I mostly got away with it.'
Dee reached out and hugged her husband.
'I expect Kate will want her mug of tea.'
'No reward for that particular guess. I wouldn't be surprised if you hear from Sharon or Kim this evening, wanting to know how it went after we dropped them. What do you want to say?'
'Oh, I must tell them how it is. I have nothing to hide from Kim and Sharon and if I had to go to London we shall need them.'
'I can hear Kate's landrover approaching so I should put the kettle on. Do you want to see her here?'
'No, I'll come downstairs with you.'
Kate came straight in, as before carrying her work bag.
'Well, what a day you must have had,' she said. 'I imagine it's been something of a shock to be told you've got a problem with the pregnancy.'
'To think that until about 11:15 today I'd never even heard of TTTS, and now I can't stop thinking about it.'
'Thank you for coming, Kate,' said André. 'We're due back in two weeks' time.'
Yes, Ruth called me to let me know about your visit. Not something that would happen everywhere, that a consultant would call a rural midwife, but given your circumstance she wants to do the very best for you.'
'Everyone was very impressive,' added André, ' and she did her best to stop us panicking about what she had told us.'

'Although I'm afraid I did panic.'
'Of course you did, Dee. I know I would. She told me that although the difference in size between the twins is already obvious, what matters more is the build-up of amniotic fluid caused by the larger twin passing more urine that the smaller because taking in more blood. That can cause pain for you and sometimes rapid swelling. If either happens I need to know immediately, whatever the time of day or night. We might get you quickly to Bristol and get fluid drained off and then take a look again at the twins. That might be the time the doctors decide you will need ablation, the laser treatment that will stop the process by cutting off the offending blood vessels, for which you would probably have to go to St George's or King's and their specialised and quite brilliant units. But I think that Ruth is hoping the development of the twins will go a little more slowly, as you're really just a little early for laser surgery.'
'One thing she didn't mention was a termination of the pregnancy. I know that by now it would be too late to do it via medication.'
'No, it would not be too late if that is what you chose, but you would be obliged to take the tablets 24 hours apart in the Women's Unit rather than at home. That option is still there for you.'
'Should Ruth have mentioned it?'
'Ruth would never stand in the way of any woman seeking a termination but neither would she recommend it if she thought there every chance of a successful outcome, and in your case, she does.'
'It isn't something we have discussed, Kate,' said André, 'and for myself I am in favour of giving our twins a chance. If one or both should die as a result of trying our best for them, then I would prefer that to causing them to die now.'
'And so would I,' added Dee hurriedly, 'and thank you, darling, for saying that.'
'Now I must go home, but I mean it – at any time, day or night, if you need or even think you might need me, call immediately. One final word, and I imagine Ruth mentioned it, don't bother watching any American TTTS videos or look on their websites. Their situation is so very different to ours.'
'She did mention it,' said Dee. 'Thank you so much, Kate.'

André cooked some supper, mainly leftovers from the previous day's feast with the girls. Knowing Ro was due a little later he was anxious about how Dee might take the news but she had to know it. At the end of their meal, the phone rang and, as expected, it was Sharon. Dee told her the whole saga of the day and André left Dee to it and he washed the dishes and then set down in his study, picking up a volume of the ONDB he hadn't yet considered. The phone call went on and on and she could hear Dee becoming more cheerful as it went on. At the end Dee came into the study.
'You haven't told me about the threat, André.'
'You were going to find out about it when Ro comes. I only learned about it

yesterday from Kim and I wanted to get this morning over with. Ro probably knew about when she called last time and that is why she has offered to take you to the range, just in case you ever need to fire a gun.'

'Sharon has offered to come and stay with us until both of these dangers are past, with Kim joining us at least every weekend. She's happy doing the shopping and driving me in and out of Exeter and the hospital. More especially she thinks three or four of us, when Kim's here, will strengthen the security of the place. Kim's a soldier and a licensed firearms officer.'

'But Sharon's not, and will you be able to behave yourself with her here all the time,' said André. 'You know you're still a bit drawn to her.'

André smiled and was met with an impish grin.

'Maybe, maybe not, but as long as I have you in bed at night, I think I will survive as a heterosexual woman.'

André stood and put his arms around his wife.

'Oh my darling Dee. I love and adore you, more than ever if it were possible. We are going to get through all this. Trust me.'

They heard a vehicle arriving.

'I'll go,' said Dee.

She opened the door and there was Ro looking relaxed in her civvies.

'Come in Ro. Are you allowed a glass of wine?'

'I'm not on duty, so yes, please. Hi André, it's good to see you again.'

'And you, and that reminds me I ought to pay a visit to your husband for a check up, and from some of the forms we received in hospital, I see that Dee can do so at no cost.'

'Yes, and do you know I'm convinced some women stay more or less permanently pregnant so they can keep coming back to their favourite Swiss dentist because, if I say it myself he's still just as dishy as when I first met him and fell for him.'

'I believe André told you about our pregnancy news.'

'Yes, indeed. I have heard of TTTS before though most people haven't and I gather there's some amazing surgery possible in London.'

'At the moment it was obvious at once to the sonologist what was happening but the doctor says that it's too soon to be clear when it's going to be a major crisis that might require surgery, but it's good to discover it early.'

'You're bound to be in a state of shock today, but human beings are remarkably resilient and we quickly adapt and then just get on much as before.'

'So give us our second shock of the day,' said André.

'I'm sure it's probably less than you learned yesterday from the major because they've only given us the bare outline. He will have said something about the backstory...'

'She,' said Dee, 'the major is a very definite she.'

'But I thought this was the head of technology.'

'Ro, we shall have to send you on a gender awareness course. It is still a she, and if I was to use the word "outstanding" it wouldn't get anywhere near

to describing what she does.'
'When she's next here could you persuade her to come for a dental check up and in return take a look at Moritz's computer? No one in Exeter can make head nor tail of it.'
'She would enjoy that.'
'As long as she doesn't fall for the dentist.'
'That's unlikely, as you would realise if you were to meet her partner, Sharon.'
'Ah! I'm pleased to hear it.'
'But I'll ask her,' said André, and I'm she'll come and take a look.'
'Thank you. Where was I? Oh yes, an approach was made to a former IRA assassin in London who may have murdered up to a dozen touts and others in the troubles, to do one more, and that one is you, André. She refused and it has gone back to the Army Council. A former interrogator both in Belfast and London, and one knighted for service, is an ideal target to keep their identity alive. I and we know no more than that. Intel has not reached us, but it may have you, as to who and when, but it was thought sensible for Dee to learn how to handle a firearm. And one other thing, the Chief Constable would like to come to see you. She would come in casual dress, just in case anyone is watching.'
André looked at Dee. 'Would that be alright with you, darling?'
'Yes. I'm looking forward to learning how to shoot – I think. The thing is, Ro, André and I met one another when I was facing considerably more danger from Islamists whom I was betraying and I think André got quite turned on by it, so another chance to have the same effect would be most welcome.'
They all laughed.
'I have to be honest, Ro, and tell you that it's true exactly as Dee tells it. Courageous hardly describes it and I knew that nothing less than such a person could ever be my wife.'
'André, you must tell Ro the whole story though, that it was really the sight of me in my manager's uniform ready for work that finally convinced you to propose.'
They laughed again.
'Oh shit,' said Dee, suddenly very serious and her hand across her mouth. 'The leak which you've been thinking came from within the Service about your title and where we live, didn't originate there. It was all freely accessible in Ilkley.'
'Ilkley?' asked Ro.
'Dee was manager of *Betty's* there and the staff all knew about what we've chosen to do, and have been greatly amused and delighted by Dee acquiring her own title of "Lady". Anyone wanting to find out details of where we are would only need innocently to make enquiries over afternoon tea.'
'I could ask the local force to look in and find out if that has happened,' said Ro.
'No. I don't think so' said André. 'The local force there is particularly

useless as Dee and I both know, besides which it should be handled by the Service. We have to call London this evening and I'll mention this and it will be best if we hand it over to them. There a possibility that one of our friends is going to come to be with us for a while, and that the major, her partner, will come as often as she can.'

'You know,' said Ro, 'that we will support you all we can but I suspect that the best way of doing that will be out of uniform, looking as if we're just casual friends calling. And in the meantime Dee, when can I take you to the OK Coral to learn how to manage a gun?'

'Well, this week I'm very busy, except tomorrow, Wednesday, Thursday and Friday. So it's up to you.'

'I'll come and get you at about 10:00 on Wednesday morning.'

'What should I wear?'

'As long as you wear something, it doesn't matter, or else the men will lose concentration.'

'And should I bring our gun?'

'Definitely not, as only André is licensed to use it and I would have to arrest you! No, we've got plenty at the range. What sort is it, André?'

'Glock 17.'

'Well the chances are, Dee, you wouldn't be able to lift it up to fire it, so we may need to do something about that and get the Chief Constable to license you.'

Ro departed.

'Have you had threats made against you before?'

'Yes, and I've always survived and we shall, all four of us, survive this one.'

Chapter Twenty Five

André did not sleep especially well for there was a great deal on his mind, but next to him Dee did seem to be fast asleep. As before, he was in awe of her capacity to accept danger without batting an eyelid. It was an amazing quality possessed by very few even within the Service, on a par with the Deputy Director herself, Martha, though she had been trained and served in the army, Dee had been the manager of a tea and cake shop in a Yorkshire town though Dee always maintained that managing customers in *Betty's* is where she learned courage!

One of their great delights was showering together before breakfast, each soaping the other. There was always a great deal of laughter as they did so and, for André the same thought each morning, that how wonderful life its unsuspected variations.

For breakfast Dee prepared one of her Ilkley specials: eggs royale with smoked salmon.

'You do know,' he said, 'that this was why I married you.'

'Of course I do, and the shower was just an aperitif.'

André laughed and then said, 'My darling, even if we lose this pregnancy, and a huge number of women do – up to 31% of all pregnancies fail I read. I want us to go on trying, my darling, not because I want a replica of me but because there should many replicas of you, the most amazing woman in the world.'

'Ah, Sir André, you're only only saying that so you will have a reason for having your wicked way with me every day.'

'What? Are you intending to restrict me to just once a day. That's outrageous. I'm a late starter, you know.'

'Oh, I love you so much, André. And that is also why you need to talk me through the implications of what Ro came to tell us about and Kim told you.'

'Yes, I spent a few waking hours in the night reflecting on it.'

'Do you agree with Ro that I need to learn to fire a gun? It seems a bit extreme.'

André laughed.

'It is, though dealing with CIRA or the IRA as it was in my day requires something of an extreme response. I think you should do it. Whoever is coming is coming for me and I shall do everything within my powers to stop him or her from hurting either of us. I hope that it will not necessitate anyone being killed but if it's a matter of us or them, I will not hesitate to make sure it's them and do so quite without apology.'

'I would like to hear from you about the woman you kept out of prison, the one who has refused the operation.'

'Ha ha, I bet you would,' said André, smiling broadly. 'Well, what can I possibly say about her? When younger she was extremely violent and to the best of our knowledge was one of the principal executioners used by the IRA to punish traitors, what they called touts. It is believed she shot 12 such people in the back of their heads, including two women. These all took place in the Republic and when we arrested her a while back they didn't want her back and I can't blame them. She had no pity in her and I believe everyone in the movement was terrified of her. When the troubles ended she moved to London and kept a watching eye over the Irish community in the East End. Like a Minotaur she fed on the young – in her case young men in her bed each night, with what I think might be called a voracious sexual appetite. We arrested her and she was brought to the Conference Centre. As I said, the Irish didn't want her back and anything we could charge her with was not up to much. She told me she'd had more than enough and wanted to get right away, perhaps to New Zealand, but I imagine they wouldn't have wanted her either, so she's still living just off the Commercial Road in Stepney, but clearly more than happy to share her bed with women now. Most important however, is that she's not wanting a return to killing.'

'Did you like her, André?'

'Her hands were too deeply stained with blood to like her and she was my enemy, but I could cope with her without total revulsion, and I could see why she had no trouble getting takers for the night watch. And I hate to admit it of someone who once had done such terrible things but part of me did warm to her.'

'So, who might come?' asked Dee.

'That's the good news, for whoever it is won't have experience and almost certainly won't know the country as you do from your walking it since we've been here. That really does give us the upper hand because whoever it is will want to approach from the north, across the moor, not wishing to be seen by anyone in the village. That's why we shall win.'

Dee stood up, walked round the table and lifted André's face to her own and kissed him.

'I fancy another shower,' she said.

Brendan had a visitor. She didn't look especially old but she certainly looked bonny, but he knew better than to engage in any kind of banter or to flirt with her. She didn't smile and spoke only about practicalities of the matter in hand.

'Here's your passport and other papers relating to your new identity, including a driving licence. You're now flying out of Shannon to Birmingham.'

'Why's that?'

'You don't ask why, you just do it. You will collect a car at the airport with this booking slip and make sure they show you how to use the satnav. Drive down the M5 to the Michaelwood services and go inside for a pee but leave your boot unlocked. When you've been away from the car for two minutes return and open the boot where there will be a small bag. Lock the boot and go for some food if you need to. Continue South to this bed and breakfast just outside Tiverton. You're booked in for two nights to give you the chance orientate on the moor. You're a keen walker. Get to the house of the target on the Sunday. Your return flight is from Cardiff to Dublin. Just leave the car in the car park.'

'What's in the bag?'

'I was told you were bright, so work it out. Afterwards bury it on the moor. Is everything clear?'

Brendan nodded.

'No papers of your own, no mobile, nothing at all that can link you to here, including any clothing with a label however innocuous and the same goes for shoes, anything that says Irish Republic to those who might have cause to look. Finally, before you leave, post your funeral arrangement to this address. Remember you are going to avenge a bastard who interrogated our soldiers both in Belfast and London, for which the British establishment have had the temerity to give him an honour. Taking him out is punishment and warns the Brits that we can do what we want when we went.'

She picked up her coat, walked to the door and without a backward glance or word, left. He looked through the papers she had given him. He was to be Eric Dennison from Tipperary on a short walking holiday, a worker with Apple in Cork. Looking at the dates he saw that this was all set to happen on the following Sunday, flying out on Friday and returning on Monday.

The girl everyone expected him to marry sometime soon, including Mary herself, though as yet he hadn't proposed, came in from work at 6:30. She was a vet in a local practice. That they lived together would have been more than frowned on a generation earlier but now drew no attention. In Brendan's life the place and influence of the catholic church had diminished massively, mainly as a result of the many paedophile scandals that been exposed. A country of the superstitious beholden to every word of "Father" had now voted to allow divorce and abortion, and most young people regarded the Church as nothing more than a hobby for aunties and grannies, and nothing to do with them. Brendan knew the stories of an earlier age when priests gave their tacit support to the IRA and regarded their Christianity as engaged in a struggle with the evil forces of the Protestant North. It was very different now. No one gave a toss.

Mary had a shower and then came downstairs to where Brendan had prepared some food.

'Have you had a good day?' she asked with a smile as they sat together.
'Days off are always good, though I've not done as much I wanted to. Falling asleep on the sofa seemed a much better idea.'
'I had to put two dogs to sleep today. The dogs behaved well and much better than the owners, poor things. I also had to turn dentist and remove a tooth from a horse which was not at all straightforward.'
'I can imagine. Oh that reminds me, I shall be away at the weekend in England. It's a conference on a new technique for treating identical twins in the womb using laser. I've heard about it and seen it on YouTube but here's a chance to begin learning about it and hopefully be eventually able to use it here. I applied ages ago but it was full and then I had a call today offering me a place. I can fly from Shannon direct on Friday afternoon.'
'Oh Bren, that's fantastic. I shall miss you of course, but you must go. Perhaps I'll go and see my mum and dad on Sunday when I'm off.'

Dee's phone rang. It was Kim.
'Hello, my darling,' she said. 'You certainly thrive on excitement and danger, whether on the outside or on the inside. Sharon and I have been learning all about TTTS and I'm sure you and André have been doing the same. I've never heard of it before. Anyway I thought I'd let you know that your hunch about someone in Betty's innocently passing on the information as to your location, marriage and new title, is the most likely explanation as to how whoever it was found out. I'm told they're so proud of you that they have a framed photograph of you in the shop with the legend "Lady Dorothea Beeson – former manager".'
'O God help us. That's terrible.'
'I'm told it's a far from terrible photograph.'
'That's not what I meant.'
Kim laughed.
'Do tell your husband that as yet we know nothing more. And have you decided whether you could bear my beloved to come and be with you both, and myself being with you at the weekends?'
'We'd love it.'
'In which case she'll get in touch and make the arrangements. I'll come late on Friday.'
Dee made coffee for André and herself and interrupted him in his study, sitting down reporting her call from Kim.
Her phone range in the sitting room again, so she quickly kissed her husband and went to answer it. It was Sharon saying she could arrive at 11:50 on Friday at Exeter Central and asking if it might be possible to be met. After this she went out for a walk upon the moor which looked quite scary under a threatening sky, but she loved it.

Chapter Twenty Six

Dee had gone out to do some shopping in Newton Abbot, somewhere she hadn't been to before. By one of those odd coincidences that happen in life, she bumped into Sam, the sonologist who had scanned her in hospital who was there an unbelievably good looking young man.

'Hello, Dee,' said Sam. 'It's lovely to see you again. This is Bryan, my partner, who volunteered on his day off to come and do the shopping with me. And this in Lady Beeson,' she added for the benefit of Bryan who smiled and then took her hand.

'Hi Sam, hi Bryan. Let me tell you how brilliant in every way your partner is in her work.'

'Of that's not necessary. She tells me that herself.'

Sam kicked Bryan gently on the shin.

'Do you normally shop here?' said Sam.

'I've never been so I thought I'd give it a whirl. It's quieter than the supermarkets in Exeter.'

'Do you fancy a coffee?'

'Yes, that would be great.'

'Ok. Sadly boy wonder here has to go to the garage to collect a punctured tyre, but I'm in need of a drink. Let's go to *Indulgence.* It's the best.'

Bryan and Sam kissed, and he said bye to Dee before heading off and the two women walked down the road and into the shop offering delights for the palate in which Dee decided to indulge, Sam joining her.

'So how are you doing, now you know what you're dealing with?' asked Sam.

'To be honest, Sam, though I know what we were told by Ruth and yourself and I've been reading all about it, I'm not sure if I've really grasped what's happening inside here. I was perhaps a little surprised in retrospective, that Ruth never mentioned the possibility of termination, not that I'm wanting to do that.'

'She's not opposed, if that's what you're thinking, but I think she set her job as being about promoting life and all its possibilities. If she thought there was no other possibility for your pregnancy, she would would have said so without hesitation. That she didn't is positive and as I said, I have seen situations like like yours come to a very happy conclusion. There's no guarantee of course and you just have to take every day as it comes. I'm not at all religious so I can't blame God when things go wrong, but women have to bear what comes.'

'Are you hoping to have children?'

'Oh I should think so, and it it happens with Bryan, they'll be good looking boys.'

'He seems so very pleasant.'

'He's lovely and I think I'm lucky.'

At that moment he came into the coffee shop to join them, his hands covered in oil and flithy dirty.

'H'm, take back what I've just said. Look at the state of him. I'll take him home but I'll pay on the way out. See you again soon.'

Sharon had not had a good day at work. She had visited the Editor and said that a major crisis had arisen to do with a close friend's pregnancy which might necessitate working away for a while.

'How long is a while and don't ask me how long a piece of string is?'

'I cannot say. The identical twins inside are competing for blood from a single placenta and one is losing which may result in death. She wants a woman friend there with her. Her husband is a good man but at this moment she needs another woman.'

'Don't most people have to cope with this by themselves.'

'Can you run the newspaper by yourself?'

'Features Editor is a key job and you're doing it so very well considering you haven't a background in journalism. But you need to be in London and where instead will you be?'

'On Dartmoor.'

'And what is the internet like?'

'For historical reasons they have a particularly high speed link. That is not a problem and if you don't believe it we can put it to the test here and now.'

'No need. You're not asking for leave of absence?'

Sharon shook her head.

'My life is one long burden with maternity leave, but this is leave for someone else's maternity.'

'I'm not asking for leave of any kind and you surely know you can rely on me to get copy in on time. I will even zoom you every couple of days so you don't forget my face.'

'When are you off?'

'Friday.'

'I agree, though very reluctantly, if you promise that you will come straight away if there's a crisis of any sort here.'

Sharon thought a while.

'Just as long as you don't pretend, otherwise you may discover on my return that your testicles will require some finding.'

He laughed.

'Ye gods. I bet no one spoke to William Rees-Mogg, when he was editor, in such terms'

'You love it really.'

Sharon crossed the room and gave her boss a peck on the cheek, turned and left.

Kim had spent two hours chatting with the Deputy Director about clothes shops in Chelsea. Kim was a snazzy dresser at the best of times and always looked so good, and it was a relatively quiet day for MI5, apart from the daily round of checking up on 20,000 jihadists, so a good gossip about things that really mattered, in this case boots for winter, took precedence over everything else.

'One work-related matter before I drag myself home after a very hard day defending the country, have you any thoughts about my being at the home of André and Dee this weekend?'

'No uniform of course, but you must be armed and you must be ready to use your weapon. This is the CIRA and they won't hesitate to try and stop you and Sharon and Dee getting in the way of André with lethal force. You must get there first.'

'How easy is it to shoot?' asked Dee of her husband as they lay drinking their tea in bed together.

'Far too easy,' said André. 'In that way far too many have died. I have never fired a gun in anger and hope I never shall.'

'Sometimes it's necessary though. Sharon was probably a second away from death at the hands of her crazy former husband when her life was saved when a policewoman shot him dead.'

'But she didn't shoot in anger; she did what was necessary and appropriate in an officer of the law to prevent a terrible crime taking place.'

'And if I learn to shoot this morning with Ro and shoot to kill someone who might be about to kill you, would that be permissible?'

'That would be for the court to decide but I think the answer would be that it was.'

'Oh, I hadn't thought about the possibility of a court.'

'It would be the coroner's court not the County or High Court, and you would have the benefit of Service counsel. So, my darling, don't add that to the other worries and anxieties you have at present.'

'You're not going to be killed, André, and neither are our two children that I'm carrying, and trust me, I shall not hesitate to kill in your defence.'

André put his cup, and that of Dee, on the bedside table, and turned towards her.

'We're quite early and expecting no interruptions which won't be the case when the boys are born,' he said, taking gentle hold of her.

'Girls, but apart from that you're quite right, so what had you in mind, Sir

André?'
'Well, Lady Beeson ...'

Afterwards there was time for a shower and a rushed breakfast before Ro was due to come at 10:00. André saw her vehicle coming up the lane.
'That's odd, she has a passenger. Oh well, we'll no doubt find out out who soon enough.'
Dee opened the door and two women stood before her. Ro was wearing what Dee thought could be described as combat uniform; the other woman was not a great deal older than Ro but had about her an air of effortless superiority that you could immediately sense.
'Good morning,' said Dee.
'Dee, this is the Devon and Cornwall Chief Constable, Arleen Hill.'
Arleen gave Dee a beaming smile and took her hand.
'Congratulations on your news though as often happens it's not exactly plain sailing. Neither of my two pregnancies were but summon up your courage and I'm sure you'll get there.'
'Thank you, ma'am.'
'You can call me Arleen, unless that is you want me to call you "my lady".'
'Come in and meet my husband, André.'
'Thank you, and you take Dee, Sergeant. Try to make sure she doesn't accidentally shoot anyone important, say above the rank of Inspector. We can more easily replace the others.'
'I'll bear that in mind.'
Dee clambered into the vehicle.
'Is this ok what I'm wearing?'
'Definitely.'
Having turned back down the lane, Dee said to Ro, 'Your boss looks pretty young to have such an important job.'
'I suspect she works hard to maintain that impression, but she's 46 and was previously head of the Regional Crime Squad in Manchester, so she's very experienced, though perhaps the Scilly Isles, Cornwall and Devon are a little too tame for her. She'll be enjoying her determination to catch whoever might be coming to take André out, and if I know her she'll have plans to have so many armed bobbies out on the moor dressed as walkers, any Irishman who meets them will feel overwhelmed.'

André was immediately impressed with Arleen and the natural air of authority she manifested and he made some coffee for them both.
'I used to hear about you in Belfast,' she said.
'You're from Northern Ireland?'
'Yes, like you, that's where my career began though after you had left but your reputation lingered as the most unusual interrogator in that you were quite likely to get them chatting about all sorts of things, their families for instance or sport or where they went for the holidays each year, and yet turned

in better results than anyone else. It was quite a reputation.

'I came from Enniskillen and so knew all about the terrible Remembrance Day bomb though on the day I was away at Boarding School in England (hence my non-accent) and later my university in Bristol, but then I went into the Police Service of Northern Ireland on a rapid promotion and loved it.'

'Belfast was tough,' said André, 'even at the end of the troubles and I have a feeling that those working for us were even more hated by the Provos than the RUC, and we lost some guys though this was never made public. Some of them were extremely brave.'

'And now this. What do you make of it?'

'I have yet to speak to my former boss about it but I trust the intel completely from my knowledge of some of the principals. I think an attempt might be made soon. Plans and arrangements are best acted on at once before there is any chance for them to leak. You and I both know that.'

'I have people at Exeter and Bristol airports.'

'Well, that's good, but I very much doubt that is how they'll come in. The ferry at Holyhead followed by a hire car would be the best bet, or perhaps Manchester or Birmingham airport, somewhere not even slightly associated with the South West and then this person will almost certainly come across the moor.'

'You have much more experience in this than me, André, so I will be guided by you.'

'Not too much. Your mind is self-evidently attuned to the criminal mind much more than mine. Please don't overlook your own instincts, Arleen, for they have served you very well.'

'Thank you, but in the gangster-ridden world of Manchester, contract killings were usually straight forward and didn't usually involve crossing moorland.'

André's phone rang and he excused himself to answer it.

'Who? You're kidding. Well, if you're only a 100 metres away, come, and I'll make you a coffee.'

He laid his phone down.

'A visitor? I'll be in the way, so perhaps I should go into another room or outside for a walk.'

'Stay where you are, Arleen. When she arrives forgive me if I don't introduce you by your title. You'll understand why.'

There was a knock on the door and opening it, there before André was none other than Nancy Carmichael.

'Sir André.'

Hello, Nancy. Tell me, have you changed your mind and are come to kill me after all?'

'How did you guess? Can I come in?'

'Of course, sorry.'

Arleen stood up.

'You must be Lady Beeson, the lucky lady married to André.'

'Alas no. My name's Arleen and I'm just a friend.'
They both sat down and Nancy began to tell of her home and life in the East End of London.'
'You're a long way from home and November's not a good time for holidaying.'
'No, I came especially to see André and talk over some important business.'
'Where do you originate?'
'Cavan in the Republic.'
'Not far from where I come from – Enniskillen.'
'What's happened to your accent?'
'My parents wanted me educating away from the troubles and sent me to England.'
'Well, Arleen, let me tell you that your parents were very wise.'
'Very wealthy, more like.'
They laughed, as André arrived back in the room with coffee for Nancy and a top-up for Arleen and himself. Arleen already had a feeling that she was in for an interesting conversation.
'Nancy, let me explain that Arleen here is my mother-confessor, someone to whom I can speak freely about anything and everything. She knows what I know which is you were visited at home and invited to come and slit my throat (metaphorically speaking) and that you refused, about which may I say how pleased I am. And you know better than to ask how I know this.'
'André, don't insult me. Of course I know how you know – it was Julie. She doesn't know I know but I have a lot more experience than her of spy spotting' Anyway I wanted this to get back to you as soon as possible.'
'Nancy, my darling, how many young men have you been to bed with over the years? Hundreds I'm sure. So can I ask why you've turned lesbian?'
'I haven't really and to my mind it's nowhere near as good. But I found myself feeling safer with Julie around and she's a good person who's been though a lot I would say, though hasn't said a word about what it might have been.'
'Have you spoken to he about your past?'
'A little. Sometimes when I think of it I am so full of self-disgust and shame it might have been better if I too had died at my own hand.'
'The last time we met at RAF Northolt you were saying this and I would have given anything to have been a priest and absolve you, but I want you somehow to absolve yourself. It's done and you all knew it was a war and in war things happen.
'Yes. You kept me out of jail last time round, André, why?'
'Because when I look at you, Nancy, I see a beautiful little girl, corrupted by events, and now has recovered. I wasn't going to get the legal and prison system mess that up.'
Arleen interrupted.
'André's quite right. Prison protects the rest of us from those who yet may do us harm, but I've known many who've been made worse by being there. It

is reported that in the troubles you did terrible things but I suspect you were manipulated by others and if André thought what he did was right, I would back his judgement every time.'

'But what brings you to South Devon today, Nancy?' asked André.

'A CIRA tweet. Last night and I'm certain it was intended as a poke in my eye for turning down the job.' She took out her phone. 'There.'

"NC xg8 22/f ☐ x♀ CU."

'The world of twitter means little to me. Can you explain?'

'NC is me. Xg8 is chess notation and in effect means that the knight, you are to be taken out on the 22nd. There is a lesbian sign followed by an indication that either Julie or I will also be taken out, and finally a promise to see me. Once I'd read it I decided I had to come and warn you and to do this I had to meet Julie urgently, explain that I knew who she worked for, and begged her to find out where you were. This she did by a rather odd route, calling a tea shop in Yorkshire, and here I am.'

'Where is Julie now, because that's really important,' asked Arleen with urgency in her voice.

'She's in a hotel in Exeter.'

'Which one?'

'Premier Inn in the centre of town.'

'In Bonhay Rd?'

'Yes.'

'I think we need to pick her up, André. Do you agree?'

'Definitely. Can you get Ro and Dee to do so when they've finished?'

'No. Ro's in a marked car. I'll get someone else who'll need to be armed.'

She stood and left the room.

'Who is that lady, André?'

'She's Arleen Hill as she said, and when she's not here chatting me up, she also serves as Chief Constable for the Devon and Cornwall Police.'

'Jesus, Mary, Joseph!.

'Yes indeed, Nancy, and if you've been followed you'll need their help at least to avoid being treated as you yourself treated touts.'

Chapter Twenty Seven

The only interruption to the silence of the next twenty minutes was a brief phonecall for André in which he hardly said a word but which told him what he had already learned from Nancy, that a local agent of the Service working in the East End of London mentoring Irish groups has disappeared and that traffic was being monitored speaking of a fatwa on her (why ever had the Irish adopted a Moslem word like that? he wondered). Carmichael had also disappeared and was to share the same fate. André's only words: "Thank you. The goods have arrived." The last words from the other end: "Tech is on her way", presumably a reference to Kim.

Arleen looked at André.

'Anything?'

'Nothing we don't know.'

Seven or eight minutes later, they heard the sound of a car arriving outside, and Arleen went to the door and opened it.

'Good morning, ma'am,' said a male voice. 'I've completed the daring rescue of the poor victim from the Premier Inn, and here she is.'

'You are so brave Andy, I would not want to risk a raid on such a place single-handed. I shall recommend you for an award from Lenny Henry! And you are Julie. Welcome to Devon. I'm Arleen Hill, the Chief Constable, though I'm about to leave you. Inside you will meet two people you know well. You're not my responsibility, but I am allowed to say how well you've done.'

'Oh thank you, ma'am.'

'Tom, just give me a few minutes.'

'Of course, boss.'

Arleen led Julie inside.

'Hello Julie,' said André.

'Sir André!'

Arleen smiled.

'An impressive set up, your lot. Even in such circumstances you get the proper title.'

'Oh she knows the form, don't you sergeant?'

' Yes, sir.'

'Sergeant?' said Nancy. 'God Almighty, lots of former comrades will be turning in their graves.'

'It's the ones still alive that we need to worry about,' said André. 'Before you leave, Arleen, if need be can I rely on you to find a safe house for these two ladies?'

'I'll set it in motion. Now I must fly. I do hope Dee has managed not to kill too many of my people.'

'Oh well, you win a few and you lose a few.'

'True. Ro will be my eyes and ears.'

'Thanks Arleen.'

'Good luck, ladies,' said Arleen and departed.

'So, my friends, we have some talking to do once we've had some coffee and we shall be joined by my wife and possibly, if she's not been massacred in a gunfight, by Police Sergeant Rowena Lehmann.'

'Oh that Ro,' said Julie. 'Smashing.'

André rose to make some coffee.'

'This is like being in a family where you know no one but everybody else knows everyone.'

'You knew André though.'

'Yes, but in peculiar circumstances. I was a prisoner if you remember and he my interrogator. He had the power to lock me up for a very long time.'

They heard a vehicle arrive and moments later the door opened and in came the aforementioned Ro in combat uniform followed by the person Nancy at first assumed was perhaps another young plains clothes officer.

"Julie,' said Ro, 'God, it's simply ages since last I saw you. What on earth are you doing here?'

'I might ask the same of you. Last I heard you'd moved to Switzerland with a man described as the most dishy dentist under the sun.'

'I'm pleased to say he's still both. And we've added a bi-lingual beauty to the world called Lotte.'

'Congratulations.'

'But I'm being bad mannered. This ladies, is your hostess, Lady Dorothea Beeson, or Dee as she is known, the wife of Sir André who, I'm pleased to say is making coffee. Dee, this is Julie with whom André and I used to work but I'm afraid I don't know your name.'

These last words were addressed to Nancy who had stood up.

'I'm Nancy, and in a manner of speaking I also used to work with André, but thank you Dee for allowing us to use your home in this way. I'm afraid your title made me expect a much older lady in tweeds, but you are so young and beautiful.'

'She is, said Ro, ' but don't stand anywhere near when she fires a gun. Three times this morning on the range she hit the target being used by someone else.'

'That's most unfair.'

'No, it's not.'

'Oh, ok, it's not,' she said with a giggle. 'But I bet I can make better cakes than you.'

'What sort?' asked Nancy.

'A bad Victoria sponge is easy to make but I make a very good one, and I can do a pretty good chocolate torte.'

'You're right about a Victoria sponge. Even when I put them in together I find it almost impossible to get both layers to rise equally.'

'Do you use a fan oven?'

'No.'

'If you're still here after dinner, let's have a go together and I'll show you my secret.'

'I'd really like that.'

Nancy smiled at Dee and decided that if she really was a lesbian now, Dee would be exactly what she would long for, though for obvious reasons she probably wouldn't mention the fact.

Armed with nothing more lethal than coffee, they sat with André at the helm.

'There's someone on her way here called Kim and when she arrives she will take over. She's a major and rather clever. Until then you've got me.'

'And of course, added Ro, 'you're not clever.'

The three women laughed.

'It's over to you, Nancy.'

She looked a little surprised.

'This is very odd, finding myself in a gathering of those I have spent most of my life regarding as the enemy and briefing you against my own people. Or at least once they were my people. Before we get down to what may or may not happen this weekend, I want to say how overwhelmed I am by your warmth and consideration. You all know that as a late teenage girl I murdered those who betrayed the cause. That is so terrible an admission I can barely live with it. What is less known is that every one of those killings was done when I was heavily under the influence of drugs and alcohol and usually after the dreadful experience of a sexual frenzy with a number of men. That combination was useful for them because it meant that I did all the very nasty things to our own people, and had not the first idea of what I was doing. That doesn't excuse me, I know, but I want you all to know that. After the troubles I came to England I was flavour of the month south of the border. I regret to say that I acquired a reputation for sexual promiscuity on a huge scale.'

No one dared speak.

'Someone called Brendan came with an order from the CIRA Council to kill you, André and in effect, I told him to piss off. Julie and I spent the night together and I told her everything, knowing it would get back to 5. I knew who she worked for and she knew I knew who she worked for. Is that right?'

'Yes, of course, though I never told her I was a sergeant in the regular army.'

'No you didn't, though you never held anything else back.'

The others looked at one another with an slightly embarrassed gaze. 'But there has been someone else reporting back to the army council who must have known about the visit of Brendan and my refusal, and who had also become aware of our relationship, though we didn't attempt to hide it. Whether or not that person also knows Julie's full identity I can't say but Julie's pretty certain she knows who it is. The IRA before them and the CIRA now have always been suspicious of members who are gay because of the potential for blackmail, and because they regard it as morally repulsive. The tweet yesterday says that both André and either Julie or I are to be taken out. But, and this is important it doesn't suggest to me that it has altered their plans for what they reveal as this weekend even a little, which is why, though they might want to kill Julie or me, they haven't twigged that she belongs here with you. It is my belief that the assassination attempt will still be on as I have had no indication at all that my information given to Julie is known.'

'Julie, how convinced are you of the identity of whoever it is passing back to wherever information on Nancy and anything else,' asked André.

Nancy interrupted.

'You have to understand, André, as almost certainly you do, that what is functioning now is little more than a rump compared with what you knew in your time, and mine. They run on a shoestring with the occasional injection of American cash, which is why they set great score by occasional triumphs – a car bomb killing a policeman, a political assassination in Devon, though it can also go catastrophically wrong as when they killed Lyra McKee by accident in Derry.'

André nodded but continued to look at Julie.

'He's called Peter Fakenham. He works in a garage and drinks most nights in *The Wig and Pen*.'

'Nancy?'

'It's him alright and I'm pretty certain he does it for the cash they provide him with in return for any info on the community, though he's not Irish himself. I suspect its blackmail: drugs and small boys, a combination his wife and two children would not appreciate knowing about.'

'Ok. Look I suggest we have a break. I'm afraid you'll have to repeat most of this to Kim a bit later, and I overheard my beloved wife offering to run a Great British Bake Off session after lunch for Nancy, so I'll go and prepare us some sandwiches and we can have a rest.'

Both Nancy and Julie fell asleep where they sat which was hardly surprising given that they had been up all night, whilst Dee and André prepared sandwiches in the kitchen and she regaled him the story of the shooting range, which, she maintained, was nowhere near as bad as Ro had reported. Ro had gone outside to receive orders and to recover a measure of equilibrium after hearing Nancy's account of the troubles. She even wondered whether she should arrest her, but realised that technically she was still an Irish citizen and had already heard from André that the Irish government didn't want her back as it would open up things best left concealed. When she finally got through to the boss, Arleen confirmed that arresting her would be pointless. None of the victims had been British and at that time we, the British, were doing our best to kill as many of the IRA as we could – she simply did much of it for us.

'Nevertheless, Ro, keep a close eye on her,' said the Chief Constable. 'It's unlikely, but she could still be the assassin and calling everyone's bluff. We're moving her later to the safe house in Ivybridge, Please take tomorrow and Friday off, other than to fully arm up ready for Sunday, and, apart from when he pays a visit to the loo, you stay with André at all times. We are not going to lose him. Is that clear?'

'Perfectly, ma'am. By the way I haven't yet returned my firearm from my visit to the range.'

'How did Dee get on?'

'Don't ask.'

'That bad eh?'

'Far, far worse. In the range I was most at risk and I was standing behind her.'

'And I've authorised her to carry a weapon. Dear God in heaven, protect us!'

'Well, ma'am in *his* absence, I'll do *my* best.'

As she finished her call, she could see a car coming towards the cottage, obviously a hire car. She didn't know, but it was Kim and Sharon. Stepping outside the car, both for a moment seemed to Ro to be glamour models given the style and quality of their clothes. She was immediately envy of their taste – and income!

'Hello,' said Ro, advancing towards them. 'I'm Sergeant Rowena Lehman once of the Conference Centre, and normally known as Ro.'

Sharon ignored the out-stretched hand and took hold of her.

'I'm Sharon and so pleased to meet you, and this is my partner Kim.'

She too hugged Ro.

'Hi Ro. I'm looking forward to doing some work on your husband's computer and his replacing a lost filling.'

Ro laughed.

'So is he.'

'And how are things here?' asked Kim.

'Well, there's a lot to tell you, not least because in addition to André and Dee, inside you will find a member of your service Julie, whom perhaps you know.'

'Yes.'

'And with her Nancy Carmichael, the former IRA multi-assassin. You will need to hear her for yourself and see what you make of her account of how she killed at least 12 people in cold blood including two women as the result of a combination of drugs, booze and sexual frenzy. I'm unconvinced but you, I'm sure, will know more about her. Even now I think she is prepared to be traitorous to her own people and possibly to André to save her own bacon. Our plan is to move her when you've finished with her to a safe house until all this is over. I wouldn't trust her as far as I could pick her up and throw her.'

'Julie I will have to debrief,' said Kim, besides which I've a had thorough briefing by my boss about Julie, and she is quite an exceptional soldier and intelligence officer, though I want to hear it from her.'

'Of course, though if I may say so, you're not exactly dressed like an army major.'

'You may need to go on a gender awareness course, Ro,' said Sharon with a big smile.

'I'll manage, but I tell you what, Sharon, whilst Kim is doing her dentist business, might you be willing to go shopping with me in town?'

'Hey, that's not fair,' said Kim.

'Shut up, major,' said her partner, all three of them laughing.

Kim took out her phone and called André.

He could see who it was but simply said 'Yes.'

'It's Curry's in Exeter, Mr Beeson, about your new dishwasher. I'm sorry but we're not going to be able to deliver it tomorrow after all,' said Kim.

'That's not good enough. This is the second time you've cancelled this week.'

'André, I would like you to be present when I see both Julie Dickinson and Carmichael. I wasn't able to bring a polygraph though I'm working on one, so I thought you'd have to do as I am a total beginner.'

'Well it looks like I have no choice and Monday morning it will have to be, but I'm not impressed and won't be using you again. Goodbye.'

The others smiled sympathetically as he shook his head.

Moments later, Sharon, Ro and Kim came in, Julie standing at once as André waved a greeting. From the kitchen, voices could be heard discussing temperatures.

'As you were, sergeant,' said Kim to Julie. 'I need a cup of tea and something to eat before anything and then we can have a full debrief. Ok?'

'Yes, ma'am.'

'Andrè, can we use your study?'

'Be my guest.'

'It would be good to have you with us.'

'Well, alright, but don't forget I'm a has-been.'

'No one could ever accuse you of that, sir,' said Julie with a mischievous grin, 'judging from the state of your wife.'

'It might have been just good luck.'

Julie smiled again.

Kim joined Sharon in the kitchen, where Dee was in full flow discussing the merits of oven temperatures with the woman she knew was Nancy. Sharon had already made the tea for both of them and pointed out some sandwiches on a plate, of which Kim took two and left the kitchen. Ro was now sitting with André and Julie, describing Lotte's early morning performance trying every scheme possible to delay her mum leaving for work

Kim finished her sandwiches and drained her tea, looked at Julie and nodded.

'Ok?'

'Yes, ma'am.'

André had moved another chair into the study and the three of them went in and sat down. Julie looked about her and then pointed at the 60 volumes of the Oxford Dictionary of National Biography.

'Have you actually read all those?'

'It contains 60,000 biographies and is made up of 72 million words, so it might take me a while or never, especially if I'm to be murdered on Sunday, but it's a quite extraordinary work and an incredible testimony to the spirit of the British people.'

'We will make sure you are able to continue reading after Sunday, sir.'

'Thank you, Julie, and it's André to you.'

She smiled again and he realised that she had a quite disarming smile which he took to at once. She turned to Kim.

' I imagine I'm AWOL, ma'am.'

'Kim. This is the Service not drill on a very cold morning at Pirbright. O God I still have nightmares about my weeks there. But I imagine you're going to tell me why.'

'I think that when you hear about the tweet Nancy received, you will understand that I had to make a rapid decision to accompany her here because it concerned the timing of the attempt on the life of André.'

André reached into his pocket and with drew Nancy's phone and showed the tweet to Kim.

"NC xg8 21/f ☐ x♀☐ CU."

'Can you make sense of it?' asked Julie.

'Yes, it's telling Nancy that the knight, using chess notation, is to be killed on Saturday or Sunday, and because CIRA doesn't approve of homosexuality, probably you too, Julie, are to be killed.'

André had previously seen lots of evidence of the extraordinary mind possessed by Kim, and this merely confirmed it.

'Julie, I need to hear from you with total honesty and no embarrassment the nature of your relationship with Nancy, and before you answer, remember that I'm gay so feel free to say whatever you choose, but I need to know the exact nature of what is happening? Do you understand why?'

'Yes. I've been observing the Irish community for about six months with the legend of a mature student researching the impact of Islamic immigration on the East End. My computer, if anyone looked, contains nothing other than material drawn from a Ph.D thesis on the subject presented in the University of Central Lancashire in 2010. Each morning I add material. For the rest of the day I look and listen.

'I had been briefed about *The Wig and Pen* as the focus of dissident activity, and of Nancy Carmichael in particular and her history. I was nearing the end of my 6 month tour, and looking forward to two week's automatic leave with my sister in Edinburgh, when I sensed something was afoot. In the first place I was invited to share Nancy's bed which would have astonished everyone else as much as it did me. Most of my previous sexual experience had been at Pirbright with randy young squaddies and I wasn't wildly keen to want more (I bet that didn't happen to you, Kim).Then one evening I saw her leaving the pub with a man I had never seen before, and later she called me to come round and in bed told me there was a plot against André. She knew by now what I was doing there (for whatever else she is, she isn't stupid and knew that it was highly likely there would be someone from 5 in the vicinity and by singularly unsubtle hints I let her think she had worked out that it was me) and that I would report this. I stayed with her at all times as I waited for orders that never came. So here we are.'

'If it were possible, Julie, and you will realise that it may take some considerable time, would you at this juncture choose to live permanently with Nancy?' asked André.

'Of course not. What has happened in the past few weeks has been done for the Service to which I am totally wedded. I do not believe her justification for the murders she committed. She is vicious and manipulative, and lies when it suits her. It's her whole way of life and if she were to know what I am saying to you, I genuinely believe she would be more than capable of putting a bullet into the back of my head.'

'You have an impressive service record, so I couldn't understand why, after tours in which you revealed exemplary courage, you were sent to Stepney,' said Kim.

Julie looked to André.

'I think I can answer that, Kim.' said André, 'as she and I spent a lot of time together when she returned from Baghdad, where she was taken hostage even though ostensibly working as a worker for the World Health Organisation. The next four months were not the best years of your life, were they, Julie?'

'Thanks to you, André, and two doctors in particular, I have made a good recovery. I'm not there yet, but without you I might never have made it this far.'

'Julie was at Buckingham Palace when I got my K. Mine was nothing more than an honorary title for long service. The Queen award Julie the MC and believe you me, Kim, she earned it.'

'Julie, I feel truly humbled to be with you and why on earth have you not been promoted?'

'At my request it has been delayed until I'm fit for active serve once again. I'm to be commissioned as a captain.'

'And would you feel up to active service this weekend or would you prefer a safe house with Nancy, because frankly, though I'm meant to be in charge I would like your experience to take charge.'

'You're my commanding officer, ma'am. I'll do as I'm told.'

'Could you have a word with Sharon and teach her how to say those words to me every day.'

They laughed.

'Ok, I need to speak with Nancy. And perhaps André I can give you a break and let Ro come in here with me instead?

'Good idea.'

Chapter Twenty Eight

Nancy and Julie briefly touched hands as they swapped over and Ro followed Kim's nod to follow Nancy into the study.

'Ro will provide provide safe passage to a safe house where you will be able to stay until we get this all over with. Until then we can't even to begin to work out what might happen next, but this place is too small for everyone. You will be looked after there.'

'With Julie?'

'I would imagine so. I also need Ro here to witness what you tell me and as she heard you the first time round, to confirm that your story has remained constant. I'm sure you understand why. So please can you tell me everything from the moment you were approached in *The Wig and Pen*?'

She did so, and also acknowledged that she had been able to discern Julie's presence among them as an agent from 5 though on reflection she wondered whether Julie had actually been cleverer than she had at first thought and deliberately let her identity show a little.

Kim then went over her record in the troubles and she repeated the claim what she had done had happened by a combination of drunk, drugs and sex enabling the men to stay completely clear of involvement in the killings.

'There was clearly someone else in the community working undercover besides Julie, someone who reported back across the sea that you were in an openly lesbian relationship. Have you any idea who that might be?'

'Peter Fakenham. He drinks and talks too much and is a mercenary over whom they have a significant hold by virtue of his love for little boys and the drugs he handles.'

'Who did the tweet come from?'

'I've no idea, but I presume it's someone who knows the details, so it's likely to come from Ireland and someone sufficiently able to use twitter and work in code. Most members of CIRA are too thick to do that. Someone young, I imagine.'

'Names?'

'None, truly. I'm completely out of touch remember.'

'Like every other woman in the world, you're hugely fond of André?

'Course I am..'

'And what about Julie? How do you feel about her?'

Nancy look at Ro who showed nothing on her face.

'She is the nearest to love that I have known in my life and together I hope we have been able to save André's life.'

'I could ask you the question again about Julie in the hope that this time you might answer it.'

Nancy grinned.

'I'm practising to be a politician by answering the question I want you to ask rather than the one you have. I think she's a smashing person and I wish she was on my side rather than yours and I couldn't have done this without her.'

'Ok, you still haven't answered my question but what you have said is a sort of answer. And excuse my asking an extremely personal question, honestly do you prefer pussy to penis?'

Both Ro and Nancy immediately pulled faces of amazement.

'Jesus, Kim! You're not kidding that it's a personal question.'

'Your personal answer will go no further than the ears of Ro and myself.'

Nancy looked down for a few moments, then lifted her head and smiled.

'Looking at Sharon, Kim, I can understand why any woman might want to be gay – she's gorgeous, but when push comes to shove, and I think I might mean that literally, it's men that do it for me.'

'Men! Plural!' said Ro with a grin, 'I only have one and he's more than enough.'

'Quiet, sergeant,' said Kim barely able to contain herself. 'Thank you Nancy, and I very much hope you never again have to answer such a question.'

Their raucous laughter was evident through the door.

By the time they returned to the living room, Dee had gone to rest and Sharon was making the bed in her's and Kim's room. The good news was that the cake was ready for cutting and Julie offered. They all thought it so unbelievably good and congratulated André on having such a talented wife. When they all drank their tea, and Sharon had rejoined them, Kim said that it would appear they had two days before they needed to be ready for action.

'Whoever is coming, whether one or two, male or female, I'm pretty certain they will approach from the North, across the moor. This cottage is marked on the OS map, so they will know exactly where they are making for, but as any reader of *The Hound of the Baskerville* knows, there's more than a few grimpens out there which they will have to survive, so it's possible that they will be doing a couple of reccies in advance..'

Julie was nodding her head.

'Julie will be running this op and we are all, including André and me directly answerable to her. However as far as possible tomorrow and Friday must be as quiet here as possible with no activities of any sort. Julie and I will now go for a walk up the back of the cottage for a short reccie of our own. My very last order of the day is to make sure there is still cake left for when we return.'

'Yes, ma'am,' was said in chorus.

The made their up toward the moor and Kim see Julie was taking everything in and working out a likely route an attacker would have to take.

'Whoever and however many (though I suspect it will be one) come there is no real alternative down to the way we have come up. Because she once worked for the service I'm happy to use Ro, though generally I prefer not to use the police.'

'Ah. That tells me you were at Hereford. That came straight out of their service book.'

'Yes. Before going out to Iraq I did 6 months there, and I loved it. There were some good people who've become friends, even though there were one or two who should have been sectioned.'

'So did you go into Iraq alone?'

'M'm. I did one of those ridiculous drops from 42,000 ft, not opening the chute until you reach 2,000 ft, all the time thinking of just two things: the intended landing target and a hope that whoever prepared my chute had got it right, because at the moment you open it you are falling very fast indeed.'

'Jesus.'

'I then had to make my way into Baghdad in the Burqa I was dropped with and go to the World Health Organisation to work with them but I was there to rescue three women, supposedly western aid workers (one of whom was CIA, one from 6, and the other a British journalist) who were being held in the city. Three weeks in, I was kidnapped and assumed I was going to die, but bizarrely they took me to the same place where the other three were being held which gave me some hope. I was tortured and on three occasions raped. Ironically it was my sexual performance that enabled our escape. One night I saw the man who had raped me return with the clear intent of repeating the performance. It was late at night and no one else was around. He opened my cage door and led me out. As he was locking the others back in I broke his neck – it made a horrible noise, but thank you Hereford for showing me how (and watch out future boyfriends!). In moments the four of us found our way out and managed to take his landrover using keys I'd taken from his body. We also had two guns, and I started up and we left at great speed in the direction of Basra. About 50 or 60 miles later we were stopped by an American patrol. And that was that. It was unbelievably shitty and scary being there but at least I left one fewer bastard behind me.'

'And it has left you with what?'

'Psychological scars I suppose but crushed vertebrae as well. I've had surgery three times and it's much improved but I shan't be jumping from an aeroplane at that height again!'

'You know David Ramsay's retiring?'

'I had heard.'
'Would working with us in HQ be too boring for you?'
'It sounds perfect to me.'
'Come and do it, Julie. I would greatly enjoy working with you and so I think would everyone else.'
'That's kind of you to say so.'
'No, it's not, because it's true, but now this is your mission, and I meant what I said, I'll do whatever you tell me. In just about every way you're streets ahead of me)'
Julie took Kim's hand for a moment and squeezed it.'
'Thank you Kim, for your confidence.'
'Now, you have a choice. You can stay here and even come shopping with Sharon, Ro and me on Friday, or you can go to the safe house with Nancy for two nights, with two protection officers looking after you.'
'I need to go for a long walk onto the moor tomorrow by myself, which suggests it would be best to remain. If the protection officers are both men, Nancy will have plenty to fill her time with and for that matter, to fill anything else she chooses!'
Kim burst out laughing.
'Julie, that's outrageous.'
'I know, but just you wait and see. Nancy is totally amoral. It's not so much that she chooses what's wrong, than she just has no idea of the difference between right and wrong. I'm not saying that I haven't sometimes enjoyed her company, but I'm under no illusions about her. If she chose she could make love and then kill her lover as simply as that. Isn't there a spider alleged to do that?
'So what should we do with her when this is over, assuming it has a positive ending?'
'If André survives it will be down to her. To arrest her, even if we knew on what charges because Ireland don't want her back and there's no international arrest warrant out for her, all we can do is what André did and let her go. She talks romantically about New Zealand but my bet would be that she will choose Stepney, always provided Peter Fakenham disappears from the scene though, believe me, she's more than capable of bringing that about herself. She is amazingly strong.'
'I think you're right and I shall have to speak about it to Ro for her to pass on her Chief Constable. She's the one with jurisdiction here and only the police could arrest Nancy. Well here we are, back at the cottage. Are you still of the mind that whoever comes, will come this way?'
'Oh yes, and that makes my walk up there tomorrow particularly important. The forecast for both days is for rain so our assassin friend will want the shortest route.'
'I take it we want him or her alive, if possible.'
'That wholly depends on the firepower he brings with him. Armed to the teeth we may have no choice.'

'One final thing. The Deputy Director thinks you are an outstanding officer of the Service, not least because like her you seen active service in the sort of way she has and I, for example, have not. She has done two tours in Afghanistan and also gone underground in the Central African Republic. She will be the next Director, that's for certain, but she has her eyes on you to replace her. So no pressure, this weekend.'

'Oh, thanks Kim!'

Briefly in the dark of a November afternoon, two soldiers gave each other a supportive hug.

It was the parting of the ways once they had eaten the pizzas that Mr Domino had brought. To her initial dismay, Nancy went off with Ro, André disappeared into his study, whilst Julie and Sharon watched tv, and Kim and Dee talked about TTTS and the laser treatment that they might have to experience in London before too long.

'It's rather a daunting prospect, and I won't deny that we've talked about a termination, but we want to give it a go.'

'That's great, Dee, and quite brave. I've been learning all about it on the internet. And if it doesn't work out this time, would you try again?

'You bet. We haven't been married for long but we still adore each other and we both love sex.'

Kim grinned and catching sight of Sharon chatting with Julie, added. 'I know what you mean.'

One of Kim's latest inventions which she was testing before extending its use within the Service was a small ultra-encrypted mobile device that could also send documents and highly sensitive papers. When it made its alarm call just at after 2:00am Kim woke knowing it was a serious matter.

'Yes, Martha.' (It wasn't a guess because only she and Martha, the person in charge of all ops so far had the equipment).

'I'm sorry to call now, but my husband and I have been out for a rare night out, so stupidly I've only just found your text about putting Julie in charge of the op this weekend. Whatever you do, don't now take that from her as it would utterly destroy her confidence but you must bear in mind all she has been through and the psychiatrist says she's by no means completely through the trauma of her horrendous captivity, so please let her take the initiative but remain with her as much as possible, adopting a subordinate role. If something should occur and you think she's losing it in any way you must revert to the major-sergeant role.

'I think you should also keep a close eye on Carmichael even though she's under protection. Take her out for lunch and bring her back to André's for some of the time. The last thing we want is her brain festering, but that brings me to the main reason I've called. The police tonight picked up Peter Fakenham. They've still got him but passed over his mobile and computer to your two boys here. The computer will go back to the yard as it's full of illegal

porn and should put him away for a while, but they need you to make sense of
his mobile. I've therefore authorised it to be brought from Northolt to you at
Exeter airport and it'll be there shortly after 3:00 which means having to get
up now. The lads thinks it's important and related to Carmichael but they need
you to see it.'
  'Ok, Martha, thank you. I'll do so now. And was the evening out good?'
  'I have an amazing husband and tonight was just brilliant. Night, night,
major.'
  'Night night, colonel.'
  She slipped out of bed and began to dress. Sharon stirred.
  'What time is it?'
  'Two o'clock.'
  'What are you doing?'
  'Got to go the airport to collect something sent from Milbank.'
  'Ok, drive safely.'
  Kim smiled and thought that the response would have been no different if
she had announced she had to pop out to the moon.
  As she crept through the sitting room towards the door, she saw a light in in
André's study where Julie was sleeping, or not sleeping. She gently knocked
on the door and opened it to find Julie wide awake and reading.
  'Come on,' she said, 'we have a job to do.'
  Julie was up and dressed in a matter of moments. She looked at Kim.
  'Boots?'
  Kim shook her head and pointed to her own light footwear. Kim ran the car
down the track for a little while before starting the ignition.
  'You're up late, so either it's a good book or regularly not sleeping.'
  'It probably sounds silly but I noticed on André's shelves a copy of John
Buchan's *John Macnab*, which is all about getting across rough ground in
Scotland which is heavily guarded, in this instance to poach a stag, or a
salmon from the loch which they will return to their owners, and of course by
guile they manage it. I read John Buchan again and again, and know it well
but I was seeking out ideas for the weekend op.'
  'Perhaps we should form a MI5 Buchan club if and when we can get you
into Milbank, because I feel the same about him. What a writer and what a
man.'
  'Kim, where are we going?'
  'Oh sorry, we're going to the airport. There's a chopper on its was with a
present for me from the two men with whom I work closely and adore. They
haven't even told Martha what it contains and won't say even over the most
secure line. I do know however that the old buggers will be chuckling in their
beds at home at the thought of getting me out of bed at this time. I first
worked with them when we were at the Yard together.'
  'You were a police officer!'
  'It caused something of a fuss when the Service decided they needed me
more than the Yard, and I've been told there was something of a row at the

morning briefing in Downing St, which the then Director won.'
'And have you proved them right?'
'They still pay me if that's any guide.'
Julie smiled, and at that very moment something clicked in Kim's mind, what without a shadow of a doubt Lancashire Dee would have called "the penny dropping".
'I've got it, Julie.'
'Got what?'
'Everyone says you're outstanding but still traumatised by Iraq – but I know now that they're completely wrong. You're not traumatised, you're haunted by the feeling that you failed on your first ever serious solo mission. It was when you asked me "have you proved them right" that I saw it. How the fuck could a psychiatrist and my senior officers and yours, fail to see that? And that's why you asked for a lowly job and refused immediate promotion because you didn't think you were worthy of it. And who, my dearest Julie, has done this to you? Who has told you, and I regret to say that I can probably guess, that only if you are perfect are you worth anything?'
By now, Julie could no longer contain her tears.
'Actually, what you did in Iraq was fucking amazing. You succeeded in your mission completely. Anyone who briefed you that it would be a matter of straight in and out should be lined up and shot. I am in awe of you and, though please don't tell Sharon, but I've just watched you get dressed and believe me, you are stunning.'
Julie laughed through her tears.
'Should a major be saying that to a NCO?'
They had reached the entrance to the airport and Kim made her way to the arrivals area.
'Come on, Julie,' said Kim, as she clambered out. They walked towards a door when they were stopped by a police office.'
'I'm sorry, ladies but you can't park there, so please move it immediately.'
Kim and Julie stopped, looked at one another and smiled.
'Thank you officer,' said Julie. 'We'll remember in future.'
She and Kim turned towards the doors again.
'The future is now. I shall arrange for the car to be towed away.'
'Ok,' added Julie, but before you do so you might just like to see what I have in my bag.' She reached inside and produced a metal badge of some sort which handed to the young, cold bobby.'
'I beg your pardon, ma'am and yours ma'am. Can I be of use to you?'
'I'm being sent by helicopter something urgent from London. Perhaps you can use your radio to find how I can collect it and from where with the absolute minimum of contact?' asked Kim.
'Yes, ma'am,' said the policeman amazed by his first ever contact with the Security Services. In a short while he was told to lead the women though a door labelled 29, to the left of Arrivals. It took them outside onto the concourse where there was an airport vehicle waiting for then with a tall

flashing amber light.

'I'm informed it will be landing is five minutes' time,' said the policeman who by now had decided he wanted to join MI5, not least because it seemed much more exciting than night patrol at Exeter Airport and these were very attractive women.

They heard the helicopter approaching and landing about 200 metres away, and at once the driver set out. The great machine was clearly not intent on staying as its blades continued to turn as they drew near. Kim leapt out and approached the door at the side which opened and a small parcel was handed to her. The crew knew her well so didn't need to check her identity, and by the time the airport vehicle had reached the terminal building the helicopter had already taken off, and on its way back to Northolt. Instead of returning to the car, Kim invited the policeman to join them in the terminal building for a cup of coffee and something to eat.

'I'd love to but I'm on duty.'

'I'm not suggesting gin and tonic. Sergeant, deal with him.'

'Do as you're told, constable and we'll tell anyone who asks that we needed you.'

'Thank you, I'd love that.'

They found one food and drink area open, and Kim sent her two subordinates off with the instruction that they were not to return without something breakfast-like. This enabled her to open the packet and consider its contents.

The breakfast wasn't bad, all things considered, and the policeman took great heart from learning that Kim had once been a police constable too. Somehow neither of the women could see him as Service material though generously did not disillusion him.

'Am I allowed to know the content of the package, Kim,' said Julie as they set off.

'I think you need to, as you're running the show. Anyway you get a mention.'

'Oh!.'

'Though mainly it concerns your friend Nancy. Here,' and she passed the phone and accompanying note. 'Turn your light on.'

'I take it this was sent to Ireland.'

'Yes, but not via WhatsApp which was unbelievably stupid.'

'Kim, can you break into WhatsApp?'

'What a suggestion, Julie. I'm profoundly shocked.'

'Yes, but can you?'

'I'm glad it's not raining. Driving in the dark when it's raining is not pleasant.'

Julie laughed.

'"Nancy and her latest love interest – the woman I mentioned – has suddenly left and I followed them to Waterloo and onto the Exeter train." But that just indicates that he followed us.'

'Come on Julie, what more?'

Julie was thinking hard and fast.

'I think it means that his presence in Stepney was not about keeping an eye on the Irish community, but keeping an eye on Nancy, and he also didn't appear to clock my identity.'

'Full marks so far, but go on.'

'It means that the target is not André though CIRA want us to think he is but would know how well-defended he would be, but Nancy. André is the decoy.'

'Well, that's the same conclusion that I have come to, and it suggests we may be dealing with two would-be assassins, though how the real one would know Nancy was in the safe house with two armed police to look after her, I don't know.'

'So what do we do now?'

'Sleep is paramount and then tomorrow we must bring Ro into the equation, even though she's technically off-duty and ask her to take us to talk to Nancy, and I think it ought to be both of us, don't you? And after that, Julie, you and I have a conversation to complete.'

'I was hoping you might have forgotten about that.'

'Of all the things we are down here to do, that is the most important.'

Chapter Twenty Nine

If Brendan had been hoping for a quiet day before heading over to England on the Friday he was to be sorely disappointed. From the moment of his first appearance in the department he never seemed to stop even for a cup of coffee. There were days (and nights) like this, he knew, but why today? Almost every woman coming in seemed to require forceps, two needed c-sections and there was an emergency haemorrhage, together with a clinic in the afternoon. The only advantage to this was that it gave little time to think about the days ahead and to face the unease inside himself, not least about having to have produced his funeral arrangements. The more he reflected on it, the more he wondered if he had, in a moment of quasi-adolescent idiocy undertaken something he did not want to do, but feared the consequence of failing to fulfil what he had freely accepted, a contract with CIRA, and for which he had already visited the Carmichael woman in London. The movement was extremely unforgiving to those letting them down, saw them indeed almost as akin to the touts once punished by none other than the Carmichael woman herself, or at least that was the story. Once you became part of the set up there was no way out. You knew too much and in fact any knowledge, however small, was too much for anyone to leave other than as a martyr or .... He didn't like to consider the alternative. And what would happen to Mary, whom he adored? Oh God it was turning into a dreadful mess and all of his own making. And all he had done was to express an interest in a pub, making conversation really, not an interest he wished to go further..

'Doctor,' said a voice behind him. 'Sorry to interrupt your thoughts but I can't find anyone else from the team. It's episiotomy time, I'm afraid.'

Brendan smiled. It wouldn't be the first time and he hoped it wouldn't be the last time, but at least he was confident about what he had to do.

For Sharon, Thursday was to be a busy day if she was going to keep her demanding editor satisfied. A lot of copy had come in which need sifting and selecting, together with no end of photographs which, of course, took up a great deal of space in the memory so before she discarded them she had to be clear about the choices she made. She had decided to focus on TTTS and on the previous day had sent off one of her deputies to Kings College Hospital in Denmark Hill to do an interview with one of the specialist consultants. Initially his secretary had blocked the possibility but apparently when she had told her boss, he insisted she get back in touch. When they met, Sharon's colleague was convinced that the doctor adored publicity! Well why not? thought Sharon. What he was doing was by any standards amazing and with luck Dee would be able to avail herself of those skills before too long and save her babies.

Kim and Julie, separately, slept late – for them, and didn't emerge until after nine o'clock. Dee prepared them some breakfast and then, with André, joined them at the table as they ate.

'I heard you leave, but what time did you get back?' asked André.

'About four, I suppose. I had to collect something that had come from the Conference Centre by helicopter,' answered Kim.

'I have a feeling that it was twice that you darling, were brought *to* the Conference Centre in the middle of the night for interrogation by me,' said André to Dee.

'It is, and in the end we decided to get married so that for any further interrogations I would be on hand.'

'Are you serious?' asked Julie. 'Why did you have to be interrogated?'

'It was thought I might be a Jihadist.'

'Ah, of course, the beard, It's obvious when you say it.'

They all laughed.

'I need to tell you about our airport visitation', began Kim. 'We knew there was someone in the East End keeping a watch on what we thought was the whole Irish community, and both Nancy and Bright Eyes here, identified him. What has only just emerged, and it emerged last night when the police collected him and handed his phone over to us, was that he wasn't there to watch the whole lot but just one person – Nancy Carmichael.

'For some reason they want her away from London and you were the obvious bait she might bite on, living in Devon. So they sent someone over to ask her to pay a visit to Devon and kill you. She refused but when he had received a text threatening – and Julie as her supposed girl-friend – they came here to warn you and escape London. This info was the last message he sent to Ireland. The Police may get more out of him but I doubt that there is more. Julie, you take over.'

'Nancy never indicated to me her intention other than to come and see you and afford us a sort of holiday. The impression I had was that she holds you in great regard as we saw when we arrived. She was keen to pass on the warning that she thinks an attempt is to be made on you this weekend, which she read on the tweet she received.

'I think it's fair to say that both the boss and I are of the same mind that you, André, are a decoy. It's quite possible that our attention will be drawn away from Nancy by protecting you, whereas someone is intent on killing

Nancy.'

'Why?' asked Dee.

'IRA justice, I would guess. Revenge we might call it,' said André, as both Kim and Julie nodded their heads. 'A son or daughter, or even a grandchild wanting an eye for an eye. The Irish government are not interested in her, and I can't blame them but in twelve families there will inevitably be one or two who seek that recrimination.'

'So what are you going to do?' asked Dee.

'First, I must inform the police in the person of Ro, on her day off, but the Chief Constable needs to know and Nancy may have to be moved. Then we must see her and talk to her. Martha said to take her out to lunch and make a fuss of her but that's not exactly safe and we'd have to have the protection officers with us too.'

'Do you think anything will happen here?' asked Dee.

'The point of a decoy is to divert attention,' said Julie, 'so I think it quite likely that we shall intercept someone heading this way on the moor who doesn't even know he or she is a decoy. It's almost impossible to approach the cottage from up there except other than in the ordinary way. Stopping someone will or should be straightforward.'

'Thanks Julie. Now I must call Ro because the police need to know this development so that they can be ready for it.'

Julie took out her phone, left the table and went out the front door.

'Have you any idea when the attempt to kill Nancy will take place, Julie.'

'I think Kim and I assume it will coincide with the use of the decoy, or else why use it?'

It was a while before Kim returned.

'Ro thought it was too good to be true to think she would actually get a day off, so she wasn't surprised. Anyway she's making an immediate Red call to the Chief Constable who will no doubt soon be in touch. It's she who will decide where Nancy will go next, though I did tell Ro that it's not impossible that there might be observers or even informers wherever they move her.'

André's phone rang and it was indeed Arleen.

'André, I probably need to talk to Kim, who I believe is in charge, but I want you to know how relieved I am to know that you might not be the target after all though I think we should still maintain the guard in case there is bluffing going on.'

'I'm hoping that it isn't a bluff, but I am in extremely capable hands, but look I'll hand you over to Julie who is managing the details of the operation. Her last op was singlehanded in Iraq and she emerged with the MC, so Kim has asked her to take overall responsibility as her last op was in a cake shop in Yorkshire.'

'Gee, thanks,' said Kim, laughing

'I'm impressed,' ignoring André. 'You do seem to find some considerably able young women.'

'These two are pretty classy, and I don't suppose you need to know but in addition to the Service, Julie remains a captain in the army, and actually spent 6 months with the guys in Hereford.'

Julie grabbed the phone.

'Ma'am, hello, are you able to spare a moment while I kill Sir André for embarrassing me in this way and save us all a lot effort this weekend?'

'Never be embarrassed to recognise your achievements, Julie, and please call me Arleen. So now what?'

'Moving Nancy is the obvious thing to do but if someone knows where she is now and I think we can assume they do, that will be exactly the same when she's in a new location, so Kim and I can't see much point in that. André being a decoy, we think that the potential assassin will want to strike at the same time as we are expecting a non-killer to come here, that is Saturday or Sunday.'

'The forecast for Sunday is not good.'

'Which is why I would choose it. Moving on the moor with low cloud means no helicopters. We need you to let your protection force know we are coming and that we wish to take the three of them to the Sportsman's Inn for lunch. No visible firearms of course.'

'That's not normal practice.'

'None of this normal practice, Arleen, and it was suggested by the Deputy Director of the Service herself, as a way reducing any tension within Nancy.'

'Make sure I get the bill then, but I insist you ensure the protection officers know that this is unlikely to be common practice in future, or the blasted Crime Commissioner will make my life hell.'

'I get the message, ma'am.'

'Thank you, captain and keep me in the loop, as they say.'

'Of course.'

She handed the phone back to André.

'Ro will be coming to take us to see Nancy. If you prefer it, Kim or I can stay here for added security.'

'The three of us will be perfectly ok. I think it best that the two of you visit Nancy.'

Shortly before they left for Ivybridge, Julie's phone called out for attention from André's study. She ran in.

'Sorry, André. I can't think who it might be. Hello? Yes, indeed, good morning ma'am.'

André rose, closed the door and left the study and Julie in private.

'You know André quite well of course.'

'I do indeed. He helped me a great deal on my return though if I may say so, ma'am, and she's not able to to hear me say this, there is another officer of the Service present who is possessed of quite remarkable insight and psychological skills.'

'That will be Kim. O God, is there nothing she can't do? I swear she's after my job and if I didn't need her and love her quite so much I would find some pretext for getting rid of her to Belize. But seriously I'm glad you're working together so well, but she tells me she's asked you to take on strategic oversight. Are you happy with that?'

'Yes, ma'am.'

'There's a slight problem with that, Julie. I know that your NCO friends in the Special Services run ops completely, but for complex political reasons I won't bother you with, the Home Office insists that they must be officer led and even then not by a subordinate. I've spoken to Rob about this and also mentioned it to Kim who won't have said anything to you about it, but we are promoting you as from now to acting major.'

'Jesus!'

'No, he was a colonel.'

They both laughed.

'On your return it will be back to captain.'

'Of course ma'am.'

'One other thing, Julie and please don't take this amiss. This is on the basis of Kim's recommendation, and if at any moment you have a sense that you need to pull back, don't hesitate for a moment to tell Kim to take over. For the next three or four days you are of equal rank. The Service thinks highly of you, so do yourself proud, major.'

'Thank you, colonel.'

Emerging into the sitting room her hands were shaking. Kim was sitting at the table with Sharon helping her with something technological but at Julie's approach, she turned her head and smiled.

'Congratulations.'

The others looked puzzled, but neither Kim nor Julie said anything. They all heard an approaching vehicle and Dee stood to look through the window.

'It's Kate,' she said. 'That's great,' as he went to the door.

'The midwife,' said André.

'Oh my God, there's a hundred here today, but that means someone can make me a cup of tea: strong, white, no sugar.'

The newly appointed major set about the important mission single-handed.

'Anyone else fancy one?' she asked.

Every hand was raised.

'How's the newspaper business going, Sharon?' asked André.

'This is the way to do it, not with the constant interruptions of Pennington Street, and my people seem to be more adventurous, more imaginative than when I'm with them, as if my presences crushes them. They're coming up with some good ideas which I imagine they talk through before they let me see them. It's giving me a great deal of food for thought.'

Julie took two cups of tea upstairs and found a half-dressed Dee lying on the bed with Kate leaning over listening to her tummy with a Pinard Horn.

Julie put the teas down and returned downstairs.

'I'd rather do what we do,' she said to no one in particular.

Sharon, Kim and André laughed.

'When Ro gets here, we have to make a detour via the Armoury in Exeter to equip you, Julie.'

'Ok. I only hope I can manage better than Dee apparently did.'

'Julie, I think that even if you were to be blindfolded, turned around two times and then fire, you would be much more likely to hit the target than Dee was,' said André.

'That's why you'll have Ro here with you at the weekend. It's a Conference Centre group here and the away team will do the safe house,' said Julie.

André smiled and nodded almost imperceptibly at Kim, who returned the smile.

Kate and Dee came downstairs into the room.

'Everything ok?' asked André.

'The donor baby's heartbeat could do with being a little stronger so I will get a message through to Ruth who will probably want to see you on Monday – she's not in tomorrow – in the meantime rest as much as possible and try to avoid excitement if you can.'

The others looked at one another.

André rose and accompanied Kate to her car.

'Is there anything you're not saying, Kate, that you might say to Ruth, for example?'

'We speak about viability at the earlier stages of the pregnancy. It is at best an estimation, even a guess, but of course is based on considerable experience. Previously the viability of Dee's pregnancy was agreed as 40%. I shall report to Ruth that in my opinion we are down to no more that 15-20%.'

'Meaning that you think a miscarriage is 80% likely.'

'I don't have any reason whatsoever that even if that happens, and over 30% of all pregnancies miscarry, that Dee will have problems next time round conceiving and coming to full term. You have been singularly unlucky this time.'

And what I should I be looking for if she does miscarry?'

'Nothing. If it happens it will be Dee who will be aware of cramping and pain in the lower abdomen, added to which will be some vaginal bleeding. Either call me or the Unit. They will want to do a scan to confirm but she should be able to come home straight away.'

'How much of this have you said to Dee?'

'All of it. I think she's been expecting it. You know, Sir André, Lady Beeson is an extraordinary woman, and I can't believe she used to work in a cake shop.'

'Kate, you don't know the half.'

They could hear a vehicle approaching up the lane.

'The police!' said Kate. 'I knew they'd catch up with me eventually.'

'I hope she's coming to give everyone a parking ticket. I'm going to install a parking ticket machine here from which visitors have to obtain a ticket to be placed on their windscreens,' said André.

Kate departed as Ro climbed down from her vehicle.

'I'll have you all know that this is my day off,' said Ro as she entered the room where everyone was sitting.

'Do you want a cup of tea,' asked Julie.

'That would be lovely.'

'I'm sorry, Ro, to have to call upon you today, and I hope Moritz and Lotte will forgive me for doing so.'

'You may find out when he looks into your mouth tomorrow.'

'Ah yes, I hadn't thought about that. But we need to get to Nancy, as I'm sure the Chief told you. Did she tell you why?'

'To take her out to lunch, she said, though she also said that you think she may be the prime target, not André.'

Julie re-emerged from the kitchen with tea for Ro.

'Yesterday,' Julie began, handing over the cup, 'we were working on the assumption that André was the decoy and to a degree I still think that, but I'm less sure now. There are two other possibilities to consider. The first is that it is Nancy who who is the decoy, that we have been led, cleverly perhaps, into switching our resources to her and leaving André less protected, making it easier for a potential killer. The second is that the aim is to kill both, and for different reasons. André, because of his work in Belfast and the award of an honour by the British establishment, Nancy because she murdered twelve members of the IRA in cold blood, even though she offered us an excuse of being drunk and stuffed with drugs and sex, which I for one don't buy.'

'In my conversations with her at the Conference Centre,' said André, we didn't talk about Ireland at all other than indirectly as it affected the matter in hand which was all to do with detecting the presence of a mole in the Service, and though there is a likeable side to Nancy with which she endeavours and clearly succeeds to manipulate others, it would be wrong to lose sight of a core of steel. Having to leave Ireland at the end of the troubles was, I suspect, pretty difficult for her though necessary to avoid reprisals for what she had done. I agree with Julie, her story was, if I may say so, pure baloney.'

'Can I make a suggestion?' asked Dee who up to this moment had not said a word since Kate's departure.

'Of course,' said Kim with a darting glance at Julie who nodded.

'I am always worried about someone who doesn't know how to make a Victoria Sponge Cake when she says she does. I decided there and then that anything and everything she said should be taken with a pinch of salt, something you mustn't add to the said Victoria Sponge. So, it seems to me, and I apologise Kim if you won't get your pub lunch, that the best two people to speak with her today, are Julie and André, both of whom I think will be better at spotting what I would call the Victoria Sponge moments when she is plainly deceiving and which the rest of us might not notice. She and Julie have been intimate, André is probably still the best "conversationalist" in the business.'

Kim and Julie once again looked at one another and a slight smile on Kim's lips indicated her approval.

'André?' asked Julie.

'You, Julie and Ro, don't know my wife as yet. Sharon and Kim will tell you that she is shrewd and wise beyond her years. I could not possibly and indeed never disagree with her.'

'Thank you, Dee. That helps clarify a great deal,' said Julie.

'Another clarification is necessary,' added Kim. 'You all know that I have handed over the running of this op to Julie with the consent of the Deputy Director. In turn Julie has been promoted to acting-major, which is pretty impressive, from sergeant to major in just a few days. By next Tuesday she will Director.'

They laughed and clapped.

'Thanks, but we've all got to prove that the lot of us are up to it, or I shall slip down a snake very quickly indeed. So, Ro, are you ready?'

'To the armoury first and on to the safe house?'

'Yes.'

'The Chief has already authorised such equipment as you may require.'

'André, are you ready?

'Being an old man, I shall be better prepared if I attend to nature first,' and he could be heard running up the stairs.'

'Old man, my foot,' said Sharon.

'Oh I can testify to that,' said Dee with a wicked grin. 'And from what my midwife has just told me, I shall need my wonderful husband to be soon performing again. She's said that the viability of my pregnancy has fallen to no more than 20%, making a miscarriage likely.'

It was Sharon who was first to reach Dee and took and held her showering her with kisses and noises of comfort. The others were all standing close by, touching and offering what became a group hug. Returning to the room, André realised that Dee must have told the others, and as they were all women he knew they would respond instinctively. Seeing him, they all pulled back and allowed him access to his wife whom he kissed and cuddled.

'I'm so sorry, André, Dee said. 'If this happens, you know it will mean even more sex.'

'But I am such an old man,' he complained.

'It's never stopped you before.'

'Sh, don't say that in front of all these ladies or they'll be shocked.'

"These ladies" feigned shock which led to laughter.

Andre looked up at Julie.

'I ought probably to stay, Julie.'

Before she could reply Dee burst in.

'No. It's important you go. If it happens it's only a relatively early miscarriage and women survive them all the time by themselves, whereas I will have my lovely Sharon and Kim here with me and a choice of cars. No, you have an important job to do which might save lives including your own. These little things inside me were clearly never meant to make it. I'm not the first and won't be the last to experience this, my darling André.'

'How on earth did you manage to find that amazing wife of yours, André? asked Ro, as she drove down the lane into town, seated next to Major Julie.

'She was twice arrested for being in league with Jihadists in Yorkshire and brought to the Conference Centre for interrogation in the form of a chat with me. Over the years I've had such conversations with a lot of people, some of them seriously unpleasant, but on both occasions she treated it as a sort of works' outing and was determined to enjoy every moment of. Her presence was utterly ridiculous and I can't imagine what anti-terrorist people thought they were doing, but I fell in love with her straight away, not least because she gave as good as she got but always with good humour. I then found reason to see her in Ilkley where she exhibited bravery the like of which amazed me. Then I saw her in her manager's uniform and almost died. She came to run the Conference Centre and I invited her to come and share my house, and that was when it happened, and she said Yes.'

'God, I'm almost in tears,' said Julie.

'Me too,' added Ro.

'What a wonderful story. I hope you don't repeat it today with Nancy,' said Julie.

'What you see with Dee is what you get. Almost the total opposite is true with Nancy, which means we shall have to work especially hard,' replied André.

'Do you want me outside in the vehicle or can I come in and chat with the Protection guys?' asked Ro.

'You can join us for lunch and I've booked a table for six anyway, but we must have full eyeball on everyone in the place.'

They were now in Exeter and Ro drove into the back of what looked like a disused cinema, which is what it had once been. André remained in the car. He had a great deal think about since Kate's visit and of he hadn't had the chance to be alone with Dee. He also knew that armouries are noisy places and as he got older he liked liked noise less and less, and indeed since his wedding had not played nor wished to attend any Wagner or large orchestral concerts. In life what he most adored was sitting quietly alone with Dee doing nothing, but doing it well.

Julie chose a Glock 17 and an assault rifle, one that she had used with Special Services to such effect that when they had a shooting competition she won it hands down. They were impressed but she forgot to tell them that she herself was amazed. She had loved her time in Hereford, not least because not a single soldier ever tried it on with her. If she had any, that was where she learned the meaning of self-discipline, and realised that having acquired it, members of the SAS were much more likely to survive in hostile conditions, and perhaps it was that got her though the Iraq experience. They had also taught her, inter alia, how to kill with her bare hands, and that had got her out of the Iraq experience. On her return she had even considered applying to move to Hereford full-time and she thought they would have her. That was when her period of self-doubt had begun.

She tested both weapons on the range and made an adjustment to the scope on the rifle. When she was ready she collected carrying equipment and at once put on the out of the waistband holster which even with the firearm in was quite invisible to the eye when work with a long pullover or light jacket. Ro marvelled at the ease with which Julie operated, and as they made their way back to the car commented on what she had just seen.

'You're totally at ease with that stuff, Julie.'

'Hereford taught me so much.'

'Did you ever think of transferring?'

'I've thought of it but I genuinely believe they need men more than anything, but the skills I learned I use on any op.'

'I hate to say it, but you're a better shot than Dee. When they heard I was bringing someone in, quite a few people expecting the return of Dee offered their immediate resignation!'

'Poor Dee. On the other hand I couldn't make a Victoria Sponge like hers.'

Ro laughed as she opened the door and explained to André why. With considerable pride he also laughed.

Chapter Thirty

Upstairs there was a Dee sandwich on the bed, with lesbians on either side. They snuggled up to one another, not least because outside it was a raw November day. They had had a cry together but ironically was Dee who settled Kim and Sharon with comforting words, until Sharon stopped her.

'Dee, we're meant to be comforting you, not the other way round.'

'And I'm loving every moment of being so close to you, but I wonder wonder whether you were shedding tears not just for me, but for you too. I'm sad that it's apparently 80-85% certain that I shall miscarry, but there'll be another opportunity before too long, all being well, perhaps even by this time next year, but how does it feel to be you two? You're both in your forties and although women do conceive and give birth at that age, and increasingly so, it struck me that using my own possible loss it had put you both in touch with your own loss of babies and children. I think it's called displacement.'

Neither Kim nor Sharon spoke for a while, and Dee began to fear that she had strayed into a difficult area or even a minefield. Eventually Sharon turned towards Dee.'

'One of the reasons I've never liked you, Dee, is because you have an awful and uncanny knack of saying the wrong thing because it's actually the right thing. It doesn't stop me loving you hugely, but neither does it stop you being a pain.'

'That goes for me too, Dee, and how your wonderful husband tolerates you I'll never know. What you said earlier about the Victoria Sponge Cake, might almost have been just funny had it not been for the observation you had made and the consequence you drew from it. It was brilliant. But as Sharon says, you and Miss Marple are a pain, always being right.'

Dee laughed and all three drew tighter together. For Kim and Sharon it was a little like being in the confessional. You could say what needed to be said without having to look anyone in the eyes, which made honesty more possible.

'I do feel that quite a lot now,' began Sharon, 'primarily because I spend so much time with Caro and Benjie. Kim knows how much I love being with them, even when Benjie is behaving really badly. I think that when we're in shops and he has a tantrum, Caro seems able to switch off her hearing to deafness again, and so doesn't take the blindest bit of notice. But I've found myself thinking when I'm with them that I want Kim and I to have a baby, that I couldn't think of anything more glorious or celebrating the wonder of our love.'

'It's really quite straightforward, my love. When we get back, or even before we leave, we make an appointment to consider the possibilities and to ask for a referral to a clinic. I am more than happy to do that because what want I most want is for you and me to be happy together. Sharing that with a new life would wonderful. But we must try hard to focus on the present and that means our care for you, Dee, and then protecting André.'

'In which case,' said Dee, 'I think we should move ourselves and go out for lunch.'

'That a brilliant idea, Dee,' said Kim.' 'The others are having lunch out, so should we.'

There was considerable tension and more or less silence as Ro, Julie and André made their into Ivybridge and the safe house where Nancy was being protected. Ro parked the marked police vehicle some 400 metres away, locked the rifle away in the gun safe, and led the other two back to the house. She was in combat dress and suddenly stopped and called the protection officers on her radio. They might well have been expecting her but knew well enough not to abandon standing orders. They gave their consent to an approach and as they did so the door was opened. Each was searched and they had been pre-warned to address Julie as ma'am,

'Is it true you're taking us out to lunch, ma'am, and without assault rifles?'

'If you prefer we can bring you back a bag of crisps and a bottle of ginger beer.'

'You're in charge. We'll do as we're told.'

'Have you mentioned this to Nancy?'

'No, ma'am.'

'Ok, debrief with the sergeant here. Will either of you be on duty on Saturday or Sunday?'

'I shall be here on Sunday from 6:00 to 2:00,' said the officer who had not spoken yet and who Julie now realised was female.'

'Ok, I'll have a word with you before you are relieved. Now take us to Nancy.'

The door to the sitting room was opened and in Julie and André went. Nancy couldn't hear their arrival because through her headphones she was listening to a concert by André Rieu on YouTube. The visitors smiled at one another. It was Julie who lifted them from her ears and she swung round in fury, then stopped herself.

'It's the wrong André. I was hoping for the one with the fiddle. Well Hello, I thought you'd forgotten about me.'

'We've come take you to lunch, believe it or not. We won't be carrying big guns, but four us will have enough firepower to protect you.'
'Is it needed?'
'Turn your chair round so we can face one another.'
Nancy was most odd. Sometimes she looked worn and a little haggard, and sometimes, as today, she looked still young.
'Peter Fakenham.'
'Oh that piece of shit.'
'Tell us what you know.'
'You've heard me on the subject before.'
'Indeed I have but we want you go over it again. By the way he's being held by the police on all sorts of unpleasant charges mostly to with small boys on his computer.'
'Good. I sussed him out quite a few months ago as a CIRA observer. It was clear they had investigated him and knew all about his hobbies. Someone in the community will have tipped them off. His role was to send back to Dublin or wherever regular reports on the Irish community in the East End though he was no more Irish than Vladimir O'Putin.'
'Did he attempt to talk to you at any time?'
'Two or three times in the *Wig and Pen* but nothing was said of substance.'
'Was he hoping for a night in the bed of Ms Carmichael?'
'Only in his dreams.'
André broke in.
'You must be slipping, Nancy.'
'What do you mean?'
'We've seen all his reports and they were about only one person: you.'
Nancy smiled but grasped at once the implication of this.
'Are you sure going out to the pub for lunch is a good idea?'
'Major Dickinson here has booked a table for six.'
Nancy stared open-mouthed at Julie.
'Major? Well fuck me. I really am losing my touch. Let me say at once that you do undercover really well, including under my covers!'
'I tried my best and neither of us complained, said Julie, blushing slightly.'
'So who's in charge? Is it still Kim or is it you?'
'That doesn't matter as well you know. My main task is to make sure that no harm comes to you.'
'Thank you.'
'Now Nancy,' said André, 'did you know any of this? You see, when one side starts playing decoys and call my bluff, it is done with the intention of lowering the cloud so that we are in the fog. It's good practice of course, but when you are on the receiving end it's less enjoyable. So who do you think is meant to be going to die in the next couple of days: you, me or both of us?'
'André, you know the esteem and even love that I have for you. There is no way I would let that happen, which is why when I did think it was, Julie and I came down to warn you at once.'

'That leaves you.'
'That's always been there and some who would say that it's a miracle it hasn't happened before now. You both know what I did. Alright it wasn't exactly as I described it the other day in front of everyone. I admit to you two what you already know that I shot each of them in the back of head and I did so because I was a stupid, murderous bitch wanting to prove myself. There's no excuses and no absolution for me. I've lived in hell ever since, haunted at night, which is why I've chosen a regular supply of young men to be there in bed with me to silence the voices.'

There was a knock on the door and Ro's head appeared.
'Ma'am, we ought to be going down the road.'
'Yes,' said Julie. 'Nancy, you will need a coat, and whilst we are walking down the road stay very close to me.'

André and Julie said nothing to each other as they waited for Nancy to return.
'Do tell me,' said Nancy with a wry smile, 'am I expected to pay?'
'No you're ok, it's my turn. You bought me a coffee on the train down.'
The pair smiled at one another.

It was no distance to walk. One of the protection officers was in front, the other behind. Ro and André stood at the side of Julie and Nancy. The two officers went ahead into the pub and soon called the others to come in. Instinctively, Julie the seat that afforded maximum eyeball on the doors and those inside. Nancy sat beside her as instructed.

As the Chief Constable was paying everyone decided to have the maximum though there no was no alcohol for anyone. The Protection Officers never ceased their watchfulness and looked tense, which was noticed approvingly by Ro. There was not a great deal of conversation, something noticed by the landlord who said to his wife that it was rummest group ever having a meal there.

The curious group reassembled for the walk back to the safe house. Once there Julie asked Ro to brief the female officer also on duty on Sunday about a possible assault on Nancy's life but told her that this info was grade 1 secret not to be disclosed to anyone, including fellow officers and her family until she arrived at 6:00 on Sunday morning when she should brief the officer on duty with her.

'I cannot even begin to tell you how important this information is. Only the Chief Constable, you and me know this. Nancy's life is at stake, as well as yours.
'You can rely on me, sarge.'

'So what now?' asked Nancy as they drank coffee in the sitting room.
'You know as well as me, Nancy, that you can't know anything other than that we shall do all we can to protect you. And we want to know who it is and where he, if it is a he, comes from and is related to, which means we would prefer to take into custody whoever it might be.'

'Judging from the fog they've plunged you into, please, for my sake do your best, because it suggests to me that if they are setting up a decoy, you are not dealing with an amateur.'

'I'm not sure why, and I don't think it's because I shared her bed,' said Julie on their way back, 'but despite knowing what she has done, which would put her into the realm of mass murderer, I still want us to make sure she comes out of this in one piece.'

'She would say she killed in war,' answered André, 'and you have done that. We didn't prosecute those who served in firing squads in the Great War and as far as I know there were no vendettas, and members of the IRA would say that Nancy simply pulled the trigger as those men back then did. No one claims she saw active service against the British army or RUC. But Julie, I have to advise great caution in dealing with Nancy. As you said the other day, she is an arch-manipulator and a very convincing liar. Even now, in telling us that she killed those 10 men and 2 women in cold blood she will have been trying to get into our heads what she wants to put there.'

'She was right about the fog though.'

'Of course she was and that is exactly what she wants us to think we are in, because it will confuse us, and is doing. For that reason we need clear-headedness and a chance to talk it over later with Kim – the four of us together.'

The lunch in Exeter was enormous fun and three women indulged themselves and although Sharon had to take three work calls, they were able to reminisce on their first adventure together in the heartland of Yorkshire. Dee kept saying that the waitresses and waiters here needed some improvement but agreed that the food did not.

'Did I hear someone mention that you were going to the dentist tomorrow, Kim?'

'Yes. Moritz, Ro's apparently dishy husband is having a persistent problem with the computer system they use. I didn't tell her that persistent problems are normally the easiest to discover and fix, so I may stretch it out and pretend to charge them the earth like some computer firms I could mention, or I'll show off and do it in a matter of minutes. Either way its a matter of quid pro quo, as I need my teeth looking at and if I take him on his my dentist on a permanent basis it will mean Sharon and I can come and see you every six months at least.'

'I know that at the moment I'm inevitably thinking about what's going inside me,' said Dee, 'though as I yet I can feel nothing at all, you'll be relieved to hear, but thank you for letting me be privy earlier to your moving conversation,' said Dee. 'There was a time, as you both know, as does André, when I thought I was in love with you, Sharon, and deeply resented you, Kim, but I now know what love is in my life with André, but I also see it there before me in the love you two have for one another.'

'I still laugh,' said Kim, 'at the thought that you were twice brought to André for interrogation, and that on the second occasion you were offered a job and invited to move in with him. God, I hope he hasn't done the same with Nancy.'
They laughed and turned their attention to the dessert trolley.

Once home, André opted for a rest on his bed, whilst Ro and Julie decided to get some fresh air and walk up the back.
'Are you happy with just the few of us? We could could almost certainly flood the area with fully-armed officers.'
'If the only concern was protecting André and Nancy, then that is what would be needed and I would hand it over to your guys, and I know what a good job they would do. My orders, however, are to take whoever it might be, one or two or more, alive, as this may be the chance for our biggest breakthrough into CIRA.'
'Even if we lose Nancy, or, God forbid, André, in the process?'
'I intend losing no one, Ro, though we both know what is at stake. You forget that you, Kim and I are all going to be in the front line.'

The others returned and wanted sleep. Ro spoke to the Chief Constable and said they had all survived lunch and suggested she prepare herself for the bill! She said that there would a planning meeting a little later which the Chief offered to attend, but was dissuaded from doing so.
'Here's a little incentive for you, Ro. If all goes well as I'm sure it will, the senior staff have agreed this morning that from Monday you will transfer to CID in the Serious Crime Unit and that your promotion to Inspector will take effect from 1st January which is the earliest date possible on your accelerated scheme.'
'That's great news, ma'am. Thank you.'
'Keep me in touch with what's happening.'
'I will.'
Ro could hardly believe her excitement at the news and doubled her determination that whatever might follow in the next few days she would come through unscathed. But first she must call Moritz and give him the news.

It was dark outside as they assembled just after 4 o'clock in the sitting room, Sharon working in André's study and Dee lying down upstairs and in the circumstances looking surprisingly well.
'Would it be wise for Dee to move somewhere safer?' asked Ro of no one in particular.
'It might take at least two armed officers first of all to convince her of that, and second to make it happen,' answered Kim. 'I haven't known Dee long, but I know her well enough that here, and close to André, is where she will be.'
André smiled and nodded.

'I've had a text from Martha,' said Julie, 'to say that no one remotely likely has entered the country from Ireland so far today, other a women's hockey team who arrived by boat in Liverpool from Belfast to play a match on Saturday against Manchester ladies, which is surely an oxymoron.'

They all laughed.

'However she assures me they'll continue to closely monitor all arrivals in the next 24 hours though that does not preclude the possibility that there is someone already here in residence. Known people are being watched especially any in the South-West which mostly means Bristol. Assuming that we shall not stop anyone at source I don't want just to adopt a strategy of wait and see. Whoever might be coming will still be working on the assumption that we know nothing, which is of course more or less accurate other than that I still think that whatever might happen will do so on Sunday, mainly because the weather forecast is still bad.'

'Did you get anything from Nancy?' asked Kim.

'How would we know if we had? replied Julie. 'If there was anything, she certainly wasn't giving anything away other just at one brief moment, which André, you may have noticed too. She asked us to do our best to save her and I had a sense that she meant it.'

She looked to André.

'Yes, that wasn't the usual cocksure Nancy,' confirmed André.

'So tomorrow when it's light enough, I'm going to do to a full recce of the moor immediately behind each location and map them in detail. I won't be alone because Martha is sending reinforcements in the form of a recent recruit, formerly a police officer and skilled in the sport of orienteering. I met her at Hereford when she was doing her firearms training but was persuaded to do an extra month training the guys there in map reading, believe it it or not. She's also extremely strong though you might not think it to look at her but she puts it down lots of sheep-shearing. I believe she will be known to some of us already though probably best known to Dee – Helen Boardman, who was her local police officer in Ilkley. She's on her way by car and should be here in about two hours' time.'

'We have space and she can always stay with us, if she doesn't mind Lotte breaking in very early and speaking German to her,' volunteered Ro.

'Thanks Ro. That would be most helpful.'

'André and I both know Helen quite well, and I was the one who recruited her. She's smashing, as they would say in Ilkley,' added Kim.

'My initial thoughts about Saturday and Sunday, are that Kim remains here but above on the moor with you, Ro. André, Dee and Sharon will be here. Helen and myself will be above the safe house. Unless otherwise necessary, we want prisoners, not corpses. Kim?'

'Fine with me. André?'

'You forget I've never been a soldier, so I go along with whatever Julie decides.'

Sharon was on cookery duty. She had managed to get a great deal of work done and the Editor had emailed her to congratulate her on the quality of what she had produced on TTTS. He was now thinking of sending all his staff to the far reaches of the British Isles and get them to work there! She smiled at her victory but was realistic enough to know that when she was dealing with her boss, it didn't mean it was the end of the war.

Food tonight was going to be basic as they had all eaten out for lunch, and consisted of M&S Ready Meals cooked in the microwave. She had been told that there would one other with them, but not told who it might be.

According to Julie, a source of endless unimportant gossip, Helen had turned quite a few hearts a-flutter in her time in Hereford, and especially the heart of one of the Ruperts (officers) who clearly had fallen for her in a big way, much to the amusement of the guys there, though some of them felt likewise. Julie was dying to know what, if anything, had come of that. From what she had seen on Helen in action, she a splendid capacity to look after herself even when in the midst of some of these hunks of the SAS. Her map-reading was second to none, and once on an exercise on which she had insisted on joining there was stunned amazement when having come across a badly injured sheep she knew nothing could help, she used her hands to kill it with a minimum of fuss. Perhaps some of them present feared that the sheep could have been one of them!

They all heard the car approaching the house, and André rose and opened the door.

'André,' they all heard, 'it's your past catching up with you. It's all those women you spurned when you married the fabulous Dee. They've decided to get you.'

'Helen, welcome. I am so pleased to see you and have your Yorkshire sense with us.'

There was a small scream from the sitting room.

'P C Boardman! Oh how wonderful. Now at least there'll be some Yorkshire brains operating.'

'Hi Dee,' said Helen. 'It's wonderful to see you.' She looked round. 'And Kim who is responsible for my leaving behind doing endless duty at the traffic lights in Ilkley.'

'And what's happened there since you left?' asked Kim.

'Hundreds of fatalities.'

'And Sharon. You are always so depressing to be with, Sharon, because however well I dress, I know I'm shabby alongside you.'

'Nonsense, Helen, besides which there are few women who look like you, and as you meant to be spending the night with Ro, Moritz and Lotte, Ro will have to watch you carefully with her husband.'

Helen turned to Ro. 'Hello sergeant. I never made it to that dizzy height so I look on you with great respect.'

'In which case take a long hard look,' said Julie. 'As she becomes an inspector very soon.'

'Oh I had one of those in Ilkley, and as André knows, he was a total tosser and time-server. And as for rapid promotion, Julie, the last time I saw you it was doing latrine duty and now you're a major, but whoever decided that knew what they were doing.'

They hugged.

Sharon said she had a M&S Microwave meal waiting for her if she wanted it.

'The only thing better than that, 'she said, would be two!'

'Ah, well, that's a coincidence,' said Dee.

Chapter Thirty One

Lotte had chatted away to Helen for ages before Helen informed her that she didn't understand a word she had said to her, which for some reason, Lotte though hilarious and dashed away to tell her mum and dad. Both she and Moritz had been in bed when she and Ro had got home last night and she was looking forward to meeting the famous dentist.

When she appeared for a very early breakfast, having to be in Ivybridge by 8:00 to meet up with Julie, she was wearing what walkers on the moor would be wearing, not combat uniform. Julie had instructed her however that she must be armed. Leaving by 7:00 meant she didn't meet Moritz but looked forward to the possibility. Perhaps she could try and lose a filling in the course of the weekend!

Kim was having to spend quite some time with Moritz today: attending to his malfunctioning network (he had complained of a faulty computer which she knew it couldn't be as it did exactly the same thing on each machine), and then he had promised to have a look at her teeth, in the course of which she anticipated a telling off because of neglect.

Dee, Sharon and Kim were setting off in good time to shop. When they asked André if he minded being alone, he merely bellowed: 'Be gone monstrous regiment of women.'

'I think that's a No,' said his wife, who knew just how much her husband was looking forward to no company whatsoever so he could read and write, without being subject to the mention of clothes and shades of lipstick!'

He did, however, have a welcome call from Kate.

'Is there any change. André?'

'I spoke to Ruth at her meeting in London, and she'll be back on Sunday evening and will see Dee first thing on Monday morning. When I described things as they are, she agreed that the chances of sustaining the pregnancy are not high. I'm sorry.'

'Thanks Kate. Although she may be covering up, she's pretty realistic about how things are and provided that a miscarriage doesn't affect further chances of becoming pregnant, she and I both will want to try again and soon.'

'It should have no effect on that at all. This didn't happen because of any deficiencies in either of you. It was just one of those statistical oddities. Dee is young, fit and healthy, and despite the fact that you enjoy giving the appearance of being old, slow and decrepit, I can see that you're none of those things, so conception should not be affected at all. Just keep at it.'

'Thank you for the vote of confidence, Kate.'

'Miscarriages and potential miscarriages matter to fathers too. I'm also smiling at the your use of the phrase "becoming pregnant" rather than "falling pregnant" which is in extensive use among most of the young women we see now. It dates you and me.'

'"Fall" is such a negative term. I think pregnancy is something good and wonderful.'

'Me too. Now remember, call me at the first sign of bleeding or abdominal cramp.'

'Thanks, Kate, I will.'

Julie and Helen met half a mile outside the village and made their approach upon to the moor well away from the safe house. The jokey Helen had not come, as Julie knew would be the case and was at once into her role of professional map interpreter, drawing what she saw and dictating notes into a recorder Julie was not aware of. Julie reminded Helen of the weather forecast for Sunday, which they agreed was most likely the day chosen, but she had already taken that in to her calculations as she often had to at home when out looking lost sheep in foggy or snowy weather when visibility was limited. Julie had seen this woman in operation alongside men in the SAS who prided themselves on their field skills and had seen her run rings round them precisely because she had learned them with sheep in the Yorkshire Dales.

They did not speak for ages, and whilst Julie was trying to familiarise herself with the basic features of the land, Helen was completely given over to her task, and was clearly enjoying what she was doing. Julie thought how much she could have done with Helen with her in Iraq though of course the land there would be totally unfamiliar to her. On the other hand she knew that guidance by the stars was also in her professional portfolio.

After almost two hours in which Julie mostly followed Helen around a large area, the cartographer among them stopped and looked at Julie.

'That's it ma'am. Job done. No is going to cross this land easily anyway nor without my knowing where he is likely to be in his approach. I certainly wouldn't recommend an assassin comes this way, and if it is raining and there is fog, the chances are that he'll enter that boggy land 40 metres to our south and struggle to emerge. A number of times I've found big yows in a bog unable to get out, with a drenched fleece. The first time somehow or other I managed to pull her out, but she died soon after having become almost frozen. Thereafter I killed them to spare them.'

'In the way you did in the Brecon Beacons, with your bare hands?'

'Well going back to get a humane killer from the hunt kennels would have just prolonged their misery. Anyway, I reckon I was almost as quick as a gun.'

'Fucking hell, Helen, when you go out with a bloke I hope you issue a health warning at the start of the night!'
They both laughed.
'And that reminds me. Did anything become of your tryst with Andrew, that nice-looking Rupert you were due to go out for dinner with, just after I was sent to Iraq?'
'I didn't break his neck, if that's what you wondering. I tend to stick to sheep unless absolutely necessary. He was so nice and we got on well together, but his vision of a housewife tucked up at home like his mother looking after the children, was not one I could share.'
They were heading back to the car.
'I broke a man's neck in Baghdad. He was total bastard who had already raped me and was clearly intent on a repeat. He turned his back momentarily and my lessons at Hereford came into their own. It was very quick and I bet he didn't even know. That enabled those I'd gone there to free to make our escape.'
'Do you think about it?'
Only when I hear stories of rape on the news and I think I should offer to pay a call on the one who did it!'
'Probably not a good idea says the former police officer, but I know what you mean alright.'
Before they entered the car, Julie opened the boot and brought out a large bag which she lifted up and showed Helen.
'Lunch provided by Dee.'
'Quality guaranteed.'
'That reminds me, Helen. Do you know about Dee's pregnancy?'
'No.'
'I thought not. Let me tell you as it could change at any moment.

Dee herself was loving being with Sharon and Ro, Kim having gone to the dentist. Although in so many ways Dee knew Kim was the better dresser, and sometimes amazed them by what she managed to get away with, she looked more to Sharon as neither were quite as slim as Kim and she knew that Sharon had wonderful taste.

Sharon and Dee both noticed that Dee was not trying on anything that would be appropriate for a pregnant woman, and eventually Sharon tactfully sought to mention this to her.

'Come on Sharon, we both know it's not going to happen this time. It's only a matter of time and I suspect I shall be induced on Monday morning if it hasn't happened by then. It will happen, I'm sure of that, as I very much hope it happens for you and Kim, but until then I want to look good for André, and you're my sure guide.'

A sure guide is what was needed by Kim when she met Moritz who was everything in terms of astonishing good looks everyone had spoken of, and it was little wonder that Ro had thrown everything up to become married to him. Just looking at hime, she thought he could almost make a lesbian turn, but only almost!

He showed the problem with the computers and indicated that it was fine until about half an hour after the team began work, which was the big clue Kim needed. It was lunch time and there were no patients.

'Please can you turn the whole network as if it was the end of the day.'

When he returned, she said, 'Sorry, Moritz, but can you now go and turn it back on exactly as you would at the beginning of the day?'

Once again he returned as the various screens in the practice burst back into life.

'Ok. I would now like to give me the dental x-rays you might have planning a little later.'

'Normally we x-ray after we have done an examination.'

Kim said nothing but continued to smile at Moritz with a persistence he found quite unnerving.

'Ok, come and sit on the chair and I'll do so.'

It took only a small while for Kim to be x-rayed with Moritz twice disappearing from the room.

He came back in and she joined him at the computer screen in the corner. He pressed a button and the first x-ray appeared.

'Don't bother with it now, Moritz, just bring up the second and ignore that too. Return to the home screen and choose the record of any patient as random.'

'It's done it again,' he said pointing to the monitor.'

'As I expected. Good. Now I know a great deal and who knows, might even be able to mend it. Tell me, was your x-ray system part of the original network package?'

'No. It was integrated about a year later and enables us to read the results almost as soon as they have been done, as you saw with yours.'

'What it means is that this is not a network problem, which is extremely good news as that would take me most of the afternoon to sort out, but a problem with the way in which the x-ray programme has been incorporated. It will be a minor programming fault but you need it resolving and I shall try and do it before your afternoon patients arrive. I can work at this monitor if that's ok with you. I shall not need to see the notes of any patient so confidentially will be totally protected. You are welcome to stay in the room after I have received a cup of strong tea, white no sugar, but I will work better on my own.'

'You really think you can sort it?'

Kim stood and stared at him.

'How would you answer that it someone said it to you about a toothache?'

'Er, yes, point taken, Kim. I shall make a cup of tea and have my lunch in the staff room.'

'Thank you'

Kim produced from her bag a piece of kit made by herself which she plugged into the back of monitor and the screen changed completely. She had designed it to pick up programming faults and it was very effective. When Moritz returned she asked for two passwords though she could have found them for herself with another of her inventions in her bag. It would take about 20 minutes she reckoned, and she was more or less exactly right in her timing. The error consisted of a repeated line which she deleted, and that was that. All she needed to do now was to repeat turning off the network, turn it back on and test it with an x-ray. One of the other dentists came and repeated Kim's x-ray. Everything was working as it should.

'How come you were able to do when all the companies who've sent people couldn't?' he asked.

'Were they men?'

'Yes.'

' Well there's your answer,' she said with glee.

Brendan was not all easy within himself as his flight began its descent into Birmingham. He had slept badly, as Mary had noticed, but he laughed it off. Now, however, he was reaching the point of no return, and maybe he would not return. Maybe he would not see Mary again, would not return to the work he loved, and he was especially anxious about showing his passport for fear that they were already looking for him. Somehow he got through, picked up the car and headed south towards the M5.

Further north in Liverpool, the women hockey players over from Belfast for their match took a coach, and failed to notice that of those who had been on the boat as if a member of the team, one of them was no longer there on the coach. She, still carrying her sports bag, made her way to Lime Street railway station in good time to catch the train to the south west. Once moving she went to buy herself something to east and drink, careful to say as little as possible and betray herself with her accent. She sat back and wondered how Brendan would be getting on. Perhaps by now he would have collected the bag at the service station and learned her little joke.

Brendan chose not to open the bag lest anyone see its content and would wait until he was in his B&B in Devon. Part of him wished he could just stop the bar and throw it into a hedge on the side of the road but knew that would be utterly reckless given that a child might might find it and, assuming it was a toy, cause untold damage. It was getting dark and he pressed on though he was enjoying the car that had been made available to him, even he wished he were driving to the conference in Birmingham he had told Mary he was attending.

As Julie and Helen finished their scrutiny of the moor behind André's cottage and were walking back, Helen stopped.

'There's something been nagging me since we were in Ivybridge.'

'Go on.'

'I'm pretty good on moorland because I know something about how it functions and so on. Any one wishing to approach the safe house would have to be at least as experienced as me, or even more to attempt the same. Conan Doyle in The Baskervilles described it as a "grimpen mire", and T S Eliot spoke of being "on the edge of a grimpen, where is no secure foothold".

'Say more.'

'What if our assassin comes to the front door as it were?'

'The protection officers are under instruction not to let anyone in without radio notification.'

'He might not need to. A High Velocity Rifle with a .220 Swift or .204 Ruger cartridge could do it for him at quite a distance away if he could get a clear shot at Nancy, and something even more powerful would destroy the front door and the protection guys with it, allowing immediate access to Nancy.'

'Any thoughts?

'Only that this has been better thought out than I had at first imagined. We shall have the three of us and the protection officers in the house. You could arrange to have the house and village flooded I'm sure with armed bobbies, with the result that he will go away and return when he's ready. So I think we should stick to the plan of us being up on the moor, but putting Kim into the house "in the wrong place" if you take my meaning – perhaps in a wardrobe upstairs or lying under the front-room window. I know that technically you and she are for the sake of this operation of the same rank, but the is actually your senior.'

'I'm not gay,' said Julie. 'but if I was it wouldn't be Sharon I would fancy though I know Dee does still, but Kim, and there is no way I would put her at risk and she knows that, so if I ask her to do something, she trusts me enough to do it. But where would the assassin obtain something big enough to smash the door down? That would require a heavy piece of kit.'

'A grenade delivered from a few metres would do it, allowing immediate access, certainly stunning if not killing the officers on guard and allowing him immediate access to Nancy.'

'H'm, and I'm sure you noticed that the front has not been properly reinforced but how would our man be aware of that? Well, we're almost there so let's go in and share our observations with Kim and André and see what they have to offer.'

The women arriving back from their shopping expedition were pretty high as they drank their tea. Dee and Sharon had bought new blouses and dresses, Ro a new coat, and Kim had bought nothing but was on a high from having defeated all the men at the dentist's, and found that her teeth were in better order than she had feared and had need only one filling, though even so, in true form, still got told off by the dentist.

Their merriment gave way to seriousness when Julie and Helen arrived carrying quite a bit of Dartmoor with them on their boots. Over tea and cake,

Julie recounted all they had done and their thoughts about how they should proceed on the following two days. André remained silent throughout which suggested that he might have much more to say when he, Kim and Helen could be alone. Helen, in the meantime had already begun turning her extensive notes in drawings. She would have welcomed the opportunity for a quiet chat with Dee but Dee was cooking so it would have to wait.

'André and I both knew from our first encounter with Helen, that she was something special, especially when it comes to moorland, and the process of thinking,' said Kim. 'She puts herself into the mind of the enemy, even if it's only a fox after lambs and she has not a trace of sentimentality when it comes to killing the fox, though that's common to most farmers.'

'The way she reads the ground so impressed everyone in Hereford that they kept her on to teach those who thought they already knew how to do to. At the end there wasn't one who failed to acknowledge how much they had learned from her.'

'If whoever is coming does so from the moor we will have the upper hand thanks to Helen – that's for certain, but I gather she wonders whether it might come through the front door,' said André. 'That would be extremely risky because of the possibility of witnesses, the fact that the police will be called and I gather from Ro that Arleen Hill is positioning two vans of armed police 3 miles from each location so they can make an instant response if needed. All the same we have to be attentive to that possibility though positioning your senior major in a wardrobe might not be regarded as tactful.'

'I think she was joking. What Helen wants is someone in the room who is invisible from outside and even perhaps from the inside and under the window seems a good idea.'

'Might he use a stun grenade? We all know what they can do even to those of us who have seen them in action and we won't have the protection. Five or six seconds might be all he would need,' said Kim. 'I suppose he may have obtained M-84s from the US but he still has to find a way of delivering them.'

The door opened and in came Helen with her completed drawings which were superb in terms of detail, showing where and how someone might try to conceal themselves.

'Helen, that simply brilliant. You are worth your weight in gold,' said Julie. 'My only anxiety is that you will be leaving us for a permanent posting with Special Forces. What you've produced today is for one necessary for us, but perhaps they might argue they need you more than we do.'

'If you don't mind my saying so, major, that's not our concern this evening.' Julie decided to shut up.

'There is however a serious matter we need to bring in Ro for,' said Kim. She stood, opened the door and invited in the wife of her dentist.

'We have a problem, Ro, and it is one which needs to be alerted to the Chief Constable, though not until Monday, and it it concerns the possibility, that someone who might be coming from the CIRA, has been fed info about the location of the safe house from someone inside the force. We can't know whether this is so until after Sunday, for we may all go home on Monday feeling rather silly if nothing happens at all, but it is possible that someone has been providing intel though as Helen might tell me, that is not our business tonight.'

'It had crossed my mind,' said Ro, and I shall be happy to deal with it if it proves that there is reason to do so.'

'Are you happy with the arrangements for tomorrow, Ro?' asked Julie.

'Yes.'

'Then, if there are no more issues, let's go and eat, meeting here for a final briefing at 6:30 in the morning.'

Brendan found his B&B easily enough, and the householder had prepared food for him, so first he put his luggage in his room, including the bag deposited in the boot, which felt strangely light, but he decided to wait until he had eaten before looking inside, not least because he didn't want to look inside and see the lethal weapon he was to use. The food was very good and the lady and he chatted for ages. He said he was getting married soon to a lovely girl (true, even if he hadn't asked her yet), who didn't love wild places as he did and with a long weekend he wanted to have a look at Dartmoor. She said November was the not the best time to do that but he was adamant that the weather was part of the appeal. They agreed on an early hour for breakfast and its content before he went back to his room.

He sat on the bed and picked up the mysterious bag and opened it. It was empty, or at least empty apart from a piece of paper. It was printed from a computer and not signed.

You are a decoy. Carry out your orders. Without a weapon of any sort, as a walker, you cannot be held and should return home.

He read it over and over trying to make some kind of sense. He assumed that someone else had now been allocated to the task for which he was just the decoy. Immediately he felt profound relief because over the hours of his driving in the afternoon he had come to the realisation that he had been totally stupid from the moment a ridiculous romanticism had swept over him and he had allowed himself to become involved with fanatics. When this was over he would do two things. First, he would ask Mary to marry him, and second, he would persuade her that they should move to England. He lay back on the bed feeling only relief.

In Exeter she left the train at the Central Station and was picked up. She had read for most of the journey and was feeling completely calm. Tomorrow they would go and take in the lie of the land, and on Sunday the forecast was still bad for the area with fog and rain most likely.

As they ate and drank, she was informed of the arrangements that had been made – two protection officers would be with Nancy in the house and some military somewhere. In addition to this, armed police officers would be held as backup 3 miles away.

'It's tempting to want to take the whole lot out,' she said with menace in her voice, 'but they'll only squeal as they did at Warrenpoint, but it's tempting and I'll give it some thought.'

'She was taken out for lunch to a pub in the village the other day. I can't think why and I've picked up a rumour that in charge of their operation are two women officers.'

'I don't understand why someone who was their enemy and who did the things she did should be protected by them unless she has turned tout and hands them juicy morsels of intelligence. In which case justice will not only be done but also seen to be done. Now, before I get to bed, show me what you've got for me.'

Chapter Thirty Two

All the principals slept badly, even those able to cuddle up to another to keep warm. Was this the day when a bullet or explosion would either end things for them or, even worse, render them helpless, candidates only for the Invictus Games? In her time in Baghdad Julie had faced these possibilities every day, though if she was honest the thing she most feared at the moment was the continuation of the conversation promised by Kim.

As they ate breakfast conversation was at a minimum, and at the end Julie said, 'Everyone knows what they have to do. Please don't mistakenly think this is a run-through. Good luck and go to.'

Outside it was still dark. Ro took her place outside the back of the house and "dug in" by the bins and compost, from the latter of which she could hear noises that suggested she wouldn't be alone – rats probably.

Julie and Helen were driven by Kim who parked almost half a mile from the house. In addition to hand weapons, each had a high velocity rifle, and were wearing proper Combat dress. Julie called ahead to the protection officers who let Kim into the house, Helen and herself going out out onto the moor behind.

Nothing happened, unless you count an occasional car passing though if anyone had noticed they would have seen one passing twice in a short time from which a young woman took photographs from her mobile, who then decided to add insult to the injury she would bring on the following day, by instructing her driver to stop at the *Sportsman's Inn* so they could have lunch. He smiled and admired her cheek.'

As they waited for their food, she asked him, 'Are you working tomorrow?'

'Yes, I shall be on the other stand-by bus, the decoy bus.'

'The decoy is my one concern.'

'Oh'.

'I'm not certain he's totally sound but there was no one else. He knows very little of what we're about at home, to be fair, but he might be encouraged to reveal the little he does know. If he were to do so and should you get the chance, might you be able to encourage him not to, if you know what I mean?'

Julie instructed everyone to stand down just after 6:00pm and they gathered back at André's for some much needed food. There was hardly anything to report other than walkers near Ivybridge.

'Same time tomorrow morning, people,' said Julie.

At breakfast the tension was much more palpable, and little was said as they divided for the separate locations and the task of waiting in what was a morning of torrential rain and low cloud on the moor. Just before they set off however, André stopped Kim by the door.

'Kim,' he said very quietly, 'if someone is about to kill Nancy, don't shoot until they've done so. That's a message for you only and won't come through Julie. Kapisch?'

She turned and looked at him.

'I know what an order is, André,' and touched his arm.

He nodded.

'I will take care of Sharon.'

Only one person was pleased with the weather and she too rose early and prepared herself. Some miles away in his B&B, Brendan told his landlady that he thought discretion was the better part of valour, and that looking out of the window at the rain, he would abandon his walking today and instead go and take a look at Exeter, which she thought was very sensible. It meant that was able to drive to within a mile of the target and make his way there with the minimum of effort and see what happened as he approached. His only fear was that they might intend to shoot first and ask questions later. The original plan had been to arrive there at about 11:00 but what the hell, he wasn't intending to get soaking wet as a decoy armed with nothing at all, not even a penknife.

She was now alone in the house and able to check her equipment. His car she would leave a mile away on the other side of the village and then walk. She would then go straight into direct action. She would use the new grenade they had obtained from Russia via Libya which combined both a demolition bomb and a powerful stunning component which would completely disorientate for far longer than a traditional stun grenade. However prepared they might be, they would not be prepared for these.

Brendan made his way across the bottom part of the moor which was far less boggy than he had been through on the previous day, and believed he might be with 200 yards of the house. His heart was pounding even though there was no evil intent in it. He now could see an upstairs light and slowly began his descent down what he rightly perceived was a lethal, muddy and soaking wet pathway. And then he slipped and went head over heels before coming to a stop with someone looking down at him pointing at him a large automatic weapon. Suddenly there was a loud bang and the person in front of him was now lying on top of him. Moments later he realised it was a woman and she shouted out : Dee, if you don't put that fucking gun down, I swear I will shoot you.'

'Sorry,' said a disembodied voice.

The woman clambered off Brendan.

'Well, I suppose that's one way of getting to know you,' she said to him. 'Can you now please stand and hold your arms out on either side.'

'Yes, but I have no weapons of any kind.'

She searched him thoroughly.

'Why not?'

'Why would I? I was simply told to come here at 11:00 am.'

"You're early.'

'I know but I can't stand the rain.'

'I don't know why you're here but I begin to think you're not cut out for this type of work.'

Brendan laughed.

'Tell me about it.'

Ro directed him to the front of the house and in through the front door where he found himself being stared at by André, Sharon and Dee.

'Hello,' said, not knowing what else to say, 'I'm Brendan and I'm soaking wet.'

'Take your coat off, ' said Dee, 'and your trousers and I'll get you some towels, and then sit down.

Brendan did as he was told but noticed that Ro was standing still with her finger on the trigger of her assault rifle.

'Honest to God, I'm not here to hurt anyone.'

'I'll fix you a hot drink, said Dee and disappeared into the kitchen.

'So what are you here for?' asked Ro, still with menace in her voice.

'I was made to come here and told that I was a decoy, but that's as much as I know. '

Ro went outside at once and called Julie.

'Decoy held.'

'Received.'

She relayed this to Helen and Kim and added: 'I'm dropping down to where I can see the front. Helen, stay.'

'Ma'am.'

It was ten minutes later that Julie found herself a concealed dip allowing her sight of the some of the road in the front of the house, but even where she was did not allow her to see the road further down to the right. Up that road, having parked her car, a young woman was approaching with a raised umbrella and a shoulder bag, as if she was walking back home from church on a Sunday morning. If you had passed her on the pavement you would have smiled and so might she. Had you been closer you might have just noticed the presence of EarPods of some sort through which which she was presumably listening to music. She stopped about ten metres away from the front of the house and took something out of her bag, and then continued. In one act as she reached the front of the house she turned and threw whatever it was she had been holding towards the front door, before stepping back a few paces. It

Rod Hacking

wasn't a bang but an explosion as all those in the surrounding area would later describe it, assuming perhaps a gas leak. She entered the house quickly. The protection officers were lying on the floor in the hall and she continued into the sitting room where she saw what she had come for completely frozen by the impact. She reached into her bag and took out a gun.

'You must have known this day would come, Nancy. Goodbye.'

She positioned the gun at the back of Nancy's head and pulled the trigger, but nothing happened as the mechanism had jammed. Moments later the woman was herself unconscious having failed to see the butt of Kim's assault rifle swinging towards her. Kim quickly disarmed and secured her.

'Target secured with a headache to follow. Urgent call to bomb disposal required to deal with remaining ordnance. Ambulance also needed.'

Moments later, Julie burst into the house and room.

'Nancy?' she asked Kim.

'A very lucky lady.'

Helen burst in and attended at once to the two protection officers who were still on the ground.

'They will survive when their brains stop rattling from the explosion. What about Nancy?'

'The gun mechanism jammed as she pulled the trigger. She was so taken aback I was able to swing my rifle and stop her having another go at Nancy. She is wearing some kind of ear pods to protect against the big bang, as I was. Julie, we need policeman to protect against locals who are already gathering outside.'

'Thank you.'

She called them at once but insisted on no weapons of any kind and no more than four officers.

She then called André, but there was no reply, nor from Ro, nor even from Sharon, which was odd and worrying.

André had continued his gentle questioning of Brendan and ascertained that he knew he had made a total ass of himself in making even the slightest contact with CIRA and had felt anxious for himself and his partner Mary, if he didn't do what they ordered him to.

Brendan stopped and looked somewhat alarmed. He stood up. At once Ro said, 'Sit down.' But he took no notice.

'Dee, Dee,' he said as he moved towards her, having noticed that she had slumped in her chair. He took her wrist and continued to call her name. He then looked down at her skirt and saw blood everywhere.

'Ro, is that your vehicle out there?'

'Yes.'

'The back seat behind the driver's will go flat. Please do that immediately. André, I need a pillow and blanket.'

'What is it?'

'Dee is having an abnormal dysfunctional uterine haemorrhage and she is

242

going to require surgery as soon as possible.'
'Shouldn't we get an ambulance?'
'By the time an ambulance gets here and turns round it may be too late.'
He was continuing to give close attention to Dee.
'How do you know this?' asked Sharon.
'Because I am what you would call a Senior Doctor in Obstetrics and Gynaecology at my home hospital. Now come on Sharon, I need your help to get Dee into Ro's vehicle. I assume we have to go Exeter.'
'Yes, said André, armed with blanket and pillow. 'She is, or at least was, pregnant with a TTTS and they have a special maternity unit there.'
'That's where we'll go. Call ahead and ask them to cross match her blood and prepare a theatre for immediate admission. Tell them that she has already lost a lot of blood.'
Brendan was strong and with help from Sharon, Dee was soon in the back and covered with a blanket.
'André and Sharon please follow. Ro, we must move. Blue light and siren all the way please and any help you can obtain as we drive from colleagues, blocking traffic can only help, but whatever you do, move fast. You're a police driver, so use all your skills.'
André called the Unit and passed on the message, but they didn't tell him that there was no one present who could do the operation. A Registrar was on call but he was almost 45 minutes away, though they called him anyway. André also called Kate, who said she was already on her way. Normally it would take about half an hour into town but Ro was amazed that almost certainly this time it was going to be under 15 minutes, nearer 10. Roads were blocked for her all the way.
In the back Brendan was trying to bring Dee back into consciousness and then he realised he would need an emergency anaesthetist in the Women's Unit and used his phone to tell them, and that they would need a stretcher to meet them and she would need an immediate drip.
In a very short time they were there.
'I knew when you were lying on top of me, Ro, that we could work well together. Thank you and thank you from Dee.'
'Is she still with us?'
'Yes, but not much longer unless we can get her straight into theatre.'
Nurses and a young doctor were waiting for them. The doctor did his best to get a line in but was clearly struggling, so Brendan took over and had it in a few seconds. The senior sister decided to take over.
'We need to get her into a side room to do an assessment.'
'And who is going to do an assessment when a Senior Obstetrician has already done one and said she goes straight to theatre.'
'Which?'
'This one. To theatre and where's the anaesthetist? And come to think of it, where's the senior reg here?'
'About 45 minutes away.'

'Sister, Dee will be dead by then and I am not exaggerating. I need you in theatre with me, and you doctor. She needs prepping and so do we.'

'But we can't just allow anyone coming in from the streets to operate on a patient.'

'Here's Sir André. By the time you've debated with him your point, you may need to tell him he can visit his late wife in the mortuary. So please let us get on with Lady Beeson's only hope.'

Ten minutes later the surgery began and of those present who still had doubts, they quickly disappeared when they saw him at work. Kate quickly joined them and having once been a theatre staff nurse took over from the sister who clearly hadn't. No one noticed another figure join them so intent on Brendan's skills were they. He communicated frequently with the anaesthetist throughout and he and Kate and the other young doctor worked together well. In time he was able to stand back and say to the anaesthetist that he was happy for Dee to go to Recovery.

'Not just good Dr O'Callaghan,' said the late arrival, 'but superb. Even our consultant Dr Ruth Timothy could not have done it as well.'

He turned towards the voice.

'Thank you. And you are?'

'Dr Ruth Timothy herself, and welcome to my department.'

'Oh my goodness, if I'd known you were here I wouldn't have dreamt of doing this.'

'And Dee would have died. I came in totally by accident on my way back from a conference. But you've given me a great idea for saving lots of money. When we have surgery, we simply go out into the street and invite the first person we meet to come in and do the job.'

Brendan laughed and went red.

'I'm joking. The fact is that if André had had to wait for an ambulance, Dee would no longer be with us. You saved her life. I take it, however, that once we've been to tell André and a lady with a gun the good news, you and I might recover together over a coffee, and you might want me to take over her further management, or will you be coming in to do that yourself?'

Brendan laughed again.

They left theatre and joined André, Ro and Sharon. Ruth gestured to Brendan.

'Sir André, I am pleased to tell you that Lady Beeson is now in Recovery being looked after. I have every reason to believe, and Dr Timothy is in agreement, that although she will need a few days to recover in here, she will soon be back with you in fine fettle. The surgery went well.'

'Oh no, it didn't,' burst in Ruth, 'it went supremely well. This young man is a superb doctor and craftsman in the theatre. Without him, Dee would unquestionably be no longer with us.'

André, and then Sharon, rose and hugged him, profuse in their gratitude. Ro came and shook his hand. She was in a quandary of enormous proportions. Here was a man sent by CIRA to mislead the authorities whilst they sought to commit murder elsewhere. He had been unarmed and admitted the whole story to them as they drank tea together. He had then saved the life of Dee, literally, by taking total charge of the situation in the house, in her vehicle and finally in the operating theatre. She ought to arrest him, but how could she possibly do that?

The two doctors said they needed to change and both wanted a drink. André and Sharon looked at one another and smiled. Somewhere outside they could hear a number of sirens, presumably arriving at A&E, work that always went on.

The first thing to strike Kim and Helen as they came up the drive was the absence of cars. They looked at one another; this was most unusual. Instinctively as they left their vehicle both took their rifles and, one on either side approached the door. Helen indicated that she would go in first and did so, shouting a warning, followed immediately after by Kim. They looked round, upstairs too, but drew a blank. Then Kim saw blood, lots of it. Something pretty dreadful had happened here. She tried Ro again and again was unable to get through. She called Julie reporting their discovery.

'Kim, take André's car from their garage. Go to the Devon and Exeter Hospital A&E and see if there's anything to report. They'll have our two protection guys there, plus Nancy. I'm now in Wyvern Barracks, Topsham St, in Exeter with the our unknown visitor waiting for the MO to come and give her paracetamol for her headache. I need Helen back at the safe house to see if she can use her instincts to find the car the visitor arrived in. I found car keys in her pocket but she'll have to collect them from me first.'

'Received'.

Kim entered the house and found André's car keys in a small bowl in his study and by the time she was back outside there was no sign of Helen's car. Kim could not work out what could possibly have happened at the house to leave such a large amount of blood and there was no residual smell of firearm discharge. And most important of all, where was Sharon, the meaning of her life?

As she drove at breakneck speed she received an email from Martha, the Deputy Director:

"Congratulations. Kim, collect me from Airport 3:00"

What on earth did she mean by congratulations when there were people missing, some perhaps fatally? She was feeling bewildered and increasingly anxious about Sharon. Arriving at the hospital she ignored all parking restrictions and went as near A&E as she could. As she went in, people stared as she was still armed and went to the Reception Desk.

'In addition to the three patients brought in following an explosion have you admitted Sir André Beeson.'

She stared at her gun.

'Erm, I'll have a look, I've only just come on duty.'

She looked at her screen.

'No, I'm sorry, oh but hang on, there was a Dorothea Beeson admitted into the Women's Unit earlier. She's now in Wynard Ward and the easiest route is via the Women's Unit. Out again and turn left.'

'Thank you.'

Kim turned and went outside. There was a policeman standing by her car.

'Give me a parking ticket at you're own risk, constable. Where's the Women's Unit?'

He pointed along the road.

'100 metres on the left.'

She reached into her pocket, pulled out the keys and threw them to him.

'Park it for me and then bring them into the Women's Unit and if I'm not there leave them at Reception.'

'I'm not sure I can let you go in carrying an assault rifle.'

'I'm not sure I can let you go in carrying an assault rifle, major. This is a terrorist incident. Do as you are told.'

'Yes, major.'

Kim ran and was there almost as quickly as Usain Bolt might have managed had he been wearing combat uniform, boots, a side gun and an assault rifle. She tried to burst in through the glass doors, only she didn't as she discovered she needed to have pressed a button. As she picked herself up feeling ridiculous, there standing before her was Sharon with a huge grin.

'Our highly trained members of the Security Services will soon receive instructions on opening rather than trying to run through glass doors.'

Kim stood still.

'Oh my darling,' she said and tried to take hold of Sharon but was wholly encumbered by her rifle.

'I fear something has come between us,' said Sharon. 'How is it that after a morning of fun and games the person I love has turned into a blithering idiot?'

'What's going on?' said Kim.

'Come on and we'll tell you.'

Kim was led into a room where Ro and a man she didn't recognise were sitting and chatting.

'Ro! Won't someone tell me what's going on. I went to the house and all I found was a great deal of blood. I imagined the worst.'

'It almost was the worst and would have been had it not been for Brendan here who's a bit like Wonder Woman and was in a moment transformed from pathetically useless potential assassin into a quite brilliant gynaecologist and obstetrician who when I arrived here with him, and Dee close to death, hijacked the operating theatre and performed miracles.'

'Not miracles, Ro. Just what we try to do every day of our lives.'

'Well, I thought it was a fucking miracle,' said Ro with finality.

'And comparing me with Wonder Woman was so cruel.'

They all laughed again.

'Where's André? Asked Kim.

'With Dee on the ward.'

'Do sit down, Kim, and take that ridiculous gun off,' said Sharon, now able to give her partner a kiss.'
There was a knock on the door which Ro answered.
It was the policeman turned parking attendant holding a set of keys.'
'Hi Tony,' said Ro. 'What are you doing?'
'Hi Sarge. Returning some keys to someone who said she was a major after she made me park her car.'
'Well, she is a real major and you can give them back to her.'
'Thank you so much, constable,' said Kim.
'My pleasure,' said Tony the constable, who couldn't take his eyes off Sharon, but had to do so in order to leave.
'Are you able to tell us what happened at the safe house,' asked Ro.
'I can't with Brendan in the room, other than to say it ended without loss of life, but with four severe headaches and a seriously big hole at the front of the building.'
At that moment Kim's radio burst into life.
'Report.'
Kim rose and left the room, and swiftly made her report.
'Tell Ro to turn her radio on and she is to rendezvous with Helen at what's left of the safe house. We're not done yet.'
'I have orders to collect Martha at 3:00 from the airport.'
'Are you willing to handcuff him to Sharon and leave them there whilst you you do that? He remains our prisoner no matter how mighty his deeds.'
'Received.'
Kim sent Ro packing and sat with Sharon and Brendan.
'Allowing for the possibility that the British government will want his head chopped off,' said Sharon, 'Brendan has been offered a job here by the Consultant Ruth Timothy as her Senior Registrar with a view to becoming a Consultant within a year. I will spare his blushes but it would have been difficult to exceed the praise heaped on him by Dr Timothy for saving Dee's life. She told me that with the sort of skills he possesses it might be possible to develop a proper TTTS Unit here, so patients don't have to go to London for surgery.'
'How did you respond?'
'I would love to accept her offer, but I've got myself caught up in something totally ridiculous as the result of my own stupidity and that might send me to prison for a long time even though I had no weapons and was not intending any harm to anyone when Dee fired her gun and Ro fell on top of me outside in the back garden.'
'Brendan, trust me, if she was aiming at you, you were perfectly safe!'
The door opened and there was André.
'She's going to be ok. Groggy but no pain, but wishes to meet her saviour. Brendan, will you come?'
'Only if Ruth says I can. Dee is her patient.'
'I cleared it with her.'

'Ok.'

'Before you go, Brendan. I have to to the airport to collect my boss, and I also have orders that you are to be handcuffed in my absence to Sharon,' said Kim.

'What?' said Sharon, as André almost fell over laughing.

'That's fine with me,' said Brendan, 'in fact I can't wait.'

After they had left, Sharon cuddled up to Kim. 'I guess I've chosen the wrong time to be gay.'

'A likely story.'

'I take it Martha is coming.'

'Mainly to sort out the problem of Brendan. A top level meeting this evening with the Chief Constable, André and the the woman who loves you. She will fly back this evening with the prisoner and Helen, and they will go to the Conference Centre. If the wrong decision is made about Brendan, he will go too. But when he comes back and you are shackled together, please my darling, can you have a conversation with him.'

'Yes. I'd already thought of that.'

There were builders and television lights outside the safe house as Helen and Ro drove past on down the road the woman had come up. It was almost exactly a mile beyond when they saw a car parked in a cul-de-sac. Ro radioed immediately for a PNC check on the number and her heart almost stopped when she received the reply.

'Holy shit,' she said.

Helen got out, and at once opened and started the car with minimal touch, and then returned to sit alongside Ro.

'Will we require backup?' asked Helen.

'Yes.'

'Arrange it.'

Chapter Thirty Three

Kim wasn't at all sure she would get away with parking where she had the other night until she caught sight of the army helicopter approaching, and then she decided to try anyway. She repeated the opening of the concealed door and walked through, thought sight of a woman wearing a gun prompted an observer to immediately call security and the police. There was an airport transport vehicle by the now landed helicopter and she could see Martha getting in. Moments later she was dropped off and came towards Kim and smiled.

'Let's go,' said Kim, and opened the outside door.

'Is this your private car park?'

'Seems to be, but it will be André who gets the parking ticket.'

Before they could start the car a group of police officers and security staff stood in their way.

'Excuse me, boss,' said Kim, opening her door.

'Who's in charge?' she asked.

No one seemed to know.

'Well one of you come here please and look at this ID.'

A constable came forward hesitantly.

'No problem, ma'am. Perhaps next time you could give us advance warning.'

They moved out of the way as the constable muttered something about her being a major in the army.

They set off heading towards the hospital which Kim thought the most appropriate place to gather.

'Is everything sorted?'

'Not quite. We're just picking up a rogue police officer. Helen radioed me when I was on my way here.'

'Should we make Helen a major as well?'

Kim laughed.

'I know I talent-spotted her, but she is very good indeed but whether we can contain her skills I don't know. It's possible she might want to jump ship and head for Hereford.'

'And Julie?'

'This will have done her a world of good – restored her self-confidence. Both of them think quickly.'

'And how did Kim get on?'

'Me? Looking forward to learning all about the Russian grenade but less keen on the instruction to let the killer shoot Nancy.'

'And did she?'

'I let her pull the trigger and when the gun jammed I gave her a gentle hit on her head with my assault rifle to prevent her having another go.'

'You're a big softie.'

'Would you have done so, ma'am?

"It's a lovely day.'

They glanced at one another and smiled.

Kim drove into the car park outside the Women's Unit. Kim turned towards Martha.

'You have a bizarre and difficult decision to make.'

'What do *you* think?'

'I think I'm glad I'm not you.'

They walked into the Unit, this time letting the doors open before her and then into the room set aside for them where they found Sharon handcuffed to Brendan.

'How did you manage to go to the loo?' asked Martha.

'I'm a doctor so it wasn't a problem for me,' said Brendan.

'Sharon?'

'I'm a doctor too, if you remember, so it wasn't a problem for me either.'

They all laughed, Kim and Martha sitting, and Sharon released Brendan and herself.

The van containing armed officers was parked about 100 metres away from the target house, and Ro drove up to the vehicle, before she and Helen left the car and climbed onto the bus.

'Hi guys. We treat this as entirely normal, what you've trained for over and over and I expect total professionalism from each of you. Yes, its Angus Cassidy, whom you all know, but he is suspected of being in close league with the person responsible for the attempted murder earlier today, including providing explosives and firearms, and a motor vehicle which will be tested by forensics overnight but which is believed to have been supplied to the said person. He may well therefore be armed and feel he has nothing to lose in attempting a shoot-out. However, if at all possible we want him alive. With me is a sergeant from the army who will go in first after we have removed the door. Any questions?'

Heads shook, but eyes looked on in wonder at the female soldier and assumed she must be from Special Forces. Slowly and quietly they made their way up the road and split on either side of the front door. Helen gave the nod and the door gave first time. She led the troops into the hall and sitting room

beyond, where she found a man holding a revolver to his head.
'You're all British scum and bastards,' and sought the trigger.
Helen's rifle not only knocked the gun from his hand but gave him such a shock that he was near-paralysed as two officers took hold of an arm each and dragged him onto his knees. Ro handcuffed him.
'Where did you learn to shoot like that, Sarge?' one of the men asked Helen, expecting the answer to be Hereford.
'Shooting pheasants on the moors in Yorkshire.'
He looked surprised, but it was in fact quite true.
Outside an armoured van had arrived to collect Cassidy.
'He's going to London tonight,' said Helen, but for now take him to the Custody Suite at the New Police Station. Armed Guard at all times outside his cell. Total strip and into a white suit.'
Cassidy was still delirious from his encounter with Helen's rifle and hardly seemed to know where he was.
Ro called Julie and then Arleen, who was on her way to the Maternity Hospital for what she later called the oddest meeting in the oddest location of her life. The news from Ro, however, was devastating. One of her own officers!
Those present at the meeting which took place in Ruth's teaching room, allowing plenty space to all were André, Arleen, Martha, Ro, Kim and Ruth, and from the beginning it was clear that Martha was in charge.
'I need to fly back to London before too long and will be taking with me at least two for a conversation in what we call our Conference Centre. I don't think there can be any doubts about these two, about one of whom we have no idea as to identity, but will be charged with terrorist offences and attempted murder. The other, Arleen, one of your own officers, will be charged with aiding and abetting a terrorist act, storing weapons and explosives with intent to cause loss of life, and maybe other things besides.'
'I'm sorry to have to report that the woman can now be charged with murder,' said Ruth, 'On my internal computer it is reported that the patient Nancy Carmichael died at 4:30. There is to be a post-mortem in the morning.'
There was a moment of silence,
'The stun grenade was not one I've come across before and if it was the same as the other we found in her bag, it was a new Russian type and is the first time we have obtained one. It was one hell of an explosion. Poor old Nancy,' said Kim
'We should never forget when we start feeling sorry for her,' Martha said, 'that she murdered twelve people in cold blood, and it seems from what you reported, Kim, that the assassin had revenge as her intention.'
'You're quite right Martha,' added André, 'but I know what Kim means. Despite all that she had done, I warmed to her every time we met and I shall not easily forget her. But she was still a rogue.'
Martha now said: 'Our main business here and now is to determine whether or not I am to take back with me to London a third prisoner – Dr Brendan

O'Callaghan. From your contact with him at your house, André, before he saved Dee's life, and strictly on the basis of your conversation with him, in which you have excelled for many years, what thoughts have you to offer Arleen and myself who have to make the final decision?'

'I would say that he told us nothing but the truth as to why he was there and wished he had never become involved with CIRA. The description he gave of the person briefing and controlling him, matches that of the prisoner you are holding in the military barracks. He held nothing back and described exactly his visit to Nancy which tallied with her account. He might need to spend time talking with someone as to why he made the stupid move of expressing interest in CIRA and the cause of Irish nationalism but all political decisions are like that, for example why did I vote to Remain?, the difference being that CIRA regard the slightest interest an application for membership, and I think he was genuinely scared as to what might happen to him and his girlfriend Mary if he withdrew – and that was when I saw what an amazing young man he is, when he stood up, ignored Ro who, still holding a gun, told him to sit down, and began attending to Dee. He was totally given to what he was doing.'

'He took charge and told me exactly what to do,' said Ro, 'from knowing which seat in the back to lower, to making sure I arranged to have traffic blocked. I couldn't see what he was doing with Dee but he never ceased his attention.'

'He was seeking to arrest the haemorrhage,' said Ruth. 'No paramedic would have known how to do that or dared to do it, as it meant staunching the bleeding inside. There is no doubt that had he not been there, Dee would have died at the house. I'm told that when he arrived here, he was extraordinary and kept heading towards the theatre regardless of objections. Once he realised that there was no one on duty who could do what was needed, he prepared for and with the help of an SHO who was totally out of his depth, Dee's midwife, Kate Perry, who he must have thought was a theatre sister, and an anaesthetist they found wandering the corridors, they set about an emergency procedure. I arrived when they well into it and I watched in fascination. Emergencies can be a bit rushed meaning not quite perfect, but Dr O'Callaghan did a job I can only say was perfect. Of course Dee needed a lot of immediate on-going care, and a lot of blood, and after she had come out of Recovery he insisted on a scan, which he might not have done in the circumstances. This is no ordinary doctor.'

'I didn't know Kate was here,' said André.

'No one did, though she gave me a wink when I arrived in theatre. She did used to be a theatre nurse. I think she slipstreamed behind Dee's trolley on her way in.'

'Is it true that you've offered him a job, Ruth?' asked Arleen.

'I certainly have. As the Bible says: he's like treasure in a field you know you have to have.'

Martha looked to Kim.

'Major, have you anything to add?'

'This so-called soldier without any weapons didn't realise that the slope at the back of André's house might be slippy and so went down like an idiot. When Dee fired her weapon which might well have endangered a passing red deer, Ro fell on top of him. After all he has done today, he told me a few minutes ago that the best part of his day, the part he most enjoyed was when Sergeant Rowena Lehmann of the Devon and Cornwall Constabulary fell and lay on top of him. This is not how a soldier thinks but in my experience it is like every male doctor thinks.'

They laughed and Ro blushed.

'Colonel and Chief Constable: We trust you to do your duty,' Kim added.

She, Ruth, Ro and André made their way out of the room but for a moment Martha left with them wanting a private word with Kim, who immediately went off up towards the main hospital. She returned to the room and closed the door.

'It must have been an awesome responsibility for the judge in a Diplock court,' said Arleen. 'Little wonder trial by jury has survived so long. No judge would want to decide guilty or not-guilty.'

'I think, Arleen, that Kim was right, and I think further we know our duty is not the enforcement of a law any barrister worth his or her salt would walk through.'

'Martha, no other thought has entered my mind. I think we should call him in, and Ruth too.'

Arleen went to the door can asked them come in.

Martha smiled first, which rather gave the game away.

'Please sit down, Brendan. You have done a terrible thing today, Brendan, by which I mean that let you Sergeant Rowena Lehmann lie on top of you far longer than was good for either of you, and greatly enjoying it. Have you anything to say for yourself?'

'Am I allowed to plead guilty as charged?'

Arleen took over.

'Technically you have allowed yourself, somewhat foolishly as you admit, to become involved with CIRA, but not in the United Kingdom of Great Britain and Northern Ireland, and within the boundaries of this country you have done nothing whatsoever that is a crime other than practice medicine unregistered. So we are in agreement that you should begin to put this right.'

'We think,' said Ruth, 'that in your present position you haven't got enough to do and that with your exceptional skills we might further the work done here in terms of fetal surgery. I think you would be ideal for this and that is why I have offered you a job.'

Martha took over.

'We will arrange to get you home tomorrow where you can talk to Mary, go down on one knee and ask her to marry you, resign from your present position and be back here soon. You will however need a briefing before you leave so that if you need to give an account for what has happened here, you can give

it. You may have a babysitter to protect you but he or she will largely be out of sight. Are you happy with this arrangement?'
'Yes, Colonel, Chief Constable and Dr Timothy. Thank you so much for what I believe is an exciting opportunity.'
'Finally, in the light of what I described as your terrible deed, I am sure you will enjoy working under Dr Timothy – but not literally, please!
Brendan and Ruth smiled at one other and both shrugged their shoulders in unison.
The four of them walked into the reception area where pizzas had just arrived.
'I don't understand it,' said Ruth. 'I went away for a conference, and when I returned I find my rooms used for soldiers and police officers to meet in, there are doctors I've never met performing life-saving surgery assisted by community midwives, and now my Reception has been turned into a pizza parlour. What is happening to my world?'
One or two laughed, but most including Ruth's own staff, were tucking into a variety of pizzas and drinks that were not good for the teeth of anyone, though only Sharon noticed the absence of Kim but didn't ask why as she had earlier seen Martha having a quiet word with her causing Kim to disappear.
Julie and Helen were preparing their prisoners for transfer to the Conference Centre and a little later an armoured van collected the two of them separately and with a police escort, directed by Helen, were driven straight inside the gates to where the helicopter was parked. First, one was brought out of the van and led up the steps and secured at the rear of the aircraft. Then the second prisoner was brought from the the second vehicle and also taken up the steps and secured at the rear but in such a way as did not allow them contact or even much in the way of awareness of the other. They now had a wait of about half an hour, first for Martha to come back on board, and then for take off clearance. Once they were in the air the prisoners would have realised that had they even been needing to speak to one another, they would not have been able to hear.
André and Brendan popped into the ward briefly to see Dee but she was fast asleep. Brendan picked up her charts and pronounced himself satisfied, The ward staff nurse chased them away with a mop she was cleaning something up with.
'I'll have you know I'm a knight of the realm,' said André in mock protest, and 'I'm Dr Who' added Brendan, as they beat a hasty retreat.
'She'll know you tomorrow, André. But only thanks to you, Brendan,'
'Experience and training.'
'I accept that but Ruth said you have something more, that very few others have.'
'I think coming to work here with her will be great, and so will be the rugby which is what I'm really coming for.'

Martha prepared to leave and thanked everyone. Unable to contain herself any further, Sharon said to her quietly, 'Kim?'

'She's ok.'

'Thank you.'

After she'd gone discussion consisted mainly in making arrangements for sleeping. Sergeant Rowena Lehman would go home and wake as an acting inspector in Serious Crime until January 1st when she would be permanent. Sharon and André would go home. Julie was to drive Brendan to where his car had been left, then collect his things from the B&B, and then lead him to a hotel near the airport, where both would stay, providing her with time for his briefing in the morning.

Sharon and André drove back to the house a little slower than they had come from it. They said little until they were about 50 yards away.

'A car and lights on', said Sharon, hoping against hope that inside she would see Kim.

The stopped and they emerged and walked towards the front door and André opened it with a key. The last person they were expecting to see greeted them. It was Nancy.

'I thought it would take more than a big bang to get rid of you,' said André'

'André, you say the kindest things.'

'How did you get here being dead?'

'I brought her,' said Kim's voice from the kitchen. 'Nancy and I didn't get pizza so I'm making some soup.'

'Darling, let me make something better than soup. After the day you've both had, including being dead and rising again, you should have something much more substantial. André, may I?

'Of course, use whatever you can find, but please include me in too. I'm not the greatest pizza lover.'

Sharon went into the kitchen and put her arms round Kim, and nuzzled her neck. 'I love you.'

Kim turned and echoed her words.

'So I guess that the time has come, Nancy, to make a final break with the past and to go elsewhere,' said André.

'Having tried to kill me today I can't assume that they won't have another go, so being dead is the best way to escape from that. I had a conversation with your Deputy Director and we agreed that probably the best place for me to go will be the United States. I will assume a new identity and seek even at my great age to find some sort of living. She said that a new passport and identity papers and history will be prepared for me and recommends that I keep my head down here in Devon until that time comes, and then tickets will be provided for me to fly. In a funny way I done remarkably well to last this long. When you when I first met I spoke of the possibility of going to New Zealand, but I don't think they would want me and I can hardly blame them. In a funny sort of way it would have been much more satisfactory had that woman succeeded in killing me but it wasn't to be and after her first attempt failed Kim saved me from her second. Of course I'm hugely grateful to Kim, but as I say, it might just have been better all-round has she succeeded. She was after all delivering the judgement I deserved.'

Kim had returned to the room and was listening.

'I'm old-fashioned enough, Nancy, to think that all life is valuable, despite all that you've lived through and participated in. If I was your Irish priest, I suppose I would say your penance was to go on living with the knowledge of what is behind you.'

'I regret to say that if you had been my old Irish priest, almost certainly you would simultaneously have been trying to get your hand into my knickers, but perhaps even he, when he began what is I think a thankless task, was a person of principle and just got lost on his way, but I thank you, Kim, for his words.'

'Kim,' asked André, 'have you any idea as to who else we should expect to be here this evening?'

'As far as I know no one else is coming. Brendan and Julie are staying in the city; Helen has gone back to London with the boss and the prisoners.'

Sharon quickly produced some food for which they were all ready.

As they were eating, Sharon turned to Nancy.

'Has it be a lonely life for you, Nancy? I know you've had a variety of regular bedtime partners, but that's not the same as having friends. So I wondered whether you feel friends were a luxury you didn't perhaps deserve.'

'You used to be a head teacher, didn't you, Sharon? I bet the girls adored you, not just because I imagine they adored in your taste in clothes, but because they knew you could as it were, see into their hearts and minds, and could strengthen and support them. As for your question, you're quite right, and it's a particular irony that I have found here with you a friendship I've long craved, and you were, back then, the enemy.'

'O God, I know that life can be very odd indeed. I married a man who turned out to be the Portsmouth Bomber and who was just a foot away from cutting my throat.'

'Mother of God! How did you get out of that?'

'It was a lady who could see what was about to happen but was there to protect me and did so with an accuracy Dee couldn't manage.'

André and Kim laughed.

'If it hadn't happened I wouldn't have met Kim. You just survived something similar and this time it was Kim who saved you and the fact the gun jammed when she tried to kill you.'

'What a pity mine never did,' said Nancy with feeling.

It was about 2:30 when Sharon suddenly sat up in bed.

'What was that?'

'What was what?'

'That loud noise outside.'

Kim leapt from bed, threw on her coat, and put on her shoulder holster with her gun, and went into the sitting room where André was standing outside his study with the door open. Nancy had slept there but the madeup bed was empty.

'André, please remain here. I will go out alone. She turned on the torch of her phone and went out the front door. Later she said she knew exactly what she was going to discover and that she could fully understand the reasons why it would be so.'

Chapter Thirty Four

'Jesus fucking Christ,' said Detective Inspector (acting) Ro Lehmann (who was well-known for her extensive use of the English language matching Sharon's) of the Serious Crime Unit who had been dragged from her bed at 6:00 am on a cold, windy and wet November Monday morning.

'How can anybody die twice in less than 12 hours? And how am I expected to let the Chief Constable know that there was a conspiracy to deceive yesterday set up a by a hospital Consultant with the full co-operation of MI5? Don't answer as they're simply rhetorical questions. Just tell me how she managed to get hold of a firearm? That's where we shall need to start, or at least someone will because it won't be me. I start a new job today.'

'The weapon you gave Dee was due to be returned to the armoury today. André's gun cabinet was full, so he put into the drawer of his desk ready to return it today. It seems that Nancy found it. It was still issued in your name.'

'She should have got Dee to fire it. She would still be with us if that had been the case. And what have you done with her body?'

'André brought it in and placed it the utility room.'

'Was death instantaneous?'

'I should think so. There isn't a great deal of her head intact.'

'Kim, look, you're the Security Service. What I would like to be able to report to the boss is that you are taking care of it completely. She's a stickler for right procedure and practice, but in this instance, as she is going to taken up with answering questions about what happened Ivybridge yesterday, I think she will see this as the best way forward for everyone, not least because she won't want anything getting out that she and the Security Service have been protecting someone who murdered twelve people in cold blood during the troubles especially as she comes from Enniskillen.'

'So?'

'As far as I know, and as far as my boss, the Chief Constable of Devon and Cornwall knows, the person you are speaking of, Nancy Carmichael, died in the Devon and Exeter Hospital yesterday afternoon from injuries received in an explosion in Ivybridge. That is what her death certificate says, I believe.'

'Yes, Please excuse my error and forgive waking you so early on the first

day of your new job.'
'You're welcome Kim.Come and see us soon and give my love to Sharon.
Oh and also to Brendan, if you see him. Tell him. I enjoyed it too!'

When Kim rang Martha, she was doubly relieved.
'First for us, because getting Nancy to the US when I know they wouldn't
want her would have been an exhaustive and expensive business that would
not have pleased the Prime Minister or Foreign Secretary, or for that matter
the President. And second, because I feel great relief for Nancy. She was
profoundly unhappy and living a pointless existence carrying with her the
twelve lives she ended. I am so relieved for her.'
'What do we need to arrange to transport the body and where to?'
'I'll send a van down and they'll know what to do. I'd also like you to
remain, and Sharon, if her work will allow it, and if André will agree, at least
until Dee comes home. In a funny way he might well be the only actually
bereaved person in this, and he might also feel guilty about leaving the gun
where she found it – which you must return to the armoury. Take good care of
him.
'Today we shall start interrogating the two we brought here last night, and I
am sending Helen to Hereford for a week to prepare herself for a mission in
Ireland, following up what has happened with you.'
'A week, ma'am? No chance. She will both need and want more, and they
will need and want more of her. Then she might be ready.'
'I have to confess that I've never liked you, Major, because you're always so
bloody right. Don't think I don't know you're after my job!'
'Martha, I don't think there is anyone capable of filling your shoes and it's
why you command such respect from everyone'
'Julie and Helen have emerged from all this so very well, and Helen is here
with us today, but you have been impressive in the way you let Julie take
responsibility for the op. Not everyone by any means can do that, Kim. I
really am not being patronising when I say how well you have done.'
'Thanks, Martha. That means a great deal to me.'
As Kim put down the phone, there was a thought in her mind which had
not been there before and not mentioned either by Martha. Had André left the
gun where it was deliberately or had he even mentioned it to Nancy when the
bedtime came. She was torn in her mind as to whether she should ask him. At
the moment he was outside emptying buckets of water on to the place where
there was blood so she took the opportunity of speaking of this to Sharon.
'I have to say it had occurred to me,'said Sharon, 'but do you think it's
something you really need to ask André about?'
'He knows how the Service works, he knows we have to keep proper
records even though in this instance he is no longer a member of the Service
and therefore not bound by its regulations. But he knows that I am and
although Martha made no mention of this I feel it is incumbent upon me as the
senior officer present to complete our work as fully as possible.'

Rod Hacking

'Yes, I can see that, but I don't imagine it will be an easy conversation.'
'It's going to be a day of difficult conversations I think. Martha has to speak to Arleen. What I wouldn't give to overhear that conversation! Martha wants us to remain here at least until Dee is out of hospital to support André and perhaps also to give you and me a brief rest. She recognised that it may not be possible for you because of your work. What do you think about that?'
'Well the Editor is not expecting me back for some time anyway and I've already shown that I can edit the features section from here, so it's no problem. The only thing I insist is that we leave the major here in the cottage when we go out and that I'm accompanied only by the woman I love.'
At that moment André re-entered the house and looked at the two with their arms around each other.
'How soon do you think it will be before I can do that with my beloved Dee?'
'I would think pretty soon,' said Sharon. 'She has no outer wounds and whilst you may have to contain yourself in bed for a little while, it won't be long before life returns fully to normal. I take it you're going in to see her today?'
'Yes I am, of course and I shall want to spend as much time with her as they will allow me to do so. And what about you two. and what about the body in the garage, which makes it sound like an Agatha Christie title?'
'That's being taken care of,' said Kim, and we don't need to do anything about it which, I imagine, is more or less what you thought would happen. The boss has a request of you however, that we remain here for just a few days on a sort of holiday, until we get in the way after Dee returns from hospital.'
'I think my wife and I would be very happy for that to be the case. I think you know how fond she is of both of you and it will cheer her when she comes home to find you here. Of course you're also welcome to go into the hospital to see her.'
'Kim needs to go into the police armoury this morning, André, to return the gun and equipment which they passed on to Dee last week when she went with Ro to learn how to shoot. Brendan certainly owes his life to those lessons, but I'm going to ask you a question that probably nobody else will dare to, and of course you are totally free to not answer, but you left the gun and ammunition unlocked in a drawer of your study desk, the room in which Nancy was due to sleep. I think you will know the rest of my question without my having to say it.'
André who had been standing, sat down.
'It could and almost certainly should have happened yesterday morning in the safe house and it pained me that Nancy was totally unconscious at that moment and would never have known what was happening. Someone would've had the revenge others have long wanted, but it wasn't to be, ironically because you, Kim, acted as you did and prevented a second attempt at killing her when the mechanism of the gun jammed the first time. Nancy

260

had reached the end of a terrible road. She did unbelievably terrible things but was operating with a mind that had been totally corrupted. As you know and strange as it may seem, I liked Nancy very much indeed and could see the person she could have been. Maybe she is the last of the victims of the troubles to die. She wanted no more. I did what I did because I cared for her enormously, even loved in a strange sort of way, so I did for her what I believe my love demanded. I have no regrets and I believe that what I did was what she wanted.'

'Do we let Julie and Brendan know?' asked Sharon.

'At the moment they both think she died yesterday in hospital. Brendan doesn't need to know more than that and once he's in the air, we can let Julie know. I imagine she'll come here afterwards anyway,' said Kim.

'What I would like,' said André, 'is to be taken to the Devon and Exeter Hospital to spend as long as they will allow me to be with Dee. We have suffered a sort of bereavement in the loss of the twins we were so excited about and we need to comfort one another.'

'André, please forgive us,' said Sharon. 'That after all is the priority we came here to save you for'.

'Thank you, Sharon.'

'Then let's go straightaway,' said Kim.

'No chance,' said André. 'I haven't had any breakfast yet, nor have either of you.'

Julie and Brendan too were sitting together at the breakfast table.

'When do you go back to work?'

'Tomorrow morning and a day when I'm completely in charge which largely means I will have no idea when I get there of what will come my way in the course of the day. There will be no shortage of appointments of course, but other happenings always occur and demand my immediate attention,.'

'Like yesterday.'

'Well not quite. No one other than myself and Dr Timothy will ever know that Dee came as near to dying as is possible without actually accomplishing it.'

'Well, that was due to you, as I'm sure Dr Timothy recognised.'

'I played my part of course, but really what kept her alive was Dee herself. She is someone so full of life and fun that she was not going out quite so easily and was determined to survive. When I am back here I shall want to see her and tell her.'

'Do you wish to do so this morning?'

'No. She's Dr Timothy's patient now. What I did should not stop her conceiving again, so she might once again be my patient.'

'You are coming back then?'

'Did you think I might not?'

'What if Mary says No?'

'Then that will be an immensely painful and sad parting.'

'I believe Martha informed you that you will have a babysitter in the form of my colleague Helen who was once a police officer in North Yorkshire and before that new up on a farm, and is incredibly strong. She is a brilliant map reader and draws in exceptional detail. She is very popular with our Special Services who constantly learn from her about how to cross land, even desert land, and I imagine most of the lads and even some of the lasses, will be in love with heShe has a broad Yorkshire accent, so with your accent, neither of you will understand the other.'

'I haven't got an accent,' laughed Brendan.

'That's what she says, or at least I think it's what she said.'

They smiled.

'What we are interested in are those who might contact you from CIRA. If they do, tell it exactly as it was. They will have known the plan. The emphasis should be on Nancy's death in hospital – we're convinced that she was the target – and also the arrest of the woman they sent, whose identity we still do not have.'

'How much should I tell Mary?'

'No more lies, no more pretence. Tell her everything including your fears of failing to fulfil their orders. And tell her you love her and want her to come to South Devon with you. What does she do?'

'She's a sister on paediatric ward.'

'Impressive and very demanding.'

'What if something goes wrong with CIRA?

Helen will make sure the pair of you know when you need to bail out and just do what she says – if of course you can understand a word of it.'

'Is her accent that bad?'

'She can turn it on when she needs to. She told me there was a particular guy from the Special Boat Section who was clearly smitten by her and was becoming a nuisance. Her ability to throw around a large sheep in shearing put him off completely, she said.'

'I shan't risk getting near her, then.'

'Oh no, Brendan. She is so lovely. I mean it. Now we must leave for the airport.'

Julie's phone rang.

'Hi, Kim. Yes of course. I'll hand you over to him.'

'Hello Kim. Of course not, we're just about to leave for the airport. No, forty's not too old, provided we got on with it. You have a choice. You could have a few days' leave and come and stay with Mary and me, and we can begin the process and complete it when I'm here, or wait until I'm functioning here though that might take a little longer as my new remit here won't include fertility. Once you're pregnant that would be different. Talk it over with Sharon and you both need to think about a potential donor, and even about the possibility of surrogacy if need be. You have my home number and my email so be in touch. Ok, and thanks for everything. Yes, I'll pass that on.'

'M'm', said Julie. 'It sounds like there may be a post coming up that requires

a major.'
'There's no telling. Anyone starting on that journey is making quite an undertaking and there be many disappointments ahead for those at any age, but if I can help I will. She also said you and she still need to have debrief on the subject go you.'
'Of shit. I was hoping she had forgotten .'

At the Conference Centre, the Director himself, Rob had come with Martha from Milbank, having given his briefing to the PM.
'What's the batting order, Martha.'
Martha smiled. Rob had been at public school and saw everything through the medium of cricket and rugby, which she took huge delight in teasing him about.
'We know who Angus Cassidy is, so we might get from him some clues as to the identity of the woman who doesn't as yet know the mission was successful in that Nancy Carmichael is dead, though doesn't know what we know that she died by suicide during the night past.'
'I suspect you'll get not a great deal from either.'
'Oh, I'm sure you're right, Rob, and it's time like this that I wish you hadn't let André retire. Alex is good but he would be the first to admit that he isn't André.'
'Any word on Dee?'
'Other than what the doctor told me who saved her life, that she will make a full recovery. They lost the babies of course, but he said that nothing he did should prevent conception.'
'That's great. I must say that when I first met Dee, and remember I'm married to the wonderful Caro, I envied André. She is certainly a very attractive woman but she exudes life and joy.'
'So does Caro.'
'I know but I worry about her living in the remote part of Surrey we inhabit. She and Sharon are such close friends that I could wish they were nearer. I fear her becoming lonely and depressed.'
They had arrived at RAF Northolt and made their way to the Conference Centre where they able to look at the "guests" via CCTV in their cells.
'Ok, Alex, take the policeman, Angus Cassidy. If you get the woman's name it will get passed on to me. I'll be with her. Normal procedure – offer coffee and tea and so on.'
Alex nodded.
'If at any stage you want to take over,' she said to Rob, 'just come and do so.'
He nodded, though knew it highly unlikely that he would wish to do so.

Martha entered the room.
'Good morning,' she said. 'Coffee or tea?'
The woman was clearly taken aback.

'Er, tea ... please. White no sugar.'
'They can hear us, so it will come soon. I have a photograph to show you. It's not very pleasant and was taken at 3:00 this morning in Devon.'
She handed it over.
'Yes, it's of Nancy Carmichael less than half an hour after she shot a lot of her face away.'
The woman stared at it. In there meantime the tea and cake arrived.'
'So your mission was fulfilled after all. You nearly managed it yourself until your gun jammed and one of my officers hit you hard with the butt of her assault rifle which I rather suspect must have hurt. And I'm right, aren't I? Killing Nancy in revenge for the 12 she killed was your purpose in being there.'
'It was more than 12. My uncle who was present at some of them maintained it was 16.'
'That would be more even than those committed by the Yorkshire Ripper. 16 cold blooded murders, but did you know that when we offered her back to the Irish government a couple of years ago they weren't interested?'
'That's why I came to bring about the justice so many people have been demanding and which the government have refused. Have you been protecting her?'
'No we haven't. All we have done is keep a close eye on her to make sure she was not still involved with what we call terrorist activities on the British mainland and we discovered that she was not.'
'I didn't actually kill her of course. Does that make it complicated in handling me?'
'Yes it does, but before we go on I really need to have your name, not least because we shall continue to talk and it helps me to know who you are.'
'Before I tell you, and I will, can I just comment that this is the strangest form of interrogation that I have ever heard of. I expected to be chained to a wall and whipped.'
'That seems to me more like an erotic fantasy than what we mean by interrogation here. In fact we don't ever use the word, preferring to speak of a conversation, which is normally what we have.'
'My name is Eileen Hagen I come from a village quite close to the border near Enniskillen. My grandmother, though she was only 24 at the time was one of Carmichael's victims, in other words my mother's mother. My mum was just four at the time. I felt that the chance of justice being available in the courts of Ireland is now impossible and with Sinn Fein now as the largest party, that day of justice is even further away, so I decided that I would take it upon myself to end Carmichael's life.'
'I dare say that if you are indeed a soldier, then it's quite possible you have fought in Afghanistan and in other places in the Middle East, where lots of the Taliban have lost their lives so it strikes me that you might understand why I set out to do this thing.'
'Yes, I've done a number of tours to Afghanistan and also been

underground, as it were in Pakistan and other places, so I do know something
of being engaged in a struggle, and I also recognise that the IRA thought of
themselves in that way but at that time I was just a girl and not involved.
Inevitably you have been. And can I take it that the equipment provided for
you, in the main Russian equipment, came through contacts you already had
with CIRA?'
'Until they were put into my hands I knew nothing about them. All I was
told to do was to go to Exeter where I would be met and given what I need it
in the way both of information as to where Nancy was being held and what I
should do when I got there. He, of course wanted something in return and
didn't get it so was rather pissed off with me. We drove past a couple of times
and I took photos from the car. He told me to stand well clear and use the ear
pods he provided when I threw the grenade at the door. Jesus. I had never
heard anything like it in my life.'
'You are in fact the first person in the west to have used such a weapon.
We'd heard that something had been made by the Russians but never come
across it. You only used one and that means that we have at least a second one
to examine and perhaps replicate, so we are very grateful to you for that. It
rendered not only Nancy Carmichael almost unconscious but also the two
policeman guarding her, but you'll be pleased to know that they're fine.
Having failed to fire your gun the first time, before you got round to doing it a
second time, one of my officers lying on the floor behind you decided that
enough was enough. She had no desire to kill you but thought that a headache
and a sleep might be the best way forward.'
'Well, you can tell her that it worked. Presumably it will be for throwing
that a grenade and that you will want to charge me and eventually lock me up,
an act of terrorism.'
Hang on a moment Eileen, I'm not a police officer, nor any of us here, and
the only way in which someone can be arrested in this country is by the police
and they make a recommendation to the Crown Prosecution Service who
alone decide whether or not a case can be made in court. We sometimes joke
but we can't arrest someone but we can shoot them, though in the main we try
not to do so.'
Eileen smiled for the first time.
'I am going to ask you a question and I should tell you in advance that a lot
depends on your answer. Tell me about the part played in all this by Dr
Brendan O'Callaghan?'
'To the best of my knowledge Brendan unwisely expressed over a drink in a
pub to a member of the council of CIRA that he was interested in the
movement. A week later there was a bombing in Belfast, a failed attempt to
kill a policeman. If that had come a week earlier I don't think he would've
been quite so keen. I'm not sure that what he said was anything other than
some kind of romantic Celtic expression but the trouble is even a sort of
expression of support is taken by CIRA as being de facto membership.
'When it began to emerge that I wanted to bring Nancy to justice, CIRA

decided that we would use Brendan for our own purposes. I'm told he had a visit from someone who clearly scared the shit out of him and after that he was pretty malleable. If I know them they would've said his girlfriend was at risk if he didn't cooperate.

'The initial plan was to get Nancy away from London and the obvious place and person was Sir André Beeson. It was never our objective to hurt him in any way so Brendan was sent to London with instructions that she was to go to Devon and kill him, even though we knew she wouldn't do this, but we reckoned on the fact that she almost certainly would get down to Devon to warn him, which of course she did.

'He didn't know it of course, but Brendan was only ever going to be used as a decoy. I would never under any circumstances do otherwise to such a good doctor. So he was given instructions but not given any weapons. I think he was genuinely terrified that CIRA would be after him if he didn't do as they demanded. I met him just the once and I thought he was a good person. Is that the right answer you were hoping for?'

Martha smiled and nodded.

'How much do you know about the workings of CIRA?'

'Very little, but you'd expect me to say that. I only met two people, both farmers. The impression I got was that they have very little money other than that which comes in from America, and it was that which paid for the weapons I was to use in Devon. They are very secretive, but the great secret above all is that there are hardly any of them. It wouldn't surprise me that you know considerably more than I do and that you know probably all there is to know. I have no interest in forcing some united Ireland. My only concern was with the murder of my grandmother, that in some way I could bring justice to bear. Ironically, I didn't manage it, and then despite me it happened.'

'I'm afraid Eileen, that I'm not able to invite you to join us for lunch, but it will give me a chance to talk to my Director who has been listening in to our conversation. It's quite possible that he might want to have a chat with you himself and that after that we can begin to think about what is the best way forward for you and for us. By the way Brendan O'Callaghan saved the life of Dee Beeson yesterday afternoon. She was 10-11 weeks pregnant with twins but had been warned by her midwife that the signs were not good. Yesterday afternoon she haemorrhaged and had he not been there, she would've died. He took her to the hospital in Exeter and in the absence of any other senior doctors operated himself. Those of us who know and love Dee dearly know how much we owe Brendan. The consultant who came in halfway through the operation watched and said that he was quite brilliant. I rather suspect he won't want to put onto his CV that he was for a short while serving as an agent of CIRA.'

'That's a wonderful story Martha, thank you for telling me.'

'And you might like to know that the quality of food we have here owes everything to Dee as she ran the place for awhile.'

Chapter Thirty Five

Alex spoke first.

'He's a particularly unpleasant sort of man, hates the British from the depths of his being, so how he could've been a copper for as long as he has been I just don't know and how he could take the oath of office beats me.

'He's pretty open about what he has done and what he thinks and believes and he is the armourer for the whole of the UK. I asked him how he had got hold of Russian weapons and he was quite open that the money came from America and the weapons came from Libya but he wouldn't say who the people involved were and knows nothing about how they got here. He did however say that he stays in close touch with certain people in Ireland but he would never under any circumstances reveal details or names. He maintains that he had no idea who the woman who came for the weapons this weekend was and still has no interest in such a question.

'When I said that it was quite likely he would be facing a long prison sentence, he shrugged and said that that was what he had been hoping to avoid by taking his own life when that interfering woman shot the gun out of his hand. He still had no idea how she could've done it. My overall judgement is that he is a dangerous fanatic and that we should hand him over to special branch as soon as possible and have him transferred to Belmarsh.'

'Thanks Alex,' said Rob, 'that was very helpful indeed. I watched your conversation quite closely and I'm bound to say I totally agree with your final observation and recommendation. My judgement would be the same as yours that he is an extremely dangerous fanatic. He might well find that prison is not a very nice place for a former police man and a terrorist. By the way Martha, who was the sharpshooter?'

'Helen. Her abilities with a gun are second to none and she says that it's because she was firing her father's 12-bore when she was just eight. The kickback on a shot gun is considerable so she did learn the hard way and we are going to have to have a serious conversation about Helen, concerning whether we should lend her temporarily or even permanently to Hereford as a trainer. In the short term I want her to go to Ireland and babysit Brendan and his girlfriend Mary, not that I'm expecting anything to happen but you just

never know what she might discover simply through observation, and believe you me she is very good at that. I very much doubt we will get any more from Eileen, because I genuinely believe she knows no more, but Helen is very canny indeed and she needs to do something working on her own.'
'It's in MI6 territory. I can't let it happen without their consent.'
'Let them know it's only babysitting and that if anything else emerges it will go straight to them.'
'I'll try but do you recall the absolute shit we landed in when told them we had lent Julie to the SAS and that she'd been dropped into Iraq? We only got away with it because the PM was so impressed that a woman was doing something so totally courageous and gave me her full support.'
'In which case she'll have to work without backup, as Julie did, and if she gets into trouble she will need to get north as quickly as possible, across the border. MI5 are still not welcome south of the border. But what are we going to do with Eileen?'
'I'd like you to go and talk with her, Rob.'
'Yes, I heard you say that to her. Whilst I do so, get Grevel Hannah down here for an urgent con. We have to do whatever we decide to with proper legal guidance or it might just come back and bite us.'
'I'll do that for you,' said Alex. 'We need someone to process Cassidy before Special Branch get here.'
'Thanks, Alex.'
Rob rose, drained his coffee cup and walked through the corridors down to the room in which he found Eileen fast asleep. The closing of the door woke her up and the sight of a good-looking man in a suit before her meant that she stood up straight away.
'I wish you could come and teach my wife to do that when I walk into a room.'
Eileen laughed.
'Have you been married long?'
'No. Please sit down, you're making me feel nervous.'
'Isn't it me whose meant to be nervous?'
'My first sight of you as I came in was of a woman at ease with herself. I've been here a few times but never known any one sleep like you were doing.'
'I was up half the night and terrified what I might find when I got here.'
'Oh, the food and coffee are much improved thanks to Dee Beeson.'
Eileen grinned.
'Martha told me her life was saved by Dr O'Callaghan. I feel really awful that my plan to get at Nancy involved him though it's a measure of consolation that he was unarmed, did no damage to anyone and saved her life. I only hope CIRA leave him alone and don't assume they can use him again.'
'Are they likely to?'
'There are very few fanatics left and when they are desperate they will try to use blackmail or the promise of dire consequences if they are not cooperated with.'

'Eileen, I can't make you a promise about this until we have spoken with one of our lawyers on his way now, but just suppose the decision was made to let you go home, would you be in a position to divert attention away from Brendan?'
'They would want a report from me much more than from Brendan – that's for certain.'
'And do you have a house of your own, or have you a live-in parent or boyfriend?'
'What a strange question. I have two bedroomed bungalow and I live alone. In the real world, I'm not an assassin but a landscape painter and quite good, if I say so myself. There's not been a great deal of time for others in my life and recently I've been tied up planning this total nonsense of pursuing Nancy.'
'A young woman of about your age needs a holiday, and Ireland would be ideal. Might there be a chance of her coming to stay with you for a while? Ironically, she's an outstanding artist herself, in terms of transforming Ordnance Survey maps into in-depth drawings. You will not be out of pocket and if you are able to understand her broad Yorkshire accent, I suspect you will get on well.'
'What is she called?'
'Helen, and she knows a lot about sheep farming.'
'Well, I know we are dealing with hypotheticals until you've been able to talk to your lawyers, but should things work that might allow me to return home, then I would be more than delighted to have your friend Helen come and share with me for as long as she wishes.'
'In that case I might also also send my wife and young son as well. Caro was stone deaf until recently and was an outstanding lip-reader. She misses social contact and would like to go back to work, but she would be such a security risk. She has one close friend who is away at the moment, and she gets quite lonely, if that is the right word for someone who has a thoroughly energetic little boy with her all the time. I try to spend as much time with her as possible but I have to present a daily security report to government early each morning and if there's anything important on the horizon, I'm often home very late.'
'That must be tough for her but not wholly unusual for the partners of those in public life, which I guess is why so many such marriages come unstuck.'
'I hope not as I love and adore her.'
'Well, I'm no marriage counsellor, but have you sat down together, or perhaps arranged for your son to be looked after, allowing you to have a few days away together providing an opportunity for you to talk and relax together and have lots of interrupted sex. I have friends who say how effective children are as a contraceptive?'
'H'm, perhaps you should become a marriage counsellor and do your painting in your spare time.'
They laughed together.
'Do you know, if someone was to express their concern for me and ask how

I might possibly survive an MI5 interrogation, and I told them as it is, nobody would ever believe me.'
'Please don't ever tell anyone.'
Rob stood, gave Eileen a big smile and nodded his head to her.
'I'll send you in a cup of tea.'

Grevel wanted to look through the entire recordings of the conversations with Eileen as hearing an account of her activity on the previous day. Sorting out the transfer of Cassidy to the police and to prison was relatively straightforward compared to the question of what was to happen to Eileen, so there was a gap of about an hour and a half before he could meet with his two superiors to discuss matters.

'I can do nothing, as I'm sure you are well aware, other than advise you. You both have the authority to release anyone being held for questioning and I have the feeling that you both can see some merit in pursuing this course of action, and I can understand why you might see this as appropriate. At the present time the courts have a considerable backlog and she might face up to three years on remand.

'As things stand, she could be charged with attempted murder, plotting a terrorist act, causing an explosion endangering human life and handling illegal explosive devices. There are already people in prison for a long time who cannot equal these offences and who perhaps were not quite as successful at sweet-talking the pair of you. I think most judges would sentence her to 20 years and given that she was engaged in matters relating to the troubles within the Republic, I cannot see the Irish government applying for extradition. They are keen to forget Nancy Carmichael and the fate of Eileen Hagen (a most unfortunate name to any Wagnerians who like the *Ring*) will only serve to raise ghosts best left undisturbed.

'On the plus side it is clear that you are hoping to turn her and housing an officer of the Service with her with the dual responsibility of protecting Dr O'Callaghan until he leaves Ireland and doing much the same for Eileen. Is that accurate?'
'Yes,' said Martha. 'It is.'
'Doesn't that put our agent at risk?'
'They are always at risk, Grevel,' said Rob.
'Surely it should be an agent of 6 as it is overseas?'
'Ireland has always been regarded as a special case and as we have been dealing with this from the beginning, we shall continue to do so, though I shall inform their head and the PM tomorrow morning's briefing.'
'And what about the Joint Intelligence Committee? Shouldn't they be told?'
'They will be in time. We've only just got round to telling them about the arrangements for the 1948 Olympic Games, so there's no rush.'
They all smiled.
'The thing is Grevel. We believe Eileen may hold the key to our being able to identify some key operators of the CIRA. We're not asking her to do it, but

we are hoping and believing that agent who will be on hand will be able to get this sorted and then call in J2, the Irish Intelligence Agency to haul them in.'
'Does J2 know anything about this?' asked Grevel.'
'Yes and our agent has a code to use when she needs them.'
'In which case as your lawyer I acknowledge that precedent takes precredence over other considerations and I consent to the release of your guest.
'The newspaper this morning said that the explosion in Devon was a gas main and had nothing to do with any terrorist activity even though it was admitted that the house was being used as a police safe house, so Eileen could not have had anything to do with it. Indeed she is being championed by locals who witnessed the event that without thought for her own safety she ran straight in to attend those hurt. Unfortunately she vanished without trace and should have been honoured for her courage.'
'Well, if it's in the papers then it must be true,' said Martha.
'When reporters wrote up any trials I was involved in it usually wasn't. Now, I will finish my report and get Cassidy away.'

Martha went into Eileen's room and found her gazing out of the window.
'Airfields are such dull places if you're a landscape painter and not even remotely interested in aeroplanes and helicopters.'
'I can believe it,' said Martha. 'Do you have hills where you live?'
'And rivers, though I've never tried fishing.'
'It's not cold so would you like to go out for some fresh air before lunch?'
'Are you serious?'
'Perfectly.'
'And will I have to be handcuffed to you?'
'No way. They hurt my wrists.'
'Ok.'
'They headed out on to the airfield.'
'Almost all of our work is taken up paying close attention to militant Islam. André was an expert on Islam and loved it greatly, spoke fluent Arabic and was deeply pained by the growth of Jihadism. We have a huge number of people we have to keep our eyes and although nothing is ever reported, we make significant steps to prevents terrorist activities. Our attention has therefore shifted almost totally from Ireland.
'Our lawyer whom we have consulted about you says that would receive not less than 20 years in prison and recommends we hand you over to the police, but I said to the Director that the facilities for landscape painting would be poor and he agreed, so we have made our decision and we're going to release you. We'll try to get you back to Ireland as soon as possible, probably by air and as near your home as can be done. I'm very much hoping Helen will come with you though to be honest I'm not sure what she will do with you other than rest. Dr O'Callaghan is already home having flown from Exeter this morning. He has accepted an appointment as Senior Registrar at

the maternity hospital in Exeter and has now to do three things which sound straightforward but are not. The first, to explain to Mary, his girlfriend, what he has been doing; second to ask her to marry him; and third, to tell her that they are moving house.'

'If she's sensible she'll jump at numbers two and three. Number one may be more difficult.'

'And whose fault will that be, Eileen Hagen?'

'Guilty, your honour, and I feel terrible about it. Do you think I should be in touch and go and see her?'

'I think he'll manage. Look, we're not "turning you" in any way and we don't expect to betray anyone. We're only asking two things. The first is that you don't get in Helen's way which is not the same as betrayal. The second is that you consider coming to live here, somewhere your work can develop and have a better market. I've seen your website and what you do is not just good but superb. The chance to live, say, in the Yorkshire Dales where you can paint and sell to the many who come looking would be great. Your parents are no longer alive and you have no dependents. You would have us to look after you. So please think about it.'

'When will I meet Helen?'

'Later today, when I've got round to telling her. There is a real chance you won't understand a word she says.'

'Is she foreign?'

'Yes, North Yorkshire!'

Brendan could hardly believe, as he opened his front door, all that happened in the course of just a few days. He was hugely relieved to find that Mary was still at work, allowing him space and time not just to put his things into the wash but to het his mind round what he had to say to the woman he wanted to marry and share his life with, when he had lied so much to her.

He had texted her from the airport but received the briefest of replies, and he knew she would would anxious about his delayed return and probably also not at all pleased with him that he didn't let her know.

He began cooking one of their favourite meals, but then stopped and instead telephoned their favourite restaurant and booked a table. It would be much more difficult for her to explode and make scene there than at home. They both had red hair and more than capable of getting a little cross with one another.

Mary was quiet when she arrived home, and when told the meal arrangements, disappeared upstairs for a shower and change out of her uniform. She returned and sat opposite him.'

'Name? I assume she has a name, Brendan. It's twice you've been to England in a short while. I telephoned the college in Birmingham where your conference was, and it is true there was such a conference, but what there wasn't was a Dr Brendan O'Callaghan.'

'No.'

'You could have been using an alias, I suppose, to hide the fact that you were there with your mistress, another doctor.'

'No, Mary, I wasn't there and there is no mistress, and I both want and need to tell you the whole truth.'

'Oh, the truth, is it? This should be entertaining.'

Brendan told Mary how it was that he found himself being blackmailed and forced into doing something for the Continuity IRA.

'Wow this is some story,' she said, her voice heavy with sarcasm.

'I was told that you might well suffer if I failed to go to London to pass on a message to a former IRA killer living there.'

Mary now listened a little more intently.

'This was followed by a woman instructing me to go to Devon, the assumption being once again that if I failed it would be you who would be either hurt or experience a serious accident. There is no other way I would have done it. I travelled to Birmingham, hired a car and en route received a message that I was there simply as a decoy and that the person being killed was the former IRA killer now in Exeter.

'I know I lied, but at the time I felt I could do no other.'

He completed his story with the events at the house and in the hospital.

'For a while I was handcuffed whilst the Deputy Director of MI5 and the Chief Constable of the Devon and Cornwall Police made a decision as to what they were going to do with me. It took them very little time, and then Dr Timothy offered me a job as her Senior Registrar with a move to Consultant in a year's time. Then they arranged my flight home.'

'What's Exeter like?'

'They're an excellent team and play some of the best rugby in England.'

'If the idiots in the CIRA don't kill you, *I* might.'

'It's a lovely city with a stunning Cathedral at its heart, a good University and what appeared to me to be a very good hospital. There's an airport offering regular flights to and from Cork and Shannon, but the countryside is probably amazing in summer but scared the living daylights out of me when I was crossing it. The hospital will help with housing and the sea is close by.'

'Could we get the boat there?'

'After the winter we could take a few days and sail it.'

'Do you think I could get registration.'

'Judging from the number of Irish nurses who have made that journey, I should think it would be straightforward.'

'Unless, of course, there was something else on the horizon.'

'Are you saying that there is?'

'Well, doctor, my period's late though I haven't done a test yet, though I felt very sick this morning.'

'H'm, sounds like appendicitis to me.'

'Probably, though of course, I had my appendix out when I was 14.'

'Ah, well almost certainly phantom appendicitis then.'

'And this is the doctor they all thought so highly of?'

'If he's going to be a dad, he can say what he likes. That's wonderful, Mary, absolutely wonderful.'

Neither would have appreciated some sort of public spectacle with him on one knee, but whilst waiting for their their food, Brendan produced from his pocket a small box which he opened with the words: 'Is there any chance you might like to make an honest of man of me, Mary?' Her eyes filled with tears.

'Indeed there is, my lovely fella, and about time too.'

Chapter Thirty Six

Helen and Eileen had got on well from the moment they met at Heathrow, though Eileen was under no illusion about her new friend. She knew only too well that she was a soldier and had also trained members of UK Special Forces. Yet she was also in the presence of a lovely young woman of her own age, possessed of a great sense of fun, who knew a lot about contemporary music and who almost certainly could drink her into oblivion – though something she was determined not to put to the test. She had been forewarned by Martha about the accent, though not about how much she talked about sheep!

They flew to Belfast where she had left her car on the way out and were soon away from the city.

'I presume you know Northern Ireland,' said Eileen.

'Only by repute. I've never been before.'

'Don't your lot still work here?'

'I've no idea. We only get to know what each of us is involved in and I guess the military world has moved on a great deal since the troubles.'

'To a degree, but that's why you and I are here now. I had an agenda from the past and it would be less than honest if you said you weren't interested in the people I liaised with.'

'True, but I'm not here to arrest them in any way. I'm here to care for and look after you and Brendan, as best I can, to protect you as far as I'm able, as you return home.'

'You could always try talking to them – they won't understand a word.'

They both laughed.

'Surely it's not that bad,' said Helen.

'What?'

They laughed again.

Dee was wide awake and drinking tea when André arrived.

'Where's the man who saved my life?' she said.

'He's gone home, but the expectation is that he will be be back permanently before long and you can then see him as often as you like.'

'Well, that's good, but it's you I want to see most of all. Ruth came to see me earlier and assured me that what happened doesn't preclude other pregnancies. Nevertheless it's a funny feeling knowing that a young man has dealt with me intimately as no other, and did so in the back of a car.'

'He kept you alive thereby. Ruth said that if it had been a paramedic you would have died. Brendan in action was simply amazing and Ruth saw at once that she wanted to claim him for here on a permanent basis.'

'And no charges against him?'

'There might have been but what he did for you stopped that.'

'Are you managing by yourself at home?'

'I did for a long time before I met you, but as it happens Kim and Sharon have asked if they stay for a little while on a much-needed holiday, getting everything ready for your return and being there to support you when you get there.'

'Oh, lucky you André, and then lucky me. That's such wonderful news. Ruth says that if all goes well I might be home by the day after tomorrow.'

'Are you in pain of any sort?'

'Physical, no. But I'm feeling sad about the loss of our twins. I'm so glad we still have the scan photographs to remind us of what tiny little things we created, not least to spur us on to try again. I feel that certainly, but what about you, my darling?'

'I share that completely, my love, but there is one thing you must promise me, and that is that under no circumstances you will never fire a gun again, even though it had the effect of causing Ro to fall on top of Brendan in the garden, something they both clearly enjoyed.'

She laughed.

'Well, ok, then, never again with a gun. But what happened to Nancy, the person the assassin came for?'

'The assassin was stopped by Kim, but Nancy took her own life in the middle of the following night with, I'm afraid to say, the gun you had been using.'

'You might think I'm being melodramatic, André, but that sounds about right to me. I think she was ready to die, ready to shed all that she carried from the past.'

'Yes. It's more than odd, for although I knew of the things she had done, there is was something in Nancy I also loved. She laughed when we told her about your success rate with a gun and said she wished she had been like you.'

'I hope you know, darling, that Nancy loved you very much.'

Four men gathered together at the Ballymote Mart on Friday for the sale cattle, sheep and weanlings, as three of them did most weeks. The fourth member of the the group had flown in earlier in the day from London and was Barry Millane, a solicitor from Dublin, now representing Angus Cassidy who would be in Belmarsh for a long time before his trial, mostly in solitary confinement for his own protection.

'He's said nothing so far and I reckon he won't, though solitary can affect any main unforeseen ways. He told me one or two things however, such as that Carmichael was dead, after effects of the new stun bomb. He also told me he thought they had turned Hagen, and it must be so because I can't understand why they've let her go and what she did. He also thought he'd heard talk of one of their women coming over with her.
'An MI5 woman?'
'Aye.'
'The fucking cheek. And what about O'Callaghan?'
'Nothing. They had to release him because other conspiracy which they know any brief could walk through, he'd done nothing wrong.'
'We can use him again, then.'
'Perhaps to sort out these two conniving bitches?'
They looked at one another and nodded their heads.

Mary knew just how innocent in many ways her husband-to-be was, no matter how brilliant in terms of the practice of medicine. He seemed to think involvement with CIRA was over and done with, but she knew otherwise. For that reason she was more than willing to move to Exeter to be rid of them once and for all. She also knew that to be forewarned was to be forearmed and although she had no wish to have a gun of any sort though of course she used one to put down large animals sometimes, she drew up a syringe with a potent content which might not kill but certainly would have s seriously detrimental effect on anyone who might threaten her or Brendan. Concealing it was straightforward and using it would be so too.

A call came into Milbank and eventually was passed up to Martha who was less than delighted that it had taken so long to reach her. Immediately she sent an encrypted message to Helen, ordering her to visit P84, which she would understand, as Barry Millane had come over early today.
    For her part Helen was still asleep when the message came through to her phone. She surfaced and picked it up.
'Thank you, Martha. Some holiday!'
"Received", she typed and sent. She quickly showered and dressed before going into the kitchen where Eillen was sitting with a cup of coffee and a bowl of cereal.
'Please will you drive me to Belfast – now.'
'Of course. Am I allowed to know why?'
'Because your life and mine may well be at risk.'
'That seems to me to be a good enough reason. Is it the same for Brendan?'
'I shall know that later possibly, but for the moment it is almost certainly you and me who are most risk. That is because Angus Cassidy has been speaking to his lawyer Barry Millane and he came here early this morning.'
'Helen, get something to eat while I get my coat.'

'We got Carmichael, or at least Hagen did, and if they've tried to turn her it seems to me we can turn her back, use her for own ends. The bitch with her is totally expendable and they'll keep it quiet as they always do. It might be a good idea if I go and pay young Dr O'Callaghan a visit and encourage him to see that he hasn't finished, that when you sign up it's for ever, and leave you two to pay a call on the others. There's no way any of us are at risk. MI5 wouldn't dare do anything to us.'

Mind you,' said one of the others, 'I admired Carmichael. There were always far few touts prepared to operate after she'd carried out the orders of the Council.'

'True,' said the third, 'but the story is that she always derived a great deal of pleasure from it, and everyone knew that no matter how close they thought themselves close to her, she wouldn't hesitate to kill anyone she was told to. We never told Hagen, but her grandmother whom she went to avenge, had been Carmichael's closest friend.'

'What do they say about all fair in love and war? Anyway, lets get going and sort this mess out tonight.'

Helen had heard of P84 during her induction and knew it to be the former base of MI5 in the city, but transformed into, of all things, a shopping mall, at the side of which was a door with the almost invisible letters P84 at the bottom. Eileen wandered round the shops in the Mall whilst Helen struggled to find a way through a door without a handle. Eventually she knocked once and moments later the door was opened.

'What is your name?' said a male voice.

'What is yours?' said Helen.

A face appeared with a smile on it.

'Helen Boardman,' she said.

'Yes you look like your photo. Have you got your badge?'

Helen had it in her hand and showed it.

'Please come in, Helen. Would you like a drink?'

'No thanks. I have work to do and I'm to collect what I need.'

The young man led her down a corridor to an armoury. Again she had to produced her ID and collected a Glock 17, ammunition and a shoulder holster which she put on. She then signed for it and made way out.

At the door she turned to the young man.

'I'd improve your personality skills if ever you want to get a girl!'

The two met up and had some lunch before heading back. On the way Helen telephoned Brendan and left a message about a possible visitor. It was Mary who received the message, wiped it off and smiled. She was prepared and wouldn't worry Brendan with it.

'You've told me very little, Helen, including why you wanted me to take you to a shopping mall quite so urgently.'

'I was ordered to go and collect a firearm to protect both you and me from

CIRA. I think, reading between the lines of Martha's message, that Cassidy has reported that you have been turned and that it's more than possible that your new friend from England is a babysitter. Without you able to give evidence the case against him will be considerably weaker and it strikes me as quite possible that he will claim you brought all the firepower and left some with him. That he had an exemplary police record will make an English jury think well of him. So, an internecine Irish conflict in which you are killed for killing Nancy will have advantages for him. Once he hears that piece of news he will begin to speak to his interrogators and tell the story he wants them to hear. I am convinced that those here will want to act as soon as possible and probably tonight. Killing me will give them pleasure because of who I work for; killing you is because it's necessary.'

'But there's some good programmes on the tv tonight,' replied Eileen, which I don't want to miss.' She turned and smiled at Helen.

'Then we must make sure we don't miss them, and to think I stopped the bastard shooting himself.'

'Who?'

'Cassidy. When we burst in he had a gun to his head and I shot it out of his hand from my hip.'

'In which case I'm totally in your hands. Jesus, you're real scary, Helen.'

'Not really. I first fired a gun when I was eight, a shotgun which threw me back about 4 yards, but I was determined that it wouldn't do so again, and it didn't.I'm a stubborn bugger and I'm not anxious about what we might have to face tonight to whenever. I promise to protect you Eileen. Once we get back I'll try and get through to Brendan again.'

As they drew nearer to Eileen's home, Helen asked her to stop and let her out, and then to turn the car around and drive for five miles before returning, which would allow her the time to make her approach to the house. Eileen handed over the house key as Helen melted away into the darkness, she turned the car and drove back five miles.

Helen left the road, clambered over a barbed wire fence and made her way as quietly as possible through a flock of sheep, disturbing them as little as possible. Again she climbed over wire, always keeping her eyes focussed on the house. For the slightest sign of a light of any kind, from a twitching curtain or a cigarette being lit, but so far she had seen nothing. She continued to circle the house and just when she thought there was nothing to be seen, she saw the tiniest of lights and it was a cigarette being lit. Anyone who had been at Hereford for even a small amount of time would have know that cigarettes are a huge giveaway, wholly disproportionate to their size.

'Very bad for your future health,' she muttered under her breath.

As she drew close to the house she was aware that Helen was now approaching in the car, affording her a little time when she could move faster without being heard as she did so. She was now at the wall of the house and could hear words being spoken by what sounded like two men. The car stopped though Eileen kept on the headlights for a while and now Helen could see two old men moving towards the car. She turned off the lights and climbed out.

'This is a surprise. What can I do for you?' said Eileen.

'Where's your friend?' said one of them.

'By now, I imagine she's back in London, if that is, her flight left on time.'

'Who was she?'

'She's called Helen and she's a police officer. She was detailed to see me safely home after the death of Carmichael.'

'Why?'

'The police and MI5 who spoke to me informed me that I hadn't actually killed her. That was just a story concocted for the benefit of the press. In fact she took a gun and shot herself, and although I had made an absolute mess of the front of a safe house with a Russian grenade which just about scared the shit out of everybody within 200 yards, they had to explain as a Gas Board leak, meaning that I couldn't be charged with anything. Helen was told to make sure I got home. But what the hell are you two doing here in the dark?'

We'd been told that you'd been turned and that you were coming back to betray us.'

'So you thought you might kill me? Is that it? Have you no fucking brains between you? You didn't use me, I used you to get the means and support I needed to get to Carmichael to get revenge for my gran. I got you to pay for the doctor's two visits to England. I couldn't give a flying fuck for your cause and never could. I might pity you but why the hell would I want to betray such useless old tossers fighting a war that was lost years ago? I passed your landcover up the way – you couldn't even conceal that properly, so go on, get back to your fantasies.'

The men stood in silence for a few moments. Then one brought out of his pocket something Helen couldn't quite see.'

'You little pile of shit. Nobody speaks to us like that.'

By now Helen could see that he held a gun in his hand and she moved quickly causing him to drop the weapon with a powerful kick as she tripped the other man to the ground. Eileen had come and forced the first man to the ground. Helen from nowhere produced two sets of handcuffs.

'Bad luck, gentlemen. I missed my flight home. Eileen, stand over these two for a little while, I need to call J2. If either of them try anything, a severe kick in the balls will be all they need. If you need more than that, shoot the bastards.'

Helen had a code to summon J2 and they responded immediately. They would send Garda at once to take the two men to somewhere appropriate. Helen also advised them that a third man would be found at Brendan's house and again they told her they would deal with it. Finally she was asked when she would be leaving the country and that it would be much easier if she could so as soon as possible.

'I fully understand,' she said. 'When do you want me out?'

'By midnight if possible.'

'I'll bear it in mind,' she replied without a promise of any kind.
She and Eileen brought the two men to to their feet, and then into the house, still handcuffed. A search revealed a second gun.
'I'm sorry you're both farmers,' Helen said. 'My dad was a farmer but wisely had nothing to do with politics. Personally speaking, I'm actually in favour of a united Ireland but too much blood has been shed over it. When you recover your liberty, stick to sheep and cattle. What sort of sheep do you have?'
'Mainly blackface upland,' mumbled on of the men.
'They're tough and hardy,' said Helen, ' a bit like our Swaledale or Herdwick.'
'More like Swaledale, I think,' said the other man.
To the astonishment of Eileen, there now followed an almost ten-minute discussion between the three of them on the merits of different breeds of sheep and the training of dogs, interrupted only by the arrival of two vehicles and the Garda.
One of the men turned back towards Helen as they were being led away and smiled at her, saying nothing but nodding his head.
When a Garda vehicle arrived at the home of Brendan and Mary they were at once greeted with drinks. Apparently the prisoner had arrived uttering threats and then, quite inexplicably, fallen fast asleep on the couch. When Brendan arrived home, he checked all his vitals and found them ok, and thought it possible he had just been overtaken with total weariness which at his age could cause him to sleep like this. By the time the officers had had their drink the man was a little less groggy and Brendan passed him well enough to travel.
When they had departed, Brendan looked at Mary.
'Did you give him something?'
'I wanted him to relax a little so I gave him a tiny injection of the sort of thing I'd give to a horse to totally relax him for up to three hours. Nothing much really though he may well have a ghastly headache when he comes round.'
'Which you just happened to have hanging around, probably to use on me!'
'That's quite an idea, but no, I had been warned by your MI5 babysitter.'
'Oh.'
'Or at least that's what I thought she said. Her accent was very strong, foreign sounding.'

Helen and Eileen drove back to Belfast where they stayed overnight, enabling Helen to visit the shopping mall and return her equipment, and then they drove up to the north coast and a whole week of holiday, even in early December. It provided them with hours for conversation and laughter and cemented a close friendship. Eileen decided to accept Martha's suggestion to move to the Yorkshire Dales and become an established Dales painter.
Brendan and Mary made a number of trips to Exeter, planning to move into temporary accommodation in the new year when Brendan would begin his

new job. Mary decided to take a whole year off to deal with what was growing within, and was glad when Ruth Timothy took over her care, her community midwife being a lady called Kate, who loved mugs of tea.

When Dee arrived home, Sharon and Kim were there to help around the place and do the shopping. Dee had been told to take it easy for three months, and one morning, after Kim had returned to work in London and André was out somewhere, Dee took hold of Sharon's hand as they sat together with a cups of tea.

'I hope you know that much though André means so much to me, you're the person I'm still wholly in love with. I was devastated in Ilkley when you went off with Kim and didn't return. I don't think I'm being melodramatic when I say that a major part of me at least, will never recover from that. It hurt and hurts even now more than you can ever know. Had Brendan not been here, or had I managed to shoot him with my gun, then I would have died. As I became unconscious the last thing I recall was you, and I think I might happily have died at that moment.'

'For a start, Dee, the only person you were likely to kill with a gun was yourself, so you saved Brendan's life as later he saved yours. But I believe you are cut out in every way to be a mum and to share that role with André. The first time didn't work out but others will. I couldn't make you pregnant just as I can't make Kim pregnant which she wants more and more. In fact we've talked about it with Brendan but I'm uneasy because it involves a third person, albeit unknown, as the donor. The person wholly excluded is me. I may become a mum in name but it won't be the same. I suppose that what I'm trying to say is that when we speak of love we are always speaking of something that is never perfect because nothing is. Despite what we are asked to say in a wedding ceremony, and especially in a wedding ceremony in church, which is that love is a 100% thing, I just don't believe it. Myself I would put it at about 60%, the remaining 40% made up of other people and concerns in our lives, and perhaps as we get older and begin to change, the 60 may drop further. I very much deprecate the nonsense of the press that promotes the lie that it is 100% or nothing. Kim is my life, but not 100% for there will always be you and the wife of Kim's boss, Caro, and perhaps more than anything, the literature of humankind.'

'Do I get 5% even?' asked Dee.

'Dee, my darling, there are days would I happily give you all.'

Dee drew near and they kissed long and deep.

Chapter Thirty Seven

Julie received a message to attend a meeting in the Coffee Shop at 10:30 but instead of finding Martha waiting for her, it was Kim. Her heart sank for she had been hoping that Kim had forgotten.

'Good morning, captain.'

'Good morning ma'am.'

'How do you think it went? Devon, I mean, for after all, you were in charge.'

'Every op could go better with better intel though I can't see how we could could have been given more. Once we knew or assumed that Carmichael was the target and not Sir André we were in a better position to prepare though even a southern approach seemed less likely, and in retrospect I failed to take that into consideration, nor were we expecting a young woman walking up the road with a shoulder bag and umbrella. That mistake almost cost lives.'

'Yes, but a brilliant disguise she took and I think just about everyone would have been fooled by it. You had no intel and its absence causes the downfall of many ops, so tell me about intel in relation to Iraq.'

'I knew where to land and where to go. For the rest I was having to rely on my wits.'

'And when you came to evaluate the mission, what did you conclude?'

'That I was much too slow and extremely lucky to find the hostages I went for.'

'You got them out safely.'

'Eventually.'

'Oh I'm sorry, I hadn't realised that you measure yourself with just two readings: perfect and flawed.'

Julie's head dropped.'

'Please look at me, captain,' said Kim gently.

She did.

'So was it parents or school?

'M'm?'

'Who was it led you to think that less than perfect was not acceptable?'

There was a long pause.

'He was called Jonny Guthrie, a boyfriend when I was 15 or 16 and he was 18.
We said we loved each other, and surprise, surprise, he then told me what that meant. I refused and he made my life something of a misery, but the more he did so, the more I felt that I was a frigid virgin terrified of growing up, in effect a total failure even though there was no way I was going to give in.'
'O God, Julie, please tell me you didn't break his neck?'
Julie laughed.
'I didn't know how to back then.'
'You did the right thing, you know, on both occasions. You should drop a line to Jonny and tell him how lucky he is.'
Again Julie laughed.
'Look, as you know I'm hoping to get pregnant. The Director has decided that some promotions are to be recommended, and the Deputy Director has asked me to interview you as the one who saw you in action in the recent op and to offer my assessment. You see, Julie, you're wrong and please bear it in mind when you come to assess others which you will soon be in a position to do, success is not the same as perfection. We have never done a perfect op and probably never can. Yours in Iraq was excellent, as everybody but you recognises. Why do you think you have the MC? You earned it as everyone but you recognises. In everything you've done in this Service you are a star, and 75% is always enough for star rating. I shall be recommending promotion to major.Well done and thank you for all you do.'
'Thank you, Kim, and I really hope something good might be possible on the pregnancy front. You and Sharon are pretty much the perfect couple.'
'I absolutely adore her and can't believe my good fortune but even for us it cannot be 100%. We also love other people and she has her literature and I have my technology and knowing my beloved as I do, I'm sure she's also a little in love with Caro, our Director's wife, her closest friend.
'Don't you mind that?'
'Not at all because that's the wonderful Sharon I love and if she was other than she is then I wouldn't love her at all, I imagine. At the end of every day we are always there for each other.

Printed in Great Britain
by Amazon